... itically-
acclai...
or...   ...nas ...
a...   ...D in English literature, thinks ever...
read more romance, and is always available to discuss
her beloved alpha heroes. Just ask. She lives in the
Pacific Northwest with her comic book artist husband,
is always planning her next trip, and will never, ever,
read all the books in her to-be-read pile. Thank
goodness.

USA TODAY bestselling author **Kat Cantrell** read her
first Mills & Boon novel in third grade and has been
scribbling in notebooks since she learned to spell.
She's a former Harlequin *So You Think You Can Write*
winner and former RWA *Golden Heart* finalist. Kat,
her husband and their two boys live in north Texas.

Amanda Cinelli was born into a large Irish-Italian
family and raised in the leafy green suburbs of County
Dublin, Ireland. After dabbling in a few different
career paths, she finally found her calling as an author
after winning an online writing competition with her
first finished novel. With three small daughters at
home, her days are usually spent doing school runs,
changing nappies and writing romance. She still
considers herself unbelievably lucky to be able to call
this her day-job.

Royal Scandals

Royal Scandals: Seducing His Queen

CAITLIN CREWS

KAT CANTRELL

AMANDA CINELLI

MILLS & BOON

First Published in Great Britain 2022
By Mills & Boon, an imprint of HarperCollins*Publishers,* Ltd
1 London Bridge Street, London, SE1 9GF

www.harpercollins.co.uk

HarperCollins*Publishers*
1st Floor, Watermarque Building,
Ringsend Road, Dublin 4, Ireland

ROYAL SCANDALS: SEDUCING HIS QUEEN © 2022 Harlequin Books S.A.

Expecting a Royal Scandal © 2016 Caitlin Crews
The Princess and the Player © 2015 Harlequin Books S.A.
Claiming His Replacement Queen © 2019 Amanda Cinelli

Special thanks and acknowledgement are given to Kat Cantrell for her contribution to the *Dynasties: The Montoros* series.

ISBN: 978-0-263-30427-5

MIX
Paper from
responsible sources
FSC™ C007454

EXPECTING A ROYAL SCANDAL

CAITLIN CREWS

To Maisey, who fixed the book once when it had all turned a bit grim, listened to a lot of ranting on street corners with very broad hand gestures, and then loved it when it was done.

CHAPTER ONE

THERE WERE SOME invitations a wise woman did not refuse.

The invitation in question tonight had been handwritten by one of the most famous men on earth on luxuriously heavy card stock and then hand-delivered to her door by a servant. The message itself had been intriguingly mysterious, asking her only to… *Meet me in Monte Carlo.*

And Brittany Hollis was many things by the ripe old age of twenty-three—including widely reviled on at least two continents thanks to her collection of strategic marriages, a reality show appearance in which she'd played the widely loathed villain and her trademark refusal to confirm or deny any and all scandalous rumors she heard about herself—but she'd always considered herself wise enough.

Too wise for her own good, in fact, or so she'd always thought. That was how an untouched virgin let herself be known across the planet as one of the most shameless women alive. Yet all the while, she stayed in control and above the snide remarks—because she, and maybe only she, knew the truth.

And no matter what names others called her, like *mercenary* when they were being polite, her ability to keep her eyes on the prize as if none of that bothered her was the best way she knew to propel her toward the tropical island paradise of her dreams.

She'd get there one day. She knew she would. She'd

spend the rest of her life in a flowing caftan sipping pitchers of mai tais with cheerful flowers in her hair, and she'd never spare a single thought for these harsh days of hustling or the cruel tabloid stories in which she was always cast as the evil villain.

Not one stray thought. Not ever again.

Brittany could hardly wait. She'd spent years sending half the money she earned back home to the family members who proclaimed her lost to the devil in public, cashed her sinner's checks in private and then shamelessly asked her for more. Again and again. Her beloved grandmother would have expected Brittany to do her part after Hurricane Katrina had wiped out what little Brittany's single mother had possessed over ten years ago, leaving them all wretched and destitute and close enough to homeless in Gulfport, Mississippi.

Brittany had done her best. Year after year, the only way she knew how, with the only weapons she possessed—her looks and her body and the wits she'd inherited straight from Grandmama, though most people assumed she was entirely witless. Her youngest half sibling was ten this year. Brittany figured that meant she had eight years left before she could suggest her family members support themselves for a change.

Though maybe she'd use stronger words.

Meanwhile, the other half of the money she made she hoarded, because one of these days she was headed for a remote Pacific Island to take up residence beneath a palm tree and the deep blue sky on a deserted white sand beach. She'd seen pictures of the archipelago of Vanuatu while still in high school, and she'd decided then and there that she needed to live in that kind of paradise. Once she made it to those perfect islands west of Fiji, she wasn't coming back to the mess of the world or her place in it.

Ever.

First, however, there was all the elegant splendor of Monaco and the man who had summoned her here to meet with him in the spectacularly iconic Monte Carlo casino where blue-blooded men like him whiled away casual evenings at gaming tables that had been specifically designed to part Europe's wealthiest from their vast, multigenerational fortunes. *To discuss a proposition that would benefit us both*, the message he'd had delivered by hand had said, though Brittany hadn't been able to think of a single thing that could possibly do that. Or anything they had in common, come to that, except a certain international notoriety—and his, unlike hers, was based on documented fact.

Documented and streamed live on the internet more than once.

Still, Brittany entered the casino that evening right on time. She'd dressed her part. Monte Carlo's achingly civilized sins were draped in the veneer of a certain old-world elegance and therefore so was Brittany. A girl liked to match. Her gown shimmered a discreet, burnished gold, sweeping from a knot on one shoulder all the way down to flirt with the gleam of her sleek heels. She was aware the dress made her look edible and expensive at once, as befitted a woman whose own mother called her a whore to her face. But it also suggested a bone-deep sophistication with every step she took, which helped a white-trash girl from Mississippi blend in with the gold-leaf and marble glory surrounding her in all directions.

Brittany was very, very good at blending.

She felt the impact of the man she'd come to Monaco to meet long before she saw him, tucked away at one of the more high risk tables in the usual throng of lackeys and admirers who cavorted about in his shadow. Even without his selection of courtiers circling him like well-heeled satellites, she would have found him without any trouble.

The whispers, the humming excitement whipping through the crowd, the not precisely subtle craning of necks to get a better view of him—it all marked him with a bright red *X*. He might as well have sent up a flare.

Then the crowd parted, and there he was, sitting at a table in a desultory manner, though his attention was on the crowd—broadcasting the fact that the man formally known as His Serene Grace the Archduke Felipe Skander Cairo of Santa Domini was so supremely wealthy and jaded he need not pay attention to his own gambling endeavors even while he was undertaking them.

Cairo Santa Domini. The exiled hereditary king of the tiny alpine country that bore his surname and the only surviving member of an august and revered family line stretching back some five hundred years. The scourge of Europe's morally compromised women, the papers liked to call him—though it was also said that a woman of impeccable reputation *became* compromised merely by standing too close to him at an otherwise staid and boring function. The living, breathing, epic scandal-causing justification for the military coup that had overturned his father's monarchy and was widely held to have assassinated the rest of his family years later, leaving only Cairo the sybaritic degenerate in their wake, like a profligate grave marker.

Largely because there was no point in targeting him, the pundits had agreed for years. He redefined *disgrace*. He did an excellent job of reminding the world why the excesses of ancient monarchies should never be tolerated, simply by continuing to draw his pampered and ill-behaved breath and cavorting about the scandal sheets like a one-man bacchanal.

Cairo Santa Domini, right there before her in the sleek, superbly fit, astonishingly handsome flesh.

His had been the name on the invitation she'd received,

of course. She'd expected she'd see him here. Yet she was somehow unprepared for him all the same.

Brittany realized she'd stopped walking and had, in fact, stopped dead in the middle of the casino. She knew better than that. Hers was a game of mirrors and sighs, of soft suggestion and affected disinterest. She did not stand about staring in shock like the yokel she hadn't been in years. That wasn't the impression she liked to give off. Yet she couldn't quite make herself move.

And then Cairo glanced over and met her gaze, bold and lazy at once, and she wasn't certain she'd ever move of her own volition again. She felt bolted to the floor—and painfully, at that.

She'd seen a thousand pictures of this man. Everyone had, and of significantly more of him than necessary. She already knew he was beautiful. Many celebrated things were from a distance, she'd found, only to prove a bit more grimy and weathered and unfortunate up close. Hollywood, for example, and many of its best-known denizens.

But not Cairo.

He had one of those full, captivating, startlingly European mouths that made her feel edgy and hollow down deep inside. That mouth of his made her imagine hot, desperate kisses in cold, unfamiliar cities bristling with baroque architecture and laden with strange pastries, when she hadn't thought about *kissing* anyone in years. He had a full head of shaggy dark hair that was obviously left mussed and careless on purpose, yet still managed to make him appear as if it had *happened* to him on the way to Monte Carlo.

And his eyes! They looked pretty enough in photographs. More than pretty. This close, a mere stone's throw across the casino floor, they were nothing short of marvelous. There was no other word to describe them. They were the color of exultantly wicked caramel and made her feel like spun sugar all the way to her toes. Her mouth watered despite herself, and she felt the heat of him in a bright blaze down deep in her belly.

This had never happened to her before. Not ever.

Brittany had been more or less immune to men since her mother's early, appalling boyfriends had raged drunkenly through their miserable trailer during Brittany's formative years. The fact she'd married three men of her own volition and for her own very practical reasons hadn't altered her opinion on the drawbacks of the male sex one bit—and not one of her husbands had affected her blood pressure like this.

Or at all, if she was honest.

It didn't make sense. She jerked her gaze from Cairo Santa Domini's too aware, slightly arrested one to take in the rest of him, not surprised to find he wore the usual uniform of all the very wealthy European men she'd ever seen out at night in this city or that, clogging up the nightclubs and restaurants and boulevard cafés. Though his version was…better.

Much better.

His dark, exquisitely tailored shirt clung to that expected glorious male torso of his that no doubt looked equally delicious framed by various Italian coasts or the yacht-choked harbors lining the French Riviera outside. His gorgeously cut dark jacket somehow made his masculine chin, with just a bit more than five o'clock shadow, seem that much more decadent and attractive. His legs, athletic and muscled and longer than most, were packed into the sort of bespoke black trousers that cost more than some people's mortgages. His shoes whispered with the quiet confidence of Milan as he stretched out his legs, continuing to lounge there, awash in his followers, as if the famed Monte Carlo tables were but a prop for a man like him.

As was she, she understood, when one of his dark brows arched high in some mixture of weary boredom and very royal command. A prop for a game she didn't yet understand—but she would. That was why she'd come.

That and she'd never before met a man who would have been an actual king, barring all that unfortunate civil unrest when he'd been a child.

Cairo crooked an imperious finger, beckoning her near, and Brittany really, truly didn't want to go to him. Every instinct inside her screamed at her to turn on her heel and run in the opposite direction. To walk all the way back up north to her efficient little flat in Paris if that was what it took.

Anything to get the hell away from him before he destroyed her.

That thought shivered over her like some kind of prophecy, bone and blood. *He will destroy you.*

She tried to shake off the feeling. She told herself she was being fanciful. Silly. Two things she'd never been in her entire life, but maybe the sight of a would-be king in a place like Monte Carlo was too much for all the broken shards of the Cinderella fantasies she knew she had rattling around inside her somewhere, scraping at her with their jagged edges when she least expected it. Making it hard to breathe in strange little moments like this one.

She started toward Cairo, affecting a faintly quizzical expression as if she hadn't recognized him. As if she'd stopped in the middle of the casino floor because she'd been uncertain where to go, not because she'd seen him and been struck by the sight. As if their gazes hadn't clashed like that, in a tangle of caramel breathlessness that was still scraping through her and making her feel almost...raw.

Brittany ignored all those inconvenient feelings, whatever the hell they were. She sauntered toward her doom, and no amount of shouting at herself to stop being so fanciful convinced her that the dissolute aristocrat who watched her approach was anything but that: her sure destruction packed into a recklessly masculine form.

"Are you Cairo Santa Domini?" she asked brightly as she drew near, letting a little more Mississippi flavor her words than usual. For dramatic effect—because people drew all sorts of conclusions about folks with drawls like the one she'd grown up using. Mostly that they were as dumb as a pile of rocks, which she'd always enjoyed using to her advantage.

As expected, her feigned inability to identify one of the most recognizable men alive was met with gasps, outraged sniffs and muttered condemnations from his entourage. Cairo's mouth, a study in carved sensuality that seemed to be wired directly into an echoing heat deep her belly, curved in appreciation.

"I regret that I am." His voice was like melted dark chocolate. Rich. Deep. Faintly, intriguingly accented, as if his use of English was an afterthought or perhaps a gift. He didn't move from his languid position, though she had the strangest notion that his decadent caramel gaze had sharpened as she approached. "But only because no one else has stepped up to take the position, no matter how I try to give it away."

"A pity." She stopped when she was *just* inside the span of his carelessly outthrust legs. She felt certain he'd appreciate the symbolism. Sure enough, that arrested, *aware* gleam in his gaze intensified. It told her she was right. And that he wasn't as bored as he was pretending to be. "Then again, no one else in all the world can boast of your indefatigable penis and its many salacious conquests, can they? What's a lost kingdom next to that?"

Brittany was aware of the ripple that deliberate slap caused all around them, ruffling the feathers of his courtiers and his more distant admirers alike. She'd meant it to do just that. And yet she couldn't seem to jerk her gaze away from the man who stood there before her—smiling, though she noticed it went nowhere near his deceptively warm eyes or the cool, calculating gleam there.

"Ms. Hollis, I presume?" he asked.

Brittany was certain he'd known her at a glance. But this was the game. So she merely nodded, all gracious condescension, as if it had been a true inquiry.

"I've been in exile most of my life," he said after a moment, his mild tone at odds with the way he was studying her. "Only the revolutionaries call me any kind of king these days. Best not to invoke their brand of fealty. It comes with toppled governments and ruined cities, generally speaking." He inclined his head, reminding her with that single, simple gesture that whatever he was now, however far he'd fallen, he'd been raised to rule. "I do hope you found your way here tonight without incident. Monte Carlo is not quite the burlesque halls of the Paris sewers— that is what we call such places in polite company, is it not? I trust you do not find yourself too far out of your accustomed, ah, *depths*."

Brittany had misjudged him. She hadn't expected a playboy royal, draped in well-dressed tarts and trailing scandal behind him wherever he roamed like some kind of acrid scent, to be anything like *sharp*. It hadn't crossed her mind that he could possibly insult her with any dexterity.

Or at all, honestly.

Some part of her shifted, deep inside, in what she told herself was grudging admiration. Nothing more.

"Water seeks its own level, I'm told," she said, and smiled all the brighter as she switched up her tactics on the fly. "And so here I am."

His impossibly carnal mouth curved again, deeper this time, and she felt it tug at her, low in her belly, where there was nothing but fire and an edgy need she didn't really understand. It seemed to intensify by the second. With every breath.

"You should, of course, feel elevated by my notice in the first place. To say nothing of my invitation." He shifted against the table at his back, propping himself up on an elbow. It only drew attention to the fact that he had to look down at her, though she stood in three-inch heels that made her nearly six feet tall. "You do not appear to be glorying in your good fortune tonight, *cara*."

"I feel very fortunate, of course," she said in an insultingly overpolite tone, as if attempting to pacify a dimwitted child. "Truly. *So* lucky."

Brittany was used to reading rooms, the better to contribute to her own tarnished legend by playing it up whenever possible. A wink here, a smile there and another rumor spread like wildfire and ended up a tabloid headline. But this was different. It wasn't only that there were no cameras allowed in this place, which made playing to them difficult. She should have been cataloguing bystander reactions to this meeting and gathering information the way she usually did—but instead, the whole of the casino seemed cast in shadow with Cairo the unlikely sun at its center, a streak of glaring brightness she found unaccountably mesmerizing.

As if he was powerful beyond measure when she knew—when everybody knew—he was at best a modern-day wastrel. He shouldn't exude anything but the latest party-boy cologne. She told herself he was a snake charmer, nothing more. Why she couldn't seem to hold on to that thought was a question she'd have to investigate in depth when she was somewhere far, far away from all this insane magnetism of his, which was far too riveting for comfort.

Cairo watched her in his oddly intent way, though every

other inch of him shouted out his pure indolence. It gave her the distinct sensation of whiplash.

"I saw your act," he said after a long, tensely glimmering moment dragged by, and Brittany found she was holding her breath. Again.

He'd been there? In the audience in that grimy little club that Europe's most pampered imagined was a walk on the wild side of their indulged little lives? Brittany couldn't believe she hadn't *felt* this intensity of his, somehow.

She hated that she felt it now. She caught herself in the act of scowling at him and softened her expression—but she was sure he'd seen it anyway.

She was certain, somehow, that Cairo Santa Domini saw a great deal more than he should.

"You have a very interesting approach to the art of the burlesque, Ms. Hollis. All that stalking about the stage, baring your teeth in such a terrifying manner at the punters. Effectively daring them to deny you their pallid offerings of a few measly bills for a glance at your frilly underthings. You'd be better off cracking a whip and dispensing with the fiction that you are at all interested in appealing to the usual fantasies, I think."

Brittany tucked her bright gold clutch beneath her arm, as languid as he was, though something in her shook at his horrifyingly accurate picture of the side gig she'd taken to make a few more scandalized headlines, and let her smile flirt with a bit of an edge.

"Are you reviewing my performance?"

"Consider it the studied reaction of a rather ardent fan of the art form."

"I don't know what's more astounding. That you sullied your aristocratic self in a burlesque club in 'the sewers of Paris,' as you call them, or that you would admit to such shocking behavior in the glare of all this fussy Monte Carlo elegance. Your desperate acolytes can hear you, you know." She leaned closer and dropped her voice to a stage whisper she was fairly certain carried all the way across the Italian border less than ten miles to the east. "You'd better be careful, Your Exiled Highness. The chandeliers themselves might shatter at the notion that a man of your known proclivities attended something so prosaic and tedious as a *nightclub*."

"I was under the impression my behavior no longer shocked a soul, or so the wearisome British papers would have me believe. In any case, do you really feel as if a return to the dance halls of your storied past are a good investment in your future? I'd thought your latest marriage was a step in a different direction. A pity about the will." That half smile of his was—she understood as it sliced through her and reminded her of the very public way her most recent husband's heirs had announced that Brittany had been excluded from the bulk his estate—an understated weapon. "I ask as a friend."

"I would be quite surprised if you truly had any friends at all." She eyed him and amped up her own smile. Polite and charming fangs. Her specialty. "But I digress. In some circles a glance at my frilly underthings is considered something of a generous gift. You're welcome."

"Ah, Ms. Hollis, let us not play these games." Something not quite a smile any longer played with that stunning mouth of his, marking him significantly more formidable than a mere *playboy*. "You did not strip, as widely advertised. You hardly performed at all, and meanwhile the chance to get a glimpse of Jean Pierre Archambault's disgraced widow in the nude was the primary attraction of the entire exercise. The whole thing was a regrettable tease."

She shrugged delicately, fully aware it made the gold fabric of her gown gleam and shimmer as if she herself was lit from within. "That must have been a novel experience for a man of your well-documented depravities."

His head tilted slightly to one side and his gaze was not particularly friendly. Somehow, this made him more beautiful. "You were a high school dropout."

Brittany knew better than to show any sort of reaction to the shift in topic. Or to what was likely meant to be a hard slap to shove her back into her place. Trouble was, she'd never much cared for her place, or she'd still be in Gulfport scraping out a miserable existence with the rest of her relatives. No, thank you.

"Did they call it something different when you failed to finish one private boarding school after the next?" she asked sweetly. His Royal Jackass wasn't the only one with access to the internet. "There were how many in a row? Six? I know the obscenely rich make their own rules, but I was under the impression your numerous expulsions meant you and I are both somehow making it through the big, bad world without a high school diploma. Maybe we'll be best friends after all."

Cairo ignored her, though she thought there was a certain appreciative gleam in those deceptively sweet-looking eyes of his. "A runaway at sixteen, in the company of your first husband. And what a prime choice he was. He was what we might call…"

He paused, as if in deference to her feelings. Or as if he'd suddenly recalled his manners. Brittany laughed.

"We called Darryl a way to get out of Gulfport, Mississippi," she replied. She let a little more twang into her voice, as emphasis. "Believe me, you make that choice when it comes along, no matter the drug-addled loser that may or may not come with it. Not the sort of choice you had to make, I imagine, while growing up coddled and adored on one of your family's numerous foreign properties."

The word *exile* called to mind something a bit more perilous than the Santa Domini royal family's collection of luxury estates; here a ranch, there an island, everywhere a sprawling penthouse in the best neighborhood of any given city. It was hard to muster up any sympathy, Brittany found, especially when her own choices had been to live wherever she could make it work or end up back in her mother's trailer.

"Your second husband was far more in the style to which you would soon become accustomed. You and he became rather well known on that dreadful television program of yours, did you not?"

"*Hollywood Hustle* ran for two seasons and is considered one of the less appalling reality shows out there," Brittany said, as if in agreement. "If we're tallying them all up."

"That's a rather low bar."

"Said the pot to the kettle." She eyed him. "Most viewers were obsessed with the heartwarming love story of Chaz and Mariella, not Carlos and me."

"The tattoo artist." Cairo didn't actually crook his fingers around the word *artist*, but it was very strongly implied. And, as Brittany recalled, deserved. "And the sad church secretary who wanted him to follow his heart and become a derivative landscape painter, or some such drivel."

"Pulse-pounding, riveting stuff," Brittany agreed dryly. "As you clearly already know, if you feel you're in a good place to judge the behavior of others despite every cautionary tale ever told about glass houses."

It had all been entirely faked, of course. Carlos had been told the gay character he'd auditioned for had already been cast, but there was an opening for a bad-girl villain and her hapless husband—as long as they were legally married. Brittany was the only woman Carlos had known who'd wanted to get out of Texas as much as he did, so the whole thing was a no-brainer. The truth was that after Darryl, Brittany didn't think too highly of the institution of marriage anyway. She and Carlos had been together long enough to get reality-show famous—which wasn't really famous at all, despite what so many people in her family seemed to think—and then, when the show's ratings started to fade and their name recognition went with them, Brittany had dramatically "left" Carlos for Jean Pierre, so Carlos could complain about it in the tabloids and land himself a new gig.

But to the greater public, of course, she was that low-class slut who had ruined a poor, sweet, good man. A tale as old as time, blah blah blah.

She raised her brows at Cairo Santa Domini now. "I wouldn't have pegged you for a fan of the show. Or any reality show, for that matter. I thought inhabitants of your social strata wafted about pretending to read Proust."

"I spend a lot of my time on airplanes, not in glass houses and very rarely with Proust," Cairo replied, a glint in the caramel depths of his gaze as he waved a careless hand. "Your show was such a gripping drama, was it not? You, the heartless stripper who wouldn't give up your tawdry dancing for the good of your marriage. Carlos, the loving husband who tried so desperately to stay true to you despite the way you betrayed him on those poles every night. The path of true love, et cetera."

Brittany felt the flash of her own smile as she aimed it at him, and concentrated on making it brighter. Bolder. It was amazing what people failed to see in the glare of a great smile.

"I'm a terrible person," she agreed merrily. "If a television show says so, it must be true. Speaking of which, didn't I see you featured on one of those tabloid programs just last week? Something about a hapless heiress, a weekend in the Maldives and the corrosive nature of your company?"

"Remind me," Cairo murmured, sounding somewhat less amused—she was almost certain. "Were you still married to Carlos when you met Jean Pierre?"

Brittany laughed. A sparkling, effortless, absolutely false laugh. "You appear to be confusing my résumé with yours."

"And speaking of Jean Pierre, may he rest in peace, what was it that drew you together? He, the elderly man confined to a wheelchair with a scant few months to live. You…"

Cairo let his gaze travel over her form, as hot and buttery as a touch. He didn't finish that sentence.

"We had a shared interest in applied sciences, of course," Brittany replied, deadpan and dry. "What else?"

"An interest that his children did not share, given they wasted no time in ejecting you from the old man's chateau the moment he died and then crowing about it to the press. A shame."

"Your invitation didn't mention that we'd be playing biography games," Brittany said brightly, as if it didn't bother her in the least to be so publically eviscerated. "I feel so woefully underprepared. Let's see." She held her bag beneath her elbow and ticked things off on her fingers. "Royal blood. No throne. Always naked. Eight thousand women. So many sex tapes. So scandalous the word no longer really applies because it's really more, 'there's Cairo Santa Domini somewhere he shouldn't be with someone he shouldn't have touched and blurred out bits in a national newspaper. La la la, must be Tuesday.'"

"Ms. Hollis," Cairo said in that drawling way only extremely upper-crust people could manage to make sound so condescending. When it was only her name. He reached over as if nothing had ever been more inevitable and then he traced a very lazy, very delicate path from the gold knot at her shoulder to the very top of that shadow between her breasts. Sensation detonated inside of her. She flashed white hot. She saw red. She *felt* him, everywhere, and that voice of his, too, all dark chocolate and stupendously bad decisions melted into something that shivered through her, dessert and desire and destruction all at once.

"You flatter me."

Brittany didn't like the way her heart catapulted itself against the wall of her chest. She didn't like the way her skin prickled, hot and cold, as if she was sunburned from so small and meaningless a touch. Since when had she reacted at all to a man? No matter what he did?

She didn't like the fact that she'd completely lost sight of the fact that they were in public, even if the public in question was mostly his circle of pseudosubjects she knew trotted around with him everywhere he went—or that all she'd really seen since she walked in here was Cairo. As if she'd come here to compete for his attention, like one of his usual horde of panting women.

She liked that part least of all, and she didn't care to ask herself why that was. It didn't matter. None of what had happened here mattered. This spectacularly messy and inappropriate man wasn't in any way a part of her grand plan, and would do nothing but delay her dreams of a getaway to her solitary tropical island paradise in Vanuatu. He had that kind of total disaster written all over him, and too much exposure to him made her worry it was written on her, too. She'd accepted his invitation because she was curious and he was Cairo Santa Domini, and now she knew.

He was her ruin made flesh. Nothing less than that. At least she knew it now, she told herself. That meant she had the chance to avoid it. To avoid *him*.

"Your Almost Highness," she breathed, in exaggerated shock.

She wanted to snatch his lazy finger away from her

overheated skin, which was why she leaned into it instead. His finger slipped into the valley between her breasts, *just there* beneath the edge of her angled bodice, but neither one of them looked down to see what both of them could feel. Their gazes were locked together, tangled up hot and a little bit wild, and Brittany was slightly mollified to see she wasn't the only one affected by…whatever the hell this was. She raised her voice so they could hear her everywhere in Monaco, the trashy American that she was, every inch of her offensive to each and every highbrow European eye that tried its best not to see her.

But Brittany wasn't any good at being invisible. "Are you *flirting* with me?"

CHAPTER TWO

A SHORT WHILE LATER, Cairo stood with his back to the disconcerting American, his brooding gaze fixed on the seductive glitter of Monaco's harbor out there in the sweet summer dark. The night pressed in on the glass windows of his penthouse suite the way that woman seemed to hammer against his composure, even when all she was doing was sitting quietly on his sofa. He could see her reflection in the glass and it irritated him that she looked so calm while he had to fight to collect himself.

That he had to do any such thing was nothing short of extraordinary for a man who was alive today precisely because he could so expertly manage himself in all situations.

But then, nothing tonight was going according to plan.

Brittany Hollis wasn't at all what he'd expected. When he'd watched that cringe-worthy television program of hers she'd been all plumped-up breasts and an endless Southern drawl, punctuated with supple flips and melting slides on the nearest stripper pole. All the advance research he'd done on her before selecting her for the dubious honor of his proposal had suggested she might possess the particular cunning native to the sort of women whose life revolved around strategic relationships with much wealthier men, but he hadn't expected any great intellect.

Cairo had been delighted at the prospect that she'd be exactly as gauche as her tawdry history suggested she was.

Someone capable of injecting the embarrassing spectacle of her risqué burlesque appearances into everyday life and making certain the whole world found her deeply embarrassing and epically shameless at all times.

The perfect woman for him, in other words. A man so famously without honor or country deserved a shameful match, he'd told himself bitterly the night he'd seen her dance. Brittany Hollis seemed crafted to order.

Instead, the woman who had walked up to him tonight was a vision, from the pale copper fire of her hair to the hint of hot steel in her dark hazel eyes, and there wasn't a single thing the least bit dumb or plastic about her. He didn't understand it. Meeting her gaze had been like being thrown from the saddle of a very large horse and having to lie there on the hard ground for a few excruciating moments, wondering with no little panic if he'd ever draw breath to fill his lungs again.

He still didn't know the answer to that.

His long-term head of security, Ricardo, who'd suggested this tabloid sensation of a woman in the first place, had a lot to answer for. But here, now, Cairo had to navigate what he'd expected to be a very straightforward business conversation despite the fact he felt so...unsettled.

"Have you lured me back to your hotel suite to show me your etchings, Your Usually Far More Naked Grace?" Brittany's voice was so dry it swept over him like a brush fire, igniting a longing in him he'd never imagined he'd feel for anyone or anything aside from his lost kingdom and its people. He didn't understand what this was—what was happening to him, when he'd felt absolutely nothing since the day he'd lost his family and had understood what waited for him if he wasn't careful. What General Estes, the self-appointed Grand Regent of Santa Domini, had made clear was Cairo's destiny if he ever so much as glanced longingly at the throne that should have been his.

"What a dream come true. I've always wanted to join such a vast and well-populated parade of royal paramours."

That the girl was perfect for his purposes wasn't in doubt, dry tone or not.

Cairo had known it the moment Ricardo had handed him her picture. Even before Ricardo had told him anything about the pretty redhead who wore so little and stared into the camera with so much distance and mystery in her dark eyes. He'd felt something scratch at him, and he'd told himself that was reason enough to conceal himself and sneak into one of her scandalous performances in Paris. He'd been far more intrigued than he should have been as he'd watched her command the stage, challenging the audience with every sinuous move of her famously lithe and supple figure.

He'd sent one of his aides with his invitation and he'd continued interviewing the other candidates for his very special position, but his heart wasn't in it once he'd seen Brittany. And that was before he'd read all the unsavory details of her life story, which, of course, rendered her an utterly appalling if not outright ruinous choice for a man some people still dreamed would be king one day. General Estes might have routed Cairo's father from the throne of Santa Domini when Cairo was still a small child, but the passing of time only ever seemed to make the loyalists more shrill and focused. And that made no one safe—neither Cairo nor the Santa Dominian people, who didn't deserve another bloody coup in a thirty-year span, much less the empty-headed playboy prince Cairo played for the papers as its figurehead.

Besides, Cairo knew what the loyalists refused to see—there was nothing good in him. He'd seen to that. There was only shame and darkness and more of the same. Play a role long enough and it ate a man alive. The desperate American stripper who'd made an international game out of her shameless gold digging was an inspired choice to make certain that even if no one listened to Cairo about who he'd become, no coup could ever happen and his people would be spared a broken, damaged king.

And then she'd walked up to him in a dress of spun gold and pretended not to know him, and he'd forgotten he'd ever so much as considered another woman for this role at all.

"Was it a lure?" he asked now. He turned to see her rolling her glass of wine between her palms, an action he shouldn't have found even remotely erotic. And yet... "I asked you to accompany me to my hotel suite and you agreed. A lure is rather less straightforward."

"If you say so, Your Semantic Highness."

Cairo had expected to find her attractive. He'd expected a hint of the usual fire deep within him and the lick of it in his sex, because he was a man, after all. Despite what he needed to do here. He'd been less prepared for the sheer wallop of her. Of how the sight of her made his breath a complication in his chest.

And he certainly hadn't imagined she'd be...entertaining.

The pictures and even the stage hadn't done her any justice at all, and the tidy little marriage of convenience he'd imagined shifted and re-formed in his head the longer he looked at her. Cairo knew he should call it off. The last thing he needed in his life was one more situation he couldn't control, and the blazing thing raging inside of him now was the very definition of uncontrollable.

And *she* was something more than a gorgeous redhead who'd looked edible in a down-market burlesque ensemble, or even a former American television star in a shiny dress that made her look far more sophisticated than she should have been. Brittany Hollis should have been little more than a jumped-up tart. Laughable in the midst of so much old-world splendor here in Monaco.

But instead, she was fascinating.

Cairo was finding it exceedingly difficult to keep his cool, which had never happened to him before in all the years since he'd lost his family. He hardly knew whether to give in to the sensation, unleashing God knew what manner of hell upon himself, or view it as an assault. Both, perhaps.

"Is this the part where we stare at each other for ages?" Brittany asked from her position on the crisp white sofa where she perched with all the boneless elegance of a pampered cat. "I had no idea royal intrigue was so tedious."

It was time to handle this. To handle himself, for God's sake. This wasn't about *him*, after all, or whatever odd need he felt licking at him, tempting him to forget the dark truths about himself in earnest for the first time in some twenty years.

"Of course it's tedious," he said, drawing himself up to his full height. He brushed a nonexistent speck of lint from one sleeve. "That's why kings are forced to start wars or institute terror regimes and inquisitions, you understand. To relieve the boredom."

"And your family was drummed out of your country. I can't think why."

Cairo had long since ceased to allow himself to feel anything at all when it came to his lost kingdom and the often vicious comments people made about it to his face. He'd made an art out of seeming not to care about his birthright, his blood, his people. He'd locked it all up and shoved it deep inside, where none of it could slip out and torture him any longer, much less trip him up in the glare of the public eye.

No stray memories of graceful white walls cluttered with priceless art, the dizzy blue sky outside his window in that particular bright shade he'd never seen replicated anywhere else, the murmur of the mountain winds against the fortified walls of his childhood bedroom in the castle heights. No recollections of the night they'd all been spirited away in the dark before General Estes could get his butcher's hands on them, hidden in the back of a loyalist's truck across the sharp spine of the snowcapped mountains that ringed the capital city, never to return.

He didn't let himself think of his father's roar of laughter or his mother's soft hands, lost forever. He never permitted himself any stray thoughts about his younger sister, Magdalena, a bright and gleaming little girl snatched away so easily and so unfairly.

He didn't have the slightest idea why the usual barbed comments from yet another stranger should lodge in him tonight like a mortal blow, as if the fact this woman had surprised him meant she could slip beneath his defenses, too. No one could do that. Not if he didn't let them.

And he was well aware that even if he'd wanted someone close to him, to that tarnished thing inside of him he called his soul, he couldn't allow it to happen. He couldn't let anyone close to him or they'd be rendered so much more collateral damage. One more weapon the general would find a way to use against Cairo and then destroy.

Why was Brittany Hollis making him consider such things?

He studied her. Her coppery hair was caught up in a complicated twist, catching the light as she moved. Her neck was long and elegant, and made him long for a taste of her. More than a taste. Her skin looked as if it was dusted a fainter gold than the dress she wore, which on any other woman might have been a trick of cosmetics, but on this one, he thought, was actually *her*. She was far prettier than her photographs and infinitely more captivating than her coarse appearances on that stupid show. She was all impossibly long legs, those lovely curves shimmering beneath the expert cling of the gown and that enticing intelligence simmering there in her dark eyes.

That same thing scratched at him, the way it had in Paris when Ricardo had given him her picture, and he knew better than to let it. This was already a mess. A problem, and he had enough of those already. He needed a clear path and a solution, or what was the point of this game? He might as well hand himself over to the general for the execution that had already been meted out to the rest of his bloodline and call it a day.

Some part of him—a part that grew larger all the time—wished he'd done just that, years ago. Some part of him wished he'd been in that car with the rest of his family when it had been run off the road. Some part of him wished he'd never lived long enough to make these choices.

But that was nothing but craven self-pity. The least of his sins, but a sin nonetheless.

"You are very pretty," he told her now. Sternly.

"I would thank you, but somehow I doubt it was a compliment."

"It is surprising. I expected you to be attractive, of course, in the way all women of your particular profession are." He waved a hand.

She smiled, managing to convey an icy disdain that would do a royal proud. "My profession?"

Cairo shrugged. "Dancer. Television personality. Expensive trophy wife, ever open to the appropriate upgrades. Whatever you call yourself."

Her smile took on that edge that fascinated him, but she didn't look away.

"I do like an upgrade." She fingered the rim of her glass and he remembered the feel of her skin under his hand, hot and soft at once. Touching her had been a serious miscalculation, he was aware. One that pounded in him still, kicking up dark yearnings and desperate long-ings he knew he needed to ignore. "Are you going to tell me why I'm here?"

"No insulting version of my title this time? I'm wounded."

"I find my creativity wanes along with my interest." She leaned forward and set her glass down on the table before her with a decisive *click*. "Monte Carlo is wasted on me, I'm afraid, as I'm not much of a gambler." Her smile didn't reach her eyes. "I prefer the comfort of a sure thing. And I loathe being bored."

"Is this what boredom looks like on you? My mistake. I rather thought you looked a bit...flushed."

"I find myself ever so slightly nauseated." He knew she was lying. The glitter in her bright eyes told him so, if he'd had the slightest doubt. "I can't think why."

He thrust his hands into the pockets of his trousers. "Perhaps you dislike penthouses with extraordinary views." He smiled. "The coast or me. Take your pick. Both views, and I say this with no false modesty at all, are stunning."

"Maybe I dislike spoiled rich men who waste my time and think far too highly of their overexposed charms." The edge to her smile and that glittering thing in her gaze grew harder. Hotter. "I've seen it all in the pages of every tabloid magazine every week for the last twenty years. It's about as thrilling as oatmeal."

"I must have misheard you. I thought you compared me to a revoltingly warm and cloying breakfast cereal."

"The similarities are striking."

"A man with less confidence than I have—and no ac-cess to a mirror—might find that hurtful, Ms. Hollis."

"I feel certain you find whatever you need in all the reflective surfaces available to you." She eyed him. "I suppose that almost qualifies as a skill. But while that confirms my opinion of your conceit, it doesn't tell me what I'm doing here."

Cairo hadn't decided precisely how he would do this. Somewhere in his murky, battered soul he'd imagined this might prove a rare opportunity to be honest. Or as near enough to honest as he was capable of being, anyway. He'd imagined that might make purchasing a wife to ward off a revolution a little less seedy and sad, no matter his reasons. A little self-deprecating humor and a few hard truths, he'd imagined, and the whole thing would be easily sorted.

But he hadn't expected to want her this badly.

"I have a proposition for you," he forced himself to say, before he made the unfortunate decision to simply seduce her instead and see what happened. He already knew what would happen—didn't he?—and the pleasures of the moment couldn't outweigh the realities of the future bearing down on him. He knew that.

He couldn't believe he was even considering it.

"I'd say I'm flattered," Brittany was saying coolly, "but I'm not. I'm not interested in being any man's mistress. And not to put too fine a point on it, but your charms are a bit…" She raised her brows. "Overused."

He blinked, and took his time with it. "I beg your pardon. Did you just call me a whore?"

"I'd never use that word," Brittany demurred, and though her voice was smooth he was sure there was something edgy and sharp lurking just beneath it. "But the phrase *rode hard and put away wet* comes to mind." She waved a hand at him. "It's all a bit boring, if I'm honest."

"Do not kid yourself, Ms. Hollis," Cairo advised her quietly. "I've had a lot of sex with a great many partners, it's true."

"That's a bit like the ocean confessing it's slightly damp."

He smiled. "The media coverage of my sex life might indeed be boring. I wouldn't know as I make a point never to follow it. But the act itself? Never."

"You'd be the last to know, of course. Even a man as conceited as you are must realize that."

"I suppose the first hundred or so could simply be interested in my dramatic personal history," Cairo said, as if considering her point, though he kept his gaze trained on the increasing color high up on her cheeks. *Interesting.* "And the second two hundred could be in it for my personal wealth. But *all* of them? The law of averages suggests not *all* of them would come apart like that, screaming and wailing and crying beneath me. The same reasoning applies if you suggest they were faking it. Some, I imagine, because there are always some. But all?"

"I'm sure you saw whatever it is you wanted to see." He could have sworn there was a huskiness in her voice and a deeper shade to the red of her cheeks, and he didn't care what she said. He knew passion when he saw it. She was as affected as he was. "Ninety times a day, or whatever the horrifying number is. The mind boggles."

Cairo was no saint, by design or inclination. But he was also not quite the epic sinner he'd played all his life. And in all the years he'd performed his role in the circus that was his life, he'd never felt the slightest urge to tell a woman that. What the hell was happening to him tonight?

"I'm only good at one thing," he told her, the way he'd have told anyone else. He pretended he couldn't hear the intensity in his own voice. He pretended he had no idea how little in control of himself he was just then. "And as it happens, I'm very, very good at it."

She swallowed, which he shouldn't have found even remotely fascinating, no matter how elegant her neck. "Is that your proposition? My answer is an emphatic no, as I said. But also, your pitch needs some work."

"That I'm an excellent lover is a fact, not a pitch," Cairo said with a small shrug. He found he was enjoying himself, which was almost as unusual as the claws of need that still raked through him. "The proposition is far less exciting, I'm afraid. I'm not in the market for a mistress, Ms. Hollis. Why would I bother with such a confining arrangement? I rarely meet a woman who wouldn't do anything I ask for free, no need to provide room, board or baubles on demand."

"I'm overcome by the romance of it all."

"Then this will delight you." Cairo eyed her, a column of gold tipped in all that sweet copper he wanted to bury his hands in, and he found his blood was pumping much too hard through his body then, as if he was out on a long, hard run in a harsh winter. He ignored it. "I find myself in need of a wife. I've been considering a number of candidates for the position, but you are far and away my first choice."

He expected her to say something scathing. Perhaps let out a scandalized laugh. He even braced himself for the lash of it, and damned if he didn't enjoy the anticipation of that, too. But she only considered him for a moment, her dark hazel gaze unreadable, and he found he had no idea what she might say.

That, like everything else with this woman, was a new experience. He told himself he hated it. Because he should have. He needed an employee of sorts, at minimum. A partner if at all possible. What he did not need was any more trouble, and Brittany Hollis had that stamped deep on every inch of her lovely skin.

God knew he had enough trouble. It lived inside him. It was his world.

"Who's your second choice?" she asked when the silence had drawn out almost too long.

"My second choice?"

Brittany didn't *quite* roll her eyes. "I can hardly determine whether to be insulted or complimented if I don't know the field, can I?"

Cairo named a famously orphaned Italian socialite, primarily well-known for her bouts of sulky nudity on board the superyachts of her questionable Russian oligarch boyfriends.

Brittany sighed. "Insulted it is."

"She's a far second, if that helps. Far too much work for too little return."

This surprising American, who he'd expected would fall at his feet in an instant and who cared if that was as much about his credit line and his title as the charms she'd called *overused* to his face, only gazed at him a moment, her dark eyes narrow. He thought he could *see* her thinking and he didn't understand why or how he could find that the sexiest thing he'd seen in years. It was that glint in her hazel gaze. It was moving through him like something alcoholic.

"You don't actually want to get married, then. You want to inflict your wife on someone—the world, perhaps? As any girl would be, I'm of course delighted to be considered an infliction. It's all my dearest fairy-tale fantasies made real, thank you."

He couldn't help but smile at her dry tone, though the curve of his own mouth felt as hard as granite. "I'm sorry, did you expect protestations of love? I could do that, if you like. You can even believe them, if it helps. But the offer is for a job. A position. Not a romantic interlude."

Those too-dark eyes held his for a moment that stretched on a little too long for comfort. Then even longer. And Cairo had never wanted to read another person's mind as much as he did then.

"I feel certain there's a middle ground." She stood, running an unnecessary hand over the sleek fall of her gown as she did, and Cairo found he wanted her with a raw fervor that shook through him, making him a total stranger to himself. Making him a traitor to his cause. Making her nothing less than a calamity—which only made the wanting worse. "I'd suggest you find it before you approach the socialite. I've heard she bites."

And then Brittany Hollis—so far beneath him that she should have been prostrate with gratitude at his attention to her and appreciative of the faintest bare crumb of his interest—actually turned on her heel, showed him her back as if he really did bore her silly and walked out.

Halfway through her burlesque performance a few nights later, Brittany felt an electric ripple go through the crowd. And seconds later, through her.

She told herself she was imagining things as she strode across the stage to the pulsing beat, but she knew better. She knew that feeling, like being lit on fire and forced to stand still in the crackling flames. That was exactly how she'd felt in Monte Carlo, burnt to a crisp where she stood on the casino floor.

Brittany concentrated on the pounding music and on the lazy choreography she could perform by rote. Something she was even happier about than usual, because she could hardly pay attention to this kick or that shimmy when she could *feel* Cairo's presence like some kind of tsunami, washing through the club. She didn't have to squint to see him past the swirling lights the club owner went a little overboard with during her number. She didn't have to try to make out his features as he moved through the dark.

She could track him by the murmur and shift in the crowd as they swiveled around in their chairs to watch him pass. She could feel the way that deceptively lush gaze of his settled on her and stayed there. It was a little too much like the dreams she kept having, the ones that spun out different, far more erotic endings to that night in his hotel suite in Monaco—when she'd never wanted a man's touch in her life. She felt that same great rush of complicated, messy feelings, the way she did each time she woke up with her heart pounding and her breath tangled in her throat, her body too warm and somehow no longer her own.

And suddenly the crimson corset she wore seemed a good deal tighter across her breasts and the black lace choker at her neck lived up to its name with a vengeance. She was aware of the creamy expanse of her upper thighs that peeked out above her garters, and the way the sleek sleeves that hooked over her pointer fingers, but covered her forearms to her elbows, left her upper arms bare. The frilly, puffy shrug she wore that made her look one step away from steampunk seemed insubstantial, suddenly, and she understood what Cairo had called "the art of the burlesque" in a different way than she ever had before.

Brittany didn't want to investigate that—much less the great swirl of *feelings* that nearly knocked her sideways on the main stage. She simply danced toward it.

Toward him.

Toward Cairo as he moved to the reserved table that had been kept empty right there in the front all night, so there was no pretending she didn't see him when—at last—he stopped showing off for the goggle-eyed audience and settled himself in the chair closest to the stage as if he owned this place and everything in it. The dancers before him, most of all.

It was Brittany's turn then, and she took it.

He'd been right about her previous performances. She'd been phoning it in, having promised the club owner eight weeks of shows and not caring too much about it after the first rash of appalled tabloid headlines. Tonight, however, seven weeks into her run, it turned out she had something to prove.

To him, a little voice clarified.

She didn't ask herself what she was doing, just as she didn't question why the things he'd said to her and the proposition he'd made—far less offensive than most of the things she'd been called and a huge percentage of the offers she'd fielded in her time—had needled her ever since. Brittany simply danced.

For him, something inside her whispered.

Up there on the stage, dressed in bright red, frilly almost underthings, she didn't care if he knew it. She danced as if there was no one else in the room. She danced as if they had long been lovers, a cheap, trashy girl like her and a man who could have had a throne. She danced as if this whole cavernous club was a king's harem, and she had no goal in all the world but to please him.

Because he wasn't the only one who was good at what he did.

The truth was, the only thing in her life Brittany had ever really loved besides her grandmother was dancing. It had gotten lost there, in the brutal reality of her first marriage and the Hollywood fakery of her second. She'd turned it into pole tricks and barely there G-strings and all manner of mugging for the camera to pay her bills. She'd used it to inform the way she moved and breathed and insinuated herself in the path of tabloid reporters and future husbands alike. But deep down inside of her was the sheer love of movement and music and the fusion of the two that, once upon a time, had been her only way out of the grim realities of her life in Mississippi.

Brittany drew on all of that now.

She danced to him, for him. She wound herself around the poles and she strutted across the stage, until she felt as if she was flying. She'd gone completely electric by the time she skidded to her dramatic finish—sliding across the stage on her knees with her hands stretched out in front of her, ending up face-to-face with Cairo as the music ended.

And it was as if she'd tipped off the side of the world, straight into that hot caramel gaze of his. Spun sugar and hot sex.

The crowd made noise all around them. She could hear the DJ on the microphone as if from a great distance. She was aware of the stage beneath her knees and the hands she'd stretched out toward Cairo in some or other form of supplication—

All feigned, she reminded herself sternly. All part of her performance, no matter how oddly right and real it felt to be stretched out before Cairo Santa Domini as if he was the only man in the whole club. Or perhaps the world.

As if nothing could possibly matter but him.

That should have set off all kinds of alarms inside of her, especially when she knew exactly what he wanted from her and, more than that, what he must think of her in the first place to offer it. That it was what she'd gone to excessive lengths to make sure everyone already thought of her didn't seem to matter.

The world didn't hurt her feelings any longer. Yet somehow, Cairo had.

Did you expect protestations of love? he'd asked, his voice scathingly amused. It had cut her. Deep.

She told herself she didn't know why.

Yet here, now, at the end of a silly dance in a stupid costume that had never affected her one bit before, all Brittany could see was Cairo. Caramel eyes burning bright and hot and that intoxicating mouth set to something far too edgy for her peace of mind. She could feel it move in her, from the breasts that wanted to break free of her constricting corset, to that low, odd ache in her belly that she tried her hardest to ignore.

"That was perfectly adequate," Cairo said, his voice pitched to slice through the clamor pressing in around them, his mouth set in a little crook.

It went straight through her all over again, little as she wanted to admit it.

Brittany shifted, rolling back so she kneeled upright on the stage above him, no longer at eye level. That felt safer, no matter that her heart clapped wildly against her ribs. She forced herself to gaze down at him coolly. Challenging and wholly unbothered, as he'd accused her of being in Monte Carlo. How she wished it was true, the way it always had been before, with every man she'd ever met in all her life. Except this one.

"Are you slumming, Your Most Graceless?" She raised her brows as she swung her legs around in front of her and then slid from the stage to stand before the chair where, once again, he lounged as if he'd presented himself for a study in aristocratic laziness. "Maybe you don't know the rules this far from the golden embrace of the Champs-Élysées. If you want a private chat, you need to pay for the privilege."

He didn't quite smile. And his eyes seemed to darken the more his mouth curved.

"Let me hasten to assure you I know my way around establishments of ill repute." He tilted his head to one side and that gaze of his went very nearly lethal. She felt it like his hand wrapped tight around her throat, rendering her choker superfluous. Or maybe that was her heart, pounding so hard she thought it might tip her over. He indicated his lap with a jerk of his chin, never shifting his gaze from hers. "Come, Brittany. Show me what you've got. I promise, I can pay."

CHAPTER THREE

HER NAME IN Cairo's decadent mouth, instead of that drawled *Ms. Hollis*, was like a lick against the hottest, sweetest part of her. It jolted through her, lightning need and the same dancing fire, making her melt. Everywhere.

Brittany couldn't seem to jerk her gaze away from his, and even knowing how dangerous that was didn't make it any easier. Her heart was a hammer against every pulse point, slamming into her again and again, but she made herself smile as she shifted position into something more pinup worthy, as was expected of a woman wearing as little as she was.

She told herself it was the game. What the costume demanded.

And so what if she'd never given an audience member the time of day after a performance before? *This is different*, she told herself, with starch. *This is our own little war, him and me, and I'll win it.*

"Was I unclear in Monaco?" she asked him. She was aware that they were attracting all kinds of stares as the music cued up the next act, but she couldn't bring herself to pay attention to that the way she knew she should. She couldn't break away from the tractor beam of his arrogant gaze long enough to read the room and react accordingly, and she didn't want to think about the implications of the situation. "I thought my walking off without a backward glance was a fairly straightforward message."

"I assumed that was a ploy," he replied in that same deceptively mild way of his that really shouldn't tear through her the way it did, making her feel hollow and needy and too many other raw things to name. "I thought I'd come here and speak to you in the language you understand."

"Rather than in Pompous Ass, the language of rich men? Don't worry, I'm fluent."

He didn't answer that directly. Still holding her gaze with his, he reached into the inside pocket of the sleek coat he wore and pulled out a leather billfold fat with euros. Very, very fat. He didn't so much as glance at it, he simply peeled a purple note from inside and slapped it on the table. Then another. And another.

"You appear to be suggesting I'm motivated by five-hundred euro notes," Brittany said. Through her teeth. "Surely not."

Cairo didn't say a word. He merely added another note to the pile. Then another. One after the next.

"I'm sure I'm mistaken," she bit out, as the pile continued to grow. "You can't possibly be calling me a prostitute, can you?"

He didn't quite laugh. Not quite.

"Of course not," he replied, in a scrupulously innocent voice that made the lie of it feel like a slap. "Your prices are much higher and you require legal vows, if your matrimonial history is any guide. Hardly a rendezvous in a back alley, is it?"

"True," Brittany replied, her voice a different sort of slap that her palms itched to replicate against that dark-shadowed jaw of his. "But I have no intention or interest in making vows of any kind with you."

That sharp smile of his edged over into something feral.

"So you say." He threw another few bills onto the table-top, carelessly and insultingly. Deliberately so, she imagined. "Then a lap dance it is."

Brittany jerked her attention away from him for a moment to see the club owner over by the bar, furiously gesturing for her to sit down. To stop blocking access to the stage, she realized, now that the next act had started. And it was simple, of course. She should merely walk away from Cairo again the way she'd done once already. She should pretend she'd never met him. She wanted nothing more than to do exactly that.

So she had no idea why instead, she settled herself on the arm of his chair and gazed down into his face as if she really was the hardened stripper she'd played on TV instead of the innocent sometimes even she forgot she really was.

"I don't give lap dances," she told him loftily, pretending she hadn't surrendered something critical in sitting down like this. As if that blaze in his caramel gaze didn't show sheer male victory and something edgier besides. As if she didn't recognize she'd lost what little ground she'd gained by denying him in Monaco. "Though I'm happy to take your money, of course. You appear to have far too much of it."

Cairo shrugged as if it was nothing to him, the thousands of euros in a purple pile on the table. What were mere thousands to a man who had untold billions in property alone?

"All I want is a dance," he told her, and he was so much closer now than he had been in Monaco. Too close.

The arms of the seats were made deliberately wide and comfortable, all the better for the girls to perch upon, so she wasn't touching him—because Brittany didn't do *touching*. Especially not with men. And she told herself she didn't recognize that craving in her for what it was, elemental and obvious, so close to that magnificent body of his as he lounged there that she could feel the heat he generated in the space between them.

Then he made everything that much more mad and wild when he reached over and started to trace a lazy little pattern against the skin of the thigh nearest him, right at the top of her stocking and below the ruffled red-and-black underwear she wore.

Back and forth. Back and forth.

She wanted to leap up. She wanted to slap his hand away. She wanted to slap *him* like the offended virgin she actually was, but she didn't dare give herself away like that. And the more she sat there and let Cairo touch her, the more she seemed to forget why allowing this to happen was such a terrible idea.

They both watched his idle finger for a while. Maybe entire years—decades—while inside, everything Brittany had ever been and everything she knew about herself crumbled into dust and shivered away until there was nothing left of her but that pulsing heat between her legs.

Her worst fear come true.

But she still didn't move.

"Or perhaps you prefer a private room after all," Cairo said, the low rumble of his insinuating voice adding to the spell he cast with that impossibly elegant finger against her thigh rather than breaking it. "Is this how you upsell the punters, Ms. Hollis?"

Brittany jerked her attention away from that mesmerizing, addictive pattern he kept drawing against her flesh, and told herself it was the insult of what he'd said—not that he'd reverted back to *Ms. Hollis*. But his gaze was worse than his touch. Too bright, too hot.

And the last thing in the world she wanted was to be locked away in some private room with this man. She knew she couldn't trust him, of course. He'd made the fact he couldn't be trusted something that practically required a celebration. But she was suddenly so much more afraid she couldn't trust herself.

"I think not," she managed to say, but she didn't sound like herself. She sounded as thrown as she felt.

Something flashed over his famous, beautiful face. She felt it echo inside of her like a roll of thunder and then, suddenly, he wasn't lounging there idly any longer. She hardly saw him move. All she knew was that one moment she sat there on the arm of his chair, barely clinging to the pretense of some civility and everything she'd ever known about herself, and the next she was sprawled across his lap.

She wanted to scream. To fight. She wanted that more than anything—so she had no idea why she simply melted against him, as if she'd lost all control of the body that had done her bidding the whole of her life.

She had never been tempted, by anyone. She had never *melted*, ever.

Cairo was hard beneath her, hot and perfect, his legs so strong they marked his studied laziness as yet another lie. His arms closed around her, holding her against his sculpted chest and she couldn't seem to *breathe*. She couldn't breathe and she couldn't speak and she had no idea why she was letting any of this happen.

Especially when he bent and brought his face so close to hers.

So. Damned. Close.

"You'd better brace yourself," she managed to tell him, though she sounded far more thrown by this than she would have liked. And still it was nowhere near as thrown as she *felt*. "The security guards take a dim view of unauthorized touching in the main room."

"When will you learn that the rules do not apply to me?" Cairo's mouth was a breath away from hers, and the thick, glossy fall of his shaggy hair brushed her cheek as he bent over her, his dark eyes gleaming. "And that sooner or later, all mere mortals do exactly as I ask?"

"I'm not giving you a lap dance," she told him, though

her heart was drumming at her again, so hard she was glad she wore that lace choker so there was no chance he could see it there in the hollow of her throat. "And I'm not marrying you, either. I don't even like you."

"What the hell does that have to do with anything?" Cairo muttered, sounding less like a king and more like a man than she'd heard him yet. "This has nothing to do with *like.*"

And then he yanked her mouth to his.

He never should have tasted her.

It was a terrible mistake in a night brimming with too many of them already. He should not have come to this crass place in a temper. He should not have indulged in that temper in the first place, for that matter. He should have laughed at the absurdity of a woman of so little breeding declining his offer to better herself so spectacularly and then moved on. Hell, he should have forgotten she existed at all the moment the door of his suite in Monaco had shut behind her.

Instead, he'd brooded over it. Over her.

"The world is full of inappropriate women, Sire," Ricardo had pointed out earlier this evening. "It's one of its few charms."

"It seems I require a particular blend of inappropriate and interesting," Cairo had replied, having spent the days since Monaco convincing himself of precisely that. It wasn't that only Brittany Hollis would do. It wasn't that he was unused to rejection. Both of those things were true. But what mattered more, he'd assured himself, was that his very *requirements* had changed. "If there are more who fit the bill, by all means, present them to me."

But Ricardo had wisely said nothing, and here Cairo was.

And this inarguably terrible mistake he was making

felt like sweet, hot glory and all manner of dark and lovely sins besides. He wanted nothing more than to commit every last one of those sins, with impunity, and with her. Cairo was only a man, after all, and he knew better than most what a terrible one he was, straight through to his core. And Brittany was sprawled across his lap, dressed in a sleek red corset and very little else, tasting of mint and longing.

He shifted, opening his mouth against hers, and he lost himself in the fire of it. The sheer, exultant perfection of the scrape of her tongue against his, the press of her breasts against his chest, the way she clung to his shirt as if she wanted him even a small fraction as much as he wanted her.

Cairo could work with a fraction.

He poured everything he had into the kiss, taking her mouth again and again. Lust and need. All the dark longings that had haunted him since she'd walked away from him in Monaco. All the sweet, hot desire that had flashed through him as he'd watched her performance here tonight.

All the fire in his twisted, haunted soul.

He wasn't surprised when she tore her mouth from his, and his arms tightened around her as if he expected her to twist out of his hold. She didn't—and it was a measure of how out of control he'd become that he counted that as a victory.

"I don't want anything to do with you," she hissed at him.

Cairo couldn't blame her. Neither did he. But that was beside the point.

"Of course not," he agreed, their lips practically touching, his hands full of her sweetness. "I can tell by the way you kiss me."

And then he set his mouth to hers once more.

Because kissing Brittany, he discovered quickly, was fast becoming his favorite vice in a life fairly overflowing with them.

This time when she pulled away, he discovered his hands had found their way to her thick hair in its tempting copper twist, and he'd pulled the fragrant curtain of it down around them. Her lips were sweet and full, her breath came as fast as his did, and her eyes had gone wide and dark.

Cairo thought he might never get enough of her, and it was a measure of how obsessed he was already that the notion failed to alarm him.

"You can't do this," she told him, and he had the strange thought that this was the real Brittany, after all her edge and flair. She sounded a little bit shaken. She looked a little bit fragile. He should have felt a surge of triumph at that, but instead, the thing that turned over inside him felt a good deal more like regret. He knew all about *regret*. "You know you can't."

"I don't think you've been paying attention, *cara*," he told her, and he shifted one hand from her thick, gorgeous hair to drag his thumb over the plump seduction that was her lower lip. He ached to taste her again. He didn't know how he refrained. "I am the last of the Santa Dominis. Some still call me a king. I can do as I wish."

"Not with me, you can't." She jerked her mouth back from his touch and shoved her way to a more vertical sitting position on his lap, and the sweet agony of it all threatened to unman him where he sat. "I want nothing to do with your little game of lost thrones, thank you. My life is complicated enough."

"Marrying me would uncomplicate it."

"Right. Because that's exactly what you are. *Uncomplicated.*"

He could see the moment it occurred to her that despite

the hard tone she'd used, what she'd said might as well be a compliment. Little did she know. He could teach darkness to the night, and that was on his good days.

"I want to be inside you," he told her then, raw and untutored, as if he was a stranger to himself. He felt her shiver, as if the electric charge of it had seared straight through her. "So deep inside you, *cara*, that neither one of us can tell who is a king and who is a stripper. Until there is nothing in all the world but that sweet, wet heat and what burns us both as we drown in it."

He was close enough that he could see the way her pupils dilated at that, so close he could feel the goose bumps beneath his hand as easily as he could see them rise up all over her exposed skin. So close he could feel all that intense heat as it burned through her, like a wild flame incinerating them both.

"I can tell who is who, though," she said, and Cairo was certain he wasn't mistaking the sheer misery he could hear in her voice, as if this was as hard and mystifying a thing for her as it was for him. That was something. He told himself that had to be something. "Just as the tabloids certainly can. And I doubt that would ever change."

"Why would you wish it to change?" He hardly sounded like himself. Or maybe he'd forgotten what it was like to be so honest, about anything. His whole life was a collection of misdirection and straight-out lies, wrapped tight around the blackened, shriveled heart of a man who should have died years ago. "You've crafted your public persona with exquisite precision. Why not take it to its logical end?"

"I know exactly where my public persona is taking me," she gritted out at him. She shifted in his lap, brushing up against the part of him that yearned for her the most, and they both froze. She swallowed, her eyes dark on his, and he had the most absurd notion that she looked *panicked* for a moment. "And it's not to your bed."

"That is why you melt against me, I am sure. Why you cannot look away."

"I'm trapped in your lap. *You* are trapping me."

"We're in a public place," he continued, and though his palms itched to move over her, to learn her in the best and most tactile way possible and prove his point besides, Cairo didn't do it. He let his voice cast that spell instead. "How many people do you think are watching us instead of the stage?"

"All of them." He didn't imagine the sheen of something harder in her gaze then, or the way she tilted her chin up. "You saw to that."

"And yet, were I to slip my fingers just a little bit higher, what would I find?" He moved the hand on her thigh a scant centimeter higher, letting his fingers toy with the satin edge of her underwear. Her breath came in a rush even as she shivered out the truth again. "How wet are you, Brittany? Right here in a strip club where everyone can see you? Would you even protest if I slid my hand beneath those silly red underthings? Or would you lean in closer so no one could be sure and ride my hand instead?"

"Neither." But her voice was soft then. Too soft. As soft as he imagined she was only a fraction of an inch from the place his hand lingered. "I'm going to stand up and get back to work."

"Work?" Cairo laughed and moved his fingers again, and the flush on her delicate cheekbones told him she felt that precisely where he wanted her to feel it. So did he. "This place is an ill-mannered salute to your late husband's family, not your work. We both know what your true calling is."

Her lips pressed together and that melting heat in her dark hazel eyes faded. "If you mean that I'm a whore, you'll have to come up with a better insult. My mother's used the word so many times I've come to consider it an endearment."

"Then marry me," he heard himself say, quite as if it was a real proposal and he was truly as raw and ruined and *desperate* as he felt inside just then. As if there was any real thing inside him at all, when he knew better. But no matter that he told himself he was playing a role, he couldn't seem to stop this electric collision course he found himself on. Worse, he didn't want to stop it. "And we shall see what words your mother uses to address my queen."

"Evidence has never persuaded my mother away from the things she's decided are true," Brittany said, and what was remarkable, Cairo thought, was how she didn't sound bitter at all just then. Only matter-of-fact. It made that same temper he couldn't afford to indulge flare inside him all over again. "But thank you. I'm sure a season as queen to the King of Wishful Thinking would be a delight. But my dance card is full." She nodded at the stage before them. "Literally."

And this time, Cairo felt a kind of hitch in his chest when she pulled away from him. He let her stand, and watched her as she stood there before him, making no attempt to hide the evidence of his need. Her cheeks burned, her eyes gleamed dark, that marvelous copper hair of hers tumbled all around her in unruly waves, and Cairo understood that role or no, he would never, ever rest until he had her.

In his bed, to start.

But no other queen would do. He ignored the part of him that questioned that—the part that reminded him he was a king without a throne and in need of any unacceptable woman to make sure he stayed without it—and indulged the part of him that had the blood of five hundred years of Santa Dominis pounding in his blood. Five hundred years of autocratic rulers who knew what they wanted and took what they wished, and brooked precious little disagreement as they did it.

He might have lost his kingdom. He might never set foot in the palace his family had built from a primitive fortress into a splendid fairy tale ever again. But he was still who he was, who he'd been bred to be, and no matter the darkness he knew he carried inside of him—or else how could he make himself such a believable disgrace?—none of that mattered in the end. He was still Cairo Santa Domini.

"You can't have me," she told him, as if she could read his mind. As if she could see the truth of him, stamped in his bones, deep in his veins, all the kings and queens who'd gone before him.

"Silly girl," he drawled, and made no attempt to sit up straighter from his lazy position. Or to rein in the desire he was certain she could see stamped all over him, from his face to his sex. "Don't you know that only makes me want you more?"

"You'll have to learn to live with the disappointment somehow," she said dismissively, and Cairo only smiled.

"That," he murmured, like the threat it was, "is one thing you can depend upon me never, ever to do."

Brittany woke late the following morning in her little flat, four narrow flights up in a weathered old building on the outskirts of Montmartre. It was laughably tiny, although if she stood on a chair in her small kitchen there was enough of a view of the Parisian rooftops and the smallest bit of the famous Basilica of Sacré-Cœur that she could forget her worries a while as she craned her head to see a sliver of its pale white dome.

She did not think about what had happened the night before. She did not think about the dreams that had haunted her through the night, waking her again and again until she finally fell into something dreamless and exhausted near dawn.

She didn't think about any of it and yet she could still feel Cairo's touch. She could still taste him on her lips.

Her body was still in that insane tumult over him, from her breasts that felt swollen to twice their size, to the shivery hot knot low in her belly that clenched and clenched and clenched. Her body, which was supposed to be entirely hers. Her body, which she'd kept a pristine little fortress ever since her first wedding night, when she'd hidden from the whiny boyfriend turned drunken lout and had decided, there and then, that she'd rather die untouched and alone than let anyone else touch her against her will.

She'd never imagined that her body and her mind could disagree about what *her will* was.

Brittany took a very long shower to wash the night away. Then she went on her daily run at her gym, moving much faster than usual today through her usual miles, but the dreams and the memories stuck with her no matter how quick her pace.

It was never a good sign when the treadmill felt more like a metaphor than simple exercise.

Brittany was already in a dark, uneasy mood when she made it back to her flat. It did not improve when she picked up the private mobile phone she'd left plugged in on her bedside table to see her mother had called at least three times.

She was scowling at the screen as she scrolled through the logged calls, no messages, when it lit up with a fourth call from her mother.

Something cold snaked down Brittany's spine. The last time her mother had called repeatedly like this, Brittany's former stepchildren—all old enough to be her parents, a fact that perhaps only she and Jean Pierre had found amusing—had taken to the tabloids to sound the trumpets about how shoddily they'd treated her and how they had "expunged that harlot" from the family home at last.

Brittany's mother had not called to commiserate about yet another tour through the slag heaps of the tabloids. She'd called, as ever, to complain that her daughter's disgraceful behavior was humiliating the whole of the Hollis clan back in Gulfport and *had Brittany no shame?*

"Do you want me to have shame, Mom?" Brittany had asked coolly. Someday, she'd vowed for the nine millionth time, she would stop answering her mother's calls altogether. Someday when she'd finally come to terms with the fact that the woman was never, ever going to treat her as anything more than a source of income. Much less love her. *Someday.* "Or do you want me to keep paying your rent?"

Today was not *someday*, regrettably, but Brittany tossed the mobile aside without answering, letting her mother go to voice mail. She powered up her laptop instead.

She didn't even have to Google herself, as she sometimes did. Oh, no. The headlines were right there on her launch page.

His Royal Stripper?
How Low Can Cairo Go?
Black Widow Brittany Trades Up!

Her heart was already causing a commotion in her chest as she clicked on the first article, as if she already knew what she'd see—

But it was worse.

Someone had taken a series of pictures in the club last night. And the pictures made the whole thing look much more sordid than Brittany remembered it. Much hotter.

Much more desperate and *much* more public. If she hadn't known better, Brittany might have assumed that Cairo actually had bought her for the evening. The papers certainly insinuated he had.

He might as well have, she thought now. It came to the same thing, and if she'd let him, she'd have a paycheck to comfort herself this morning. Meanwhile, that scraped-raw, heavy feeling in her chest wasn't going to help a soul. It was better to ignore it. Starting with the little sound she didn't mean to let out as she sat there gaping at those awful pictures that told her far too many hard truths about herself and her own longings. She lifted up a hand to try to rub that harsh, hollow feeling out of her own chest.

It didn't really work.

She felt betrayed. By herself, not by the devastatingly handsome man whose entire life was a monument to wreck and ruin. She should have seen this coming. She should have known there was no way *Cairo Santa Domini* could turn up in her life *without* leaving his dark mark all over her.

This was what he did. Exactly this.

She should have assumed not only that someone would have photographed the whole of their encounter, but also that, of course, they'd sell it to the voracious tabloids. In point of fact, it was likely Cairo had engineered the whole thing and the photographer in question was on his payroll. Why hadn't she thought of that last night? *Of course* he'd play this up to the paparazzi. *This was what he did.*

She should have been prepared for this—why wasn't she?

But she knew why. Brittany hadn't been thinking after that kiss, which looked even more carnal and impossibly sexy in the pictures than she remembered it. And her memories were explicit. She hadn't been thinking when she'd staggered away from him and hid backstage, where none of the other girls talked to her and she could pretend she was utterly at peace as she changed back into her street clothes. She hadn't been thinking when she'd opted to walk home despite the hour and the questionable neighborhood, hoping the exercise and the night air might clear her head.

He'd kissed her. She'd kissed him. It had been the most sensual experience of her life, and she hated herself for that. She hated that she'd responded to him like that.

That kiss had been the only thought in her head.

The truth was, she hadn't been doing a whole lot of actual thinking since she'd walked into that casino in Monaco.

The fact that Cairo was certain to destroy her had loomed so large inside of her from her first glimpse of him that even now, it was making it hard for her to breathe. It was clouding her judgment, confusing her, making her *react* to him rather than act in her own best interests the way she always had before.

The way she'd been doing all her life, or she'd never have made it this far.

"Pull yourself together, Brittany," she ordered herself, her own voice loud in the quiet of her little studio, her own face much too big and exposed on the laptop screen before her, looking vulnerable and needy and entirely too aroused.

It horrified her to see that expression. Or it thrilled her, because she could still *feel* that kiss.

Or maybe she couldn't tell the difference. "This is an opportunity. Since when do you turn down an opportunity?"

Destruction wasn't a good enough excuse to avoid something. If it was, she'd never have left Gulfport at sixteen in the company of Darryl, whom she'd known perfectly well was nothing but trouble.

The kind of destruction Cairo was likely to cause, she understood in the wake of his kiss in a way she hadn't before, was purely internal. He wouldn't take a swing at her the way Darryl had. He might rip out her heart with his royal hands. He might tear it into pieces, mash it into a pulp beneath his feet. She didn't understand why a man she should find laughable in any real sense instead posed such a risk for her neglected little heart, but there it was. She didn't know why. She only knew it was an inescapable truth. She'd known it the moment she'd laid eyes on him.

"But so what?" she asked herself now, digging the heel of one palm into her chest as if that could make the feeling of immensity and inevitability go away.

Because other than the small issue of her inevitable ruin, Cairo Santa Domini was perfect for her purposes. More than perfect. He was *Cairo Santa Domini*—he was a dream come true. Richer than sin, possessed of more blue blood in the tip of one toe than her entire family tree put together and not in the least put off by her sad, tacky and deeply checkered past. Most of the wealthy European men Brittany had met after marrying Jean Pierre, including his own sons, had indicated that they would be happy to sully themselves with her in private of an afternoon, but would never allow anyone to see them in her gauche presence in public, lest their ancient claims to aristocracy collapse into so much deeply inferior dust.

Cairo was quite the opposite.

And if she still felt that strange pang at the fact he wanted her *because* of the image she'd crafted instead of despite it, to say nothing of her low-class upbringing, well…of course he did. Why else would a man like him notice a woman like her? That silly *pang* was between her and the heart he was going to break without even trying very hard, and the truth was, she could as easily live on her far-off island with a shattered heart as without it.

The point was the palm trees and the fruity drinks and the solitude. Who cared what happened to her heart?

So when her other mobile phone rang—the one she kept for paparazzi, tabloids and whoever else wanted to reach her yet didn't know her personally—she answered it.

"Please hold for His Serene Grace the Archduke Felipe Skander Cairo of Santa Domini," the cultured voice on the other end of the line intoned.

Brittany didn't hang up, despite that spike in her pulse. Because her own internal destruction was a small price to pay. Cairo Santa Domini might be as dangerous as he seemed. After last night, she knew he was.

But he was her only escape. He was the light at the end of the tunnel as much as he was also the train.

She had no choice.

"Darling," she purred when he came on the line, that voice of his dark and sinful and good enough to eat. God, she was in so much trouble. But she told herself it would all be worth it. One day, all of this would be worth it. Vanuatu waited for her across the planet, white sand beaches, peace and anonymity at last. "I saw our engagement announcement in all the tabloids. You shouldn't have."

CHAPTER FOUR

CAIRO APPEARED IN so many tabloids with so many women that even when the woman in question was notorious in her own right, like Brittany, it could only cause so much comment. There was the initial carrying on and then it was on to the next set of celebrity shenanigans. Football players were forever embroiling themselves in bitter custody disputes with B-list actresses, politicians were ever hypocritical and blustery in turn and the papers never lacked for seedy stories to tell in their breathless, insinuating headlines.

"We appear to be less interesting than the custody tussles of a striker for Real Madrid," Brittany said brightly when they met after the initial frenzy started to fade that first week, to plot out their next few moves. That sweet smile she could produce on cue did absolutely nothing to soften the edge in her voice—which was a good thing, Cairo thought, since he was a perverse creature who liked the edge better. "The entire world has been overexposed to Cairo Santa Domini scandals. A few pictures in a strip club are too run-of-the-mill to captivate the public interest after a steady diet of far worse. I'm afraid your shenanigans are good for a shudder, nothing more."

"It's usually more than a shudder," Cairo assured her, because he couldn't seem to help himself. "It's really more of a drawn-out scream, with many a religious conversion along the way. Oh, God. Oh, Cairo. *Oh, God.*"

Brittany sighed as if he was a deep and enduring trial to her. A sound Cairo was certain no woman—no *person*—had made in his presence in all his life, except himself.

"I'll keep that in mind," she said, as if placating a child having a tantrum.

"You do that," he murmured, and then they discussed how best to prepare for the second phase of their plan.

Cairo very rarely appeared with any woman more than once. It was difficult to maintain a reputation as an inveterate playboy if he seemed interested in quality rather than quantity, so he'd never tied himself down to anyone for more than a long weekend. Sometimes he'd throw in a repeated date or weekend years later, just to keep people guessing, but that didn't happen very often.

"I become rather boring after three consecutive days," he'd once told a smarmy journalist in Rome when questioned about this pattern of his, flashing a knowing smile as if he could already read the fan letters his secretary would be forced to wade through, each declaring him anything but *boring*. Some complete with enclosed panties, as punctuation. "It is less a pattern and more of a public service, you understand."

The second time the paparazzi "caught" him and Brittany in the sort of restaurant famous people would only patronize if they were trying to avoid being seen, five days after that night in the strip club, it caused a buzz. It suggested that an actual relationship of some kind had survived both what was called *Cairo's Scandalous Lap Dance* and the resultant tabloid screeching over the photos of the two of them kissing.

"Had I known this would cause such a commotion," Brittany told the pack of cameramen who surrounded her when she emerged from an expertly timed trip to Cartier, flashing her megawatt gold digger's smile and a sizeable cocktail ring on her right hand featuring a deep blue sapphire the approximate size of the Mediterranean Sea, "I would have asked for something a whole lot bigger."

Then, days after that dinner, they were seen exiting Cairo's private residence in the unfashionable morning light, suggesting they'd spent the night there. Or perhaps several days *and* nights, now that Brittany had finished her run at the strip club.

"Are you *dating*?" a clearly appalled television tabloid reporter asked Cairo as he made his way through the heaving mass of paparazzi outside a charity event in London a few days later. "You and the Queen of Tacky?"

"You will be the first to know." He smiled, all teeth and noblesse oblige. "You and all of your viewers are foremost in my thoughts as I navigate my romantic life, I assure you."

"Why isn't she with you tonight?" another reporter demanded. A bit too hotly, Cairo thought, as if these people had personal stakes in Cairo's continuing bachelorhood. He supposed they did. And in that darkness in him he paraded around in so many fine clothes, calling it a man and letting them call him the worthless one he'd always known he was. "Did you already break up?"

"I cannot keep track of this relationship according to all your conflicting headlines," he told them. "On, off. Playboy, gold digger. Maybe she and I are simply two people who enjoy each other's company. But of course, that makes no snide headlines for you, so that will never be printed as a possibility."

Cairo Calls Bad-news Britt a Gold Digger, screamed the papers the following day, right on cue.

After that, Cairo squired Brittany to the lavish wedding of an old boarding school friend of his, currently one of the richest men in Spain. The speculation about what they meant to each other surged into what could only be called a dull roar.

Had Cairo ever attended a wedding with a date before, therefore keeping him from finding several dates there? Answer: no. Did a man who was only after a bit of fun take that fun to a very old friend's wedding in the first place? Answer: of course not, as there was nothing fun about a date with high expectations that a man was only going to dash cruelly. The papers were agog. Could Cairo Santa Domini possibly be getting serious about the most unsuitable woman in the world—even after she'd finished her stint in that horrible Parisian club?

Answers on that last varied, especially after "a wedding guest" released a photo of Cairo and Brittany in their wedding finery, clinging to each other on the dance floor in what was called "the would-be king at his most tender and affectionate—friends claim they've never seen playboy Cairo lose his head like this before!"

"I had no idea you could dance so well with your clothes on," he'd murmured to her as they'd swayed to the wedding band.

"How many of the bridesmaids here have experienced what *you* do so well without your clothes?" she'd replied, not missing a step as she smiled up at him, and he was certain only he could see how razor-sharp that smile was.

After that, they took it to a new level and introduced a series of romantic holidays.

First a weekend in Dubai. Then a week in sun-drenched Rio, and an endless series of photographs of the happy couple on the famous beaches in very, very little. "The better," one online gossip magazine asserted dryly beneath a photo of Brittany in a tiny bikini, "to remind you why Brittany Hollis is dating your husband Cairo Santa Domini and you aren't." Then, after a low-key week or so in Paris, they embarked on an elaborate fortnight in Sub-Saharan Africa, from the sweeping deserts of Namibia to the glory of Victoria Falls to an elegant, fully catered safari in Botswana.

All photographed extensively and then carefully curated to look like a sweepingly luxurious trip so epic it redefined romance. A love letter to all the world, from two of the least likely people to fall in love around. A masterpiece.

If Cairo said so himself.

"Oh, please," Brittany replied when he actually did say it, sitting on one of the camp chairs in the spacious tent they shared, piled high with rugs and linens and tables laden with succulent foods, that had been set up for them a stone's throw from the nearby river bristling with hippos and crocodiles. She was reading yet another book on her e-reader while he tracked their headlines on his mobile, and they were the only ones in the entire world who knew that they slept on opposite sides of that tent the same way they'd slept in different parts of all the hotel suites he'd booked. Night after torturous night, not that it was driving him mad. "*Romance* is not the word being used when people discuss us. I think you know that."

He did know it. What he didn't know, out there in the deep Botswanan night so thick with stars, was why he wanted to change the conversation. Or why some part of him hated it every time another tabloid skewered her. When that, of course, had been the whole point from the start.

Has Brittany Stripped Her Way into Cairo's Heart? howled one New York gossip rag.

Will Cairo Be Lucky Number Four for Much-wed Brittany? asked a British paper, pretending to be slightly less salacious.

Another British paper was far less circumspect: *Brittany's Big-game Hunt in Botswana—Will She Nab Herself a Crown?*

And more starkly by far, in the most popular Santa Domini paper over a picture of the two of them gazing adoringly at each other: *Queen Brittany?*

He should have been pleased, Cairo told himself. Everything was going according to plan. He should have been *exultant*.

But he didn't sleep much on that holiday, and he told himself it had nothing to do with the fact she was in that tent with him, yet a world away. He told himself it was for the best, and he should *exult* in the fact this woman seemed so immune to him.

Exult, he told himself as they smiled and laughed and pretended so well the whole world gasped and carried on over every new photograph.

Exult, he ordered himself when they were in private and she held herself so far away, all cool smiles and distance and her face forever in a book.

He shouldn't find her a mystery and he shouldn't want so badly to solve that mystery that he was up half the night. If this was exulting, Cairo thought as the safari wrapped up and they returned to their regularly scheduled lives in Europe, he was going to require a whole lot more caffeine to survive all the nights he spent asking himself if she really was the only woman he'd ever met who saw only the darkness in him.

That and why, if she was, he was masochistic enough to find that attractive.

"I'm getting the sense that the world is not so much rejoicing in our relationship or even avidly watching it unfold so much as they're craning their necks at us, the way people do at a terrible accident," Brittany said as they flew back to Paris from an exceptionally glorious charity ball in Vienna one night.

She set aside the paper she'd been reading and eyed Cairo as he lounged on the sofa across from her in his preferred position: lying flat on the white leather sectional with his feet propped up on the far arm, his dark suit in disheveled disarray all around him because the more rumpled he looked, the more the papers speculated about his sexual prowess and giddily imagined he performed sex acts behind every potted plant in Europe.

Who was he to deny his public?

He waved a negligent hand and let the ice cubes rattle around in the drink he held. The more noise the ice cubes made, he'd discovered long ago, the drunker people assumed he was. And it was astonishing, the things people said and did when they assumed another person was too drunk to remember, respond or protest.

Cairo wondered if he'd ever simply live through a moment, without mounting any kind of performance to survive it. Or if he even knew how to do that, when there was nothing in him but lies atop lies.

Then he wondered why, when it had been this way since he was a young man, he found the realities of his life and all its necessary untruths so terribly constricting now.

"We are a delicious accident, *cara*," he told her, and experimented with a faint, fake slurring of his words. "That's the whole point."

"My mistake," Brittany replied. "I was starting to think the point was you cavorting about the globe so you could better rub your wealth and careless lifestyle in the face of every last person alive."

"That is a mere side benefit. One I greatly enjoy."

Cairo swung around to sit up, raking his hair back from his forehead as he did. He put his drink down on the coffee table in the expansive jet cabin that better resembled a hotel suite, and he told himself there was no reason in the world for this *gnawing* thing inside him.

She'd agreed to everything after that night in the strip club. After that kiss he'd been torturing himself with ever since, as if it had been his first. She'd come to his residence in the car he'd sent for her in the middle of the night that week, to keep the meeting a secret. All the hints he'd seen of some kind of vulnerability in the strip club had been gone by then. Long gone, leaving her as smooth as glass. She'd merely discussed their strategy with him, offered her own thoughts and ideas and then signed all the papers. No theatrics. No hint of any emotion at all, as if everything between them was strictly business.

Brittany had insisted that was how it should remain.

"You must be joking," Cairo had protested after she'd dropped that little bomb. It had been well into the wee hours that night in Paris, and she'd sat there across from him in one of his ecstatically baroque salons as if she'd been carved from stone.

"I rarely joke at all," she'd replied, deadpan. "And never about sex."

"But sex is one of the great joys of life. Surely you must know this."

"No wonder you are widely held to be such a bright beacon of happiness. Oh, wait. Laziness is more your style, isn't it, Your Indolent Majesty?"

He hadn't known quite what to make of such a strange, stilted conversation about sex with a woman whose taste was still tearing him apart. A woman who, even then, had that same high color on her cheeks that told him she wanted him as badly as he wanted her, no matter what cold, repressive things she said to deny it.

"I know you want me," Cairo had said, baldly. As if he'd never finessed a situation in his life. As if he didn't know how. As if he couldn't help himself or keep himself from being more alarmingly honest with this woman than he was with anyone else alive. "Do you imagine you're hiding it?"

"I don't care who you sleep with, of course," Brittany

had continued as if he hadn't said a word. She'd waved a negligent hand in the air, but he'd seen the way her eyes glittered. He'd been certain that meant something. Or he'd wanted, desperately, for that to mean something. "I only ask that you keep it discreet, so as not to distract from what we're trying to accomplish, and that you make certain to keep it far away from me. That's only courteous."

"No threesomes, then?" he'd asked. Drawled, really. Entirely to watch her reaction—but she'd given him nothing but that glass exterior of hers, smooth and clear.

"You can have all the threesomes you like." Her brows had arched and he'd felt skewered on that hard gaze of hers. "Unless, of course, a man of your appetites finds that number restrictive. Believe me when I tell you I couldn't care less where you put your, ah, royal scepter. As long as it isn't anywhere near me."

"That's hurtful." He cocked his head to one side as he considered her. "My scepter is considered the toast of Europe, if not the entire world."

A faint gleam in her dark eyes then. "I doubt that."

"Naturally, the savage, rutting creature you seem to think I am will only view your denial of what we both feel as a great challenge."

"I don't feel anything." Her voice then had been crisp, her gaze clear, but he still hadn't believed her. Wishful thinking or the truth? How could he still not know? "Am I attracted to you? Of course. You're a remarkably handsome man. I can't imagine any woman alive wouldn't react to you, especially when you decide to turn all of that smoldering on her to get your way."

"Is that what I did? I thought I kissed you and you kissed me back and we very nearly broke a few decency laws right there in that strip club. It wouldn't have bothered me if we had. I have an unofficial diplomatic immunity. You, of course, might not enjoy a stint in a French prison."

"I don't find it necessary to act on every attraction I might feel," Brittany had said, again as if he hadn't spoken. He hadn't been able to think of any other person alive who'd ever treated him as if he was annoying. What was the matter with him that he found that as intriguing as anything else she did? How much must he hate himself? But, of course, he'd already known the answer to that. And she'd still been speaking, still fixing him with that stern glare of hers that he'd doubted she knew made him almost painfully hard. "And I feel certain that as time goes on, the attraction will fade anyway."

"I'm told that never happens. Such is my charm." Cairo had smiled when she'd shaken her head at that. "I'm only reporting what others have said."

"How would they know?" she'd retorted, settling back in her chair as if its stuffy, hard back was comfortable so long after 2:00 a.m. "You never spend more than a weekend with anyone. I'm signing up for far more exposure to your…"

"My scepter?" he supplied.

Her smile in return had been that sharp, edgy thing he found far too fascinating. "Your charm. Such as it is."

"I think you're kidding yourself," he'd said softly then, because he couldn't seem to maintain his game with this woman. "Sex is inevitable."

"I'm sure you believe that," she'd replied, her tone crisp, as if she didn't care either way, and he'd found that needled him far more than if she'd seemed horrified. "And I told you I don't care who you have it with, so I certainly don't need to hear about it." Then she'd shrugged as if she'd never encountered a topic more tedious in all her life. "Have at, with my blessing."

Except the most curious thing had happened since that conversation. Cairo had discovered that he hadn't had the slightest urge to touch any woman but her. He told himself it was because she'd proven herself to be such an excellent partner. A perfect costar in this little bit of theater they were performing for the masses and for their own complementary ends.

He told himself a lot of things. But the only woman he saw was her.

"Why would you do this?" she'd asked him that first night when Ricardo had ushered her into the elegant salon that had stood more or less unchanged for centuries. "What can you possibly hope to gain?"

He'd only shrugged. "I need an infliction, as you said, for any number of shallow reasons. Why are you doing it?"

She'd sniffed. "I want to retire to Vanuatu and live on the beach, where no one can take a single photograph of me, ever."

Cairo didn't think they'd believed each other, but there it was. And here they were now, weeks into this thing. She dressed perfectly, reacted perfectly, gazed at him with the perfect mix of adoration and mystery whenever there was a camera near. She was tailor-made for her role.

That had to be why he'd lost his drive for his favorite vices, women and whiskey, in no particular order. He was too busy taking in the show.

"Why are you staring at me like that?" she asked now.

She'd changed from her stunning ball gown the moment they'd boarded the plane, almost as if she couldn't bear to be in all that couture a moment longer. She did it every time. The moment she could be certain no cameras would follow her, she threw off all the trappings of her larger-than-life presence and left nothing behind but a real, live woman.

Cairo was fascinated. He found he liked her in what he considered her backstage uniform. Low-slung, high-end athletic pants that clung to every lithe curve and long-sleeved T-shirts made of the light, remarkably soft cotton she preferred. Usually, like tonight, she also wore an oversized cashmere scarf she would wrap several times around her neck. He liked it. He liked her gleaming copper hair piled high on the top of her head, so he could see her delicate ears and the line of her neck and that sweet, soft nape he had every intention of getting his mouth on, one of these days.

"Forgive me," he said when moments dragged by and he was still staring. "It occurred to me that you're the only woman I've ever seen in casual clothes." He smiled, and had no idea why it seemed to come less easily than usual. "My lifestyle has never really leant itself to such intimacies."

Brittany blinked. Then again. Her expression shifted from that bulletproof cool he despised and admired in turn to something else. Something that made that gnawing thing in him dig deeper and start to actually hurt.

"You work so hard to pretend otherwise," she said after a moment that dragged on far too long and made his chest hurt. "But beneath all the smoke and mirrors, beneath the Cairo Santa Domini spectacle, you're a completely different man. Aren't you?"

Cairo didn't like that at all. He'd worked too hard for too long to make certain no one ever bothered to take him at anything but face value, because he knew exactly how black and cold it was beneath. Why was this woman the only person on earth who never seemed to do that?

"There is no 'beneath the spectacle.'" His voice was too grim. Too gritty. Too damned revealing. "There is only spectacle. The spectacle is how I survive, Brittany. Believe that, if nothing else."

It was possibly the most honest thing he'd ever said to her. Or to anyone.

"Sometimes I think you're a monster," she told him. "I think you want me to think it. And then other times..."

Her voice softened, and everything inside him ran hot and wild, terror and need. "I think you're possibly the loneliest man I've ever met."

His heart kicked at him. Cairo wanted to kick back. At her, and this situation, at his whole wasted, twisted life.

"I don't know an orphan or refugee who is ever anything else," he said quietly. He knew he shouldn't have said it. He should have made a joke, laughed it off. Said something appalling or shallow, as expected. But he couldn't seem to look away from her. He couldn't seem to breathe. He didn't understand what was happening to him or why he couldn't stop it. There was nothing in all the world but her lovely face and that searing gleam of recognition in her dark hazel eyes, and the words coming out of his mouth, filled with a truth he knew he shouldn't tell. "I am both. All I have—all I will ever have—is the spectacle."

He slumped back down after that, pretending to lapse off instantly into sleep like the lazy ass he was so good at playing would.

But he felt the weight of her dark gaze on him for a long time after.

"The general is rumored to be in ill health," Ricardo told him some days later. "It has been widely suggested that this ill-conceived fling of yours at a time the kingdom might actually need you may finally have put you beyond the pale, even in the eyes of your most die-hard supporters."

Cairo did not look up from his laptop, where he was managing his investment portfolio with a shrewdness he knew most would not believe he possessed, but then, he had worked hard to live down to any and all expectations. He sat at the gleaming, polished table in his Parisian residence that had welcomed all manner of European royalty in its time. It, like everything else in this house he'd inherited from his late family and got to rule over like the high king of ghosts, was a monument to nostalgia.

He included himself in that tally.

"I would have thought that I was so many shades lighter than pale that I'd gone entirely translucent before my eighteenth birthday," he said, more to the screen than to Ricardo. "That was certainly the goal." He sat back then and eyed the closest thing he had in the world to a friend, this man who had been at his side since before his family had died and who would support him to the bitter end. "What will it take? A murder conviction?"

"The loyalists would only claim you'd been framed, Sire. And then you'd simply be in prison, a situation that I doubt would suit you."

Cairo did not state the obvious: that he was already in prison. That he had been born into one sort of prison and then, after the revolution that had sent his family into exile, thrust into an entirely different one. And that the way he'd lived since he'd survived his adolescence was yet another jail cell, all things considered, no matter how elegantly appointed.

No one had any sympathy for a man like Cairo Santa Domini. Cairo, least of all. He knew he deserved it.

"You are correct," he said instead. "A life sentence would not suit me at all."

Ricardo smiled slightly, as if he knew exactly what Cairo hadn't said. "The scandal sheets are having a field day and there appear to be more than the usual number of appalled citizens registering their dismay at your antics, but I'm afraid the rumblings from the most deluded of your followers grow ever louder. It's as if they think they must act before you commit an unthinkable crime."

"Not an actual murder, I assume. A marriage." Ricardo nodded and Cairo rubbed a hand over his face. "But the general is unwell?"

His murderous heart, one of the many reasons he would
never be a good man, wanted that evil man dead, as painfully as possible. It would be a good start.

"The palace is trying to keep it quiet, but my sources
tell me it is serious," Ricardo said quietly. He aimed a
swift, dark look from Cairo. "The loyalists think this relationship of yours is a distraction. Merely a game you
play as you bide your time and wait for the usurper to die."

Cairo thought of the loyalists, true believers who had
opposed the general's coup thirty years ago and had only
grown stronger and louder in the years since. The more
the general hunted them down and attempted to silence
them, the louder they got and the more furiously they agitated for Cairo to return and take his throne.

They didn't seem to realize that his attempting to do
so would lead to nothing but slaughter. Had they learned
nothing from his family's "accident"? General Estes was
as much a butcher today as he had ever been. Perhaps even
more so, if his power was slipping away.

"The loyalists believe what they want to believe," he
said now.

"The key points they wished me to pass on all concern
your current companion," Ricardo told him. "She is inappropriate, they claim. Unacceptable, though stronger language was used. She is a slap, and I quote, 'in the face of
centuries of the Santa Domini bloodline.'"

"Heaven forfend the bloodline that ends in me suffer
a slap. The monarchy might be lost in shame forever—
ah, but then, there is no monarchy and hasn't been for
thirty years."

Ricardo had heard all of this before. He inclined his
head. "They want to meet."

They did not want to do anything so innocuous as *meet*.
They wanted to plan, to scheme. They wanted to talk strat-
egies and possibilities. The practical loyalists wanted their

seized lands and confiscated fortunes back. The idealists wanted the country of their forefathers, the fairy-tale perfection of "the kingdom in the clouds," as Santa Domini had been known in previous centuries. Cairo was as much a figurehead to them as he was to their enemies.

And figureheads too often ended up sacrificed to the cause, one way or another. What the loyalists failed to realize was that they'd be served up along with him. Cairo had been trying to avoid that very outcome since the general had assassinated his family.

As long as the general lived, nothing and no one Cairo cared about was safe.

"Impossible," he murmured now. "My social calendar is filled to bursting and I am, quite publically, falling head over heels in love with an American temptress reviled on at least three continents, rendering me stupendously unfit to be anyone's king."

"That is what I told them, more or less. It was not received well."

This was the problem with royal blood. History was littered with the executed and deposed relatives of this or that monarch, all of whom had been pressed into service by exactly the sort of people Cairo knew better than to actually speak to directly. The fact of his existence was enough of an irritant to General Estes. The general had claimed the throne of Santa Domini, but everyone knew he'd taken that throne by force and, because of that, there would always be whispers that he could only hold the throne by the same force. Meanwhile, Cairo hadn't set foot on Santa Dominian soil since he'd been a child and had made himself one part a laughingstock and two parts too scandalous to bear, but there was no doubt that he was his country's legitimate heir.

If he'd hid himself away somewhere and stayed out of the public eye as his parents had advised him to do when he was a child, Cairo wouldn't have survived to adulthood. That he lived, that he drew breath daily, was a constant reminder to the general that he was not legitimate and could never be legitimate no matter whom he bullied. That he had not won his position by popular vote or historic right, but by violence and betrayal.

Cairo had spent a very long time making sure no one could possibly imagine a known fool like him, vapid and excessive and usually scandalously naked besides, as any kind of king. Secret meetings and murky discussions with those who would use him to take back the country would undo all of that work. It would put not just Cairo at risk, but all of those who had ever supported his family. From the sweet nannies who had raised him and his lost sister, to Ricardo, to say nothing of the ancient families that had stood with the kings of Santa Domini for centuries.

He might have risked himself, now that he was no longer a grieving and terrified boy. But he had already lost everyone he'd ever cared about. He could not risk anyone else.

He would not.

"I suppose there is only one course of action, then," he said after a moment, when the air in the old room, so much like a mausoleum, grew tight. "To put the final nail in my coffin."

"Not literally, I hope." Because Ricardo would always do what was asked of him, Cairo knew this as well as he knew his own heart within his chest, but that didn't make the man any less of a loyalist at heart.

He made himself smile, and pretended, as he always did, that he didn't know how deeply the other man longed for Cairo to stand up one day and announce he'd had enough—that he was taking back the kingdom. That day would never come. Cairo had made certain of that, as surely as he'd made sure to become exactly the sort of creature his beloved father would have loathed.

"Indeed, that is what we always hope, Ricardo," he said instead, and for the first time in a long while, he found he actually meant it.

Cairo turned his attention back to his laptop, telling himself that he was perfectly calm, because he should have been. That his heart was not beating too hard, that he was not tense with sheer anticipation—for all the wrong things—because he should have been as composed as he was when he handled his investment portfolio.

That he was not should have concerned him a great deal more than it did.

Because it was finally time to propose to Brittany, his inappropriate consort who functioned as the perfect sucker punch against his splendid ancestry, royal blood and claim to the throne of Santa Domini.

He would make her his wife and ruin the dreams of all those loyal to him, once and for all.

He should have viewed this necessary step with a measure of satisfaction. Possibly with a touch of nostalgia for the country he'd not laid eyes on since he was small boy.

But he found that instead of his kingdom, what he thought about was Brittany. Copper fire and the sweet, hot insanity of her slick mouth against his. Her lean, muscled curves in his lap and her scent all around him like a fist. The torture of these last weeks, of having her so close and yet so far away. Every touch he stole in front of the cameras that he relived for another sleepless hour when alone at night. The agony of her smile, of that mysterious distance in her eyes. It had been unbearable from the start.

But the time had come at last.

He would finally, finally make her his.

Cairo found he couldn't wait.

CHAPTER FIVE

"Pay attention, please," Cairo said from across the small table, which was how Brittany realized she'd been lost in her own head somewhere. She snapped her gaze back to his and saw that same brooding, amused impatience in those caramel depths that she was starting to crave a little bit too much.

Maybe more than a little bit.

She shoved that thought aside and cranked up her smile to something melting and adoring, as befit the occasion. She assured herself it was completely feigned. She'd worn a gown of glorious red that clutched at her breasts and then tumbled down to flirt with her knees, and the sort of fancifully high and delicate shoes that impressed even the most glamorous French women. She'd pulled back the front part of her hair and let the rest of the heavy mass of it swirl down from that gleaming little clip to tumble past her bare shoulders, a sleek fall of copper that she knew caught the light.

She would look beautiful in all the engagement pictures. Elegant, even; the better for all the nasty "compare and contrast" photos the papers would run the moment they heard the news. This side a future almost-queen dressed for the part, that side a stripper in a G-string and a bikini top upside down on a pole.

The vicious articles wrote themselves.

Brittany told herself, the way she seemed to do more

and more these days, that she didn't mind at all. That this was what she wanted. That she was as pleased with the public persona she'd created as she ever had been, and welcomed the way she and Cairo were using it to their own ends.

I have never been happier in all my life, she told herself now, surrounded by fine china and Michelin stars. Again and again, hoping it would sink in. *Not ever.*

Cairo looked devastatingly gorgeous. Cairo always looked devastatingly gorgeous. The things the man did to a jacket and a pair of dark trousers defied description. It was as if a light shone upon him from a great height, making him seem something like angelic despite his rather more earthy reputation. He turned heads. He inspired sighs. He couldn't walk across an empty street without someone gasping aloud, and there'd been a chorus of dreamy sighs all the way across the restaurant floor when they'd entered.

He was the most dangerous man Brittany had ever met, and sometimes, when he lost that smirk of his and stopped saying his usual absurd and provocative things, she was sure it was as obvious to the world as it felt sloshing about inside her.

Tonight he'd chosen the best table in Paris's current darling of a restaurant, where the paparazzi could crowd about outside and take telephoto pictures of their meal. He'd picked her up from her flat in a flashy sports car, a muscular Italian bit of fancy in a deep, glossy black, and had swept her into the restaurant in a hail of flashbulbs that hardly seemed to register to him at all. A surreptitious glance at the mobile phone in her evening clutch told her the pictures were online before they'd ordered their first course.

There's no getting out of this, a little voice kept whispering to her from that place, deep inside her, where everything was fluttery and terrified and all because it recognized how susceptible she was to this man. How vulnerable. He made her *feel things* and that was unforgivable. *There's no taking it back.*

"You seem bored," Cairo said after one silent moment bled into the next. He leaned back in his chair in that exultantly male way of his, a negligent finger tracing the stem of his wineglass as he spoke. "Surely not."

From a distance she would look enthralled with him, she knew. Or she hoped. She leaned forward and rested her chin on her hand, to underscore that impression. Too bad it made it far too easy to forget that she was supposed to be acting.

"It's only that I've done this so many times before," she said.

Laughter flashed over his extraordinary face, and that didn't help. Brittany might as well have plugged herself into an electrical outlet and switched on the power to full blast. She *felt* it when he laughed. Everywhere.

She was in so much trouble. That truth shivered through her, making her stomach flip over and then knot tightly, and it took everything she had to pretend it wasn't actually happening.

Cairo watched her, close and hot, as if he knew every last thing she wanted to hide from him. "Did your teenage first husband propose to you in the finest restaurant in…wherever you came from?"

"In fact he did," she said loftily. Brittany forgot herself again and grinned at him, remembering. "It was the parking lot of a McDonald's with a bag of cheeseburgers from the drive-thru."

"Be still my heart."

"That counted as highly romantic to a sixteen-year-old girl with no prospects, I'll have you know. Darryl had even bought the cheeseburgers, which made the whole thing especially fancy."

He smiled at that. Brittany looked away. The sapphire ring she wore on her right hand caught the candlelight and reminded her exactly how far she'd come from a fast-food parking lot in Gulfport, Mississippi.

Cairo wasn't done. "And what about poor Carlos, who you treated so hideously on television like the callous creature the papers tell us daily you truly are?"

"He came into the bar where I was working—"

"Is that a euphemism? Do you mean another strip club?"

"I mean the bar where I was working as a waitress," she said, shaking her head at him. Then she relented. "The strip club was my second job."

Cairo's mouth moved into that smile of his that she'd discovered made her silly straight through. Completely and utterly foolish, and something like shattered besides. The only defense she had against it was to act like an icicle. But somehow, she couldn't seem to do that tonight. Her ability to freeze had disappeared, lost somewhere in the dancing flames of the candles between them. Or in that smile of his that made her feel like just another flickering bit of the light surrounding him.

Maybe it wasn't the worst thing, to be caught up in this man. To flicker and dance around him like the candles on the tables, or his loyal subjects, who followed him from party to party without end, or every woman who'd ever laid eyes on him. Maybe she was trying too hard to resist the inevitable. It was possible that giving in to it would make this latest transactional, cold-blooded marriage... easier.

Sweeter, anyway. She had to believe it would make it so much sweeter.

"Carlos came into the bar and he said he was moving

to Los Angeles and I should go with him." She shrugged away the other parts of the story that had little to do with what he'd asked. She didn't like to think about that time. The usually angry, rough clientele and the places they tried to put their hands. That ever-present sense of danger that, still, had been better than a life dodging Darryl's fists. She might have been a virgin, but her experiences had made sure she never felt anything like innocent. "He was pretty sure he could get us both on a television show if I did."

"Better than a sonnet."

"I asked what the catch was, because who walks around claiming they can get on television shows? He said we had to get married, I said okay. The end."

Cairo didn't actually move to put a hand over his heart, but the gesture was implied in the way he watched her then, his caramel gaze looking darker in the candlelight. More like whiskey than candy, and it made Brittany feel a little tipsy, instantly.

Maybe more than just a little tipsy, she thought.

"Sheer poetry," he said, his mouth in that tempting curve. "And Jean Pierre? Or did he have one of his nurses do the honors as he lay in his sickbed?"

"That one was much more fun." Brittany couldn't seem to stop smiling at him tonight, when she knew better. These past weeks had been sheer torture. Cairo was not the sort of man whose potency wore off the longer she spent time with him, like every other man she'd ever known. Not Cairo. He intensified. He got *worse*. "He came backstage after one of my shows."

"This time we really are talking about a strip club again, yes? For the purposes of clarity?"

"He said some lovely, complimentary things." She raised her brows at him, daring him to comment.

"I'm sure he praised the strip club's choreographer to the moon and back." Cairo nodded, that sharp gleam in his gaze telling her he knew very well Jean Pierre had done no such thing. "Or perhaps the set design?"

"Something like that," Brittany murmured.

Jean Pierre had told her something that bordered on filthy, that he'd somehow made sound charmingly bawdy instead—but Brittany suspected that Cairo, with that sharp gleam still in his gaze as he waited, wouldn't find it nearly as amusing as she had at the time.

She didn't want to dig into how she knew that. Much less what it meant.

"And then he told me he had very little time left to live and a handful of deeply ungrateful children. 'Marry me, *cherie*,' he said." She affected a dramatic French accent and had the enormous, very complicated pleasure of seeing Cairo's dark amber gaze gleam with pleasure. "'And we'll give them hell.'"

"This proved sufficiently compelling for you? I'll make a note."

"Jean Pierre had a certain charm."

"By which, of course, you mean his net worth."

There was no particular reason for that to slice through her, especially not tonight. Brittany didn't know what was the matter with her, especially because it was true. She didn't know why she felt so…fragile. She couldn't scowl at him with so many people watching them, inside the restaurant and out, so she had to settle for a bright sort of smile that made her own mouth hurt.

"I make no apologies for that or any other choice I made, then or now," she told him, and she chose not to concentrate on how difficult it was to keep her voice in the neighborhood of calm. "Only people who never have to worry about money look down on those who do nothing but. Besides—" she let her gaze sweep over him, from that reckless dark hair to his careless smile, and the sheer masculine beauty of that body of his he packaged to perfection "—you're no different from me."

"I must beg to differ, *cara.* I do not sell myself to the highest bidder."

Her smile still hurt. Worse, then. "Keep telling yourself that. Tabloid after tabloid after tabloid."

Cairo's eyes flashed with an emotion she couldn't read. He inclined his head slightly, very slightly. He did not say touché. Brittany supposed he didn't have to say it out loud. The fact she'd scored a direct hit seemed to simmer in the air between them.

"Cairo," she said, and she didn't know what she was doing. She was performing, yes, but all she wanted was to...do something about the fact it seemed she'd hurt him, when she'd have said that was impossible. "You're not the man you play in public." She didn't know where that came from, only that the moment she said it, something shifted inside her. She knew it was true. She reached her hand out across the table, but he didn't take it. "It won't kill you to admit that, if only to me."

He let a bitter sort of laugh, and Brittany had the impression he was as surprised by the sound as she was. He leaned forward. He still didn't reach for her hand.

"That is where you are wrong," he told her, and she went still. His dark eyes were so dark and something like tortured, and she realized in the same instant that she'd never seen him look like this. Not remotely indolent. Not the least bit lazy or pampered. No trace of that smirk on his beautiful mouth. "It very well might kill me. Did you imagine this was a game?"

That sat there between them, stark and harsh. Brittany's head spun. Then he pulled his gaze away and ran an unnecessary hand down the perfect line of his lapel.

"What do you mean by that?" she asked, her voice

barely above a whisper, her hand still reaching across the table. She couldn't seem to move a muscle.

"I mean nothing by it." But it took him another long moment to look at her again, and she didn't believe him. "I am a creature of well-documented extremes, that is all. The theater of it all goes to my head sometimes and I imagine I am starring in some great tragedy. I think we both know I am not the tragedy sort."

"Cairo…"

But he changed again, right there before her eyes. He didn't appear to move a muscle, and yet he changed. He looked as useless and lazy as ever, that stark moment gone as if it had never been.

"This proposal will be unmemorable, I'm sure," he told her, his voice amused and his gaze more like his usual caramel again. Light. Easy. Why couldn't she believe it? "Especially for a woman as vastly experienced in this area as you. Are you ready?"

Brittany pulled her hand back from the center of the table and told herself this was none of her business. *He* was none of her business. She should never have acted as if she wanted to know *the real him* anyway. What an exiled king chose to hide behind his public mask was his affair, not hers.

"It can't possibly be as heartwarming as cheeseburgers in a parking lot, or off-color remarks in a strip club," she replied, and it was a fight to make her voice cool again. As if that strange moment that still spiked the air between them hadn't happened. "But you do like a challenge, don't you?"

Cairo's mouth moved into its usual amused curve, though his eyes remained dark on hers. He reached into the pocket of his suit coat and pulled out a small box. An instantly identifiable jeweler's box that could really only contain one thing. And still, Brittany found herself staring at it as if she didn't know what it was. As if she didn't know what was happening. As if they hadn't decided he would do this here, now, tonight.

The frightening part was, she was only partially acting. She felt too hot, then too cold. Her tongue felt glued to the roof of her mouth.

He moved then, shifting from his seat to kneel down beside her chair, and her heart started drumming wildly in her chest. She couldn't tell if the restaurant around them went quiet. She couldn't tell if the earth had stopped spinning. The point of this was the spectacle he'd mentioned, the endless show that was both their lives—but all she could see was this. Him.

The last man in the world who should ever have been kneeling down before her, and yet there he was, doing exactly that.

The whole world narrowed as he took her hand in his.

Then disappeared entirely.

This isn't real, this isn't real, this isn't real, she chanted at herself.

But the truth was, it felt more than real. It felt like a fairy tale, the kind she'd lectured herself against loving or believing in all her life. It felt like magic and hope and something sweet besides.

His Serene Grace the Archduke Felipe Skander Cairo of Santa Domini smiled at her, Brittany Hollis, from the worst trailer park in Gulfport, Mississippi, as if she thrilled him. As if she really, truly did. That treacherous part of her, not buried as deep inside her as it should have been, wished that was possible. Oh, how she wished it.

He cracked open the small box he held and presented it to her with flourish, and Brittany's heart stopped.

She knew that ring. Everybody knew that ring. That glorious, incomparable diamond for which songs had been written and blood had been shed, across the ages. She knew its sparkle, its shape, even the delicate, precious stones that surrounded it like a whimsical halo. It had been painted by any number of great masters over the centuries, was known as one of the finest legacy jewels in all of Europe, and was so beloved by so many that various paste representations were sold all over the world.

"It was my mother's," Cairo said quietly, his eyes on hers. She knew that. He must have known that everybody alive knew that. "And my grandmother's before her, going back hundreds upon hundreds of years. It was commissioned a very long time ago, crafted by my kingdom's finest artisans, and is known as the Heart of Santa Domini. I hope you will wear it proudly."

"Cairo…" Her voice was a whisper. She couldn't wear such a ring. She couldn't bear it. It was a symbol of hope, of love, and this was nothing but a sideshow performance for a baying crowd. But she couldn't seem to open her mouth and tell him so.

She'd forgotten her internal chant entirely. She'd forgotten her own name. She'd forgotten the fact they were in public, the paparazzi right there outside the window, even the fact that all of this was staged.

There was only the look in Cairo's caramel gaze. That hot, dark, gleaming thing that wrapped around her and pulled tight. There was only the way he took that fairytale ring from the velvet box and then slid it onto her finger, as if she was the princess in the tale, not the joke he was playing on the world.

"Marry me," he said, and his voice was different, too. Deeper. Richer.

As raw as she felt.

And Brittany understood how foolish this game of theirs was. There was nothing the slightest bit cool about her then. No icicle. Nothing even close. She felt… everything. She didn't know if she wanted to cry or if she wanted to scream. If she wanted to fall into his arms or run away. She only knew that she'd been married three times and not one of them had ever felt like this. Not one of them had ever made her shake, inside and out.

Not one of them had ever been anything but expedient.

She tried to remind herself that Cairo was the same, if on a grander scale. That it was all he was. She tried to tell herself this was no different from the rest, and no matter that she was wearing one of the most romantic diamonds in the history of the world on her hand.

"Must I beg?" he asked then, though he looked as comfortable on one knee as he did lounging in a chair or sprawled out on a sofa. As if he could inhabit whatever posture he found himself in and make it his own, and easily.

"Of course not," she said quickly, and she wasn't faking the way she shook. Or the sting of tears that threatened to spill over from behind her eyes. "Of course you don't have to beg."

"Say it," he ordered her, every inch of him the king he wasn't, even as he kneeled in what ought to have been a supplicant position. It took her breath away. It made her imagine that all of this was something much, much different than it was, and that, she knew on some distant level, was the most dangerous thing of all. "I find I require it."

"Yes," she told him, this exiled king on his knees before her. *Her.* Brittany Hollis, reality-show villain and scourge of Europe, destined for nothing but infamy and then irrelevance. In that order, if she was lucky. "Yes, I'll marry you."

"I hoped you might." He didn't move. His eyes were lit up with that drugging heat she didn't want to recognize, but she did. God help her, but she did. She could feel it echo inside of her, making that sweet, hot knot in her belly bloom into something more like an ache. "Come now, Brittany. We need to sell this scene for our adoring public."

"I said yes. What more do you want? A song and dance?"

"I think you know." He smiled when all she did was stare at him, so outside herself she hardly knew where she was, and shivering inside as if she'd never get warm again. She wasn't sure she wanted to. "Kiss me, please. And make it good."

Brittany felt dizzy then. Hot and wild and pierced straight through.

But it didn't occur to her not to obey him.

You want *to obey him*, that voice inside her accused her.

She sat forward in her seat. She let go of his hand and indulged that part of her she'd been denying all this time, sliding her hands over that marvelous, ever-roughened jaw of his to cup his beautiful face between her hands.

Her breath caught. She saw nothing but fire in his hot, sweet gaze, this stunning man whom she should never have met. Whom she should never have touched. Whose kiss weeks ago still worked in her like a fire she couldn't stamp out and whose gorgeous male body, sculpted to impossible perfection, had been *right there within reach* on all those little holiday jaunts they'd taken, in all those rooms and tents they'd shared without ever sharing a bed.

She hadn't touched him. She hadn't dared. She didn't know what would become of her if she followed that flame. She couldn't imagine what waited for her on the other side—and she hadn't known how to handle the fact she'd *wanted* things she'd never, ever wanted before, from anyone.

But tonight, she'd agreed to marry him. Tonight, they were in public, where it was safe. Where they could both wear the masks they preferred. Where there could be no real surrender to lick and scrape of all that fire inside of her.

Tonight, she felt as if she could dare anything. Even this. Even him.

Even the terrifying things she felt inside.

So Brittany slid forward and pressed her mouth to his.

It was better than she'd remembered—better than she'd dreamed. She tested the shape of his lips, shuddering at the warmth, the contact. He tilted his head to change the angle and took the kiss deeper, hotter.

His taste exploded through her, fine wine and devilishly perfect man.

God help her, but he was perfect.

Brittany kissed him as if fairy tales were real, and as if the two of them were, too. She kissed him as if they were nothing more than a man and a woman, and this kiss was all that mattered.

No kings, no strippers. No tabloid personas. No calculation whatsoever.

She couldn't seem to do anything but pour herself into him, no ice and nothing hidden or left back. No self-preservation at all.

Brittany kissed him as if she was falling in love with him, raw and wild and heedless, and her heart flipped over in her chest at the very thought.

And as if he knew it, Cairo pulled away. He brushed her hair back from her cheek, handling her as if she was infinitely precious to him. Something bloomed within her, warm and bright. Because she wanted that. She wanted to be precious.

To him.

"I promise you," he said, his voice husky with what she might have called a kind of pain, or maybe it was the honesty she'd asked for earlier, "you won't regret this."

"Neither will you," Brittany heard herself say, her voice as swollen as her lips, but a solemn vow even so.

It hung like that between them, shimmering and real.

And that was when the first paparazzo reached their table.

Six frantic and over-photographed weeks later, Brittany stood in a tiny stone chamber high in an ancient castle built into the side of the Italian coast, letting a set of smiling attendants lace her into her wedding gown. She kept her eyes trained on the tapestries that adorned the walls, all showing this or that medieval battle or glorified feast.

She tried to remind herself that this day, like all the conflicts and celebrations on display before her, would fade into blessed obscurity soon enough.

In five years, ten, a hundred, no one would care that Cairo Santa Domini was the first of his bloodline in three hundred years to marry outside the iconic cathedral that had stood for centuries in the Santa Dominian capital city, not far from the grand palace where his family once ruled. No one would care that he was—as a particularly vicious reporter had said to Brittany's face with obvious relish—polluting himself and the Santa Dominian line of ascension by consorting with her at all.

Time would pass. They would be messily and extravagantly divorced, as planned. They would make sure to drag it all out across the tabloids, the better to ensure the entire planet was heartily sick of them both. And then Brittany would fade off into obscurity and be remembered as nothing more than a tiny little footnote in the long, celebrated tale of Cairo's family that would end, ignominiously, with him.

It was too bad this particular footnote was fighting off a panic attack.

"Are you well, my lady?" one of the attendants asked

in heavily accented English as they finished the lacing. "You look pale."

"I'm fine," Brittany said, though her tongue felt strange in her mouth. She made herself smile. "I'm excited, that's all."

The women smiled back, the bustling and fussing continued, and then the church bells were ringing out the hour and it was really about to happen. In sixty short minutes she was going to walk outside to the chapel set high above the Mediterranean Sea and marry Cairo Santa Domini.

She dismissed the women from the room and stood there in the middle of it, fighting to keep her breath even and her eyes dry. Fighting to keep upright instead of sinking to her knees and staying there. Or worse, crawling into the four-poster bed that commanded the whole of one wall, hauling the covers up over her head and pretending she was the child she didn't think she'd ever been. Not really.

"Vanuatu," she muttered to herself. Fiercely. "Palm trees and white sands. Freedom and mai tais and life in sarongs."

Get your head into this, she ordered herself, in a pitiless sort of voice from down deep inside her that sounded a great deal like her harsh, bitter mother. *Right now. You have no other option.*

Brittany only realized her hands were clenched into fists when her fingers started to ache. She straightened them as the door to her chamber opened behind her, and then she smoothed the dress where it billowed out below her waist and—according to the mirror angled on its stand before her—made her look like a confection. She looked past it and out to the Italian hills that sloped toward the deep blue sea, dotted in marvelously colorful houses seemingly piled on top of each other while the staunch cypress trees stood like sentries beside them. She tried to breathe.

She kept trying.

"I'd like a few moments to myself," she managed to say after a moment, and was proud that her voice sounded much, much calmer than she felt.

"It is my role in life to disappoint you, I am afraid."

Cairo.

Of course.

Goose bumps swept over her, and she hoped he couldn't see them through the filmy, gossamer veil she wore pushed back to cascade over her shoulders toward the stone floor. His voice was richer than usual. Deeper and darker, and suddenly there was a lump in her throat that made it hard to swallow.

Then she turned to look at him and it was all much worse.

He was resplendent in white tie, lounging there in the doorway like a decidedly adult version of Prince Charming. The long tails of his morning coat did marvelous things to his lean, powerful frame, as if he'd been born to wear such formal clothes. A bubble of something giddy and inappropriate caught in her chest, and she had to swallow down near-hysterical laughter, because, of course, he had been. Bred for centuries on end to look nothing short of perfectly at his ease in attire most men found confining and strange.

"You are staring at my boutonniere as if you expect it to rise from my lapel and attack you," he said in his lazy, amused way, as he shut the heavy door behind him.

Brittany had never been a coward. She'd never had that option. And she didn't think she was one now, no matter how she felt inside. Still, the hardest thing she'd ever done in her life was to lift her gaze to meet his.

This glorious man. This would-be king. This inscrutable creature who was about to become her fourth husband.

Fourth, a small voice whispered deep inside of her,

with a certain feminine intuition she chose not to acknowl-edge, *and last*.

She shrugged that away, and the shiver of foreboding that crept down her spine, and let herself drink him in.

He looked exactly the way she'd expected Cairo Santa Domini would look on his wedding day. If, perhaps, more stunning. That careless dark hair of his was ac-tually tamed. He'd even shaved his deliberately scruffy jaw, so he looked a bit less like a renegade than usual. He looked every inch the gleaming, impossibly wealthy and powerful royal he was.

And his eyes were more whiskey than caramel again. They seemed to see straight through her, pinning her to the wall like yet another decorative tapestry.

"What are you doing here?" she asked, and she hated that she sounded so much more stern and *bothered* by him than she'd intended. Or was wise. She cleared her throat. "Aren't you supposed to be waiting for me in the chapel?"

"It is not as if they can start without me." He eyed her, and she had no idea what he saw. No idea what that dark awareness that gleamed in his gaze was, only that it seemed to echo inside of her, growing bigger and wilder by the second. "I wanted to make certain you were not seized with any bright ideas about tossing yourself out the windows. A bridal suicide, while certainly bait for the tabloids, would simply mean I needed to start this process all over again. And I do hate to repeat myself."

"The papers we signed were clear. Death means no money at all. And if I abandon you at the altar I only get a quarter of what I would if I go through with it." She made herself shrug, as careless as he always was despite the fact she felt so soft and shivery. "It wouldn't be in my best interests to climb out the window, even if it wasn't a steep fall off a very long cliff to the sea."

Something occurred to her then, and gripped her so hard it was like a brutal fist around her heart.

"Why?" She didn't want to ask the next question, but she forced herself to do it anyway. "Have you changed your mind?"

Brittany understood far too many things in that airless, endless moment while she waited for his response. Too many things, too late. Too much she didn't want to admit, not even to herself.

This wedding was nothing like her others, two rushed courthouse visits and the small civil ceremony on the grounds of Jean Pierre's chateau that had been all about the gown she'd worn specifically to infuriate the old man's heirs. It had done its job. It had proclaimed her more Vegas showgirl than the solemn bride a man of Jean Pierre's standing should have been marrying, just as he'd wanted. She'd expected the dress for this even more dramatic performance today to be along those same lines. She'd been prepared for it, despite some drawings Cairo had showed her weeks ago that suggested a more classic approach.

But instead, the gown her attendants had dressed her in really was the one Cairo had showed her. Simple, elegant. It made her look like an actual, blue-blooded princess worthy of marrying a royal, not a tabloid sensation. Her breasts were not the main attraction. They weren't even on display. Her legs and thighs were not exposed every time she moved. Her veil, handed down in his family for generations and smuggled out of Santa Domini years ago, was almost as old as Cairo's title.

This wedding—this man—was nothing like the others.

And it made her feel things she'd never felt before. *He* did.

"I have not changed my mind," Cairo said.

His gaze was too bright and too assessing at once, and he seemed to fill the whole of the room, stone walls and the four-poster bed and ancient tapestries be damned. Then he stepped closer to her and that was worse. It was as if he took over the entire world while her heart simply hammered at her, telling her things about herself she didn't want to know.

Brittany had to order herself to stand still. To simply hold her ground, tilt her head back to keep her eyes on his face and keep herself from reacting when he reached over and took her hand in his. Idly, lazily, his fingers found the Heart of Santa Domini and moved the famous ring gently this way and that on her hand.

It was such a small, civilized sort of touch. It was so restrained, so conservative—nothing like that kiss in the burlesque club or the one staged for the slavering press in one of the finest restaurants in Paris. They were both wearing so many fine, carefully crafted clothes today, all of them formal and stuffy and exquisite. There was almost no flesh on display at all, in contrast to almost every other time they'd been together.

Not to mention, they were alone.

That word seemed to pound through her. *Alone.*

Maybe that was why his seemingly inconsequential touch *hummed* in her, stark and wildly electric, as if he'd done something far more wicked than take her hand in his. Something in her wished he had. She felt soft and desperate and deep inside her, high between her legs covered in yards and yards of shimmering white, something clenched hard and then pulsed.

She wished she wasn't a virgin. She wished she was as experienced as she pretended. Then she would know how to handle this. Then she would know what to do.

"Have you?" Cairo asked. Quiet and close, his attention trained on the ring.

"No," she said. It was not quite the set down she'd wanted to give. She was lucky she got the words out at all. And was that relief she saw chase across his gorgeous face? But that made no sense. It disappeared and she told herself she'd imagined it. "No, I haven't changed my mind."

There was no reason on earth that she should. Except, of course, that overwhelming sense of doom and ruin and longing and insane hope that was filling her nearly to bursting. She planned to keep right on ignoring the lot of it, straight on into the financial benefits of this arrangement that would have her feet sunk deep in the South Pacific sand within five years, tops.

All she had to do was keep herself from toppling over. Especially while Cairo was watching her...and touching her.

How could he manage to do this to her with so meaningless a touch?

"The guests have assembled," Cairo told her, as if none of this was getting to him. She envied him that. "The overbred scions from all the noble families in Europe or their more embarrassing relatives in their place, depending on how personally offended the sitting monarch is by my assorted shenanigans over the years."

"Of course, your friends and very distant family are here, as expected."

"In the sense that all of Europe's aristocratic families were related at some point or another?" He shrugged at that, though Brittany knew that he was listed in the lines of succession of at least five different kingdoms. "I would not call them my family. It would be rather presumptuous, among other things. But I cannot help noticing that your family are nowhere in evidence."

She wanted to tug her hand from his, but she suspected that would be too telling. Too revealing, when she already felt wide open and much too vulnerable, and this was the man who had showed her his real face in a restaurant in

Paris and then claimed she'd misread him. She needed to remember that. Cairo *wanted* these masks they wore.

She had no idea when she'd stopped wanting it, too.

"Mine weren't invited," she said. Abruptly.

Cairo's brows rose. He opened his mouth to say something that would no doubt cut her to the quick, and Brittany couldn't take it. She felt too exposed already. And suddenly she didn't care if he knew it. She pulled her hand back, but that didn't help. She could still feel that deceptively simple touch everywhere, as if he'd branded her.

"My family didn't sign up for this spectacle." She did nothing to ease that snap in her voice. "And it's not as if our marriage will last long anyway. It would take longer for them to get here than we'll stay together. Why bother?"

Brittany regretted her words almost the instant she said them. Cairo seemed turned to the same stone as the walls around them, and she knew, deep inside, that she'd offended him.

He looked away for a moment, toward the cliff and the sea and the Italian villages clinging to the hills in the distance as if the view could soothe him. When he looked back, there was a speculative expression on his face.

"You cannot be nervous, *cara*, can you?" He adjusted his crisp cuffs, one after the next, though his gaze never left hers. "This should be like falling off a log, as you Americans say, should it not? I am the wedding virgin here, after all, not you."

Later, she would reason that it was *that word*. She hadn't heard that ridiculous, archaic word in a long time, because who would bother to use it in the vicinity of such a well-known slut and, according to the more salacious papers, possible prostitute? It hardly came up in the strip clubs or dive bars where she used to spend all her time. Much less in Hollywood, the most virginless place she could imagine.

But here, now, in an old castle on the Italian coast, it hardly mattered *why* she flinched at the sound of the word. Only that she did, right there where Cairo could see her do it.

And then, much worse, she blushed.

Bright red and unmistakable.

She could feel the heat of it sweep over her, making her sweat and let out a harsh, loud breath. Her dress felt itchy all around her, suddenly. The combs that held her swept back veil felt prickly against her skull.

And worse than all of that was Cairo, who watched her with wholly undisguised fascination.

That and a very hungry sort of focus.

"Brittany," he said softly, so softly. "Do you have something you want to tell me?"

"No."

He laughed at her reply, but the way he watched her with those dark whiskey eyes of his only seemed to deepen. And then expand inside of her. "Can it be? Is it possible?"

The mortification and all that red heat seemed to roll tight inside of her, and she didn't know what to do with it. Only that if she didn't do *something*, she'd explode. She fought for some composure—but then came up hard against the far wall of the small, ancient room.

She hadn't even realized he'd been coming for her, or that she'd backed away from him. All the way across the room.

And now it was too late.

Cairo leaned in close as if he wanted to inhale the fine tremors that moved over her body, one after the next. Then he laid his hands on the cool stone wall, one palm on either side of her head, caging her where she stood.

"Stop lying to me," he ordered her, in that same quiet voice that did nothing to disguise the fact it was another steel-tipped royal command.

"We're about to get married for money so we can lead a tabloid life," she managed to bite out in some semblance of her usual composed, measured tone. "I thought lies were a given."

"Brittany," he said, and again, her name in that mouth of his *did things* to her she wished she could ignore, "are you the best-disguised and least likely virgin in the whole wide world?"

CHAPTER SIX

SOMETHING SHOOK THROUGH BRITTANY, long and deep.

She had to stop this. She had to distract him. She couldn't let him think she was an innocent, not today of all days. She didn't think she'd manage to survive it if he thought she was anything but the hard-shelled, cold-eyed creature she'd spent so many years pretending she was that she sometimes believed it herself.

Because she couldn't allow herself to be vulnerable. Not here. Not with him.

She didn't know how to handle the fact that Cairo was the only person she'd met in years who didn't see exactly what she wanted him to see when he looked at her.

Masks, she snapped at herself. *This relationship is about masks, not what's beneath them.*

"Of course I'm not a virgin," she said crisply, frowning at him. "Do people still use that word? Did it become the seventeenth century while I wasn't looking?"

He didn't look convinced. And Brittany knew, with every last fiber of her being, that she had to convince him he was mistaken and she had to do it *right this very minute* before it was too late—

Some part of her whispered that it already was.

That it had been too late from the moment she'd set foot in Monte Carlo.

And still Cairo looked at her in that deeply unsettling

way of his, as if he could see straight through to her battered old soul.

As if he already knew she was a virgin, whether she bothered to confirm it or not. As if a small fact she'd considered essentially meaningless for years told him everything he needed to know about her.

She couldn't have this. She couldn't let him think this, especially because it was true. It would ruin everything, she knew it.

"Impossible," she said when he didn't respond, but continued to watch her in that same considering way. It was much harder than it should have been to affect her trademark arch, amused voice. "Everyone knows I'm a whore, Cairo, and here's a news flash. They're not wrong."

"Including your own mother, I believe you mentioned."

Brittany would have said the names her mother had called her over time were a collection of very old scars set over wounds that had long since healed, and yet she ached when he said it. Still, she made herself smirk at him as if there were no scars, no ache, and never had been. Not beneath *her* mask.

"Especially my own mother."

That it wasn't strictly a lie gave her voice a little power, she thought. After all, some members of her family believed that listening to certain kinds of music rendered a woman instantly and irrevocably fallen. It was a slippery, easy slope from that to whoring about. Her mother had always been the first to say so, when it suited her.

Cairo shifted then. He left one hand on the wall as the other moved to trace a lazy pattern along the line of her jaw. Down the length of it, from near her ear to her chin. Then back again. And the look in his eyes was more than simply dangerous, then. It was possessive. Triumphant.

And very, very male.

Brittany felt that shaking thing inside of her again,

insistent and terrible. Some part of her wanted nothing more to surrender to it. To tell him the truth he'd already guessed. To stop lying about herself for one little second in all these years of living those lies to the hilt.

Just here. Just to him. Just to the only man whose kiss had made her feel like a woman, not a means to an end.

But that was insanity. That bordered on *intimate* and she knew better than to risk such a thing. Not with *Cairo Santa Domini*, in the name of all that was holy, given his version of intimacy likely involved cutting down to three orgies a week from seven.

What the hell was she thinking?

She blamed the dress. The elegant princess dress that gave a woman *ideas*, even a woman who should know better. The dress that looked as if it had fallen from the pages of a fairy tale and made even a trailer-park Cinderella like Brittany imagine princes were real and charming and right here in front of her at last.

Life had taught her better than that. Over and over again.

So she smiled at Cairo, suggestively and wickedly. She reached up and covered the hand he held to her cheek with hers, and arched herself into him. She pressed her breasts against his chest and she tilted back her head to keep her gaze on his, and she did her best to ignore the way those things made the fire inside her sear through her.

"I can play a virgin if you want me to," she murmured, her voice sultry. "Why am I not surprised that the most famous playboy in Europe likes a little role play?"

That hot blaze in his eyes deepened. The air between them seemed to pull tight, as if something huge clenched around her, then squeezed. Hard.

"Are we playing?" he asked quietly.

"A marriage like this is nothing but a game." Brittany made herself pout at him when he only continued to stare down at her, as if he really was trying to see inside of her. He shifted, dragging his chest against hers so that tendrils of flame curled through her and made it hard not to squirm where she stood. And harder still to remember she was supposed to be acting. "Why not take it into bed as well?"

"You told me there was to be no sex in this marriage." His gaze was on her mouth. Her heart pounded hard, like a sledgehammer.

"You told me that wasn't your style," she countered.

She didn't know when she noticed that he'd angled his torso into her. That he was holding her there against the wall that easily, and Brittany knew she should have hated it. She should have felt caught. Captured. *Compromised.*

She didn't.

His eyes glowed that dark amber that made her chest feel tight, and she couldn't seem to pull in a full breath to save her life. His palm was surprisingly hard and warm against her cheek. She could feel it in her toes. His chest pressed against hers and made her breasts ache, the peaks pinching into hard points. And that beautiful mouth of his was set in a stern, resolute line that made something giddy and wild race through her, then coil tight low in her belly.

"I already told you I want to be inside you, Brittany," he told her, and it had the ring of a vow. Of something stitched together, need and command as one, and a red hot punch straight to that place that already melted for him. "That hasn't changed."

She rotated her hips, pulling him closer to her, and then she slid both of her hands around his neck. Her pulse was a riot, hammering through her veins and striking rapid blows in her temples, her throat, her wrists. And deep between her legs, where she ached and melted and ached some more.

And Brittany forgot that she was playing a role. She forgot everything but the fact she wanted him, as extraordinary as that was. *She wanted him.* And the whole world already thought he'd had her a million times, so who was she saving herself for if not this curious man who got beneath her skin as no one else ever had?

"Then why aren't you?" she asked. Cairo seemed to freeze there before her, save the hand that had gripped her jaw. He dropped it then, but his eyes stayed locked to hers. "Why aren't you inside me, when you are renowned the world over for your inability to keep it in your own trousers? Why have we spent our entire relationship so chastely and demurely?" She laughed at that, because she didn't know the answer herself when the only thing inside her was this edgy, delirious need. "Or is this terrible reputation of yours no more than the fevered imaginings of an overworked publicist somewhere?"

His gaze took on a light she'd never seen before, but she felt it. God help her, but she felt it, deep inside of her, where she was nothing but slippery longing and very bad ideas.

"Why don't we find out?" he murmured, his voice like silk.

Silk and danger and too much heat besides.

He shifted again, then. He reached down between them and began pulling up her heavy white skirt, never moving that demanding gaze of his from hers.

Brittany couldn't have said a word if she'd tried.

She didn't try.

And this time, when he traced patterns over the top of one thigh and then dipped into the valley between her legs, he didn't stop there. He found the silken panties she wore and smoothed his way beneath them, and then it was happening. It was really happening.

He was touching her where no one else had ever touched her.

Him.

Cairo.

He made a low, approving noise that rolled over her like another caress, as if finding her heat made him feel as raw as she did, and she surrendered herself all over again.

She had the distant thought that she always would.

Cairo stroked her tender flesh with his fingers, his eyes glittering darkly as her lips parted. Brittany did nothing—could do nothing—but lean back against the wall. And die from the pleasure of his touch, over and over and over. And let her hips rise to meet him with every slippery, decadent stroke, as if she was learning how to dance for the very first time.

As if he was teaching her the steps to the most perfect dance of all.

"It almost feels as if I know what I'm doing," he murmured, his voice a low, throbbing thing that mixed in with the slick, delicious movement of his hand, there against an old castle wall. "I can almost imagine no publicist has been involved in the creation of my reputation. What do you think?"

But everything else was lost in that fire he built in her and she couldn't respond. She wasn't sure she would have responded if she could. Not when she could disappear into the sweet glory of his touch instead.

And that was when he found the center of her need. He pressed against it once, then again, making her moan out loud. She told herself an experienced woman wouldn't react the way she did—but she couldn't seem to help herself, not when he ground his hand against her.

"Let's consider this an object lesson," Cairo murmured, dropping his head beside hers, his breath against her neck. "You have a habit of saying things no other person alive would dare say to me. Perhaps I have finally found the appropriate way to respond."

He twisted his wrist, plunging a finger deep inside her

molten heat while the rest of his hand rocked hard against the place where she ached the most.

It was an invasion. *It was perfect.*

He did it again, then again, then added a second finger and did it once more.

And Brittany simply…broke apart.

She shook and she shattered, and she fell into a thousand pieces right there in her wedding dress with her fingers dug deep into his arms, and the only thing she knew in all the world was his hard hand and his rough voice at her ear. She might have fallen apart forever, tumbling this way and that into a million little shards of who she'd been. She felt as if she had.

And when she came back to herself she was slumped against the smooth wall and the only thing holding her up was the arm she hadn't realized Cairo had put around her waist, securing her there against him.

He was watching her closely when she finally focused on him again, with an expression she'd never seen on his royal face before. Hard and solemn at once, and lit from within with a kind of hunger that made her clench tight all over again, against the fingers she could still feel inside of her.

Inside of her. Brittany let loose a shudder, low and deep, through a brand-new lick of need and heat.

Cairo smiled at that. He took his time pulling his hand away. He smoothed the silken fabric over her heat and then he drew his hand away entirely, letting the heavy wedding dress fall back into place to cover her weak knees and legs.

As if none of it had happened, when she was still soft and soaked and trembling.

"Brittany," he began, as if that wasn't the same sensual hunger that stormed through her turning his gorgeous face stark.

And something surged in her then, shocking her back

from that syrupy sweet place he'd thrown her into so easily, so expertly. Some kind of heightened awareness, or desperation. She didn't know what it was, she only knew with every inch of her body that she had to act instantly or lose everything.

"Is that it?" she asked, and she'd never sounded more bored. She heaved a sigh and pushed away from him, taking advantage of the look of arrogant astonishment on his face to swish her great skirts around him and start toward the other side of the room. "Clueless teenagers commit more interesting sins while fully clothed in the hallways of their high schools. I expected a little more finesse from a man who calls himself a king."

"Finesse," he repeated, as if he was unfamiliar with the word, and he sounded far closer to her than she'd expected. And far more cutting. Every hair on the back of her neck stood, but she didn't turn around. "The excitement of our wedding day must be playing havoc with my hearing. I just imagined you questioned my *finesse* mere seconds after you climaxed in my hands. Surely not."

She turned around then and her stomach flipped over, because he was *right there.*

He kept coming. Brittany decided to stop moving and stood there at the foot of the four-poster bed, trying to exude bored experience while her knees still felt like jelly.

"It's okay," she murmured, as insincerely as possible. She rolled her eyes. "I'm sure you're great."

His head tilted slightly to one side and the way he smiled then, slow and hard, made her think of a wolf.

"Oh, I am at that." Cairo reached over and ran a finger down the length of her hair, then tugged on the end. Once, then again. Not precisely hard—and yet that small hint of sharpness seemed to rebound through her overheated body, blooming into something much hotter and more intense in the place that still ached for him the most. "But by all means, *cara*, do not take my word for it."

And then he bent down and swept her up off her feet, huge dress and veil and all, and tossed her onto the bed.

Cairo hardly let himself think.

She landed on the bed with a soft exhalation and then he was there with her, levering himself above her and holding himself up on his elbows.

"Cairo—"

"Quiet, *cara*. Allow me to meet the challenge you issued, if you please."

His voice was a lash of command. He hardly recognized it. But that didn't seem to matter. Nothing seemed to matter except this woman dressed in white, with those dark eyes still so hot and wild and all for him. This woman who would shortly be his wife. *My wife*, he repeated, and the words seemed to reverberate inside of him, growing so big and so loud they filled him up—then crowded out everything else.

The world. His sense. *Everything.*

Cairo didn't care. He traced her lips with his fingers and hoped she could taste her own need when he did. She flushed that intoxicating red again, and it made him feel dizzy. It made a beast he hadn't known that lurked so deep inside him roar.

For once in his life, he didn't calculate the outcome of this encounter or worry about his performance. He'd left that somewhere behind them on the stone floor, tangled up in those abandoned little moans she'd made that left him so hard and so wild for her he ached.

He ached.

"Cairo," she said again, and this time her voice was little more than a whisper. But he recognized the heat in it. The impossible fire that burned in him, too.

He forgot how they'd come to be here. He only knew that finally, *finally*, Brittany was beneath him. *Where she belonged*, that beast in him growled.

What else could possibly matter?

He reached between them and pulled her dress up and out of his way. She made a soft, high sound, but when their gazes clashed she pulled her lower lip between her teeth. Then rocked her hips against him as he settled himself between her soft, leanly muscled thighs in wordless welcome.

God help him, but she was perfect.

He leaned in close and took her mouth with his, with all the desperate ruthlessness of a man about to explode. Her taste washed through him, sweet woman and all Brittany. He lost himself in the sheer perfection of it. He tasted her again and again, then angled his head for a hotter, slicker fit and did it all over again.

She lifted herself to meet him, her tongue meeting his and then driving him slowly, inevitably, gloriously insane.

Cairo had been acting a part for a long time. He'd pretended to be lost in a thousand kisses, usually for the benefit of the cameras that always waited nearby. But there were no cameras here and the longer he indulged himself in this woman, the more he forgot he'd ever treated a kiss like a stage.

This time, he really was lost.

He wanted her naked. He wanted her without a stitch of clothing on her perfect, delectable body, spread out before him like the feast she was. He wanted to take his time. He wanted to wallow in sensation, bathe in passion, throw himself completely into this woman and never come up for air—

But the bodice stopped him. It was a piece of understated elegance, embroidered and close-fitting, and it penetrated the fist of need that had him locked in its grip.

Just enough to remember that there were people waiting.
That there were other things he needed to do to Brittany
today, like marry her.

He could think of only one thing he wanted more, just
then.

He deepened the kiss. His mouth mated with hers,
taking her and taunting her. Making her flush and buck
against him, her hands clutching at him and urging him
on.

"Are you ready?" he asked her.

"I've been ready for weeks," she retorted, as he should
have expected.

Cairo reached down between them and worked at his
trousers, then smoothed his hand back beneath her silken
panties, still beautifully damp from before. She was still
molten hot and mind-numbingly soft, and she was *his*.

He'd been waiting for this moment since the moment
he'd seen her picture, so long ago now. He'd longed for this
since the night they'd met in Monte Carlo. He'd imagined
this a thousand different ways since she'd walked out on
him that night and left him to stew in his own wild need.

Cairo had never wanted another woman more.

He lined himself up with her slick, ready entrance *at
last*, then thrust himself home.

It hurt.

He was huge and hard and so deep inside her, and the
sensation that burst within her was too much. *Too much*.

Brittany went stiff, unconsciously slamming her hands
in fists against his chest, and Cairo froze.

She'd imagined she could play it off. She'd been so sure
that all her years of dancing would have loosened her up,
made this a nonissue, the way so many of the other girls
had claimed it had for them. She'd wanted him so much
that she'd been positive she could simply throw herself

into this thing without him pausing or even noticing that it was her first time.

But his eyes were dark and faintly accusing as they met hers now. His beautiful face was taut. He held himself very, very still above her, but there was no mistaking the steel length of him still sunk deep inside her, or the utter foreignness of the big, hard, decidedly male body nestled tight between her thighs.

He was stretching her. He was inside her and he was stretching her and she could *feel him* everywhere. With every shuddering breath she took.

But far worse than that, he had definitely noticed.

Brittany felt tears pool in the corners of her eyes, when she hadn't *cried* in longer than she could remember, and she couldn't believe she felt so *undone*.

"Do you care to explain this turn of events?" Cairo asked, conversationally, which only made that particular hot gleam in his eyes seem more dangerous.

She tried to blink back the tears in her eyes and swallow down that lump in her throat, but only made a snuffling sort of sound instead. She *snuffled*. She was flat on her back in the most beautiful wedding dress she'd ever seen, His Serene Grace the Archduke Felipe Skander Cairo of Santa Domini braced above her and deep *inside* her, no longer a virgin no matter what happened next if she understood the mechanics of these things correctly, and she'd *snuffled*.

Like some kind of animal.

"Do not cry," he ordered her. His gaze gentled as it met hers and it was astonishing how comforting Brittany found that. "Don't you dare cry, *tesorina*. You have lived through far worse things than me, I am confident."

A moment ago she'd had a sob inside her chest, so big she'd been afraid it would burst straight out through her ribs like some kind of alien creature and engulf them both, and now she wanted to laugh. She loosened the fists she still had clenched against him, uncurling her fingers and then smoothing them over the elegant morning coat he wore. Almost as if she was comforting *him*.

She opted not to analyze that.

"I haven't yet determined whether or not I'll live through this," she pointed out after a moment, and though her voice was thicker than normal, there were no tears in it.

She could feel him, hard and so astonishingly hot, still wedged deep inside her. The very thought of it made her a little bit breathless, and then there was how it *felt*. Or maybe it was just him, braced above her so that thick hair of his fell down his forehead the way it always did. But there were still no tears. And then his mouth curved, and Brittany couldn't imagine why she'd ever felt like crying.

Cairo lowered himself to his elbows and cradled her face in his hands. It made him move the slightest bit inside of her, the faintest bit of friction where she was nothing but tender and new and scared, and it hurt again. She stiffened in the same instant she recognized that the pain was far less than before.

"You will live," he assured her. He held himself still again. "I promise."

He was heavy and hard, and her dancer's thighs, which she'd thought could handle any amount of stretching, felt... different. They almost ached from this strange position, pressed down and wide open by another person so much larger and more solidly muscular than she was. Still, it wasn't a painful ache. Not quite.

"It is your maidenly virtue that we must mourn here today," Cairo continued, sounding almost as lazy as he normally did, despite that caramel gleam in his dark eyes. "That and your penchant to lie directly to my face are two topics I imagine we will spend some time discussing in the days to come."

"Let's not get carried away." She frowned at him. "I might not have had sex before, but that doesn't make me—"

"A virgin? I think you'll find that is, in fact, the text-book definition."

"Virtuous." Her frown deepened. "I haven't been remotely virtuous since I was a kid and I was never much of a maiden, either. I have three husbands who would agree."

"Three husbands, yes." His gaze held hers, hot and gleaming, and he moved then. A simple little slide. An adjustment, nothing more, and it made her breath catch as she clutched at him. But it didn't hurt. Not at all, this time. "But no one has ever been here but me."

She scowled at him.

"I will take that as the confirmation I do not actually require," he murmured.

He pulled her closer to him, and Brittany was astounded to feel herself begin to melt all around him again. That look in his eyes changed again, and this time, the flush she felt was from something that felt a great deal like shame.

"You should have told me." Cairo's voice was reproving, and there was that edge to it she didn't quite understand. Once again, she had the wild notion she was looking at a Cairo no one else had ever seen, this man who looked at her with something akin to tenderness in his gaze. Deep inside, she trembled. "I did not wish to hurt you. I am not quite that monstrous. Not quite."

"I…" This was so far outside her experience. She didn't know what to do, what to say. She'd never *felt* so many things at once, physical sensation mixed with a flash flood of emotion, and all the while Cairo simply held himself there. Not hurting her. Not rushing her. Not leaving her. As if he could stay like that forever. "I didn't want you to know."

"Because you thought I would mind?" he asked, and though his voice was mild enough she thought she heard an edge in it. He still didn't move. "Or because you thought it would give you better leverage to throw your virginity at the highest title in your vicinity?"

She tipped her chin up as if she wanted to fight him for saying that. Maybe she did. Or maybe that was her only defense when he accused her of something so outside her imagining that she felt lacerated.

"I can't imagine a single person alive who would imagine that Cairo Santa Domini, patron saint of the lascivious, would have the slightest interest in whether or not someone was a virgin. You are whatever the opposite of a virgin is. Times a million."

His dark eyes gleamed. "As it turns out, I find myself deeply interested and also deep inside you. Perhaps they are related states."

She tilted her head back to glare at him more fully. "If I'd known the possibility of a truly white wedding mattered to you, because you are apparently a giant cliché masquerading as a man, I would have made certain to demand more money for going through with it." Her voice was as icy as possible, and yet even she could hear she sounded much too rough. And that it was far too revealing. She soldiered on, "And if I'd known you were a walking caveman, I would have turned you down the way I wanted to do from the start, no matter how many provocative pictures you sold to the tabloids."

"I am a king, Brittany."

That rang out between them, and she thought she saw something like amazement on his face for a moment, though he blinked it away. He seemed to get harder, bigger. Propped over her like that, still lodged inside of her, he became the whole world.

And Brittany found she couldn't seem to say another word.

"Not a cliché, not a caveman, not common in any way," he told her, in that same quietly ringing tone. "And I may not have a kingdom or the subjects I deserve, but I will have a wife before this day is done. I will have you. Like this. As long as we are together, I will have you exactly like this."

Cairo said it as if they stood at the altar already and these were the promises he was making to bind them together. She shook again, deep inside. Then, following an urge she didn't entirely understand, she moved her hips. She rocked them against his. His eyes darkened. And she pulled in a breath.

Because that didn't hurt at all. In fact, it felt…interesting.

"And whatever games we play in public, Brittany, what we do in private is ours. More specifically, mine."

"Cairo," she whispered. "I think I want you to start moving now."

Something flared in his gaze then, a deep, male satisfaction and that same hunger she recognized.

"Your wish is my command, *tesorina*," he told her. "But first you must say it."

"What do you want me to say?" She rocked against him again, against that impossible length of his buried so deep inside her, and shivered when sensation swirled through her. Lighting her up from the tips of her ears to the hard points of her nipples, past the molten place where they were connected, down into the toes that curled in the delicate shoes she still wore.

"Tell me," he urged her, and he pulled back then. Slowly. Slowly and steadily, inch by inch, and it made Brittany flush. Then try to meet him when he reversed himself and sank back into her. Deep and sure. "Tell me that in this, I am your king if no one else's. That here, you are mine."

She would have told him absolutely anything just then. Anything at all.

"Yours," she agreed, her head moving against the bed as he repeated that luxurious slide. Even more intense, delicious sensations coiled in her and flashed like wildfire through her entire body. Again and again. "I'm all yours."

"You have no idea how true that is, *tesorina mia*," Cairo muttered, dark and urgent, and then he really began to move.

And Brittany simply surrendered herself into a mass of pure sensation.

Cairo set a lazy, easy pace, and he encouraged her to meet him. Brittany moved her hips as he directed her, growing bolder with each stroke until she wrapped her legs around his hips.

He built the fire between them high and bright and so intense she didn't see how anyone could live through it. She also didn't care. He thrust harder, deeper, and she gloried in it. In him. As if she'd spent her whole life searching for this. As if this, right here, was exactly where she was meant to be.

As if her body knew things her mind didn't want to examine.

Still, he urged her on. Still, he swept her along with him, until she was hovering on another precarious cliff of his making.

"I can't..." she whispered.

"But you will," he replied, fierce and sure. "For me."

He reached between them and stroked her where she needed him the most. Brittany tipped her head back and gripped him tight as he pounded into her. Again and again—

Until finally, she hurtled off into nothingness, breaking apart into too many scattered little bits to name.

And this time, he called out her name and followed her right over that edge.

She had the vague notion they floated out in that silken, beautiful darkness together for a very long time. It could have been years.

But Cairo was already up and moving when she finally thudded back into her own skin and opened her eyes again.

"Stay where you are," he told her, in that bossy tone of voice she thought she really ought to object to.

But she didn't say a word. Nor did she move. She felt loose and lazy as she lay there on the old four-poster bed. There were all manner of thoughts and problems and issues hovering there, waiting for her to acknowledge them, but she ignored them. She listened to the cries of the seabirds on the other side of the windows instead, wafting in on the sweet summer breeze. She felt the sunlight dance over her face. She imagined she could hear the sea against the rocks, far below.

She felt bright and sunny straight through, as if she could drift away into the blue sky forever.

Cairo came back to her then, and she blinked, because he looked immaculate as he stood there at the foot of the bed. Not a wrinkle, or a hair out of place. As if none of this had happened when she could still feel him between her legs, where she was deliciously tender. She knew that should have bothered her. It should have done *something* other than make her shudder with a little more of that heat. He moved to put a hand on her belly and she shivered at his touch, then again when he used the cloth in his other hand to tend to her.

"You did not bleed much," he told her matter-of-factly, and she flushed at that. As if the words were more intimate than the act they'd shared. He tucked the cloth into her panties, pulled them back into place over her hips and then helped her to her feet, smoothing her dress down around her as she stood. "Leave that there until just before you walk down the aisle."

"What?" She wanted the floor to swallow her whole. She stared at the stones, willing it to do just that. "I don't want to talk about this with you."

"Brittany." She couldn't help but obey him when he used that voice, but he took her chin in his hand to make certain. "You are wearing a very white dress and you will be standing in it before a large congregation and a great many cameras. This is no time for modesty."

She pulled away then and stepped around him, amazed that her legs held her up when she felt as if she'd been swept away. As if she wasn't entirely herself anymore.

As if the mask she'd worn all her life had shattered, leaving her with nowhere to hide.

"This was a mistake," she said, sounding stilted to her own ears. "That shouldn't have happened."

It took everything she had to pull herself together. To lift her chin, run her hands over her veil, manage to smooth out her expression. She moved to the mirror and was as amazed as she was oddly disappointed that she looked exactly the same. The same as she had before he'd come into this room and more, wholly unruffled. As if nothing had happened between them but a little chat, like all the other little chats they'd had over the past weeks. All she needed to do was reapply her lipstick and no one would ever be the wiser.

She decided to take that as a sign. A portent, even.

"That will never happen again," she told him, raising her gaze to meet his in the mirror.

He moved to stand directly behind her, and her body knew him. It ached for him. She felt herself soften, everywhere, and had no idea what to do about it. As if he knew it simply by looking at her, Cairo smiled. He slid his hand around to hold her there before him, stretching his palm against the tight waist of her gown.

She felt the heat of it everywhere, like a promise. She wanted to lean into it, into him. She would never know how she kept herself from doing it. How she kept her spine straight and her knees locked.

"You are going to marry me in approximately five minutes," Cairo told her, and she couldn't help but remember the way he'd said "I am a king," as if he'd never said such a thing out loud before. She could hear the echo of it again now, and more, feel it deep inside her. Like a command from on high. "You are going to remember what happened here with every step you take down that aisle. I have no intention of a carrying on a sexless marriage, Brittany. Certainly not with a woman who wants me as badly as you do. Almost as badly as I want you."

"I…"

But she didn't know what she meant to say. What she could say, when every last cell in her body wanted nothing more than to throw herself back onto that bed again. To tear off her clothes and all of his and actually explore him this time. Then lose herself in all that marvelous shattering all over again. Right here, right now, and who cared how many noble personages waited for them below?

"I was always planning to seduce you, Brittany," Cairo told her as he pulled his arm from around her body. He righted her when she started to slump over because her knees really weren't working, and she flushed at his touch all over again. His firm lips moved into that small curve that set off explosions all through her. "Now I will simply take comfort in the fact that inevitably, I will ruin you for all other men. I likely already have. What a great pity."

"That's a lovely sentiment," she managed to say, trying desperately to sound as composed and as dry as she wished she was. "I'm signing up to be your wife for a little while, not become your..."

She faltered, not knowing what word to use. What this was, what she was.

Or, worse, what she wanted to be. With him. For him. Much less for herself.

Cairo smiled at her then, and this time, it reached his eyes. And it was as lethal to her as the way he'd touched her, as the way he'd moved inside her, as the way he'd made her feel. It was almost too much to bear, too bright and too perfect, like the impossible Italian summer on the other side of the window.

He was her ruin made real and today she'd ensured it. She felt something inside her crack wide open and she was terribly afraid it would suck her in and destroy her right then and there, whatever it was. It felt that brutal and that permanent.

The trouble was, some part of her wanted to see what would happen. Some part of her imagined the wreck of it—of this—would be worth it, no matter what came after.

"Don't worry," Cairo told her, as if he felt it, too, that great, wide, open thing that was already changing everything. As if he knew exactly what it was and what it meant. As if this was as real as it felt—as real as that silly, fairy-tale-headed fool inside of her wanted it to be. "You will be both. My wife, yes. My countryless queen in all your glory. But most of all, Brittany, you will be mine. Do you not understand? You already are."

CHAPTER SEVEN

THE LAST OF the Santa Dominis married his stripper bride in a private chapel that dated back to the Italian Renaissance, the first of his family to marry in a place other than the Grand Cathedral in Santa Domini's capital in centuries.

Three whole centuries, to be exact.

As the old hymns were sung and the old words intoned, Cairo stood at an altar his ancestors had built with a woman for whom he felt entirely too many complicated things to name and found it hard to remember that he was baiting a trap. It was much too difficult to focus on the real purpose of this performance.

Because all he could think of, all he could see, all he could concentrate on was Brittany.

Who had somehow seen beneath every last mask he wore. And was already his.

Princes and counts and the assorted minor arcana of Europe sat in the pews arranged behind him, yet all Cairo could think about was the fact of her innocence and his taking of it. Her sweet heat and her addictive taste. The untutored rawness of the way she'd moved beneath him and the greedy little sounds she'd made as she'd found her release. He had to shift slightly as he stood to mask his body's response to the onslaught of memory, lest he appall the gathered throng of European nobles even more than he already had by making them bear witness to this ceremony in the first place.

Pay attention to the game, you fool, he ordered himself as the priest waved his hands over his bride's elegantly veiled head and intoned sacred words down the length of the chapel.

He was making this woman his in every conceivable way today, and despite the niggling sense that he was forgetting something critical, he exulted in it. If was up to him, he thought, he'd lock her up somewhere far away and out of the public eye, and indulge himself in her forever.

But that, of course, was not the game they played. No matter that she wasn't at all the practiced trollop she'd pretended she was for years. Nobody alive could possibly know that except Cairo—and in any case, it changed nothing.

The fact he felt he could show her the truth in him didn't mean he should, or that it altered the course they'd set out. It only made him hate himself that much more.

"I don't understand," Brittany had said weeks ago. It had been a few days after their engagement dinner. Enterprising paparazzi were attempting to scale the gates of his Parisian residence and the sketches he'd commissioned from his preferred Italian dressmaker had been spread out between them on the coffee table in one of his salons. "This looks like something a proper English princess would wear. I assumed we'd be taking the loud and tacky route."

"Everyone will be expecting that, of course." He'd eyed her, all copper fire and that distance in her gaze. He'd had the fleeting notion she'd been protecting herself—but he'd dismissed it. Why should she need protection? She was the one marrying up. "I have something else in mind."

A different sort of color bloomed high on her lovely cheeks, his mother's ring gleamed on her finger and it was a dangerous game he'd been playing. He'd known that all along, but perhaps never so keenly as in that moment.

"I don't understand." He'd had the impression she'd thought about how to respond. Her words were too precise. "I thought the point was to horrify the entire world with your marriage to a bargain-basement upstart like me."

"I want something slightly more complicated than a circus of a ceremony and a parade of bad taste," he'd said quietly. "That would be an obvious stunt. And not only because that was how you did it the last time you married above your station."

There had been a hint of misery in her dark hazel gaze. Then she'd blinked it away and lifted her chin, and he'd wondered if he'd only wanted that kind of reaction from her. If that was why he kept baiting her.

If he'd *wanted* her to feel all the things he was terribly afraid he felt himself.

"You want them to pity you," Brittany had said softly.

She hadn't met his gaze then. The iconic ring he'd slid onto her finger so recently had seemed to dance in the Parisian morning light between them, hoarding the sunshine and then sending it cartwheeling across the room.

Like joy, he'd thought. Not that he would know.

Brittany had still been talking. "You want them to think you believe that the sheer force of your feelings for me makes me somehow appropriate. You want to present a sow's ear all dressed up like a silk purse and pretend you can't tell the difference. You want them to laugh at you. At me."

She'd met his gaze then and it had taken everything he had to keep from flinching. He, who had never so much as blinked at all the tawdry things he'd done in his lifetime. He, who had always known precisely what his mission was and how best to achieve it, no matter how many reports he received that the general's health continued to decline.

"I do," he'd said, and he'd pretended that he hadn't seen

her pretty eyes go darker at that. Or, more to the point, he'd pretended he didn't care.

He said the same words now.

His voice was strong and sure to carry throughout the chapel and dispel any possible doubt that he was marrying this woman—*his woman*. He kept his fingers clasped tight around hers. And he waited.

But it wasn't until she replied in kind, sending relief arrowing through him, that Cairo realized he hadn't known what she'd say. Some part of him had truly believed that Brittany might change her mind at the last moment and take off running, like some captured bride of old. Another part of him wouldn't have blamed her if she had.

Here in this church, as he slid a new ring onto her finger to proclaim her his without any doubt or wiggle room, Cairo found absolutely nothing amusing about the idea of Brittany anywhere but here. With him.

The whole world thought they knew her, but only he did.

She was his in every possible way.

"You may kiss the bride," the priest intoned.

Cairo wanted to do a great deal more than simply kiss her.

But this was a stage, he reminded himself. This was an act. This was his opportunity to paint himself the besotted fool for the cameras.

He told himself he was a lucky man, indeed, that it was so easy.

Brittany tilted her face up to his, her pretty eyes darker than usual. He wanted that to be evidence. He wanted her to be as swept away in this as he was. He hated that he couldn't quite tell how much of her was real and how much of her was a performance.

It had been different up in that old stone chamber. When he'd been able to feel the truth of her, of them, in the way she shook apart in his hands and then again beneath him. When he'd ridden them both into all that glorious fire and let them burn and burn and burn.

God, how he wanted to do it again.

He pressed his mouth to hers. He felt her tremble against him when he deepened the kiss, holding her against him a beat or two longer than was strictly polite, and he saw the vulnerable cast to her temptation of a mouth when he finally released her.

She was thinking about what had happened between them, too. About him sunk deep inside her and her legs wrapped around him. He knew it as well as he knew his own name.

"Next time," she murmured, right there against his lips, "why don't you brand me with your initials instead? Or perhaps urinate in a circle around me, like a dog?"

"Is that a request?" he asked, in a low voice pitched for her ears alone. "Or a dare?"

And then he pulled back and presented her to the assembled crowd, before she could answer back in her usual tart way. His queen at last, and who cared what those vultures thought of her?

He knew what he thought: that his honeymoon couldn't come fast enough, because one taste of her wasn't nearly enough.

Cairo couldn't remember ever wanting a woman the way he wanted this one. *His wife*, he thought as they made their way down the chapel's long aisle and then stepped out into the exuberant Italian sunshine. It was such a small word, and yet he couldn't seem to process it. *His wife*.

There was only one other thing in all the world he'd ever wanted so badly it had consumed him whole. Thinking of his lost kingdom as they moved, Cairo thought he should be ashamed that he'd lost sight of it for even a moment. No matter how his new queen's smile caught the sun and made the whole world a little brighter all around her as they walked from the chapel. The wedding breakfast that waited for them, arranged in artistically laden long tables in the old castle keep, was not the place to forget who he was or the role he needed to play here.

Because it had never been more crucial to keep up his usual act than it was today.

"I never thought I'd see the day," one of his supposed best and oldest friends said with an entirely feigned congratulatory grin, slinging his arm over Cairo's shoulders in a show of his usual drunkenness as Cairo made his rounds sometime later. Cairo could see right through it, but then, there wasn't much of Harry Marbury—a man constructed of as many impeccably pedigreed English forebears as cast-off morals—that wasn't entirely transparent. "It's not as if you must marry to secure the kingdom, Cairo. It's been lost all your life and no matter those rumors that the old soldier is on his last legs. What *is* this preposterous wedding all about?"

"We all must fall in our time," Cairo replied lazily, as if mention of the general didn't scrape at him. And he hated himself when he continued, as he knew he must. "Better to cushion that landing in a woman who knows her way around a stripper pole, in my opinion."

"One does not marry the trash, friend," Harry said, laughing in his condescending way—and raising his voice just enough that it carried across the gathering and over to where Brittany stood with that fake smile on her face. Cairo saw her stiffen and he hated all of this. These lies, these performances, when what had happened between them had been real. Raw and real and entirely theirs. The most real and unscripted he thought he'd ever been in his life. "One uses it and then one's servants puts it out. In bins, I'm told."

Cairo would never know how he managed to keep himself from murdering the man—his supposed oldest, dearest friend—with his own two hands just then, right where they stood in the medieval courtyard of the old castle keep.

But he didn't, because this was exactly what he'd wanted. What he'd gone to such great lengths to make happen, precisely like this. He had no one to blame but himself if he didn't like how it felt now.

Now that she was his wife. His exiled queen.

His, damn it.

That was the part that mattered. That and the headlines Harry's little comment would likely generate from all the hangers-on that Cairo knew full well spent half their time in his presence texting the tabloids with choice snippets that usually bred headlines. And that was why Cairo laughed indulgently and clapped Harry on the back as if he'd told a rousing great joke instead of exterminating him like the cockroach he was.

You deserve a medal of valor for letting him live, he told himself grimly as he smiled and laughed and encouraged all these parasites to pity him as the reception wore on. Just as he'd planned.

Though it was hard to mind any of that when he had Brittany in his arms again.

She tilted her head back as they danced together for the first time as husband and wife, exiled king and nominal queen, smiling up at him for the benefit of the crowd.

"You look as if you are head over heels for me," he told her, and tried to sound as if he was chiding her when all he could think about was keeping his hands where they belonged. Instead of where he longed to put them. He was sure everyone could see it and with it, his real face. His true self. And yet all he wanted to do was continue to gaze down at her. "The papers will not know whether to call you smitten or materialistic."

"It must be the romance of the day," she said dryly. "It's

going to my head. Next thing you know I'll be reciting poetry and telling all the papers it was love at first sight, right there in that nightclub in the sewers of Paris where they think we met."

Two things happened then, in an instant.

First, a hard kick in the vicinity of Cairo's chest, making him clasp Brittany tighter as he fought it off. He tried to tell himself he didn't know what it was—but he did. Of course he did. Anticipation, desire... As if he wanted this to be real. As if he wanted this to be the mad, epic romance they were pretending it was.

As if it already was.

But that wasn't possible. He knew that as well as he knew his own, cursed name.

Because the second thing that happened was a vicious punch, straight to the gut. Cairo knew what happened when love was involved. He'd lived it. He was still living it. Grief and horror and crushing, interminable loss. A lifetime of pain and guilt when the people he'd loved were taken. He wouldn't go near it again. He *couldn't* go near it again.

But God help him, he wanted things today he'd never imagined he'd ever want. *Ever.* It was the way she'd come apart for him earlier, so soft and hot beneath him. It was the way she'd watched him in the chapel, her eyes solemn on his.

It was the simple, searing fact that no one had ever had her but him. No one had ever touched her and therefore nobody truly knew her, except him. Cairo didn't need to be told that she'd given him a gift far more precious than her maidenhead today.

He'd spent his whole life doing what he had to do, not what he wanted to do. He always made the smart choice no matter how it hurt him, no matter what it cost. He'd learned long ago to think of himself and his own feelings last, if ever, because what the hell did *he* matter when there were so many lives on the line? He'd never questioned any of it. He'd become his own worst nightmare, an utter disgrace to all he held dear. And because of that, he'd survived.

He gazed down at the woman who fit as perfectly in his arms as he had inside her, and he didn't know if he could do it this time. For the first time in as long as he could remember, Cairo wanted to do more than simply survive.

He wanted *more*.

"You're staring at me." She sounded edgy, despite the smile she aimed at him. Because, of course, they were still in public. They were always in public.

"You are my wife." He sounded like the man he'd taken such care, all his life, to keep from becoming in word or deed or public perception. He sounded like his memories of his father, commanding and sure. His father, who had refused to fight the coup because he'd thought that meant fewer of his subjects would die. His father, who had always viewed his exile as a mere interlude. His father, the king of Santa Domini Cairo would never, ever become. "My queen."

Her dark eyes glittered despite the sunlight, and she seemed as far away then as if she was up on the stage in that club again. On display to all, available to none.

But he'd seen beneath that mask. He'd removed his own.

Everything was different now.

He didn't want to watch her distance herself from him or what had already happened between them today.

He wanted anything but distance, even when they were out in public for all to see.

He dipped her then, slow and romantic and not entirely for show, and let himself enjoy the way her gaze spit fire at him despite the smile she kept welded to her lips. He pressed a kiss against that smile when he pulled her back to standing, and let that kick between them.

That lick of fire. That spiked edge of need.

And the murmurs and applause from the crowd he'd half forgotten all around them.

"That felt like a threat," she told him through her teeth, her smile as bright as her clever eyes were dark, making her even more beautiful to him, somehow.

"It was a promise," he retorted.

Searing and hot, that promise.

One he had every intention of keeping.

And keeping and keeping, until he wore them both out.

Soon.

Brittany woke up sprawled across the wide bed in one of the private jet's guest chambers. She was still wearing the pale yellow shift dress that had been set out for her to change into after the wedding breakfast, and in which she'd been photographed by a sea of paparazzi as she and Cairo had boarded his plane in Italy the night of their wedding.

She'd staggered on board, put as much distance as possible between her and the brand-new husband who'd gotten under her skin in more ways than she could possibly count already, and then slept like the dead the moment she'd tossed herself across the soft coverlet.

She was all too aware he'd let her go. Let her retreat from him.

And now you're waking up married, she told herself—perhaps a little more sharply than she should.

After all, it wasn't as if that was anything new.

The fact that she was no longer a virgin, on the other hand, was.

Lying there on her stomach, she pulled her hand out from beneath the pillow and stared at her rings. She'd worn wedding sets before, of course. Her first husband had been as deficient in that department as in everything else, but Carlos had dutifully presented her with not only the expected solitaire engagement ring and a platinum band to match, but also a bill for her half of the investment they were making in their Hollywood future. Jean Pierre had preferred yellow gold and had given her an ornate ruby he'd claimed was a family heirloom when they'd gotten engaged, then two guard bands of rubies and diamonds at their wedding ceremony. His fifty-year-old matron of a daughter had sneered at the rings and told Brittany it looked like her hand had been dipped in blood.

"Success," Jean Pierre had murmured into Brittany's ear, the conniving old fool.

But today she wore the Heart of Santa Domini and next to it, an eternity band of heart-stoppingly perfect diamonds that sparkled with their own, deep fire.

Because this time she was married to a legend. She was Cairo Santa Domini's queen. Whatever happened next, however their fake little marriage worked and then ended, she would always—*always*—be the first woman he'd married. She would appear in all his biographical information, in history books and encyclopedias alike.

Just as he would always be the first—something inside her whispered *only*, but she shoved it aside as so much damaging wishful thinking—lover she'd ever taken.

Brittany rolled over and sat up, looking around the compact room as if she expected to see her new husband lurking somewhere. As if Cairo was the sort who lurked. But she was alone. The little room was dark. She had no idea what time it was, how long she'd slept, or even where they were flying. Cairo had announced that they would honeymoon for a month or two and that had been all the information he'd offered. She hadn't asked where they were headed because it hadn't much mattered. The Maldives, New York City, the moon—who cared?

Their act was their act wherever they took it.

She scraped her hair back into a knot at the nape of her neck, wishing she'd had time to comb it all out and shower after the wedding. Wishing she hadn't slept in all her makeup, come to that. She ran her index fingers below her eyes and sighed when they came away smudged with black mascara. *How regal and queenly*, she chided herself. No wonder Cairo had married her for the sole purpose of parading her embarrassing low-class behavior in front of the whole world. She couldn't even manage to wash her own face.

None of this felt real to her, the fact she'd married the most famous exile alive, and not just because she didn't like thinking about *why* Cairo had married her.

Her other marriages had felt real. Too real, in all the wrong ways. Her first wedding night had been spent locked in the bathroom of the run-down motel Darryl had taken her to before he'd started drinking himself into a rage. She'd been so naive then, thinking *drunk* was the worst thing a man could be. Darryl had quickly taught her otherwise. Her marriage to Carlos had been pure business all the way through, and their life together had been entirely conducted to be filmed, from their choice of apartment in the gritty outskirts of Los Angeles's Echo Park neighborhood, a far cry from the Hollywood tourists loved, to their plotted outings to Southern California hot spots. Even her time with Jean Pierre, which had been all about creating a commotion, had been conducted as a shared vision and business enterprise.

Her new marriage didn't feel particularly authentic in that sense. She certainly didn't feel like any kind of queen, exiled or otherwise. But *she* felt something far more than real. Cairo knew her deepest, darkest, best-kept secret.

She felt raw all the way through.

Brittany moved to the edge of the bed and helped herself to the bottle of spring water that had been left there, gulping down half of it in greedy swallows, but she still felt parched.

You are going to remember this moment with every step you take down that aisle, he'd promised her, and he'd been right. She'd felt soft and shivery all the way through the ceremony. She'd *felt* the vows he'd made as if he was still moving deep and wild between her legs, and she'd hardly managed to get her own out in turn.

There were a thousand things she should have been thinking about now that she was awake. She knew that. That they hadn't used any protection, for one thing. But she couldn't worry about that. Not now. Her mind skidded away from that and she found all she really wanted to know was where her brand-new husband was and why he wasn't in this bed with her, teaching her more of all the many marvelous things he knew.

She wanted to learn each and every one of them, and she didn't care how vulnerable it might make her feel. Or she'd care later, she told herself firmly. After he was gone and she had the rest of her life to live without him.

Not that she wanted to think about that inevitability. It would come soon enough. And in the meantime, she could indulge the sensual side of herself she hadn't known she possessed. Until Cairo.

Brittany heard a muffled buzzing sound then and it took her a long moment to realize it was her mobile phone. She looked around the room, finally spotting her handbag on the floor near the foot of the bed, where she must have dropped it in her earlier exhausted haze. She moved to yank the bag up from the floor, thinking as she did that the fact it was buzzing at all meant they had to be above land somewhere, not an ocean, or there wouldn't have been a signal.

Brittany glanced at the display, saw it was her mother and then answered the call anyway.

A choice she regretted almost instantly.

"Well, well," Wanda Mae Hollis said in her gravelly smoker's voice, thick with its usual resentment. "How nice of your uppity majesty to pick up the phone. I've been calling you for weeks."

"Hi, Mama," Brittany said, and it was harder than it should have been to mask her emotions. It annoyed her that there were any to mask. Phone calls from her mother were always assaults of one sort or another. She should have been used to it by now—and she was. That was why she usually avoided them. "I've been a little bit busy."

She sounded more Mississippi when she spoke to her mother than she did at any other time, ever. Her voice flattened out into the drawl she'd worked so hard to leave behind her when she'd left home, as if she was still that miserable child trying to make herself small in the corner of her mother's trailer while another drunken adult fight raged on.

"You don't need to tell me what you've been up to," Wanda Mae said bitterly. "It's all anyone can talk about today, no matter where we go. I hope you're happy with yourself."

This was why Brittany limited phone conversations. She didn't know why she'd answered this one. Did she want to punish herself? But she suspected she knew what it was that had made her pick up the call: that tiny little shred of hope she kept tucked away, deep inside of her, and only took out from time to time when it whispered things like, "maybe your mother might be happy for you for once."

That little shred was always wrong. Hope, she'd discovered long ago, was a big fat liar.

Brittany snuck an arm around her own waist and held on tight, then dug her bare toes into the carpeted floor beneath her as if she needed to remember that she was solid. That she was real. That she had a whole life that had nothing to do with Wanda Mae Hollis, and nothing her mother said could matter one way or the other unless she let it.

But she still didn't hang up. She didn't know why.

"Thank you," she said instead, and made an effort to sound as if she'd never visited Mississippi, much less grown up there. "I appreciate you calling with your good wishes."

Wanda Mae snorted. "I couldn't walk three feet today without someone else throwing your latest exploits in my face. Do you know what they're saying about you? Do you care?"

"I'll assume they're not praising me and calling me the next Kate Middleton," Brittany said, and was proud of the fact she sounded amused. Or close enough to amused, anyway, that the mother who barely knew her wouldn't be able to tell the difference. "But that's just a guess."

"Trust you to marry a king and screw that up, too," Wanda Mae snapped.

Brittany sighed. "I did it to hurt you, of course. You've discovered the truth."

"You think you're so smart, don't you?"

Her mother didn't wait for an answer. She kept right on talking, the way she always did.

The sick part, Brittany understood then as she listened to the usual litany of complaints and accusations that followed after that rhetorical question, was that she found this comforting on some level. She clenched her free hand into a fist and felt her rings dig into her flesh, but still, this was some kind of cold, bracing comfort. It reminded Brittany who she was and, worse, who she might have become.

Nothing had ever made Wanda Mae treat her eldest

child as anything but an embarrassing burden, no matter how much money Brittany had sent home over the years, which was never, ever enough. Nothing had ever made Wanda Mae act as if she loved Brittany at all, for that matter. Not Grandmama. Not her other kids, most of whom Brittany had basically raised herself while Wanda Mae was out cavorting in bars. Not the fact Brittany was the only one who hadn't gotten in any trouble. She hadn't gotten pregnant and she hadn't gone to jail. She'd just left.

And still, somehow, Brittany found her mother's predictable fury soothing. She knew what to expect, and no matter that it was the same endless font of vitriol every time. It was her mama. It was the way things had always been. *You probably need to take a look at that*, she told herself, not for the first time.

After all, she'd lost her virginity at last. She'd never thought that would happen. Didn't that suggest anything could?

But not today. Not when she felt so…ripped up inside. It was as if those stolen, heated moments in the castle had done a whole lot more than throw her over a cliff she hadn't known existed. They had crumbled her foundations into dust.

Cairo had.

She didn't know what to do about it. She didn't know if anything could be done about it, come to that. And her mother was still shooting off her mouth, the way she liked to do when she got going.

No wonder she'd answered this call. Somewhere deep inside, Brittany had obviously wanted to know that something, somewhere, would remain the same no matter how much she might have changed. No matter how much Cairo had already changed her, from the inside out, leaving her flailing about without a mask when she needed one the most.

"Only you could manage to marry the one person on earth more sinful and shameful than you are," Wanda Mae was saying as if personally affronted by this. "How am I supposed to hold my head up in town, Brittany?"

"I've never known how to answer that question, Mama," she replied, unable to keep the weariness from her voice. "But I'd imagine you should use your neck, like anyone else."

"I'm glad you can still make smart remarks. I'm glad you think this is one more big joke, like everything else in your life. Everyone knows exactly what kind of sick pervert that man is. Everyone knows what he's like. It's probably why you chose him. You *like* degenerate, disgusting—"

Brittany didn't know she meant to move and she had no memory of doing it, but then she was standing there by the side of the bed as if she'd *jumped* up. Her heart pounded at her, suggesting she had.

"Careful, Mama," she said, and her voice was cold. A kind of blade, slicing through her mother's stream of words and shocking them both, if her mother's gasp was any indication. "Be very careful. Keep running your mouth about him and you might find the bank dries right up. Then how will you keep yourself in cigarettes and beer?"

"You would threaten your own mother?"

"I don't want to hear your thoughts on this marriage."

Wanda Mae sniffed. "This is the influence that man has on you. This is the kind of ungrateful, selfish creature you've turned into, in such company. Flaunting yourself all over the world and then taking it out on your poor—"

"This is your last warning," Brittany said, even colder. "I'm not playing with you, Mama. He is off-limits to you."

Her mother fell quiet, and Brittany couldn't seem to feel that shocking little victory the way she should. She felt too unsteady. Her stomach was twisted into a knot and her heart was pounding at her. And she couldn't remember the last time she'd defended her choices to her mother. Had she ever?

But she refused to listen to her mother vent her spleen on Cairo.

She refused.

She didn't really want to ask herself why.

"You listen to me, Brittany," her mother said after a long pause, and her voice had gone quiet. Brittany closed her eyes and braced herself. "You think I don't know anything. You lit out of Gulfport and never looked back and believe you me, your opinion of the folks you left behind couldn't be more clear. You think we're all dumb country trash."

"I think nothing of the kind," Brittany gritted out, and what she hated herself for the most was how guilty she felt when her mother said these things. As if Brittany's snobbery had been the problem instead of Wanda Mae's patented blend of neglect and malice. "I think you'd find just as much about me to criticize if I lived next door."

"But I know a few things about rich men and poor girls," Wanda Mae continued as if Brittany hadn't said a word. "There's nothing new about it."

"Haven't you heard, Mama? I'm not all that poor any longer. If I was, you wouldn't get all those checks."

"This is one of the oldest, saddest, most run-of-the-mill stories around." Her mother's voice was upsettingly even. Not harsh. Not cruel. As if she was relaying a simple fact, nothing more. "Rich men like to play their games. They like to put a pretty girl on their arm and make a show out of it. They like to make sure everyone knows what a sacrifice they're making, taking on a charity project like her, so young and so desperate. And then they make those girls pay for the privilege. They make them pay and pay and pay. You might end up with more money, but you better believe that man will take whatever's left of your soul."

Brittany opened her mouth to say "you don't know him," but stopped herself just in time, horrified.

As if she did? As if anyone did? He'd been *inside her body* and she didn't know him at all.

"Thank you, Mama," she forced herself to say through lips gone stiff. "I'll keep that in mind."

She ended the call as her mother launched into another part of her lecture, then tossed the phone on the bed.

But she couldn't control the way she shook. The way her stomach flipped, end over end. Or the way her mother's words spun around and around in her head. As if Wanda Mae knew exactly how precarious this all was. As if she'd seen what Cairo had done to Brittany in that castle. How he'd touched her and, worse, how he'd made her feel.

What was going on with her that she'd tried to defend Cairo to her own mother when she hadn't defended *herself* in years?

"She's a lonely, bitter woman," Brittany told herself furiously, scowling at the mobile phone on the coverlet as if it was her mother's face, flushed with her usual anger. "You shouldn't listen to a word she says."

But her words disappeared the moment she said them, as if sucked out of the plane's windows and tossed off into the dark.

And her mother's words seemed to echo there instead, like a curse.

Like something worse.

Like prophecy.

CHAPTER EIGHT

THEY LANDED ON the small, private island in the Vanuatu archipelago as the South Pacific dawn eased its deep blue and fresh pink way across the sky.

"Vanuatu," Brittany murmured as they made their way down the jet's stairs to the private runway. She sounded shell-shocked. "You brought me to Vanuatu."

Cairo found he couldn't look away from her as she stopped at the bottom. There was the sea and the white sands and the sprawling house he'd bought on this faraway spot, but all he could see was his wife in a crumpled yellow dress and her hair in a tangled coil at her nape.

His wife, who he'd had to force himself not to pursue when she'd barricaded herself in that cabin for the whole of their twenty-hour flight. He'd reasoned she needed time. Space. Some peace and quiet after the circus that was their wedding. To come to terms with what had happened between them in that castle, perhaps—before they'd exchanged vows. To accept that they were truly married, in the classic sense of the term that involved the kind of consummation she'd never experienced before.

And if he allowed her space, he could pretend he hadn't needed it himself. That he wasn't shaken by what had happened. That it was nothing but sex, that moment she'd given herself to only him. That this marriage was yet one more circus sideshow, nothing more.

But she was his wife even so. The morning breeze from

the sea all around them was cool and soft, and teased the ends of the hair she'd braided to one side and tossed over her shoulder. She swallowed hard as she looked around, and he found himself watching the lovely line of her throat as if there were clues there. Answers to questions he didn't know how to ask.

"It looks exactly as I imagined it would," Brittany said quietly. Perhaps too quietly.

"Did you not wish to come here?" Cairo asked.

His own voice sounded unduly harsh in the quiet morning, with no other sounds but the surf and the breeze. He felt like a parody of himself. Even the clothes he wore seemed to brand him a fraud. A T-shirt that clung to his torso. Casual linen trousers. He felt like a beach bum instead of a king, or even the Euro-trash version of a king he'd been playing to the hilt all these years, and he found that made him…uneasy.

As if she would forget who he was if he gave her the chance. Or he would.

"I've always wanted to come here." She swallowed again, then blinked, as if she was shaking something off. Him? Their wedding? He didn't much care for that notion. "Eventually, I wanted to come here and stay forever."

"The island is yours," he said shortly. Gruffly.

Her gaze moved to his and he didn't like that it was troubled. He didn't like that at all.

"Mine? What do you mean, 'mine'?"

Cairo nodded to the waiting servants to handle their baggage and then took Brittany's arm, threading it through his. She didn't resist, and he found himself turning that over and over in his head like some hapless boy obsessing over his first sweetheart. It appalled him. Deeply. He was frowning as they started up the winding path toward the house that waited at the widest part of the small island, all rolled-up walls and high ceilings to let the tropics inside. An island paradise, if he said so himself.

But all he could concentrate on was the feel of her skin against his. Her arm on his. The smallest, most innocuous touch he could imagine, and yet it pounded through him like fire.

He had never felt so naked in all his life.

"Consider this place a wedding gift." His voice was even rougher then.

Cairo didn't know what was wrong with him. He'd spent twenty hours sitting on a jet plane becoming more and more of a stranger to himself. As if he'd left every careful mask he'd ever worn behind at that castle in Italy. As if here, with this woman, he was a man. Not an exiled king. Not a disgrace.

He didn't have the slightest idea what that meant, only that it spun in him, making him feel something like drunk.

Brittany was frowning now. At him. "You can't hand out islands as presents. That's insane."

Cairo ignored that. He reveled in the simple feel of her arm against his. Her lithe body moving beside him as they walked through the gathering daylight. The silky tropical breeze that danced around them and over them, making him remember those moments he'd been deep inside her—

Remember them. Who was he kidding? He hadn't thought of anything else since it had happened. He hadn't really tried.

"I was beginning to think I'd married Sleeping Beauty." He thought he felt her stiffen slightly beside him, and he thought there must be something deeply wrong with him that he'd view that as a good thing. Or any other reaction she had, for that matter. As long as he got to her. "And here I am, a king without a country instead of the necessary Prince Charming. It would have been quite the PR disaster, don't you think?"

She glanced at him, then back toward the path that stretched ahead of them. "I was tired."

"Are you certain?"

"Am I certain I was tired?" She frowned at him then. "Yes. But if I'd been confused, the fact I've slept for hours and hours would have cleared it up for me."

"It was a twenty-hour flight, give or take."

"Then, yes, Cairo. I'd say I was tired."

He tried to smile. That same casual lazy smile he'd used all his life. It should have come easily to him, the way it always had, but his own mouth betrayed him. "Because I was starting to think you were hiding in that bedroom."

She didn't pull her arm from his and Cairo didn't know why that felt like a gift.

"Do I have a reason to hide from you?" she asked. Carefully.

He thought they were both a little too aware that she hadn't exactly denied it.

"You tell me."

But she didn't. They walked for a moment in silence. The waves surged against the shore and the palm trees clattered overhead. Her bright copper hair, thick and wild, unwound itself from her makeshift braid as it moved and flowed around her, and he knew how she tasted, now. He knew how soft and molten she was for him, and the noises she made when he moved deep inside her. He knew her.

Maybe that was why his heart kicked at him, making his whole chest hurt.

"I appreciate the thought," she said in what he thought was a remarkably stiff voice, here on a tropical island in the middle of a perfect blue sea in all directions. "But I can't accept an entire island. As a...bridal present for a wedding that has the shelf life of organic fruit."

A swift glance her way showed him nothing. Her expression was smooth. Composed. The way it always was, as if he'd never held the heat of her in his hand.

His chest hurt. Worse than before. He was fairly certain it was that temper of his he normally kept locked away. Or worse, the truth of himself he'd been hiding from all these years.

"I am afraid it is already done." He stopped moving when the path ended at the bottom of the sweeping lawn that led up to one of the house's many lanais. "The island is yours, as is everything on it. My attorneys transferred ownership the moment you said 'I do.'"

She managed to pull her arm from his without seeming to do it on purpose. Cairo might have admired the sheer efficiency of the gesture if he hadn't hated that he was no longer touching her.

"No."

Her voice was low. She crossed her arms and frowned out toward the horizon. And Cairo could have pretended he hadn't heard her. That she hadn't spoken.

He didn't know why he didn't.

"I apologize that the gift does not please you," he said stiffly. "Is it the size of the island? The house? Would you prefer something larger or more ornate? Dubai, perhaps?"

"Of course not." She shook her head, but she still didn't meet his gaze. "I grew up in a trailer with my mother, whatever boyfriend she had that week and four other kids. Any house containing a room I don't have to share is like heaven to me. This…" She jutted her chin toward the house and when she finally looked at him again, her eyes were much too dark. "The house is beautiful, Cairo. Everything here is beautiful. It's so much more than I imagined."

"Then I fail to see the problem."

He felt rooted to the ground. Frozen into place. Completely out of his element—and how could that be? How had this woman turned him so upside down? What the hell had she done to him?

But he thought he knew. He hadn't expected her to be a virgin. To be innocent. There was no place in his sad, soiled life for *innocence*. And because he hadn't been prepared, even after she'd given herself away and he'd guessed the truth, he'd simply…reacted. He hadn't planned out what he'd do. He hadn't performed his usual role.

Those moments with her on the bed in that castle were the most genuine he'd been in at least twenty years, and it was addictive. He wanted more. He wanted her. He wanted to be the man he was with her, not the role he played.

He wanted everything.

"This is the problem," Brittany said, and her tone was too even. "This is my dream. I told you that. *Mine*. You have no right to use it as part of this sick little farce we're acting out for the world's amusement."

"By which I am to assume you mean our marriage."

"Marriage, performance art—whatever you want to call it." She shrugged. "It's not real. Coming to Vanuatu is a dream that's sustained me for years. It's what I've held on to through every single horrible thing that's written about me or said to my face. It's what allows me to shrug it all off. How could you possibly imagine I'd want to pollute it with this thing? With—"

She cut herself off.

"Me?" Cairo supplied coolly, because she did not see a man. She saw the game. The roles he played. The creature he'd become.

"I don't know what you dream about," she threw at him, and his particular sickness was that he found that to be progress, that little show of temper. "I couldn't begin to guess."

"I am a king without a kingdom." Cairo laughed at that, though the sound was hollow, and he thought the breeze stole it away anyway. "What exactly do you imagine it is I dream about, Brittany?"

"I dream about something that's mine," she snapped at him, and he saw the way she gripped herself tighter, as if she was holding herself back. Or holding herself together. "All mine. Where no one is watching me and speculating about me and making up stories about me. I dream about a perfect, unspoiled place a million miles away from the rest of the world, where I can disappear. Do you have the slightest notion what that means?"

"I'd imagine it means a well-staffed house accessible only by boat or by air, in the farthest reaches of one of the most remote island nations on earth." He eyed her, standing there with her feet in the sand and the South Pacific around her because he'd imported her straight into her fantasy. "Wherever will we find such a place, do you think?"

"I play a part, Cairo. A role." Her words came fast and hard now, and he found he enjoyed watching her unravel far more than he should. It meant this was getting to her, too. That he was. Cairo couldn't regret that. "I've been playing it since I was a kid. Vanuatu was supposed to happen when I finally left it all behind, not while I'm neck-deep in the middle of yet another performance!"

Something eased inside him then, though that pressure in his chest remained. He thought the way she scowled at him was beautiful. He thought *she* was beautiful—even more so than the island paradise that waited all around them.

He saw the way her lips trembled slightly before she pressed them together. He saw the way she leaned back, as if she'd wanted to put more space between them, but had forced herself to stand still.

This wasn't affecting only him. He wasn't the only one without a mask.

"Come here," he said. It was more of an order.

Cairo had the distinct pleasure of seeing that melting expression move over her face before she balked, visibly, and straightened where she stood. He *felt* it, everywhere. In that pressing thing in his chest. In his sex.

"I'm standing one foot away from you," she said, crossly, and he was insane to find that tone of voice comforting. He was a madman, there was no other explanation.

But he didn't care.

He sighed in the officious manner that had servants at aristocratic balls leaping to tend to his every whim, and then he merely reached across that one foot of space, hooked his hand around her neck and hauled her to him.

She hit his chest an instant later, made one of those soft noises that made the hunger in him burn white-hot and threw her head back to look up at him. She was scowling, of course. She was always scowling. But that meant she wasn't hiding behind her mask of composure, and Cairo loved it. He craved it. He wanted more.

"Cairo—"

"This is not a performance," he told her, holding her where he wanted her, her body flush against his. *Where she belongs*, something in him whispered. "You, me. Here. None of this is for public consumption. It is only ours. It is real."

The truth was the way she flushed at that. The way her eyes darkened with the same need he felt careening around inside of him, changing him. Changing the whole world.

"There's no such thing as *ours*," she whispered. "There's nothing *real* here."

"Tesorina," he murmured, "of course there is. It tastes like this."

And then he bent his head to claim her mouth, and showed her exactly what he meant.

* * *

The weeks that followed were like a dream. The best version of her favorite dream, in fact.

Brittany never, ever wanted to wake up.

It wasn't only that the house and island were even more beautiful than she could have imagined they'd be. It wasn't that they were staffed to the extraordinary level of discreet, nearly psychic level of service that Cairo demanded. That meant that almost the moment they had a thought or a desire, often before it was expressed, the plate of food was laid out or the tray of drinks was presented. That meant fresh towels and a selection of new, tropical clothing to better while away the days every time they exited one of the property's pools, or wandered out of the sauna. That meant the tiki torches were always lit the instant the sky began to turn colors at the end of the day and there was always a hammock waiting between two palm trees should they take a walk along the beach.

All of that was divine. Luxurious pampering far beyond anything Brittany had ever imagined. But far more remarkable than the level of service was the solitude. Their first night there, after Cairo had carried Brittany off to the vast master suite they'd shared ever since and after they'd worked off their jet lag in the most delectable manner possible, they'd agreed to simply…shut out the world.

"No one will miss us for five weeks," Cairo had said when evening had started to creep across the sky, orange and red, outside the open floor-to-ceiling spaces where walls would be in another house. "They will barely notice we are gone, with so many other headlines to keep them occupied."

He'd been sprawled out on his back on the bed, the sheets in complicated tangles at his feet. Brittany had been stretched out over him, the dizzying heat they'd built in each other still there where she pressed against him, even as the lazy ceiling fan moved the cooler air around on her back. Her head had been a cascade of images of all the ways they'd had each other already in that single, perfect, endless day. All the things he could do with his hands, his mouth. All the places on that stunning body of his she'd tested with hers.

Her body had still been humming. She thought perhaps it always would.

"I suppose we have the rest of our lives to be terrible," she'd agreed drowsily, unable to think of much beyond the simple perfection of the way their bodies fit together. The way they seemed perfectly crafted to come together like this and drive each other wild—

There had been something in her that had balked at that, deep down beneath the layers of satisfaction. She might not have had sex with anyone before Cairo, but she wasn't a complete idiot. She knew sex made people crazy. It made them imagine intimacies that didn't exist outside the bed. Hadn't she watched her own mother make that mistake again and again? Brittany had always vowed she'd never be one of those deluded fools, no matter what.

But she could put that aside for a little over a month, too, she'd thought then. She could simply sink into this thing and not worry about what came after or how she'd have to play it when they went back to their carefully scripted, relentlessly public lives. She could decide not to worry about it—about anything that wasn't Cairo, or herself, or how they made each other feel—until this honeymoon was over. And until then, they could lock their phones and laptops in one of the cupboards and let themselves soak in the peace and quiet of this little island so far away from anything.

"I think this is the purpose of a honeymoon," she said.

Cairo smiled, his hand moving lazily down the length of her spine, then back up again. "I thought it was an opportunity to post pictures from exotic locales onto one's social media pages, the better to maintain one's presence and public brand. No? Are you sure?"

"Ask me in a month," Brittany replied, grinning as she buried her face in that tempting hollow between his pectoral muscles.

Their days bled one into another, long and sweet. They walked on the beaches in the sun and in the intermittent rains that kept the plants lush. They sat beneath the impossible confusion of stars at night, out on one of the terraces or huddled together on a blanket on the sand. They talked, ate, swam. They argued politics and classic movies. They read books from the house's eclectically stocked libraries, discussed them, then read more.

And they explored each other, with a ferocity and focus that would have shaken Brittany to her core if she'd stopped to think about it. She didn't. It seemed part and parcel of these stolen blue-sky weeks. It seemed as inevitable as the afternoon rains, the kick of the tropical winds, the smudged blue line of the horizon far away in the distance. She abandoned herself to Cairo's touch the same way she lost herself in a novel or sank beneath the sea to listen for whale songs. No thought, no concern, no self-preservation.

There were no kings on this island, no class divisions, no strippers and no scandal. There was only the glory of the way her body took him in, again and again. There was only the sweetness of the way they came together in the lazy heat, the bold explosions of need and hunger they weathered in the pool, on the beach, standing near the trees, down on the floor of the room they liked to read in.

Brittany had never known another person's body as well as she came to know Cairo's. Every inch of his skin. Every tiny imperfection that made his intense male beauty that much more fascinating to her. She tasted her way across the acres of his sculpted chest and lost herself in the taut ridges of his abdomen. She licked him where he was salty and slept tangled up with him in that great big bed. She learned how to straddle him and take him into her, how to ride them both blind, and how to tease him with the slow, careful rhythm of her hips until he could only groan. She learned how to love him with her mouth, sucking him and licking him until he sank his fingers in her hair and bucked against her, emptying himself between her lips.

And she had never been known so comprehensively in return.

Oh, the things Cairo taught her about herself. About her appetites and her capacity for both pleasure and need. There was no boundary he wouldn't cross, no limit he wouldn't push, if he thought it would make her scream.

It usually did.

He was insatiable. She lost count of the times he reached for her at night, or the times their gazes snagged during the day and led to more of that bone-melting fire they fanned high in each other again and again.

It couldn't last. She told herself that *of course* it couldn't last, but perhaps that was what made it so poignant.

Or that was what Brittany told herself as the weeks rolled by, slow and bright and more beautiful than anything she'd ever dared imagine. Better than she ever could have dreamed that night she'd rejected his initial proposal in Monte Carlo. Just…*better*.

Because the other thing they did with all their time together was talk. Rambling conversations that started one day and ended the next, and that Brittany only realized later were deeply revealing. Stories comparing their very different childhoods, painted in broad strokes and told as if they'd been amusing, when they weren't. Current events, popular culture in at least three countries, even the odd conversation about sports—all these things, taken together, meant not only that she knew the exiled king of Santa Domini better than anyone alive, but that he also knew her the same way.

Inside and out, that little voice inside her reminded her daily. *No masks. No act. Just you.*

She told herself it didn't scare her, such astonishing intimacy. Because she wouldn't let it.

One night, after they'd had their usual dinner of fresh grilled seafood and an array of perfect fruits, they sat out on one of the terraces beneath the night sky. The flames on the tiki torches danced in the faint breeze from the water, and they were tucked up together on one of the loungers. Brittany sat between Cairo's legs, her back to his chest, and absently ran her fingers through his.

It had been a month, and the fact of that had been echoing inside her all day. It reminded her that this wasn't forever. That this relaxed, smiling man who was all caramel and whiskey when he looked at her here would disappear, and soon. They would put on more clothes and walk back onto the stage where they conducted their lives and had already made plans to end their brand-new marriage, and these weeks would be the anomaly.

She would have to wake up, and she didn't want that. More to the point, she would have to deal with the growing worry deep inside of her that the fact she'd missed her period for the first time in her life, two weeks into their stay, was from something more than the stress of such a major life change.

Brittany didn't want to consider that, much less what it might mean if her suspicions were correct. All the things it might mean, when their relationship had a built-in expiration date. A child was forever, no matter their messy divorce.

A child would change everything.

"You seem far away."

Cairo's voice was rich and lazy, but Brittany knew that, here, it was because he was actually relaxed. She couldn't bring herself to ruin that. She felt the words on her tongue and swallowed them back.

They had so little time left before they were back in the world. It could wait.

"We only have a week left here." She blew out a breath and told herself it was kinder to wait until she knew for certain. Better. "It's going to be hard to leave. To get back onstage and into the headlines."

Her hair curled as it pleased in the humidity here, and after the first day or two of fighting it she'd simply let it do what it would. Behind her, Cairo wrapped a long curl he found around his finger, winding it tighter and tighter, then let it loose only to start all over again.

"What would you do?" he asked idly. Or perhaps not idly at all. "If there were no headlines. If there was only a normal life to live."

"A normal good life or a normal bad life?" she asked, tipping her head back to better rest against his shoulder.

His mouth, still the most gorgeous thing imaginable, grazed her forehead in a glancing kiss that still managed to make that glowing heat deep inside her spike.

"I believe that is the trial of normal life, is it not? One cannot tell, day to day. One is without the constant intervention of the press, there to interpret every move and fashion it into a narrative that sells papers. If that is good or bad is up to you."

"I want picket fences," Brittany said, surprising herself. But once she said it, she warmed to the idea. "I want to cook things, feed a family, worry about the school run and the ladies at the PTA. I want the life they live in minivan commercials, with golden retrievers and a good soundtrack."

She felt his laughter, deep in his chest.

"You would not get to dance in that life. The picket fences forbid it, I think."

She smiled at that. "I'd dance for fun, not money. That's the problem with being good at what you love. You turn it into your job and then it can't be about love anymore. It has to be about bills." She laughed. "Not that you'd know much about bills, I think."

"I pay my bills." Cairo's voice was ripe with the same laughter she'd felt in his chest, and that wealth of affection that she knew would fade, out there. Out in all those spotlights and flashbulbs. And it would likely happen very quickly if she really was pregnant. She shoved that aside. "Larger ones, I imagine, than most."

He pulled her closer to him. She could feel the heat of him through the gauzy layer of the flowing dress she wore. The heat and the steel-edged strength that was all Cairo. With his arms around her and his body surrounding her, Brittany felt hollowed-out and whole at once.

"What would you do?" she asked. "If you could choose a normal life, what would it be?"

He was quiet for a long time. Brittany could feel the solid weight of him behind her and feel the soothing beat of his heart against her back. She listened to the waves in the distance as she waited, and tried to tip herself over and out into the stars spread out so thickly above them.

"I do not think I know what normal is," Cairo said, when she'd stopped expecting that he might respond. He sounded quieter than before. "I do not know what it looks like."

"You could be an accountant," she said, crinkling up her nose at the image of his highness, the imperious accountant. "Or, I know, a traveling bard. Can you sing? That would work better if you sang, of course."

"The only thing I know how to be is me," Cairo said, and there was a strange note in his voice then.

Brittany didn't think. She shifted around on the lounger, moving so she could straddle him and loop her arms around his neck. She looked down into his perfect face. Those impossible cheekbones, that purely Santa Domini jaw he deliberately left unshaven, as if that could obscure the truth of him. As if anything could, exile or a thousand mocking headlines or his own penchant for self-destruction.

She felt him stir beneath her, and felt her own body, so attuned to him now, instantly ready itself for his possession. But she made no move to impale herself on him, to throw them both back into that slick, breathless heat. She only searched his royal face in the starlight, and that odd expression in his dark amber eyes.

"Then that's normal," she said. "That's your normal life. Why should you change?"

Cairo's mouth curved. "I like it when you are fierce on my behalf, *tesorina*. The truth is I have never adapted." He shrugged, and she expected him to kiss her. To change the subject with his touch as he usually did. She was shocked when he kept speaking. "I was bred to be the king of Santa Domini. My father might have been exiled, but he always imagined that was a temporary state of affairs. He had every intention of reclaiming his throne." His jaw hardened, and though his hands were at her hips she could see his attention was far in the past. "Even after he died, nothing changed. I was the unofficial king. I was always me. It didn't matter how many ways I made it clear I was unfit to rule. Every person I trusted expected that someday, I would take back the kingdom. All these years later, they still do." His gaze found hers, hard and stirring and filled with a darkness that tugged at her. "What is normal for me, Brittany, is to be the greatest disappointment my people have ever known."

"No." The word was out before she knew she meant

to speak, but she didn't stop. She continued, feeling very nearly furious—but *for* him, not *at* him. "Nothing about you is disappointing."

Something sparked in his gaze then. He lifted a hand to slide it over her cheek, anchoring his fingers in her hair as if he'd hold her there forever. As if he could.

"You cannot be trusted," he told her softly. "You make me imagine I could be not only a decent man, but the man I was intended to become. You are so far under my spell you cannot see straight."

"You're wrong, Your Majesty," she whispered back, still fierce and sure, and finally using the title that he deserved. *His* title. "You're pure magic."

The way he looked at her then, so certain that that was the sex talking and it could never, ever be true, broke her heart.

And that was when she knew. It wasn't a jolt or a shock. It was as inevitable as the next wave against the gleaming white sand. The sun sinking into the sea. It washed through her, changing her completely from one moment to the next, though nothing had changed. She loved him. She wondered if she always had, even back in that first moment when she'd seen him across a casino floor and had been struck dumb. She'd known this would happen from the start.

This was the ruin, the destruction, she'd feared all along. *Love.* As simple and as terrifying as that.

She'd spent a month here with absolutely no mask. She'd given him her virginity. She'd opened herself up to him in a thousand ways she hadn't known were possible, and she thought that no matter what happened next, even if she really was pregnant, she couldn't regret it. She wouldn't.

But she couldn't tell him, either.

Because she knew without having to ask that love was

the one thing that could ruin everything between them. Worse, perhaps, than the possibility of a child.

"No, *tesorina*," Cairo said, that look in his eyes that made her heart feel shattered. Sad and wise and lost, as if they were already back in Europe. As if she'd already had to give him up, the way they'd planned. As if he'd known all along that this dream of theirs could never last. She'd known that, too. And it hadn't done a single thing to stop this. Any of this. "You are the magic."

And then he pulled her mouth to his.

She kissed him back, a sharp desperation snaking through her. Because every kiss was measured now. Every touch was closer to their last.

She wriggled against him, lifting herself up so she could find him in his linen trousers and free the satin length of him between them. The fire that always raged in them both was a madness tonight, the flames wild and almost harsh, and Brittany shook as she waited for him to handle their protection, as he'd done every single time save their first. She let out a soft sound of distress when he pulled his mouth from hers, and he didn't laugh at her the way he usually did.

Neither one of them was in a playful mood.

She felt the blunt head of his sex against her softness, and she rolled her hips to take him inside of her. She worked herself down, rocking gently until she was seated fully against him.

Cairo let out a long, hard breath. Brittany wrapped her arms around his shoulders and then, giving in to an urge she didn't want to name, tipped her forehead to his. For an eternity, they sat there like that, drinking each other in. Her husband. Her king. Possibly the father of her child. For as long as she had him.

He was huge and hard within her, she was soft and trembling. Their mouths were so close she could breathe with him if she liked, and it was as if they'd both realized how close they were to losing this. How very short, indeed, the week they had remaining to them was.

She started to move then, and this time, it was a dance. It was joy.

It was love.

Brittany couldn't say it, she didn't dare say such a thing to the man she'd married purely for the headlines, so she showed him. Every roll of her hips, every lift and every slide. He peeled the straps of her dress down and took one of her hard nipples into his mouth, driving her wild as she loved him with every last part of her being. He pulled hard and she let her head drop back, and then it really was as if she'd fallen off into all those stars.

It was hard to tell who did what. There was only sensation and fire, bliss and longing.

Love, she thought, with each delirious thrust, but then she stopped thinking altogether.

And there was only Cairo.

He reached down between them and pressed hard where she needed him most, and Brittany exploded—but he didn't stop. He surged into her, pounding her straight through one exultant climax and high again toward another.

He flipped them over on the lounger, coming over her in the soft, silken night as he thrust himself home.

Deeper. Harder. Better than perfect.

Again and again and again.

Until they flew over that edge together.

And stayed there beneath the quiet glory of the southern stars until the first hint of a brand-new morning, when everything changed.

CHAPTER NINE

RICARDO ARRIVED ON the island via very noisy helicopter from Port Vila, Vanuatu's capital city, not long after the break of dawn.

He was not welcome, Cairo thought uncharitably as he watched his most loyal subject walk toward him over the otherwise deserted beach, the crisp suit he wore that was so appropriate in Paris looking nothing but out of place here.

It was a stark reminder of how far away Cairo had been from the world this last month—and how much he'd like to remain here forever.

"Was I expecting you?" Cairo asked. He led Ricardo onto the lanai where breakfast was usually served, and nodded toward the carafe of strong, hot coffee he knew the man preferred. "I feel certain I was not."

It was more of an effort than it should have been to keep his tone light. Lazy and careless, as expected. He'd grown unused to speaking to anyone but Brittany—and he'd thought he'd be able to keep it that way a while longer.

The truth was, he didn't *want* to speak to anyone but Brittany. He hadn't wanted to leave her when the sound of the helicopter had woken them both where they'd drowsed off together beneath the light blanket he'd pulled over them sometime in the middle of the night. He'd had to let her go, and he didn't like that edgy, pointed sort of feeling that had moved into his chest lately, to go along with that pressure that never really eased.

He didn't like any of this.

"You have been out of reach for a month, Sire," Ricardo replied, pressing a mug of coffee to his lips. He took a pull, relaxed his shoulders, then focused on Cairo again. "Completely out of reach. There were rumors that you were dead."

Cairo waved a hand. "There are always rumors."

"These were more convincing, given the absence of the usual photographic evidence to the contrary."

"I would never die in so obscure a fashion," Cairo murmured, and some part of him was dismayed at how easy it was to pick up his role again. To slip back into that second skin of his and treat it like it was the only one he knew. "Especially not so tragically young. I would make certain to die theatrically in a major city, the better to leverage good media coverage of my pageant of a funeral."

"Sire." Ricardo's expression was...not grim, exactly. *Solemn*, Cairo thought. And something rather more like *expectant*. "General Estes suffered a massive heart attack a few days ago. He collapsed in the palace and was rushed to the hospital, where, after many attempts to revive him, he died." He watched Cairo's face as if he expected a reaction. When Cairo only stared, he cleared his throat. "His ministers have stepped in and are trying to maintain the peace, but they have never been anything but puppets. You know this. And, Sire. The people..." Ricardo made no attempt to hide the gleam in his gaze when he trained it on Cairo. The fervor, the belief. "Sire, the people are ready."

Time seemed to spread out. To flatten.

Cairo remembered his father's hand, heavy on his shoulder as they'd walked together through a foggy British morning on a remote estate, years ago now.

"What if we never go home?" Cairo had asked. He

could not have been more than eight years old. His father, then the exiled king to Cairo's crown prince, had seemed so old to him then. So wise and aged, when in truth he'd been an athletic man midway through his forties.

"It is your duty to carry Santa Domini within you wherever you go, whether we return home or not," his father had said. "You must serve the kingdom in all you do and say. All you are. Every step and every action, Cairo. That is your calling. Your destiny."

He'd never forgotten it. Not when they'd come to get him out of his history classroom that rainy winter day, bundling him off to a room where grim strangers frowned at him and pretended to be concerned for him. Not when they'd told him everyone he loved was dead and his world was forever altered. Not when he'd realized that he must be next on the general's assassination list, no matter that the man's involvement was never officially confirmed, and no matter how many people told him that it had been an accident.

Not when he'd wondered, in his grief, if he should let the general exterminate him, too. It would have been so much easier than fighting.

He'd thought of the kingdom then.

"There's only the prince now," the woman had said on the news. She'd been a village woman from one of the most remote spots in the kingdom. He'd watched her from a guarded hotel room somewhere outside of Boston, while the authorities investigated his family's death. He hadn't been permitted to attend their funerals, but he'd watched his people mourn. "He's all that we have left of our history."

He'd served the kingdom then, and lived. Santa Domini's history—but ever unfit to lead. He'd made sure of it.

He thought of the kingdom now.

He thought of the general, dead at last with all the

blood of Cairo's family still there on his hands. And the things that roared in him then had sharp claws. They left deep marks that he knew, from experience, would never go away.

He thought of the woman who had called him magic, who had seen him as no one else in all the world had ever seen him. And no one else ever would. He told himself he didn't understand what it was that tugged so hard and so insistently at his heart then, leaving him bleak.

He had made himself unfit to be a king. He could not undo that now. He could not erase the things he'd done, nor allow the man who'd done them—the man his father would have loathed—to sit upon that throne.

Cairo had no choice but to gaze back at Ricardo blandly.

"Ready for what?" he asked, and, oh, what it cost him to sound so bored. So disengaged. "The funeral? I'm sure the general's men will give him a good show." He paused, as if something occurred to him. "You must know *I* cannot set foot on Santa Dominian soil, Ricardo. Not even all these years later, when no one could possibly care either way."

He saw the incredulity on his man's face, followed by a flash of something as close to pure rage as he'd ever seen a servant show in his presence. And if that made him feel sick, if he loathed himself as much as his father might have had he lived to see what his son had become, that was neither here nor there.

This wasn't about him. It never had been.

"Ricardo," he said gently, "what game do you think we've been playing here? The goal is to remind the world at every turn that I am not fit to lead. Has that changed?"

"I thought…" Ricardo looked lost. "Sire, that was a game you played, but now it's ended. I assumed we were merely biding our time."

"You know what they say about making assumptions, I am certain."

Ricardo put his coffee down as if he feared he might otherwise drop it. Cairo opened his mouth to say something else, to hammer in the man's low impression of him even harder and deeper, but heard the faintest sound from behind him.

Cairo knew what he'd see before he turned to confirm it. He'd grown accustomed to the sound of that particular light step. Those particular bare feet against the stones. He'd know her anywhere.

Brittany stood there in the wide-open entry to the lanai, in the deep shadows of the house. She'd thrown on a different dress, this one a bright riot of colors that cascaded from a neat bow around her neck all the way to the ground. Her hair fell in the careless abandon he found endlessly compelling here, copper and bright, but her hazel eyes were too dark and fixed on him.

He'd kept telling himself that he was scratching an itch. Week after week after week. That one of these mornings he would wake up and find himself as bored with Brittany as he'd always been with every other woman alive. But an entire month had passed, and all he felt was this ceaseless *hunger*.

Cairo wanted to know what she thought. About the book she was reading, about the weather, about what she'd had for her breakfast, about the cloud formations stacked in the sky. He wanted to see what she would say next, on any topic. He loved the stories she'd tell about her Mississippi childhood, the drawl that slipped into her speech and the evident affection she had for the grandmother she'd lost when she was only nine.

He hated not touching her. He hated that she stood across the lanai from him and didn't come any closer, which felt like a slap after all these weeks. And he felt something very much like shame that she'd seen him transform, so easily and so heedlessly, from the man she'd woken up with into Cairo Santa Domini, professional joke.

"Did you hear?" he asked her, and he thought he was the only one who'd be able to see the way she reacted to that smug, bored voice he used like the weapon it was. The faint widening of her eyes. The quick breath she took, then held. "Ricardo has come all this way to update me on events that cannot concern me in the least."

"Sire," Ricardo tried again. "The ministers are the ones most interested in these rumors of your death. They want to move fast and elect another regent while pretending they think you've abdicated."

"Then I should stay where I am," Cairo said, sounding even more bored than before. "I cannot imagine anything less amusing than a riot. Let them work it out amongst themselves, without my involvement."

"Don't be silly." Brittany's voice was cool, composed. As sharp as it had been so long ago now, in Monte Carlo. It made him as hard as he'd been then. But this time, it came with a pervasive sense of sorrow at everything they'd lost when that helicopter landed. At all the things that must happen now. They'd agreed on it long before the general had died. "Of course, you must return to Europe."

"He needs to take his rightful place," Ricardo said, turning to Brittany as if he expected her to agree with him.

But her eyes met Cairo's from a distance that seemed much, much farther than merely across the lanai. And he thought he could feel that pressure in his chest cracking into pieces and shattering all around him, so loud and harsh he was surprised no one else seemed to hear it.

"I think my husband's rightful place is in the tabloids," she said, and it slid between his ribs like steel. Like a killing blow. Like love, he thought, vicious and deadly.

Because she knew him best, this woman. She knew him better than anyone, his destiny and his heart alike. She knew exactly how best to hurt him, and she did it. It made him wonder how he'd hurt her, to make her respond like this. But then it hardly mattered as she kept going. "The more lurid, the better. That is, after all, how we make our money."

Brittany waited for Cairo outside his expansive master suite in the historic Parisian residence. The one she didn't share. The one he'd told her was his before locating her and her things far away from him, down two floors and all the way in the other wing of the grand old house.

It had been a very long handful of days since they'd flown back from the island.

Paris had welcomed them with a glum drizzle and packs of paparazzi, and Brittany had felt...off. She'd assumed it was the culture shock. She'd assumed it was the difficulty in transitioning from a life lived in a sarong and a hammock to all the appearances at parties and balls and charity events that were expected of her, all to be recorded in snide detail in the papers.

She'd assumed it was that little secret deep inside her that she'd still been pretending might be something other than what she'd known, on a deep, feminine level, it was.

"I can't imagine they think you'll discuss the lines of ascension here," she'd said that first night as their car inched closer to the red carpet outside some or other film festival Cairo had insisted they attend. The cameras were everywhere. Squat, grizzled men had poured over the cars like ants, and waiting her turn to be picked apart was making Brittany feel anxious and faintly queasy. "I wish they'd leave us alone."

"You had better hope they do not," Cairo had replied from his side of the seat, where he kept his face buried in the paper. "As that would render you obsolete and wholly useless to me."

He'd been about that charming the entire way back from Vanuatu.

Two nights ago, he'd swept a cutting glance over her when she'd met him in the grand foyer of his museum of a residence.

"You look tired," he'd said flatly.

"How flattering." She'd hated that she had to work so hard to sound crisp and unbothered. That she couldn't switch back into her old role as easily as he had. "That was, of course, my goal for the evening."

He'd looked impatient. "There is no need to look so tragic. I am thinking only of the photographs." He frowned faintly as he took in her exquisite gown and the jewelry he'd picked out himself. "Perhaps that shade of red is not your color."

It had been the precise shade of red as the dress she'd worn at their engagement dinner.

"Cairo." She'd wished she hadn't bothered when he'd stared back at her as if he hardly recognized her. As if she was nothing to him. She'd felt like nothing, and later, she'd imagined, she would lie awake in her lonely bed where no one could see her and if she cried a little bit about that, nobody need know. "There is no need for you be *quite* so brusque. People might mistake you for a Royal Jackass."

She'd thought she'd seen the Cairo she knew in there. Just the faintest glimpse of him, behind all that dark amber. It had made her foolish.

"I know this isn't you," she'd said.

"Do you?" he'd asked icily, dangerously. "Because I find I have no idea what awaits me in that mirror every morning. I was meant to be a king, but I made myself a clown. A disgrace to my name. I have no earthly idea who I am—but you think you do?"

She'd shaken at that, but she'd met his tortured gaze. "I know you are a good man."

"You know nothing of the sort," he'd said coldly, furiously. "What you know is that I am good in bed, as I told you I was when we met. Do not paint me with all your feverish little fantasies, Brittany. I am not a good man. I have only ever been a monster, and it hardly matters why."

"Cairo—"

"You are no use to me run-down and dragging," he'd said then, cutting her off. "My suggestion to you is that you see a doctor and sort yourself out, or leave. Your choice."

The bastard.

She'd only realized she'd said that out loud when his mouth had curved in a far icier smile than the ones she'd known and basked in on their island. It made her heart ache inside her chest.

"I am afraid I am distressingly legitimate," he'd replied. As if it hurt him. His mouth had been grim, his caramel gaze dark. "Therein lies the problem."

Yesterday, she'd summoned Cairo's private physician. She'd paged through articles on her phone while the brisk woman bustled around her and gave her the news, and she'd tried to imagine what it must feel like for Cairo with the general finally dead and a kingdom he'd made certain he couldn't claim clamoring for his return. She'd told herself to be calm, to be understanding, and if all of that failed, to be quiet.

Because she'd known going into this that it would hurt. Why was she surprised that, sure enough, it did—if in a different way than she'd anticipated?

"What are you doing here, Brittany?"

She jerked back into the present to find herself on the little upholstered bench in the hall outside Cairo's bedroom. He stood a few feet away, dressed in one of his three-piece bespoke suits and his hair a calculated mess, his expression as distant as if they'd never met.

Brittany told herself she should hate him. But she didn't.

She didn't. She couldn't.

I have only ever been a monster, he'd said, and that made her want nothing more than to prove him wrong. It made her want to do all kinds of foolish things, like tell him she loved him.

She didn't dare.

"It's lovely to see you, too," she gritted out.

He managed to look as if he was sighing heavily while not actually moving, a skill she might have admired under different circumstances.

"We do not have an appointment," he told her. "If we did, it would not be in my bedroom. I will see you this evening as planned, for the—"

"Will we just pretend that it never happened?" she demanded, and she was horrified to hear her voice crack. But she pushed on. "That whole month was nothing more than a dream, is that it? Have you truly convinced yourself of that?"

"The honeymoon is over." His voice was like steel. "It never should have happened in the first place. This was always a business arrangement. We should have kept it on that level."

"It's a bit late for that," she said, and couldn't help the laugh that bubbled up then. "Much too late."

Another look of impatience flashed over his beautiful face, and he shook his head at her.

"Do you know who I am, Brittany? Have you met me? Read about me in any tabloid?"

She had an inkling of where he was going, of what he might say, and it felt like a car crash. As if she'd spun out of control already and there was nothing she could do to stop it—all the while perfectly cognizant of the tree she was seconds away from smashing against.

"What," Cairo asked, ruthless and cold, "ever gave you the impression that sex with you would distinguish you in any way from the thousands of women who came before you?"

Everything inside of Brittany went horribly still, then. Frozen solid.

It occurred to her that was a blessing.

She stood, carefully. She smoothed her hands over the sleek line of the dress she wore. She remembered herself, at last. It had been so hard to pull her public persona back onto her and wrap herself up in it again—but look at that. He'd just made it remarkably easy.

"Calm yourself," she told him, from miles away. Her voice was crisp and cold, and the great thing about the way he'd yanked her heart from her body and crushed it on the floor beneath his shoe was that it couldn't hurt her any longer. It was simply gone. "I wasn't forming the queue for a chance in your bed. Been there, done that, thank you."

His harsh expression didn't change.

"Then as I said, I will see you tonight. We have a very precise plan, Brittany. I suggest you stick to it."

"With pleasure," she replied. Then smiled pure ice at him. "One small wrinkle in the plan, however. I'm pregnant."

One sentence and the world crumbled. Cairo knew that better than most.

He'd never thought it would happen again. It had already happened twice. He'd never imagined he would once more find his world divided so tidily into *before* and *after*.

"How?"

That hardly sounded like him.

Brittany looked smooth and perfect, which he'd come to hate. She was so different here in Paris. So far from his island lover she might as well have been a different woman. Her hair was pulled back in a sleek chignon. She wore a tailored dress and her usual impeccable shoes. She looked like a glossy photograph of herself. She looked untouchable, and no matter if she was slightly pale.

She made him ache. She made him wish he was a different man—a better one.

Her expression turned faintly pitying.

"You're the one with battalions of experience, as you are so happy to share with me and every tabloid reporter in Europe. Surely you can figure out *how*."

Cairo could only stare at her, the world he knew falling apart in great chunks all around him, though the hall was quiet. Deceptively peaceful.

"You cannot be pregnant," he told her.

Another cool smile. "Funny, that was what I told the doctor. Almost verbatim. Apparently, it's not up to me."

"You don't understand."

"I assume it was that first time, in the castle before our wedding," she continued, her voice as falsely merry as her eyes were hard. "How romantic, I'm sure you'll agree. I took the liberty of paging through our contract this morning and it seems there's no provision for pregnancy—"

"Of course there isn't." Dimly, he understood that he was raging. That he'd shouted that. "I am the last of the Santa Dominis, Brittany. It ends with me. There cannot be another."

Her composure cracked at that, and all the things he'd tried so hard to ward off and keep at bay swept over him then as her hands crept over her flat belly. As her mouth softened, even trembled.

He had always been so careful. How had he let this happen?

"Cairo." He had never heard her so tentative, and that tore at him. "Is it really so bad?"

"Do you think I spent my wasted life in the tabloids for fun?" he threw at her. "I did it for protection. The more irredeemable I was, the less likely anyone would ever see me as a king. The moment I became anything like a king, the general would have me killed."

Brittany shook her head, her eyes flashing. "The general is dead."

She had to understand. She had to see the danger.

He closed the distance between them, wrapping his hands around her shoulders and putting his face in hers.

"I cannot have a child." He heard the thickness in his voice, the decades of grief and pain. "I cannot condemn an innocent to this life. I have never been a good man. I have never lived up to a single expectation. But I will not be that kind of monster, selfish beyond imagining. I will not lock a baby in this prison with me."

He didn't know when tears had begun to fall from her eyes, only that they tracked down her face. And the hands he'd put on her shoulders to keep her at a distance curved to hold her instead.

"You don't have to do this alone, Cairo," she whispered. "Don't you understand? You're not alone in this any longer."

"We have a plan—" he started.

"I love you," she said, very distinctly.

Again, the world was cleaved in two. And again, he could do nothing about it but mourn the split—and the inevitability of what he had to do.

"No," he said, very clearly, so she could not possibly mistake the matter. "You do not."

"Of course I love you." She scowled at him. "You're the only man I've ever let touch me. I not only let you touch me, I threw myself into it without a single thought about the consequences. Please. I know exactly where babies come from, Cairo. I knew about condoms before I knew my own telephone number. None of these things are accidents."

"None of those things matter," he said. He shook his head, trying to clear it. Trying to think. "We will have to fabricate a lover and have him claim the child. It will be a huge scandal. The baby you tried to pass off as mine—"

"No."

She didn't scowl. She didn't shout. She simply stood there, her hand curved over her belly, her face pale, as if she was carved from marble, and as movable.

"No?" he echoed.

"No," she said again, even more firmly. "This is your baby. I am your wife. I'm done playing these games, Cairo."

"You already agreed to play them."

"I agreed to play tabloid tag with a man who doesn't exist," she said, and though her voice was still thick with emotion, she didn't waver. "But then I fell in love with you. The real you. The man who, deep down when everything is stripped away, is a king. The true king of Santa Domini, no matter what happened in the interim."

"The true king of Santa Domini died in a car crash years ago." Cairo's voice was harsh with the past. Bitter. "I am nothing but his embarrassing shadow."

"The general stole your country. He killed your family. He forced you into this terrible game and, worse than that, somehow got you to believe that the act you put on is who you really are."

"It is no act. How else can I tell you?"

But he couldn't bring himself to drop his hands, to step away.

"Is that what you want for this baby?" she asked him softly, her dark hazel eyes hard and beseeching at once.

"You want to condemn him to the same game? The same lie of a life in public, until it starts to feel real in private, too?"

"You have no idea what you're talking about." But he dropped his gaze to that belly of hers. "You have no idea what is involved."

"Here's what I know." And Brittany pulled herself away from his grasp, stepping back so he had no choice but to let her go. He saw the sheen of emotion in her eyes and the resolve, too. "Neither one of us had any choice. We did what we had to do, and our lives played out in a hundred different tabloids because of it. But our child deserves better."

"I agree," he said fiercely. "That is why no one must know it's mine."

She drew herself up to her full height and there was no pretending she was anything but regal. She had been from the start.

"I won't run. I won't hide and I won't lie. I am your queen and this baby is the heir to your kingdom. Don't you understand?"

She searched his gaze and he didn't want to hide from it any longer. From her. When he knew she was the only one who'd ever really seen him in years.

The only one who had ever known the man he'd hidden beneath a series of masks, each more elaborate than the next.

"It doesn't matter if you love me," she told him, and his heart twisted in his chest at the quiet resolve in the way she said that. "What matters is the future. The future you never had, but your child can. The general is dead. It's *your* throne, Cairo. All you have to do is claim it."

CHAPTER TEN

THIRTY YEARS AFTER escaping it in the middle of the night, His Serene Grace the Archduke Felipe Skander Cairo of Santa Domini walked back into the Royal Palace that his family had held for generations.

It had been remarkably easy to retrace his family's steps. Up into the mountains and over the border, then down through the farthest villages, making his way through the very heart of the alpine kingdom he had been born to protect.

And with every step, he knew. That this was right. That this was home. That even if what was left of the general's military executed him the moment he set foot in the palace, this was where he belonged.

In his country, with his people, taking back what was his so that no child of his blood would be forced to live as he had done all these miserable years.

The white-covered mountains were deep in his bones. The green hills, the crystal-blue lakes—they pumped in his blood. They made him who he was.

By the time he reached the palace gates, he had attracted followers and the inevitable press. But he didn't stop to read headlines or gauge public sentiment.

He didn't care what the papers said. This was right. Finally, he was doing what was right.

Ricardo stood proud at his side. Hundreds of loyalists stood at his back. The police had met them outside the

capital city, but rather than arresting them all, had only escorted the procession along their route toward the palace.

"You are a movement, Sire," Ricardo told him.

Cairo knew better. He was a man. He was a mediocre
husband and he was already well on his way to being a
terrible father. He was famous for all the wrong reasons
and he'd squandered the better part of his life in fear.

But none of that mattered, because one woman had
looked straight into the monster in him and seen only
the king.

Today, at long last, he would claim that crown.

He walked through the palace gates that the general's
remaining cronies didn't dare close against the rightful
heir to the Santa Domini throne. Not when he had made
this so public. He climbed the ceremonial steps, as aware
of the news helicopters buzzing overhead as he was of the
brave men and women who walked with him, ushering
him toward his uncertain future.

But he would walk to meet it with his head held high.
As his father would have wanted him to do, he knew without question.

He hadn't been in the palace since he was five years
old, but Cairo knew his way. He marched past the ancient
canvases that depicted his ancestors, the frescoes and the
marbled halls, to the grand throne room that he knew full
well had not been used since his father had last sat there
thirty years ago.

That was where they met him, a pack of fat, old men
with soft hands and shifty-eyed guards.

Cairo did not wait for them to speak.

"Good afternoon, gentlemen," he said, stopping halfway across the polished floors and standing there beneath
the statue of his grandfather, aware that there were cameras on him, as there were always cameras on him. Today
he was grateful for it.

And he was aware that no matter what happened here, he would be remembered for this moment above all others in his life.

Better make it good.

"I am Cairo, the last of the Santa Dominis. I believe you have been waiting to execute me for the crime of possessing my father's blood for the past thirty years." He inclined his head, though his eyes glittered and he felt his rage inside him like a drum. "Here I am. Do with me as you will."

Brittany watched the dramatic reclamation of the Santa Domini throne with the rest of the dumbstruck world—on television, hidden away in a safe house in one of Cairo's lesser known properties in the remote Scottish highlands.

It had been part of the bargain they'd struck when Cairo told her what he planned to do, and what he needed her to do if he did not live through it.

It hadn't been lost on her that Cairo had not expected to survive. But it was one more thing she couldn't allow herself to examine too closely.

She and a Hollywood actor as well known for his collection of children by assorted famous mothers as for any actual acting waited out the march into Santa Domini together in the drafty old manor house. Meaning she had watched it live on the twenty-four-hour news channel in the cozy den while the blandly attractive, deeply boring man in question had done push-ups in the gallery and spent several hours on his mobile phone shouting at his agent.

"You don't have to stay any longer," she'd told him after Cairo walked into the palace. When the remaining ministers resigned on the spot and the bells of all the Santa Domini churches began to ring out across the land after lying dormant for thirty years.

Long Live the King! the news sites and the people cheered.

As if Cairo had never been scandalous in all his life.

Because he was the king, she understood. She was his scandal.

"I don't understand why I was here for this," the actor told her, annoyed. "Why would anyone pay that much money to have me just…sit around for a week?"

"Rich people are strange," Brittany said coolly. "Royals are worse."

Then she'd dismissed him and waited for the car to take her to the plane that would deliver her to her own fate.

She landed in Santa Domini the following morning.

Aides whisked her from the plane into a fleet of gleaming black cars with tinted windows, hurrying her into the palace as if they were trying to hide her from the public. She imagined that was exactly what they were doing. It was exactly what she'd expected they'd do.

Cairo might have been instantly forgiven his scandalous past by virtue of his being, in fact, a king. But she was a girl who'd taken her clothes off for a living and then married a few men for obvious practical reasons. There was no forgiveness for her. Especially when the king himself didn't love her.

She told herself it didn't hurt, because it shouldn't. This wasn't about her or her feelings or her battered heart. It was about the baby that grew inside her daily. It was about a different sort of love altogether.

She told herself that had to be enough.

Brittany didn't see Cairo again until they led her out onto the balcony high above the palace's famous square, where kings had addressed the nation for centuries. She had been dressed and styled by a pack of palace attendants, then brought here to wait for him with everyone else.

He strode from the great doors and did nothing more

than slide a swift, intense look her way on his way to his podium. She made herself smile. Because what mattered was that he claimed his throne and took back his kingdom so that his child would never have to hide as he'd done.

She smiled dutifully in her lovely silver gown, her hair sleek and sophisticated, as if she really was a queen. And then watched the man she'd never meant to fall in love with, the father of the baby she carried within her, take his rightful place before his people.

It didn't matter that he didn't love her, that no one could or ever had. What mattered, she told herself as he stood there so proud and tall and beautiful, was that she loved him. She hadn't known she could. She'd worried she'd been broken by her family, her squalid, public life. But she loved him, and that was a good thing, regardless of what happened next.

"I have been hiding in plain sight the whole of my adult life," Cairo told the huge, cheering crowd, and all the world. "I believed I served my country by disappointing it, day after day. By rendering myself the least likely king, I ensured not only that I survived, but that the vile enemies of this kingdom could not vent their spleen on any who supported me."

He stood there in the same sort of suit he'd always worn, the very height of male elegance and every inch of him royal. He was the same man he'd always been, so beautiful it almost hurt to look at him. But now, Brittany knew, the whole world saw what she'd always seen beneath all of that. The real man within him, brave and true, who had always been more than the role he'd played.

The man she loved desperately and totally, with every fiber of her being, but could never truly have as she had during those stolen weeks on the island.

He was the King of Santa Domini.

She was a jumped up stripper whose own mother was ashamed of her antics.

His voice was sure and true as he addressed his subjects. Brittany called on all her years of pretending, all the acting she'd done and all the situations she'd had to weather, and stood there smiling as if her world wasn't ending right there in front of her.

The pain of it would pass. Or fade, anyway. She was sure it would, some day. She would always be his footnote. And the mother of his child.

But because she loved him, she would step aside as soon as she could do so without causing him any further scandal, and let him marry the sort of woman fit for a king.

It wouldn't make her child any less his heir, and that, she told herself firmly, was the only thing that mattered. That and the life the child could live, a life not on the run, a life that Cairo hadn't had.

Out there in front of her, Cairo was still speaking. He talked of his parents. He talked of his sister, the lost princess, Magdalena. He mourned the dead and promised that he would see to it that any citizen of the kingdom who had suffered under the general's rule would meet with him if they wished, so he could personally see to it that their suffering was ended.

Brittany thought she'd never seen a man better suited to be a king.

That was why, when her phone had rung beside her while she'd been getting ready earlier, flashing her mother's number and promising the usual punishment, she'd ignored it.

She didn't need that abuse anymore. She didn't need to feel badly about herself to know who she was.

She would survive this. She would do more than merely survive this. She loved a man who loved his country, and she wasn't afraid of the sacrifices ahead of her, no matter that they might prove difficult. Life was often difficult. That didn't mean it wasn't good.

For the first time since she'd left that island, and since she'd found out she was pregnant, Brittany felt at peace.

And Cairo was still speaking, his voice ringing out over those famous palace steps, down into the fairy-tale courtyard, and all across the world that had always hung on his every word, but never so much as today.

"Some have asked, why now? What prompted me to find my way back to my people, my country, my life?" He shifted, and glanced over his shoulder, his caramel gaze grazing hers. It was a swift, quick glance, and yet it was as if he looked straight into her soul. Brittany found she was holding her breath. "It was not the ignominious fall of a vicious man who fancied himself a dictator, let me assure you. It was something far less noble than the urge to do my duty. I found myself a woman who wasn't the least bit impressed with me and I made her my queen."

That statement went through her like a lightning bolt. And it hurt.

She'd imagined he'd issue a tasteful statement, released quietly sometime after the world had grown used to the return of the king. Not...here, now. With so many people as witnesses.

Brittany had to remind herself that the whole world was watching. That this was not for her or even about her. This was about a kingdom that deserved better than a stripper queen. Better than an infamous woman who had only ever learned how to make money and headlines. She reminded herself that Cairo was not hers. That he had never been hers, not really, no matter that she carried their baby inside of her or wore the Heart of Santa Domini on her hand.

He belonged to his people. He had only ever been on loan.

But she cradled the precious ring with the fingers of

her other hand anyway, as if she thought someone might come and try to take it from her right there where she stood. She would give it back when asked, of course. She would do the right thing.

Until then, she'd pretend this was the fairy tale that deep down she'd always dreamed about, no matter how many times life kicked her in the teeth instead.

She lifted her chin. In front of her, Cairo smiled, then turned back to his subjects and all those cameras.

Brittany braced herself. And she smiled.

"I made her my queen and she made me a man," Cairo told the world. "And as I learned to be the kind of man who deserved such a queen as Brittany, kind and true, strong and brave, I understood what I owed not only to her, but to you, the people of Santa Domini. I did not know if I would claim my throne or lose my life when I returned here. I only knew that I could not live with myself if I stayed in hiding, forever on the run, forever a man unworthy of both his queen and his country."

He lifted his arm and raised it toward the crowd. "I pledge to you that I will always strive to be the king you deserve, and to serve this country with every breath and bone in my body."

Then he turned.

King Cairo, resplendent and fierce in the clear mountain air, with thousands of adoring subjects cheering him on from below.

Today, Brittany knew exactly what that glorious mouth of his tasted like, and how it felt against every part of her skin. She knew the heavy silk of his dark hair and how it felt to run her hands through it. She missed the careless scruff he'd shaved from his astonishingly handsome face, the better to show off that perfectly cut Santa Domini jaw.

And, oh, his eyes. They were caramel and they were

wicked and they were focused on her as if there was nothing else in all the world but the two of them.

He held her gaze for a moment.

Then the rightful king of Santa Domini dropped to his knees before her. Her heart stopped. Then pounded into her, wild against her ribs, so hard she almost toppled over.

"Brittany," he said, as if they were alone, though the microphone on his lapel transmitted his words around the globe, "I love you."

The crowd roared. And Brittany didn't have it in her to fight the tears that spilled over and poured down her cheeks.

"No," she told him, because she had to. Because he deserved a real queen. A good one, who was proper and good and had never been featured in a burlesque ensemble in a tabloid—much less on a reality television program. "You can't. You're a king."

"And you are a queen," he replied, the maddening man. "My queen."

And Brittany forgot the crowds, the cameras. She forgot where they were. They might as well have been back on their own private island, with nothing for miles in all directions but the deep blue sea.

Cairo held out his hands, then waited.

Brittany pulled in a breath, then let it out. She needed to walk away. She knew she needed to walk away. She knew she didn't deserve to be here, with him. She was supposed to be the joke he played on the world. She couldn't stay with him and let him become the joke because of her...

But she couldn't bring herself to do it.

She didn't *want* to walk away from him.

So instead she reached out and took his hands, feeling the heat of his instant, sure grip go through her, warming her like the sun.

"You married an exiled royal with a terrible reputation," he said, his voice low and sure and his eyes on her. "And you made him into a king. You wear the Heart of Santa Domini on your hand and you hold my own heart between your palms. I want you to marry me again, in the cathedral where generations of Santa Dominis have pledged their lives to each other, so I can make you the queen in my people's eyes that you have always been to me."

She opened her mouth to refuse him. To sacrifice the very thing she wanted most, the only man she'd ever loved and the only person she'd ever let get close to her—but she looked into Cairo's warm, steady gaze, and she found she couldn't do it. Not to him, not to their baby.

Not to herself.

The truth was simple. She didn't want to live without him.

Maybe, just maybe, he wasn't crazy. Maybe they could do this.

She knew she had to try.

"If you think I can be the queen you need," she said, and heard her voice echo back at her from all over the vast palace complex and the Santa Domini mountains that surrounded them, "then I promise you, I will do my best to live up to that honor every day of my life. I promise."

Cairo's smile broke across his face, brighter than the summer's day around him. He surged to his feet and he pulled her into his arms, and the whole of his kingdom cheered for them, loud and long.

So loud and so long that nobody could hear him when he leaned in closer, his gaze hard and hot and hungry on hers, just the way she liked it.

"I love you," he told her again, this time for only her. "I will never let you go, *tesorina*. Never."

"You'd better not, Your Maddening Majesty," she said. Then smiled back at him, hope and love and the whole of their future dancing there between them. "Just think of the headlines."

"I always do," Cairo replied, arrogant and sure.

And entirely hers, forever.

Then he bent her back over his arms, a dashing king and his Cinderella queen, and kissed her like a fairy tale come true.

Because, Brittany knew with a rock-deep certainty, it finally had.

* * * * *

THE PRINCESS AND
THE PLAYER

KAT CANTRELL

One

Auwck. Auwck.

Bella Montoro's eyelids flew open at the raucous and unwelcome alarm clock. One of the pair of feral blue-and-gold macaws who lived in the tree outside the window of her Coral Gables mansion had chosen today, of all days, to wake her early.

Miami was full of wild macaws and normally, she loved them. Today, not so much.

Groaning, she smooshed a pillow over her head but the pressure didn't ease her champagne headache and the barrier didn't muffle the happy squawks of her feathered friend. Fine. It was time to drag herself out of bed anyway.

She sat up. A glance through the bay window confirmed which bird it was.

"Good morning, Buttercup," she muttered sarcastically, but with the window closed, the macaw couldn't hear her.

She didn't dare open the window for fear she'd frighten her away. Both Buttercup and her mate, Wesley, were as wild as the day was long, and Bella enjoyed it when they deigned to hang out with her. She watched them groom themselves for as long as she dared since she wouldn't get to see them for a while once she left Miami for the small country of Alma—today's destination.

Bella had always known she was descended from royalty, but a dictator had been ruling her ancestor's country for ages. She'd never expected the political climate to shift. Or for the Montoros to reclaim the throne. But it had happened and though her father was first in line to become king, his divorce rendered him ineligible for the crown due to Alma's strict laws. Then her oldest brother, Rafe, had abdicated his place so he could focus on the new baby he and his fiancée, Emily, were expecting.

Her other brother, Gabriel, had stepped up, adopting his new role with an ease Bella admired. And while she liked the tiny island country of Alma well enough to go back for her brother's coronation as the new king, the promise of bigger and better parties didn't fully make up for having to leave behind the things she loved in Miami.

She was also leaving behind her great-aunt Isabella, who might draw her last breath any day now. Rafe would check in on her of course, and Bella could call. But still. It wasn't the same as having daily access to the woman who always had a kind word and gentle piece of advice, no matter what the occasion. Bella had been named for her father's aunt, and they shared a kinship that transcended age.

Her father owed her for agreeing to this move to Alma. Big time.

Bella watched Buttercup groom her feathers for a moment, and then turned away from the beautiful view of the grounds. She might not see this house again either, and she'd taken for granted how much she loved living here. Now that the day of her departure had arrived, everything had gotten real, really fast. She'd been an American her whole life and while she'd always enjoyed the privileges of being a Montoro, becoming a member of Alma's royal family carried heavy responsibilities with few tangible rewards.

Not that anyone had asked her opinion.

With far too much racket for Bella's taste, her maid, Celia, bustled into the bedroom and frowned at the crumpled, glittery dress on the floor as she stepped over it. "They have plenty more hangers at the store if you've run out, Miss Bella."

Bella grinned at the woman who'd been her friend, confidant and occasional strong shoulder for years, blessing her for sticking to their tried-and-true teasing instead of becoming maudlin over the irreversible changes that had ripped through the Montoro family recently.

"Got hangers," Bella informed her around an involuntary yawn. "Just not the will to use one at three a.m."

Celia sniffed as if displeased, but an indulgent smile tugged at her mouth nonetheless. "Seems like a gal about to get on a plane in a few hours might come home at a decent hour."

"Oh, but it was my last night in Miami!" Bella protested without any real heat and stretched with a moan. "I had lots of people to see. Lots of parties to attend."

"Hmpf. Lots of money to talk your friends out of, you mean."

Celia was one of the few people who recognized that Bella's involvement in wildlife conservation wasn't just a rich girl's cute hobby. It was Bella's passion and she used her connections. Shamelessly. And it wasn't an accident that she'd been named the top fund-raiser in Florida by two different conservation groups.

"You say that like it's a bad thing." Bella shook her head as Celia selected an outfit from the overflowing closet and held it out with a raised eyebrow. "Not that one. The blue pantsuit for the plane. With the cropped jacket."

Like a well-rehearsed ballet, Bella and Celia danced around each other as they navigated a bedroom that closely resembled a post-hurricane department store. Everyone joked that you could always tell when Bella had whirled through a scene because nothing was in one piece afterward. It was a reference to Bella's birth during the harrowing hours of Hurricane Andrew, before FEMA had started cracking down on evacuations.

Both mother and baby had emerged from the storm without incident, but Bella held the private belief that the experience had branded her soul with hurricane-like qualities she couldn't shake. Not the least of which was a particular talent for causing chaos.

Celia began packing Bella's suitcases while her mistress dressed and they laughed over Bella's account of the previous night's parties, as they'd done many a morning over the years. But this would be the last time for a long time. Maybe forever, depending on what happened in Alma.

Bella kept up the light banter, but she was pretty sure the shadows in Celia's eyes were reflected in her own. As the hour grew near for Bella to leave for the sun-drenched islands of Alma, she couldn't stand it any longer. "I wish you could go with me to Alma!"

And then to her mortification, Bella burst into tears.

Celia folded Bella into her arms and they clung to each other. When Adela, Bella's mom, had finally ditched her cold, unsatisfying marriage the day after Bella's eighteenth birthday, Celia had been the one who stuck around to make sure Bella didn't get into too much trouble. Best of both worlds—she had someone who cared, but who also couldn't tell her what to do. Bella did not like being told what to do.

"There, now. Your brother will look out for you and besides, you'll be having so much fun as the new princess, you won't even notice I'm not there."

"That's not true," Bella sniffed and hugged Celia tighter. "Gabriel will be busy with king stuff and spend all his free time with Serafia now that they're getting married. What if I'm banished to some out of the way place—*alone*?"

She wouldn't put it past her father to lock her up in the palace dungeon or do something else equally archaic since he seemed bent on rediscovering his old-fashioned side. That last photo of her to hit the tabloids? Totally not her fault. How was she supposed to know the paparazzi had hidden in the foliage surrounding Nicole's pool? Everyone else had shed their swimsuits, too, but Bella was the only one they'd targeted, of course.

Rafael Montoro the Third was not amused. Apparently it was problematic that her father's business associates and soon-to-be-king Gabriel's future subjects in Alma could easily access naked photos of Bella.

No one seemed to remember that she was the victim in that scandal.

Celia snorted. "With Gabriel about to take the throne, your father will want the whole family in the public eye, gaining support for your brother. You're the only princess Alma's got, sweetie. They'll love you and so will your fiancé. Your father can't lock you away *and* expect you to marry the man he's picked out."

"Yeah, I've been trying not to think about that." Her head started pounding again and that fourth glass of champagne last night started to feel like a bad idea. But her friends had been determined to send her off in style to her new life as the sister of the king of Alma, so how could she refuse?

Besides, anything that helped her forget the arranged marriage her father was trying to force down her throat was a plus in her book. Fine time for her father to remember he had a daughter—when it was important for the Montoro family to strengthen ties with Alma through marriage. How come Gabriel and Rafe didn't have to marry someone advantageous? Her brothers had chosen their own brides. It wasn't fair. But her father had made it clear she was to get on a plane and meet this man Will Rowling, who was the son of one of Alma's most powerful businessmen.

Maybe she should be thankful no one had thought to match her with Will's father. Seemed as if that might be more advantageous than marrying the son. She shuddered. *No* marriage sounded like fun, no matter who the guy was.

If Alma turned out to be horrible, she'd just come home. Rafe and Emily were going to make her an aunt soon, and she'd love to hang out in Key West with the baby. Nobody dictated Bella's life but her.

"Mr. Rafael isn't completely unreasonable. After all, he did agree to let you meet Will and see how things go. Just remember why you're doing this," Celia advised.

Bella's guilty conscience reared its ugly head and she eased out of Celia's embrace before the older woman sensed it. "It's my royal obligation to help Gabriel ascend to the throne," she mimicked in her father's deep voice. "The whole family needs to be in Alma to prepare for the coronation."

But that wasn't really why she'd agreed to go. Miami had grown too small to hold both Bella and Drew Honeycutt. Honestly, when you told a guy that you just wanted to have fun and not take a relationship seriously, he was supposed to breathe a sigh of relief.

He was not supposed to fall to one knee and propose after two months of casual dating. And then plaster his second proposal on twenty billboards around the city, along with Bella's picture and a cartoon heart around her face. The third proposal spread across the sky in the form of a "Will you marry me, Bella Montoro?" banner behind a small plane, which flew up and down South Beach for six hours while Bella was at a private cookout on the penthouse terrace of Ramone, the new guy she'd been seeing. A fan of drama Ramone was not. Thanks to Drew, he'd bowed out.

And Bella had really liked Ramone, dang it; the more

he drank, the more money he handed over for her wildlife charities.

Drew followed her around, popping up at parties and museum openings like a bad penny, espousing his love for Bella with horrific poetry and calf eyes galore. It would be great if she could tell him off, but Honeycutt Logistics did a lot of business with Montoro Enterprises and she couldn't afford to irritate her father further. Plus, she was 97 percent sure Drew was harmless and worse, he seemed genuinely baffled and brokenhearted over her continual rejection of his proposals.

Each Drew sighting was another kick to the stomach. Another reminder that she was the hurricane baby, destined to whirl through people's lives and leave havoc in her wake. If only she could find a way to *not* break everything into little pieces—even though it was always an accident—she'd feel a lot better. She hated hurting people.

It was probably not a bad plan to disappear from the Miami scene for a while.

Celia managed to get Bella into the car on time and with all her luggage. The gates parted and Bella waved goodbye to Buttercup, Wesley and the house she'd grown up in as the driver picked up speed and they exited the grounds. Sun sparkled across Biscayne Bay and her spirits rose with each mile marker along the highway to the private airstrip where the Montoro Enterprises jet waited to fly her to Alma.

This was an adventure no matter what and she was going to enjoy every second of the sun, sand and royal parties ahead. By the time she'd boarded the plane, buckled her seatbelt and accepted a mimosa from Jan—the same flight attendant who'd given her crayons and coloring books once upon a time—Bella's mood had turned downright cheerful. Cheerful enough to sneak a glance at the picture of Will Rowling her father had sent her.

He was classically handsome, with nice hair and a

pleasant smile. The serious glint in his eye might be a trick of the light. Serious she could do without and besides, this was the guy her *father* had picked. Chances were Will and Bella would get on like oil and water.

But she'd reserve judgment until she met him because first and foremost, Alma was about starting fresh and Will deserved a chance to prove they were meant for each other. If he came out strong with a fun-loving nature and swept her off her feet, she'd be okay with a fabulous love affair and passion to spare.

Though she couldn't deny that one of the big question marks was what kind of guy would agree to an arranged marriage in the twenty-first century. There was probably something really wrong with Will Rowling if he couldn't meet women on his own. She probably had a better chance of her plane flying into an alternate universe than finding her soul mate in Will Rowling.

For the fourth time, someone kicked sand in James Rowling's face and for the fourth time, he ignored it. If he let loose with a string of curses—the way he wanted to—he'd only alert someone to his presence here, and James was trying to be invisible.

Or at least as invisible as one of Alma's most notorious failures could be. Maybe in fifty years he could fade into the woodwork, but every single citizen of Alma—and probably most of the free world—had watched him miss that goal in the World Cup. Anonymity was scarce.

So far, no one had recognized him with Oakleys covering his eyes and a backward ball cap over his hair. The longer he kept it that way, the better. The last thing he wanted was a bunch of questions about why Real Madrid had dropped his contract. It wasn't hard to look that one up…along with pictures of James leaving a bar in Rio with a prostitute…not that she'd mentioned money to *him*. Or worse, questions about whether he planned to stick around

his adopted homeland and play for Alma's reserve football team—*soccer* team if the questioner was American.

No comment.

A reserve team was for beginners. He would get a new
professional league contract, period. If not around here,
then maybe back in England, where he'd been born. There
was no other alternative. Football was his life.

Peeling his shirt away from his sticky chest, he leaned
back into his short-legged beach chair, stuck his legs
straight out and closed his eyes, somehow sure the elu-
sive measure of peace he sought would be within reach
this time. He almost snorted. When had he turned into
an optimist?

There was no peace to be had and if there was, it sure
as hell wouldn't be found in Alma, the capital of boring.
Not to mention his father's presence permeated the entire island, as if Patrick Rowling's soul lived in the bed-
rock, sending out vibrations of disapproval on a regularly
scheduled basis.

That's why James was at the beach at Playa Del Onda,
soaking up the sun instead of doing whatever it was his
father thought he should be doing, which would never happen because James lacked the capacity to do what his father said. It was like a mutated gene: his father spoke and
James's brain refused to obey. He automatically did the
opposite.

"Ooof!" Air whooshed from his lungs as something
heavy landed square on his chest.

Then his beach chair flipped, tossing him into the sand
on top of something. It squealed.

Some*one*. When his vision cleared, the tangle of supple-
bodied woman and blond hair underneath him captured
his complete attention.

He gazed down into the bluest set of eyes he'd seen in
a while. Something shifted inside as the woman blinked
back, her beautiful heart-shaped face reflecting not an iota

of remorse over their risqué position. Her body had some-how slid into the grooves of his effortlessly and the slight-est incline of his head would fuse his lips to hers.

She'd fully gobsmacked him.

Their breath intermingled. She seemed in no hurry to unstick her skin from his and in about two and a half seconds, his own body would start getting into the moment in a huge and inappropriate way.

Sexy strangers signaled big-time problems and he had enough of those.

Reluctantly, he rolled off her and helped her sit up. "Sorry about that. You okay?"

"Totally." Her husky voice skittered across his skin and he was hooked on the sound of it instantly. American. His favorite. "My fault. I was focused on this thing instead of where I was going."

She kicked at a Frisbee he hadn't noticed lying in the sand two feet away. But who'd pay attention to a piece of plastic when a fit blonde in a tiny bikini landed in your lap? Not him.

"I like a girl who goes for the memorable introduction."

It was certainly a new one. And he'd experienced his share of inventive ploys for getting his attention. Knick-ers with cell phone numbers scrawled in marker across the crotch, which he discovered had been shoved into his pocket. Room keys slipped into drinks sent over by a knot of football groupies at a corner table. Once, he'd gone back to his hotel room after a press junket to find two naked women spread out across his bed. How they'd gotten in, he still didn't know.

The logistics question had sort of slipped his mind after ten minutes in their company.

"Oh, I wasn't angling for an introduction." She actually blushed a bit, which was oddly endearing. "I really didn't see you there. You kind of blend into the sand."

"Is that a crack about my British complexion?" he teased. "You're pretty pale yourself, darling."

She laughed and rearranged her hair, pulling it behind her back so it didn't conceal her cleavage. A move he thoroughly appreciated. This gorgeous klutz might be the best thing that had happened to him all week. Longer than that. The best thing since arriving in Alma for sure.

Maybe it wasn't so bad to be stuck here cooling his heels until a football club whose jersey he could stomach wearing knocked on his door.

"No, not at all. I wouldn't be so rude as to point out your flaws on our first meeting." She leaned forward, her vibe full of come-hither as she teased him back.

Intrigued, he angled his head toward her. "But on our second date, all bets are off?"

Glancing down coquettishly, she let loose a small smile. "I'm more of a third-date kind of girl."

His gut contracted as the full force of that promise hit him crossways. She was a unique breed of woman, the most fascinating one he'd met thus far on this stupid rock he was being forced to call home for the time being. The memory of her hot flesh against his was still fresh—it was enough to drive him mad. And he suspected she knew exactly what she was doing to him.

"I have a feeling you'd be worth the wait."

She picked that moment to stand and for some reason, the new angle cast her in a different light. It tickled his mind and he recognized her all at once. Pictures of the new princess had graced every news channel for the past couple of weeks, but she'd been clothed. Regardless, he should have recognized her sooner and maybe not disgraced himself by flirting with a woman who probably really had no clue she'd stumbled over a former football player for Real Madrid.

A princess—especially one as fit as Bella Montoro—wasn't running around the beach at Playa Del Onda looking to meet guys, whether they were semifamous or not. Which was a dirty shame.

He shoved his hat back onto his head and repositioned his sunglasses, both of which had flown off during the sand tango.

Ms. Montoro... Princess Bella... Your Royal Highness... What did you even call her when her brother hadn't been crowned yet? Whatever the form of address, she was way out of his league.

But that didn't mean she thought so. She hadn't bothered to hide the frank attraction in her gaze when she'd been in his arms earlier. If there was anything he knew, it was women, and she might be royalty but that didn't necessarily make her off-limits.

He quickly scrambled to his feet in case there was some protocol for standing when princesses stood...even if she was wearing a postage stamp–sized white bikini that somehow covered everything while leaving nothing to the imagination.

No point in beating around the bush. "Am I permitted to call you Bella or is there some other title you'd prefer?"

"What, like *Princess*?" She wrinkled her nose. "I'm not really used to all that yet. And besides, I think we're a little past that stage, don't you?"

The feel of her soft curves flush against his body flooded his mind and his board shorts probably wouldn't conceal his excitement much longer if he didn't cool his jets. "Yeah. Formality isn't my specialty anyway. Bella it is."

Strangely, calling her Bella ratcheted up the intimacy quotient by a thousand. He liked it. And he wanted to say it a bunch more times while she lay stretched out under him again. Without the bikini.

She smiled and glanced down, as if the heat roiling between them was affecting her, too, and she didn't know quite what to do with it. "This is all so awkward. I wasn't sure you knew who I was."

Shrugging, he stuck his hands behind his back because he had no clue what to do with them. It was the first time he'd been unsure around a woman since the age of fourteen. "I recognized you from your pictures."

She nodded and waved off her friend who'd most likely come to investigate the disappearance of her Frisbee partner. "Me, too. I wasn't expecting to run into you on the beach or I would have dressed for the occasion."

Ah, so she *did* know who he was—and dare he hope there was a hint of approval there? She'd gotten rid of the friend, a clear sign she planned to stick around for a while at least. Maybe he wasn't so far out of her league after all. "I'm a fan of your wardrobe choice."

Laughing, she glanced down. "I guess it is appropriate for the beach, isn't it? It's just not how I thought meeting you would go. The picture my father sent painted you as someone very serious."

"Um…you don't say?" He'd just completely lost the thread of the conversation. Why would her father be sending her pictures, unless… Of course. Had to make sure the precious princess didn't taint herself with the common riffraff. *Stay away from that Rowling boy. He's a boatload of trouble.*

His temper kicked up, but he smoothed it over with a wink and a wicked smile. "I'm every bit as bad as your father warned you. Probably worse. If your goal is to seriously irritate him, I'm on board with that."

He had no problem being her Rebel Against Daddy go-to guy, though he'd probably encourage her to be *really* bad and enjoy it far too much. Instantly, a few choice scenarios that would get them both into a lot of trouble filled his mind.

Her eyes widened. "He, uh, didn't warn me about you… Actually, I'm pretty sure he'd be happy if we went out. Isn't that the whole point of this? So we can see if we're suited?"

This conversation was going in circles. Her father wanted them to date? "He's a football fan, then?"

She shook her head, confusion clouding her gaze. "I don't think so. Does that matter to you, Will?"

"Will?" He groaned. This was so much worse than he'd anticipated. "You think I'm Will?"

More importantly, her father had sent her a picture of Will for some yet-to-be-determined reason, but it wasn't so she could flirt with Will's twin brother on the beach. And this little case of mistaken identity was about to come to an abrupt halt.

Two

Bella laced her fingers together as she got the impression all at once that she wasn't talking to the man she thought she was. "Aren't you Will Rowling?"

He had to be. She'd studied his picture enough on the plane and then again last night while she tried to go to sleep but couldn't, because she'd been wondering what in the world her father was thinking with this arranged marriage nonsense. And then she'd come to the beach with the daughter of one of the servants who was close to her age, only to trip over said man her father had selected.

Except he was staring at her strangely and the niggle of doubt wormed its way to the surface again. How could she have made such a mistake?

"Not Will. Not even close," he confirmed.

He grinned, and she let herself revel in his gorgeous aqua-colored eyes for a moment because she didn't have to fight an attraction to him if he wasn't the man her father picked out for her.

The sun shone a little brighter and the sea sparkled a bit

bluer. Digging her toes into the warm sand that suddenly felt heavenly against her bare feet, she breathed a sigh of relief and grinned back.

This was turning out better than she'd hoped. Geez, she'd been one heartbeat away from believing in love at first sight and trying for all she was worth to shut it down. Because she'd thought he was Will Rowling. Imagine *that*. Her father would be insufferable about it and demand they get married right away if she'd become smitten so fast. It would have been a disaster.

But if this extremely sexy man wasn't Will—*perfect*. She slid her gaze down his well-cut body, which a T-shirt and long shorts couldn't hide. Of course she'd felt every single one of his valleys and hard peaks. Intimately.

No. This was *not* perfect. She was supposed to be meeting Will and seeing if they got along, not flirting with some look-alike stranger who made her itch to accept the wicked invitation in his gaze, which promised if he got her naked, he'd rock her world.

With no small amount of regret, she reeled back her less-than-innocent interest.

"Well, sorry about that, then," she said and held out her hand. Might as well start over since this whole thing had blown up in her face. "Bella Montoro. I guess you already knew that, but I'm at a disadvantage."

His rich laugh hit her a moment before he clasped her hand in his and the combination heated her more than the bright sun or her embarrassment. "I'm the one at a disadvantage, if you were hoping I was Will. I'm James. The other Rowling. Will is my brother."

"Brother? Oh," she drawled as it hit her. "You and Will are twins."

"Guilty." His eyes twinkled, sucking her under his spell for a moment.

"Then I'm doubly sorry." Mortified, she racked her brain, but if her father had told her Will had a twin brother, she surely would have remembered that. "I've made a complete mess out of this, haven't I?"

"Not at all. People confuse us all the time. It's fine, really."

It was not fine. It was so the opposite of fine, she couldn't even wrap her head around how *not fine* it was. Because she'd just realized this sensually intriguing man she'd accidentally tripped over was the *brother* of the intended target of her father's archaic arranged marriage plan.

If that didn't complicate her life a million times over, she didn't know what would.

Her hand was still gripped tight in his and he didn't seem in any hurry to let her go. But he should. She pulled free and crossed her arms, wishing for a cover-up. Why did that glint in James's eye cause her to feel so exposed all at once?

"I'm curious," James said casually as if the vibe between them had just cooled, which it most definitely had not. "Why did your father send you a picture of Will?"

"Oh, so I would know what he looks like." Actually, she'd demanded he do so. There was no way she was getting on a plane to meet someone blind.

"I'm sensing there's more to the story." His raised eyebrows encouraged her to elaborate.

"Wouldn't you wonder about the appearance of a person your father wanted you to marry? I sure did."

Surprise flew across James's face. "Your father wants you to marry Will? Does Will know about this?"

"Of course he does. Your father was the instigator, actually. You didn't know our fathers cooked up this idea of an arranged marriage?"

His laugh was far more derisive this time. "The elder Rowling doesn't share much of what goes on his head. But somehow it doesn't shock me to discover dear old Dad wants his son married to a member of the royal family. Did you agree?"

"No! Well, not yet anyway. I only agreed to meet Will and see what happened. I'm not really in the market for a steady relationship, let alone one as permanent as marriage."

Groaning, she bit her lip. Too late to take that back, though it had been the God-honest truth. Regardless, spilling her guts to the brother of her potential fiancé wasn't the best plan. James would probably run off and tell Will his future bride had felt up his brother on the beach—totally not her fault!—flirted with him—maybe partially her fault—and then declared marriage to be worse than the plague.

Instead of falling to his knees in shock, James winked and dang, even that was sexy.

"Woman after my own heart. If you don't want to get married, why even agree to meet Will?"

Why was she still standing here talking to the wrong brother? She should go. There was nothing for her here. But she couldn't make herself walk away from the spark still kicking between them.

"It's complicated," she hedged.

She sighed and glanced over her shoulder, but there was no one in earshot. She didn't want to draw the attention of a camera lens, but surely it couldn't hurt to spend a few minutes chatting with the man who might become her brother-in-law…so she could keep reminding herself that's who he was to her. If nothing else, she could set the record straight in case he intended to repeat this conversation verbatim to his brother.

"I'm the king of uncomplicating things," James said with another laugh that curled her toes deeper into the sand. "Try me."

It wasn't as if anyone was expecting her back at the gargantuan house perched on the cliff behind them. Gabriel was never home and her father... Well, she wasn't dying to run into him again.

She shrugged. "We're all new at this royalty thing. I don't want to be the one to mess it up. What if I don't try with Will and it has horrible repercussions for my brother Gabriel? I can't be responsible for that."

"But if you meet Will and you don't like him, how is that different than not meeting him in the first place? Either way, you don't end up with him and the repercussions will be the same."

How come she'd never thought of that? "That's a good point."

"Told you. I can uncomplicate anything. It's a skill." James's smile widened as he swept her with an impossible to misinterpret look. "I just figure out what I want to do and justify it. Like...if I wanted to kiss you, I'd find a way."

As his gaze rested on her lips, heat flooded her cheeks. And other places. She could practically feel the weight of his kiss against her mouth and he hadn't even moved. A pang of lust zinged through her abdomen and she nearly gasped at the strength of it. What was it about him that lit her up so fiercely?

"You shouldn't be talking about kissing." She inwardly cursed. That should have come out much more sternly, instead of breathy with anticipation. "Flirting as a whole is completely off-limits."

A hint of challenge crept into his expression and then he leaned in, stopping just short of touching her earlobe with his mouth. "Says who?"

"Me," she murmured as the scent of male and heat coiled up low in her belly, nearly making her weep with want. "I'm weak and liable to give in. You have to be the strong one and stop presenting me with so much temptation."

He laughed softly. "I'm afraid you're in a lot of trouble, then."

"Why?"

"Because I have absolutely no reservations about giving in to temptation."

The wicked smile spreading across his face sealed it—she *was* in a lot of trouble. She was supposed to marry his brother. And the last thing she needed was to set herself up for a repeat of the Drew Debacle, where she accidentally broke James's heart because she ended up with Will. Better all around to stay away from James.

Why did the wrong Rowling have to be so alluring and so delicious?

Maybe she could find Will similarly attractive if she just gave him a chance.

"I'll keep that in mind." All right, then. She was going to have to be the one to step away. Noted.

So step away. Right now.

Through a supreme act of will, she somehow did. James's gorgeous aqua eyes tracked her movement as she put one foot, then two between them. He nodded once, apparently in understanding but definitely not in agreement.

"See you around, Princess."

He stood there, one hip cocked in a casual stance that screamed Bad Boy, and she half waved before she turned and fled.

As she climbed the stairs to the house, she resisted looking over her shoulder to see if she could pick out James's yellow T-shirt amidst the other sun worshippers lounging on the white sand. He wasn't for her and there was no getting around the fact that she wished otherwise.

James Rowling was forbidden. And that might be his most attractive quality.

Bella entered the Playa Del Onda house through the kitchen, and snagged a glass-bottled cola from the refrigerator and a piece of crusty bread from the pantry. Both the colas and the bread tasted different in Europe but she didn't mind. All part of the adventure.

Thoughts still on the sexy man she'd abandoned on the beach, Bella munched on the bread as she climbed the stairs to her bedroom. She almost made it before a dark shadow alerted her to the fact that her least favorite person in the house had found her.

"Isabella." Her father's sharp voice stopped her dead, four steps from the landing on the second floor.

"Yeah, Dad?" She didn't turn around. If you didn't stare him in the eye, he couldn't turn you to stone, right?

"Is that how you dress to go out?"

"Only when I go to the beach," she retorted. "Is there something new you'd like to discuss or shall we rehash the same subject from last night? You didn't like that outfit either, if I recall."

Ever since Adela, Bella's mother, had left, this is how it went. Her father only spoke to her when he wanted to tell her how to run her life. And she pretended to listen. Occasionally, when it suited her, she went along, but only if she got something out of it.

"We'll rehash it as many times as it takes to get it through your scattered brain. Gabriel is going to be *king*." Rafael stressed the word as if she might be confused about what was happening around her. "The least you can do is help smooth his ascension with a little common sense about how you dress. The Montoros have no credibility yet, especially not with that stunt your brother pulled."

"Rafe fell in love," she shot back and bit her tongue.

Old news. Her father cared nothing for love, only propriety. And horror of all horrors—his eldest son had gotten a bartender pregnant and then abdicated the throne so he could focus on his new family. In Daddy's mind, it fell squarely into the category of impropriety. Unforgivable.

It was a reminder that her father also cared little for his daughter's happiness either. Only royal protocol.

"Rafe is a disappointment. I'll not have another child

of mine follow his example." He cleared his throat. "Face me when we're speaking, please."

She complied, but only because the front view of her bikini was likely to give him apoplexy and she kind of wanted to see it.

He pursed his lips but, to her father's credit, that was his only reaction. "When have you arranged to meet Will Rowling?"

Ah, of course. Complaining about her bikini was a smoke screen—this was actually an ambush about her arranged marriage. With the scent of forbidden fruit lingering in her senses coupled with her father's bad attitude, she'd developed a sudden fierce desire to spend time with someone who had clearly never met a good time he didn't like.

And his name wasn't Will. "I haven't yet."

"What are you waiting for, an invitation? This is your match to make, Isabella. I'm giving you some latitude in the timing but I expect results. Soon." The severe lines around his mouth softened. "This alliance is very important. To the entire Montoro family and to the royal legacy of Alma. I'm not asking this for myself, but for Gabriel. Remember that."

She sighed. "I know. That's why I'm here. I do want to be a credit to the royal family."

Hurricane Bella couldn't whirl through Alma and disrupt the entire country. She knew that. Somehow, she had to be better than she'd been in Miami. The thought of Miami reminded her of Buttercup and Wesley, her feathered friends she'd left behind. Some said the wild macaws that nested in southern Florida were people's pets set free during Hurricane Andrew. She'd always felt an affinity with the birds because they'd all survived the storm. Buttercup and Wesley could continue to be her source of strength even from afar.

"Good. Then arrange to meet Will Rowling and do it soon. Patrick Rowling is one of the most influential men in Alma and the Montoros need his support. We cannot afford another misstep at this point."

It wasn't anything she hadn't heard before, but on the heels of meeting James, the warning weighed heavily on her shoulders. Gabriel hadn't wanted to be thrust suddenly into a starring role in the restoration of the monarchy to Alma's political landscape. But he'd stepped up nonetheless. She could do the same.

But why did it matter which Rowling she married anyway? Surely one was as good as the other. Perhaps she could turn this to her advantage by seeing where things went with James.

"I'll do my best not to mess this up," Bella promised.

If it didn't matter which Rowling she picked, that meant she didn't need to call Will anytime soon. The reprieve let her breathe a little easier.

Her father raised his eyebrows. "That would be a refreshing change. On that note, don't assume that you left all the tabloids behind in Miami. The paparazzi know no national boundaries. Stay out of scandalous situations, don't drink too much and for God's sake, keep your clothes on."

She saluted saucily to cover the sharp spike of hurt that she never could seem to stop no matter how many times she told herself this was just how he was. "Yes, Father."

Escaping to her room, Bella took a long shower but it didn't ease the ache from the showdown with Rafael.

Why did she still care that her father never hugged her or told her he was proud of her? Not for the first time, she wondered if the frosty temperature in her father's demeanor had caused her mother to leave. If so, Bella hardly blamed her. She hoped Adela had found happiness.

Happiness should be the most important factor in whom you married. The thought solidified Bella's resolve. If her father wanted a match between the Montoros and the Rowlings, great. Bella would comply—as long as the Rowling was James.

She'd rather see where that led than try to force a match with the right brother.

Why shouldn't she be allowed to be as happy as Rafe and Gabriel?

The loud, scornful whispering at the next table over started to annoy James about two bites into his paella. Couldn't a bloke get something to eat without someone publicly crucifying him? This time, the subject of choice was his lack of a decision on whether to take a spot on Alma's reserve team.

The two middle-aged men were in complete agreement: James should be happy to have *any* position, even though Alma wasn't a UEFA team. He should take his lumps and serve his penance, and then it would be acceptable to play for a premiere club again, once he'd redeemed himself. Or so the men opined, and not very quietly.

The paella turned to sawdust in his mouth. He was glad someone knew what he needed to do next in his stalled career.

Playing for Alma was a fine choice. For a beginner. But James had been playing football since he was seven, the same year his father had uprooted his two sons from their Guildford home and moved them to the tiny, nowhere island of Alma. Football had filled a void in his life after the death of his mother. James loved the game. Being dropped from Real Madrid had stung, worse than he'd let on to anyone.

Of course, whom would he tell? He and Will rarely talked about anything of note, usually by James's choice. Will was the perfect son who never messed up, while James spent as much effort as he possibly could on irritating his father. James and Will might be twins but the similarities ended there—and Will was a Manchester United fan from way back, so they couldn't even talk football without almost coming to blows.

And Will had first dibs on the woman James hadn't been able to forget. All without lifting a finger. Life just reeked sometimes.

Unable to eat even one more bite of the dish he'd found so tasty just minutes ago, James threw a few bills on the table and stalked out of the restaurant into the bright afternoon sun on the boardwalk at Playa Del Onda.

So much for hanging out at the beach where fewer people might recognize him. He might as well go back to Del Sol and let his father tell him again how much of a disappointment he was. Or he could swallow his bitterness and get started on finding another football club since none had come looking for him.

A flash of blond hair ahead of him caught his eye. Since Bella had been on his mind in one way or another since he'd met her the day before, it was no wonder he was imagining her around every corner.

He shouldn't, though. She'd been reserved for the "right" Rowling, the one who could do no wrong. James's black sheep status hadn't improved much. Frankly, she deserved a shot at the successful brother, though he had no clue if Will was even on board with the match their father had apparently orchestrated. When Bella mentioned it yesterday, that was the first he'd heard of it. Which didn't mean it wasn't legit.

The woman in front of him glanced into a shop window and her profile confirmed it. It *was* Bella.

Something expanded in his chest and he forgot why he wasn't supposed to think about her. Unable to help himself all of a sudden, James picked up his pace until he drew up alongside her. "Fancy meeting you here."

Tilting her head down, she looked at him over the top of her sunglasses and murmured something reassuring to the burly security detail trailing her. They backed off immediately.

"James Rowling, I presume?" she said to him.

He laughed. "The one and only. Getting in some shopping?"

"Nope. Waiting around for you to stroll by. It's about time. I was starting to think you'd ordered everything on El Gatito's menu." She nodded in the direction of the restaurant he'd just exited and leaned in to murmur, "I hope you skipped the cat."

She'd been waiting for him? The notion tripped him up even more than her wholly American, wholly sexy perfume, for some odd reason.

"I, uh, did. Skip the cat," he clarified as he caught her joke in reference to the restaurant's name. "They were fresh out."

Her smile set off a round of sparks he'd rather not have over his brother's intended match.

"Maybe next time."

"Maybe next time you'll just come inside and eat with me instead of skulking around outside like a stalker," he suggested and curled his lip. What was he *doing*—asking her out? Bad idea.

One of her eyebrows quirked up above the frame of her sunglasses. "I can say with absolute authority that me noticing you heading into a restaurant and accidentally-on-purpose hanging around hoping to run into you does not qualify as stalking. Trust me, I'm a bit of an expert. I have the police report to prove it."

He had a hard time keeping his own eyebrows from shooting up. "You're a convicted stalker?"

Her laugh was quite a bit more amused this time. "Not yet. Don't go and ruin my perfect record now either, okay?" She shrugged and slipped off her sunglasses. "I picked up a stalker in Miami a couple of years ago. So I'm pretty familiar with American law. I would hope it's reasonably similar in Alma."

Sobering immediately, he tamped down the sudden and violent urge to punch whomever had threatened Bella's peace of mind. She'd mentioned it so casually, as if it wasn't a big deal, but it bloody well *was*. "What do you mean, you picked up a stalker? Like you went to the market to get milk and you just couldn't resist selecting a nutter to shadow you all the way home? No more jokes. Is he in jail?"

That may have come out a little more fiercely than he'd intended, but oh, well. He didn't take it back.

Wide-eyed, she shook her head. "He was practically harmless. A little zealous with his affections, maybe. I was out for the evening and he broke into my bedroom, where he waited for me to come home, bouquet of flowers in hand, like we were a couple. Or at least that was his sworn testimony. When my father found out, he immediately called the police, the mayor of Miami and the CEO of the company who'd sold him the security system installed on the grounds. I'm afraid they were rather harsh with the intruder."

Harmless? Anyone who could bypass a security system was far from harmless.

"As well they should have been." James developed an instant liking for Bella's obviously very level-headed father. "Was that the extent of it? Do I need to worry about the nutter following you across the pond?"

James had had his share of negative attention, invasions of privacy and downright hostile encounters with truly disturbed people. But he had fifty pounds and eight inches on Bella, plus he knew how to take care of himself. Bella was delicate and gorgeous and worthy of being treated like the princess she was. The thought of a creepy mouth-breather following her through the streets of Alma in hopes of doing depraved things made him furious.

"I doubt it. I haven't heard a peep from him in two years." She contemplated James with a small smile and crossed her arms over the angular sundress she wore. "You seem rather fierce all of a sudden. Worried about me?"

"Yes," he growled and shook his head. She was not any

of his concern—or at least she shouldn't be. "No. I'm sure your security is perfectly adequate."

He waved at the pair of ex-military types who waited a discreet distance away.

"Oh, yeah. My father insisted." Her nose wrinkled up delicately. "I'm pretty sure they're half security and half babysitters."

"Why do you need a babysitter?"

He couldn't leave it alone, could he? He should be bidding her good afternoon and running very fast in the other direction. But she constantly provoked his interest, and it was oh-so-deliberate. She wasn't walking away either and he'd bet it was because she felt the attraction sizzling between them just as much as he did.

Hell, everything he'd learned about her thus far indicated she liked the hint of naughtiness to their encounters… because they weren't supposed to be attracted to each other.

"I have a tendency to get into trouble." She waggled her brows. "These guys are here to keep me honest. Remind me that I have royal blood in my veins and a responsibility to the crown."

That was too good of a segue to pass up. "Really? What kind of trouble?"

"Oh, the worst kind," she stressed and reached out to stroke his arm in deliberate provocation. "If you've got a reputation to uphold, you'd best steer clear."

The contact of her nails on his bare arm sang through him. This was the most fun he'd had all day. "Sweetheart, I hate to disillusion you, but I've managed to ruin my reputation quite nicely all by my own self. Hanging out with you might actually improve it."

"Huh." She gave him a wholly inappropriate once-over that raised the temperature a few thousand degrees. "I'm dying to know. What did you do?"

"You really don't know?" That would be a first.

When she shook her head, he thought about glossing

over it for a half second, but she'd find out soon enough anyway. "Mishap in Rio. Some unfortunate photographs starring me and a prostitute. I swear, money never came up, but there you go. The world didn't see it as an innocent mistake."

Gaze locked on his, she squeezed his arm. "Man after my own heart. Of all the things I thought we might have in common, that was not it. I'm recovering from my own photographer-in-the-bushes fiasco. Cretins."

"Oh, that's too bad. Sorry."

A moment of pure commiseration passed between them. And it spread into something dangerously affecting. They shared a complete lack of reverence for rules, their chemistry was off the charts and they were both in Alma trying to find their footing. It was practically criminal that he couldn't explore her gorgeous body and even more attractive mind to his heart's content.

But he couldn't. While he might have competed with Will over women in the past, this one was different. James wasn't in a good place to start anything with a woman anyway, especially not one who would live in the public eye for the foreseeable future. She needed to be with Will, who would take care of her and not sully her with failure.

Not to mention that his father seemed to have struck some kind of bargain with the Montoro family. Until James knew exactly what that entailed, he couldn't cross the line he so badly wanted to.

She'd flat out told him he'd have to be the strong one, that he should stop tempting her. So that was the way it had to be.

James smiled and slipped his own sunglasses over his eyes so she couldn't read how difficult this was going to be for him. "Nice to see you again, Bella. I've got an appointment I'm late for so I've got to dash."

Casual. No commitment to calling her later. Exactly the right tone to brush her off.

She frowned and opened her mouth, but before she could say something they'd both likely regret, he added, "You should ring Will. Cheers," and whirled to take off down the boardwalk as fast he could.

Being noble tasted more bitter than he would have ever anticipated.

Three

James's rebuff stayed with Bella into the evening.

Apparently he wasn't of the same mind that a match between the Rowlings and Montoros could work just as easily between James and Bella as it could with his brother.

Being forced into a stiff, formal dinner with her father didn't improve her mood. Gabriel and Serafia were supposed to be there, too, which was the only reason Bella agreed, but the couple had yet to show.

Five bucks said they'd lost track of time while indulging in a much more pleasurable activity than dinner with Little Sister and Frosty Father. Lucky dogs.

Bella spooned up another bite of Marta's gazpacho, one of the best things the chef had prepared so far, and murmured her appreciation in case her father was actually paying attention to her today. But her mind was back on the boardwalk outside El Gatito. She'd have sworn the encounter with James would end with at least a kiss in the shadows of a storefront. Just to take the edge off until they got behind closed doors and let the simmering heat between them explode.

"Isabella." Her father's voice startled her out of an X-rated fantasy that she shouldn't have envisioned at all, let alone at the dinner table.

Not because of the X factor, but because it had starred James, who had cast her off with the lovely parting gift of his brother. *Call Will.* As if James had already grown tired of her and wanted to be clear about what her next steps should be.

"Yeah, Dad?" He must have realized that they were actually sitting at the same table. For once. She couldn't remember the last time they'd eaten together.

"You should know your great-aunt Isabella has decided to spend her last days in Alma. She arrived this morning and is asking after you."

Sudden happy tears burned Bella's eyelids. "Oh, that's the best news ever. Isn't she going to stay here with us?"

"The restoration of the monarchy is topmost on your aunt's mind." Rafael's gaze bored into her; he was no doubt trying to instill the gravity of royal protocol. "Therefore, she is staying in Del Sol. She wished to be close to El Castillo del Arena, so that she may be involved in Gabriel's coronation to the extent she is able."

Bella swore. Del Sol was, what? An hour away? Fine time to realize she should have taken her father up on the offer of a car…except she hadn't wanted to learn all the new traffic laws and Spanish road signs. Too late now—she'd have to take the chauffeured town car in order to visit Tía Isabella.

"Playa Del Onda is practically like Miami." Bella grumbled, mostly to herself. "You'd think she'd prefer the coast."

Her father put his spoon by his plate even though his bowl of gazpacho was still almost full. It hadn't been long enough since the last time they'd dined together for her to forget that meant a subject of grave importance was afoot and it wasn't her aunt's preference of locale.

"I have another matter to discuss. How was your first meeting with Will Rowling?"

Biting back a groan, she kept eating in a small show of defiance. Then she swallowed and said, "I haven't scheduled it yet."

Her father frowned. "I have it on good authority that you spoke to him today. On the boardwalk."

Spies? Her father had stooped to a new low. "I wasn't talking to Will. That was James."

Oh, duh. Her brand new security-guards-slash-babysitters had spilled the beans. Too bad they were the wrong beans.

Rafael's brows snapped together. "I cannot make myself more clear. Will Rowling is the man you should be pursuing."

Bella abandoned her spoon and plunked her elbows on the table to lean forward, so her father didn't miss her game face. "What if I like James better?"

Never mind that James had washed his hands of her. Regardless, it was the principle of the thing. Her father liked to try and run her life but failed to recall that Bella's typical response was to tell him to go to hell.

"James Rowling is bad news wrapped with trouble," Rafael shot back with a scowl. "He is not good enough for my daughter."

It seemed as if James had quoted this exact conversation to her yesterday on the beach. What was he, psychic? James's comment about the photographs that had gotten him into trouble crossed her mind and she realized there must be more to the story. She actually knew very little about the man other than the way he made her feel when he looked at her.

She eyed her father. What if Rafael had *told* James to brush her off? Would James have listened? She wouldn't put it past her father to interfere and now she wished she'd chased James down so she could ask. Shoot. She'd have to arrange another accidental meeting in order to find out.

"Maybe I'd like to make that decision on my own."

"Perhaps you need a few more facts if you're determined to undo the work I've already done on your behalf." Her father rubbed his graying temple. "Will Rowling is the next CEO of Rowling Energy, and he will be of paramount importance to your brother's relationship with the entire European oil market. How do you suppose the Montoros will lead a country rich with oil if we do not have the appropriate alliances in place?"

"Gabriel's smart. He'll figure it out," she said, but it came out sounding a little sullen. As smart and capable as Gabriel may be, he'd never been king before and besides, Alma hadn't had a king in a long time, so her brother would be a bit of a trailblazer.

She owed it to Gabriel to give him a leg up.

"Have you given any thought to Will Rowling's feelings, Isabella? You haven't reached out to him in the three days since you've arrived. You could not have insulted him more if you tried."

No, she hadn't thought of that. She swore. Her father had a very small point. Miniscule. But a point nonetheless. How would she feel if Will had come to Miami to meet her and then didn't call her, choosing instead to flirt outrageously with her best friend, Nicole, for example?

She'd hunt Will down and tell him to his face what a dog he was. So why should she get a pass to do whatever pleased her? It didn't matter if her father had scared off James—this was about doing what she said she'd do.

"I'll meet Will. Tomorrow, if he's free," Bella promised and turned her attention to eating. The faster the gazpacho disappeared, the faster she could as well.

It didn't go down as well this time. Righteousness wasn't as fun as it looked in the brochure.

* * *

Will Rowling took Bella's call immediately, cleared his schedule for the next morning and agreed to take her on a tour of Alma. He'd been very pleasant on the phone, though his British accent sounded a bit too much like James's for her liking.

When Will picked her up at 10:30 a.m. on the dot, she flung the door open and actually had a bad Captain Obvious moment when she realized Will *looked* like James, too. *Duh.* As common as fraternal twins were among the moneyed set of Miami, she'd never actually met a set of identical twins.

She studied him for a long second, taking in the remarkable resemblance, until he cleared his throat and she found a dose of manners somewhere in her consciousness. "I'm so sorry! Hello. You must be Will."

"I don't know if I must be, but I am Will," he agreed.

Was that a joke? Trying not to be too obtrusive, she evaluated his expression but it was blank. With James, she never had to wonder. "I'm Bella, by the way."

"I assumed so. I have your picture."

Of course he did. And this was her house. Wasn't this fun? "Are you ready to go?"

"Yes, if you are." With a smile that didn't reach his eyes, he held out a hand toward his car, and waited until she left the house to follow her so he could help her into the passenger seat.

Will climbed into the driver's seat and buckled his seat belt carefully before starting the car, which guilted Bella into fastening hers as well. Seat belts. In an itty-bitty place like Alma, where nothing happened.

She sighed and pasted on a bright smile. "Safety first."

Usually she trotted that line out during a condom discussion. She almost cracked a joke along those lines, but something told her Will might not appreciate the parallel. Sinking down in her seat, she scouted for a topic of discussion. They were supposed to be seeing how they meshed, right?

Will must have had a similar thought process because he spoke first. "Thanks for arranging this, Bella. I'm chuffed to show you around Alma, but I'd like to know what you might be interested in seeing. Anything jump out at you? I'm at your command."

Did he mean that in the double-entendre way? A provocative rejoinder sprang to her lips that she'd have let fly if she'd been in the car with James. Should she flirt with Will, the way she normally did on a date, or would that just lead to him taking her up on it, when she wasn't even sure she wanted him to? Maybe she should just be herself, but what if Will hated her immediately? Would her father lay another guilt trip on her?

All of this second-guessing was making her nuts. She wasn't with James, and *everyone*—including James—wanted her to make nice with the proper Rowling. Yeah, she'd looked up James last night, finding far more information about him than she'd expected, and little of it would fit the definition of the word *proper*.

No one, not even James, had thought it relevant to mention the man was a professional soccer—*football* in Europe, apparently—player. Since he appeared to have quite a bit of fame, maybe he'd assumed she already knew. Regardless, bad press followed James around like it did her. No wonder her father had nearly had a heart attack when she mentioned James's name. He was the very opposite of the proper brother.

Proper pretty much covered Will's personality. Five minutes in, and judging by the stiff set of Will's shoulders, he wasn't as much of a fun time as his brother. Hopefully, she'd judged wrong and would soon discover otherwise.

"Thanks," she responded. "I've only seen the coast and a bit of Del Sol. Why don't you pick, since this is your home?"

"No problem." He shot her a small but pained smile, cluing her in that this whole set up might be as difficult for him as it was for her.

She should give him a break. "So, Will. How long have you lived in Alma?"

An innocuous enough subject, hopefully, and given the brothers' accents, it was a safe bet they hadn't been born here.

"Since I was seven. My father moved us here from England."

"Oh, that must have been quite an adventure."

She'd lived in Miami her whole life and living someplace new did have appeal for that reason alone. If only this arranged marriage business hadn't soured the experience of coming to Alma, she'd be having a blast. And that was why she still didn't think of it as her home... She still reserved the right to go back to Miami and play aunt instead of princess if the royal pressure grew too great.

Though with Tía Isabella's arrival in Alma, going home held much less appeal.

Will's face remained expressionless, but he tapped his pinky on the steering wheel in a staccato rhythm as he drove north out of Playa Del Onda along the coastal road that circled the main island.

"The move was difficult," he said shortly and paused so long, she wasn't sure he planned to continue. But then he said, "My mother had just died."

"I'm sorry," Bella murmured. "That *would* be difficult on young boys."

All at once, she realized this was James's history as well as Will's. And now she was absurdly interested in learning more. The gorgeous deep blues of the bay unfurled as far as the eye could see on her right but she ignored the spectacular view in favor of watching Will.

"Thanks." He glanced in the rearview mirror and double-checked the side mirrors before changing lanes. Will Rowling might very well be the most careful driver she'd ever met. "Look, let's just get all of it out on the table, shall we?"

"Depends on what you mean by *all* and *table*," she countered, a little puzzled by his abrupt change of subject.

Was this the part of the date where he expected her to air all her dirty laundry? She'd never had a long-term relationship, never wanted one, never thought about what went into establishing a foundation for one. Maybe they were supposed to spill deep, dark secrets right off the bat. She was *so* not on board with that.

"About the arranged marriage," he clarified. "We should clear the air."

"I'm not a lesbian looking for a fake husband and I don't have a crazy uncle chained up in the closet, if that's what you're fishing for."

He flashed a brief smile, the most genuine one yet, giving her a glimpse of what he might be like if he loosened up a little. "I wasn't fishing. I meant, I wanted to tell you that marriage wasn't my idea. I'm not after your title or your fortune."

"Oh. Then what are you after?"

The smile vanished as his expression smoothed out into the careful nothingness he'd worn since the first moment. "Aligning myself with the Montoros through marriage is advantageous for Rowling Energy. It would be fitting if we suited each other. That's the only reason I agreed to meet you."

Ouch. That was kind of painful. Was she actually disappointed his motives for this pseudo-date nearly matched hers word for word? Well, not really, but no woman liked to find out a man was only interested in her connections. At least he'd admitted it up front.

All on the table, indeed.

"Yeah. I get that. My father pretty much insisted that I get on a plane and fall in love. Not necessarily in that order." Her lips twisted into a grimace automatically.

"Since we're on the subject, would you really go through with it?"

"Marriage, you mean?" A shadow darkened his gaze though his eyes never left the road. "Rowling Energy is on the brink of gaining a starring role on the world's oil stage. Our alliance makes very good sense. My assumption is that you thought so as well."

"Wow." Bella blinked. Had he memorized that careful statement in one sitting or had he repeated it to himself in the shower for the past week so he could get it out without stumbling? "I bet you say that to all the girls."

If she'd ever had any shred of doubt about her ability to tolerate an arranged marriage, it had just been crushed under the heel of Will's ambition. There was no way she'd marry *anyone* unless the words *deliriously happy*, *scorching passion* and *eternal love* entered into the conversation about a hundred times first, and even then, vows would be far, far in the future.

His eyebrows rose slightly. "Meaning?"

She rolled her eyes. "I just hadn't pegged you for a romantic. That's all."

"It wasn't intended to be romantic," he explained, and she had the distinct impression he really thought she'd needed the clarification.

As nightmare dates went, this one hit the scale at about eleven point five. So much for being herself. *Check, please.*

"Will, I have a confession to make. Instead of seeing the sights, I'd really like a ride to Del Sol to visit my great-aunt Isabella." She blazed ahead before he could say no. "She's very sick and I'd like to see her. The timing is terrible, I realize, but my mind is just not where it should be for this outing."

Hitching a ride hadn't been her intent when she'd called him, but a savvy woman knew when to cut her losses and she might offend Will if she screamed bloody murder in his ear…which she might very well do if forced to spend five more minutes in his company.

This was not going to work out. Period. The last thing she wanted was to be stuck in a horrible marriage to a cold-hearted man, as her mother had been. If it didn't make you happy, why do it? Why do *anything* that didn't have fun written all over it?

"No problem." Will checked forty-seven points of the car's position and did a U-turn to head to the interior of the island. "I sensed that you were distracted. Glad to know the reason why."

Yet another reason they would never work—obviously Will read her about as well as she could read Spanish. She'd been the opposite of distracted, but only because she'd been hoping for a scrap of information about James, God knew why.

"Yeah, I'm a mess. My aunt has Parkinson's and her prognosis is…not good." Bella left it at that and choked back the wave of emotion for a situation she couldn't change and hated with all her heart.

Good thing Will wasn't her type. Now she had the morning free to visit Tía Isabella and she didn't even have to feel guilty about it because she'd gone out with Will, as ordered.

"I'm sorry," Will said earnestly. "You should definitely visit her. We can go out another time when you're feeling more in the mood for company and conversation."

Oh, so *she* was the problem in this equation? She scowled but didn't comment because then she might say something she couldn't take back about the stick up Will's butt. "Sure. That would be nice."

"Well, this may be an ill-timed invitation, then, but Rowling Energy is throwing a party tonight at my father's house for some of our elite associates. Would you care to attend as my date? Might be less pressure and more fun than being one-on-one like this, trapped in a small car."

How…reasonable. Oh, sure it was strictly an opportunity for Will to trot her out around his snobby business partners who only cared about whom he knew. She wasn't stupid. But a party was right up her ally and the magic word *fun* only sweetened the pot. With enough champagne, she might even forget the whole setup reeked of royal responsibility and actually have a good time. Less pressure, as advertised.

Maybe she'd misjudged Will Rowling. "I have the perfect dress."

"It's settled, then."

In no time and with only one internet map miscalculation, they found Tía Isabella's narrow cobblestone street in the heart of Del Sol. Like a true gentleman, Will helped Bella from the car at the door of her great aunt's rental house, and had a word with Tía Isabella's housekeeper to ensure Bella would have a return ride home. The housekeeper promised to have a car sent from Playa Del Onda, so Will took his leave.

All in all, Will seemed like a nice, upstanding guy. He was certainly handsome enough and had gorgeous aquacolored eyes. Too bad she couldn't get the sexier, more exciting version she'd tripped over at the beach off her mind.

"Patrick James Rowling!"

James groaned and thought about ducking out the door of the sunroom and escaping Casa Rowling through the back gate. When his father three-named him, the outcome was never fun nor in his favor.

Actually, any time his father spoke to him it was unpleasant. Even being in the same room with Patrick Rowling reminded James that his mother was dead and it was his father's fault. Time healed all wounds—except the ones that never should have happened in the first place. If his father hadn't yelled at his mum, she wouldn't have left in tears that night back in Guildford. Then his mum's single-car accident would never have happened. He and

Will wouldn't have become motherless seven-year-old boys. The fractured Rowling family wouldn't have subsequently moved to Alma, where James didn't know anyone but Will, who was too shell-shocked to do anything other than mumble for nearly a year.

But all of that had happened and James would never forgive *or* forget.

As a result, James and Patrick gave each other a wide berth by mutual unspoken agreement, but it was harder to do when under the same roof. James should really get his own place, but he still wasn't sure if he planned to stay in Alma, so here he was.

Patrick Rowling, the man who'd named his first born after himself in a moment of pure narcissism, stormed into the sunroom and shoved a newspaper at James's chest with a great deal more force than necessary. "Explain this."

"This is commonly known as a newspaper." James drew out the syllables, ladening them with as much sarcasm as possible. "Many civilized nations employ this archaic method of communicating information and events to subscribers. Shall I delve into the finer points of journalism, or are we square on the purpose of this news vehicle?"

His father's face had grown a deeper, more satisfying shade of purple the longer James baited him. A thing of beauty. James moved his half-empty teacup out of the line of fire, in case of imminent explosion. It was Darjeeling and brewed perfectly.

"You can dispense with the smartass attitude. I've had more than enough of it from you to last a lifetime."

What he really meant was that he'd had enough of James doing the opposite of what Patrick commanded. But if James toed the line, how could he make his father pay for his sins? Of course, his father could never truly pay in a lifetime. The sad part was that James might have settled for an apology from his father for all the horrible things he'd caused. Or at least a confession. Instead, his father heaped praises on Will the Perfect Son and generally pretended James didn't exist.

Until James managed to get his attention by doing something beyond the pale. Like whatever had gotten the elder Rowling's dander up this time.

His father poked the paper again. "There's a rather risqué photo of you on the front page. Normally, I would brush it off as further proof you care nothing for propriety and only your own self-destruction. But as it's a photo of you with your brother's fiancée, I find it impossible to ignore."

"What?" His brother had a *fiancée*? "What are you talking about?"

James shoved his father's hand away and shifted the paper so he could see the front page. There it was, in full color. He whistled. What a gorgeous shot of Bella in his arms. Her hair all mussed and legs tangled in his. He might have to cut it out and frame it.

Wait... *Bella* was Will's fiancée? This was news to James. Last he'd heard, Bella planned to see how things went before committing to marriage. Had Will even *met* Bella yet?

"Your timing is impeccable, as always. Now that we're all caught up, please explain how you managed to create a scandal so quickly." Dear old Dad crossed his arms over the paunch he liked to pretend gave him a stately demeanor, but in reality, only made him look dumpy.

Obviously they were nowhere near caught up.

"Maybe that's Will—did you ever think of that?" James challenged mildly and went back to sipping his tea because he had a feeling he'd need the fortification.

"Your brother is with the Montoro princess as we speak and it's their first meeting."

Montoro princess. Really? James rolled his eyes. His father couldn't be more pretentious if he tried. "If they hadn't even met until today, how are they already engaged?"

Waving his hand with a snort, Patrick gave him a withering look. "Merely a formality. They will be engaged, mark my words. So as far as you're concerned, she's your brother's fiancée. Will is quite determined to woo her and I've never seen him fail at anything he set his mind to."

Despite what should be good news—his father had deliberately thrown the word *fiancée* in James's face even though it wasn't true—James's gut twisted at the thought of Will and Bella together. Why, he couldn't explain, when he'd been the one to suggest Bella should ring Will. Obviously, she'd taken his advice and rather quickly, too. He'd just run into her in town yesterday.

"Smashing. I hope they're having a fantastic time and fall madly in love so they can give you lots of royal babies, since that's the most important accomplishment a Rowling could hope to achieve." The sentiment had started out sincerely but halfway through, disappointment had tilted his mood. James lived his life with few regrets but stepping aside so Will had a fair shot with Bella ranked as a decision he'd questioned more than once.

"Don't change the subject. If you deliberately staged that picture with the princess to ruin your brother's chances, the consequences will be dire," his father warned.

James couldn't quite bite back the laugh that burst out. "Oh, please, no. Perhaps you'll disown me?"

What else could his father possibly do to him besides constantly express his displeasure in everything James did? Being signed with Real Madrid hadn't rated a mention. Being named captain of the Alma World Cup team wasn't worthy enough of a feat to get a comment.

Oh, but miss a goal—that had earned James an earful.

Patrick leaned forward, shoving his nose into James's space and into his business all at the same time. "If you don't stay away from the Montoro princess, I will personally ensure you never play football again."

James scoffed. "You're off your trolley. You have no power in my world."

And neither did James, not now. It pricked at his temper that his father would choose that method to strike at him. Patrick clearly failed to comprehend his son's life crisis if he didn't already know that James had managed to thoroughly subvert his own career with no help from anyone.

The threat gave him a perverse desire to prove he could come back from the twin failures of a missed goal and a dropped contract. He needed to play, if for no other reason than to show everyone James Rowling couldn't be kept down.

"Perhaps. Do you want to wager on that?"

James waved nonchalantly with one hand and clenched the other into a tight fist. What colossal nerve. A supreme act of will kept the fist in his lap, though letting it fly against the nearby wall might have ended the conversation quite effectively.

"Seems like pretty good odds to me, so don't be surprised if I roll the dice with Bella." He waggled his brows. "I think that picture is enough of an indicator that she fancies me, don't you think?"

Which might have been true when the picture was snapped, but probably wasn't now that he'd stepped aside. Will would be his charming self and Bella would realize that she could have the best of both worlds—the "right" Rowling and her father's blessing. Probably better for everyone, all the way around.

Deep down, James didn't believe that in the slightest. He and Bella had a spark between them, which wouldn't vanish with a hundred warnings from the old geezer.

"The monarchy is in its fledgling stages." Patrick hesitated for the first time since barging into the sunroom and James got the impression he was choosing his words carefully. "Rowling Energy has a unique opportunity to solidify our allegiance and favor through the tie of marriage. There is only one Montoro princess."

"And only one heir to the company," James said sourly. "I get it. Will's the only one good enough for her."

His father sighed. The weariness that carved lines into his face around his mouth had aged him quickly and added a vulnerability to his expression that James hadn't been prepared for. Patrick had never been anything other than formidable for as long as James could remember.

"I would welcome you at Rowling Energy if you expressed but a smidgen of determination and interest." Then his father hardened back into the corporate stooge he'd become since entering into the high stakes oil market. Dad had too many zeroes in his bank account balance to truly be in touch with his humanity. "Will has done both, with remarkable success. If you would think of someone other than yourself, you'd realize that Will has much to gain from this alliance. I will not be at the helm of Rowling forever. Will needs every advantage."

Guilt. The best weapon. And it might have worked if James truly believed all that drivel. Marrying into the royal family was about his father's ambition, not Will's.

"Maybe we should let Bella sort it on her own, eh?" James suggested mildly. He didn't mind losing to Will, as long as the contest was fair.

"There's nothing to sort," his father thundered, growing purple again. "Stay away from her. Period. No more risqué pictures. No more contact. Do not ruin this for your brother."

To put the cap on his mandate, Patrick Rowling stormed from the sun-room in much the same manner as he entered it. Except now Bella Montoro had been transformed into the ripest forbidden fruit.

James had never met a scandal he didn't want to dive headlong into, especially when it involved a gorgeous woman who clearly had the hots for him. Pissing his father off at the same time James introduced himself to the pleasures of Princess Bella was just a sweet bonus.

Four

Bella spent two wonderful hours catching up with her great aunt Isabella, but the sickly woman grew tired so easily. Coupled with the fact that Isabella's advanced Parkinson's disease meant she was bedridden, it was difficult for Bella to witness her once-vibrant aunt in this condition. Regardless, she kept a bright smile pasted on throughout their visit.

But even Bella could see it was time for her to leave lest she overtire Isabella.

Before she asked her aunt's nurse to call a cab, Bella took Isabella's hand and brought it to her cheek. "I'm glad you decided to come to Alma."

"This is where I choose to die," Isabella said simply with a half smile, the only facial expression she could still muster. "I will see Gabriel become king and my life will be complete."

"I wish you wouldn't say things like that."

It was depressing and wretched to think of the world spinning on without Isabella, whom Bella loved unconditionally and vice versa. Her throat burned with grief and unreconciled anger over a circumstance she couldn't change.

Geez, she'd been less upset when her mother had left. That had at least made sense. Parkinson's disease did not.

"It is but truth. All of us must make our lives what we can in the time allotted to us." Isabella paused, her voice catching. "Tell me. Have you visited the farmhouse yet?"

"What farmhouse?" Had her father mentioned something about a farmhouse and she'd been too busy ignoring him to remember? Shoot. She'd have done anything Isabella asked, even if the request came via her father.

"Oh, dear." Her aunt closed her eyes for a moment. "No, I don't believe I imagined it. It's white. In the country. Aldeia Dormer. Very important. My mother told me and Rafael of it. My brother is gone, God rest his soul, so I'm telling you. You must find it and…"

Trailing off with a blank expression, Isabella sat silent for a moment, her hand shaking uncontrollably inside Bella's as it often had even before her aunt's disease had progressed to include forgetfulness and the inability to walk.

"I'll find the farmhouse," Bella promised. "What should I do when I find it?"

"The countryside is lovely in the spring," her aunt said with bright cheer. "You take your young man with you and enjoy the ride."

"Yes, ma'am." Bella smiled. Wouldn't it be nice to actually have a "young man" in the sweet, old-fashioned sense that Isabella had meant? Bella had only mentioned Will because her father had apparently told Isabella all about the stupid arranged marriage. It was the first thing her aunt had asked after.

"Wear a red dress to the party tonight and take photographs." Isabella closed her eyes and just when Bella thought she'd fallen asleep, she murmured, "Remember we all have a responsibility to our blood. And to Alma. I wish Rafael could be here to see his grandson take the throne."

"Red dress it is," Bella said, skipping over the royal responsibility part because she'd had enough of that for a lifetime.

Wasn't it enough that she was going to the party as Will's date when she'd rather be meeting James there? And if James happened to show, would it be so much of a crime if she danced with him once or twice? She'd still be Will's date, just the way everyone wanted, but would also give herself the opportunity to find out if James had pawned her off on his brother because he didn't like her or because of some other reason.

Guilt cramped her stomach as her aunt remained silent. Yeah, so maybe Bella considered it a possible bonus that she might run into James at the party. Was that so bad?

"Isabella, I—" Bella bit her lip before she spilled all her angst and doubt over what her father had asked her to do by giving Will a chance. Her aunt was tired and didn't need to be burdened with Bella's problems.

"The farmhouse. It's part of the Montoro legacy, passed down from the original Rafael Montoro I, to his son Rafael II. And then to his son Rafael III. Remember the farmhouse, child," her aunt wheezed out in the pause.

"I will." Before she could change her mind again, Bella went for broke. "But I might take a different young man with me than the one my father wants me to marry. Would that be a bad thing?"

"You must make your own choices," her aunt advised softly. "But beware. All choices have consequences. Be sure you are prepared to face them."

Isabella's shaking hand went slack as she slipped off into sleep for real this time. Bella took her leave reluctantly and slid into the waiting car her father had sent for her, wishing her aunt wasn't so sick that they could only have half of a conversation.

What had Isabella meant by her warning? During the hour-long ride back to Playa Del Onda, Bella grappled with it. Unfortunately, she had a sinking feeling she knew precisely what her aunt had been attempting to tell her. Being born during a hurricane hadn't infused Bella with a curse that meant she'd always leave broken hearts in her wake. It was her own decisions that had consequences, and if she wanted to be a better person than she'd been in Miami, she had to make different, more conscious choices.

Hurricane Bella couldn't cut a swath through Alma, leaving broken pieces of her brother's reign in her wake. Or broken pieces of her father's agreement with Will's father. Mentioning all of Bella's ancestors hadn't been an accident—Isabella wanted her to remember her roots.

Either she had try for real with Will and then tell him firmly it wasn't going to work, or she had to skip the party. It wasn't fair to anyone to go with the intention of running into James for any reason.

By the time the party rolled around, Bella was second-guessing the red dress. She'd never worn it before but distinctly remembered loving it when she'd tried it on at the boutique in Bal Harbour. Now that she had it on... the plunging neckline and high slit in the skirt revealed a shocking amount of flesh. But she'd promised Isabella she'd wear red, and it was too late to find another dress.

And honestly, she looked divine in it, so... Sexy red dress got the thumbs up. If she and Will were going to get along, he'd have to accept that she liked to feel beautiful in what she wore. This dress filled the bill. And then some. If a neckline that plunged all the way to the dress's waistband caused a problem with Rowling's business associates, better she and Will both find out now they weren't a good match.

The chauffeur helped her into the back of the Montoro car. Thankfully, Will hadn't offered to pick her up so she had an easy escape if need be. *Please God, don't let me need an escape.*

Within ten minutes, the car had joined the line of Bentleys, Jaguars and limousines inching their way to the front steps of the Rowling mansion. Like the Montoros' house, the Rowlings' Playa Del Onda residence overlooked the bay. She smiled at the lovely sight of the darkened water dotted with lighted boats.

When Bella entered the double front doors, Will approached her immediately, as if he'd been waiting for her. His pleasant but slightly blank expression from earlier was still firmly in place and she bit back a groan. How long were they going to act like polite strangers?

Jaw set firmly, Will never glanced below her shoulders. Which sort of defeated the purpose of such a racy dress. What was the point of showing half her torso if a man wasn't even going to look at it?

"Bella, so nice to see you again," Will murmured and handed her a champagne flute. "That dress is stunning."

Okay, he'd just earned back all the points that he'd lost. "Thanks. Nice to see you, too."

His tuxedo, clearly custom-cut and very European, gave him a sophisticated look that set him slightly apart from the other male guests, most of whom were older and more portly. Will was easy on the eyes and commanded himself with confidence. She could do worse.

Will cleared his throat. "Did you have a nice afternoon?"

"Yes. You?"

"Dandy."

She sipped her champagne as the conversation ground to a halt. Painfully. Gah, normally she thrived on conversation and loved exchanging observations, jokes, witty repartee. Something.

The hushed crowd murmured around them and the tinkle of chamber music floated between the snippets of dialogue, some in English, some in Spanish. Or Portuguese.

Bella still couldn't tell the difference between the two despite hearing Spanish spoken by Miami residents of Cuban descent for most of her life.

She spotted her cousin Juan Carlos Salazar across the room and nearly groaned. While they'd grown up together after his parents died, he'd always been too serious. Why wasn't he in Del Sol managing something?

Of course, he looked up at that moment and their gazes met. He wove through the crowd to clasp Will's hand and murmur his appreciation for the party to his hosts. Juan Carlos was the kind of guy who always did the right thing and at the same time, made everyone else look as if they were doing the wrong thing. It was a skill.

"Bella, are you enjoying the party?" he asked politely.

"Very much," she lied, just as politely because she had skills, too, just not any that Juan Carlos would appreciate. "I saw Tía Isabella. I'm so glad she decided to come to Alma."

"I am as well. Though she probably shouldn't be traveling." Juan Carlos frowned over his grandmother's stubbornness, which Bella had always thought was one of her best traits. "Uncle Rafael tried to talk her out of it but she insisted."

The Montoros all had a stubborn streak but Bella's father took the cake. Time for a new subject. "How are things in the finance business?"

"Very well, thank you." He shot Will a cryptic glance. "Better now that you're in Alma working toward important alliances."

She kept her eyes from rolling. Barely. "Yes, let's hear it for alliances."

Juan Carlos and Will launched into a conversation with too many five-syllable words for normal humans to understand, so Bella amused herself by scrutinizing Will as he talked, hoping to gather more clues about his real personality.

As he spoke to Juan Carlos, his attention wandered, and Bella watched him watch a diminutive dark-haired woman in serviceable gray exit by a side door well away from the partygoers. An unfamiliar snap in Will's gaze had her wondering who the woman was. Or rather, who she was to Will. The woman's dress clearly marked her as the help.

Will didn't even seem to notice when Juan Carlos excused himself.

"Do you need to attend to a problem with the servants?" Bella inquired politely.

She'd gone to enough of her parents' parties to know that a good host kept one eye on the buffet and the other on the bar. Which was why she liked attending parties, not throwing them.

"No. No problem," Will said grimly and forced his gaze back to Bella's face. But his mind was clearly elsewhere.

Which told her quite a bit more about the situation than Will probably intended. Perhaps the dark-haired woman represented at least a partial answer for why Will seemed both pained by Bella's presence and alternatively agreeable to a marriage of convenience.

Bella had come to the party as requested by God and everyone and she deserved a chance with Will. He owed it to her, regardless of whether he had something going on with the diminutive maid.

"Look, Will—"

"Let's dance." He grabbed her hand and led her to the dance floor without waiting for an answer, off-loading their champagne glasses onto a waiter's tray as they passed by.

Okay, then. Dancing happened to be one of her favorite things about parties, along with dressing up and laughing in a private corner with someone she planned to let strip her naked afterward.

For some reason, the thought of getting naked with Will made her skin crawl. Two out of three wasn't bad, though, was it?

The quartet seated in the corner had switched from chamber music to a slightly less boring bossa nova–inspired piece. Not great, but she had half a chance of finding a groove at least.

Was this how the people of Alma partied? Or had the glitzy Miami social scene spoiled her? Surely not. Alma was one of the wealthiest countries in the European Union. What was she missing?

Halfway into the song, Will had yet to say a word and his impersonal hand at her waist might as well have belonged to an eighty-year-old grandfather. This might go down in history as the first time a man under thirty had danced with her and not used it as an excuse to pull her into his strong embrace. It was as if Will had actually wanted to *dance* or something.

None of this screamed, "I'm into you."

Perhaps the problem with this party lay with the host, not the country. Will might need a little encouragement to loosen up.

When the interminably long dance finally ended, Bella smiled and fanned herself as if she'd grown overheated. "My, it's a little warm in here."

Will nodded. "I'll get you another glass of champagne."

Before he could disappear, she stopped him with a hand on his arm, deliberately leaning into it to make the point. "That's okay. Let's go out on the terrace and talk."

The whole point was to get to know each other. The car trip hadn't worked. Dancing hadn't worked. They needed to try something else.

"Maybe in a few minutes," Will said with a glance around the room at large. "After I've played the proper host."

Disappointment pulled at her mouth but she refused to let a frown ruin her lipstick. "I hope you won't mind if I escape the heat for a bit by myself."

For a moment, she wondered if he'd really let her go.

He'd invited her, after all, and hadn't introduced her to one person yet. This was supposed to be a date, wasn't it?

"Certainly." Will inclined his head toward the double glass doors off the great room. "I'll find you later."

Fuming, Bella wound through the guests to the terrace—by herself!—and wondered when she'd lost her edge. Clearly a secluded terrace with a blonde American in half a dress didn't appeal to Will Rowling. What did—dark-haired housekeepers?

Great, she thought sourly. Bella had come to the party with the genuine intent of seeing where things might go with Will, because she said she would. Because she'd bought into the hoopla of being a princess, which came with responsibilities she'd never asked for nor wanted any part of.

But she'd done it, only to be hit over the head with the brutal truth yet again. The man her father wanted her to marry had less than zero interest in her as a person. She wouldn't be surprised to learn Will was perfectly okay with a hard-core marriage of convenience, complete with separate bedrooms and a paramour on the side.

Sounded an awful lot like her parents' marriage, and *that* she wanted no part of.

She shuddered, despondent all at once. Was it asking too much for someone to care what she would actually have to sacrifice with this mess her father had created?

The night was breathtaking, studded with stars and a crescent moon. Still, half the stone terrace lay in shadow, which went perfectly with her mood. Leaning on the railing, she glanced down into the crash of ocean against the cliff below.

"Thinking of jumping?"

The male voice emanating from behind her skittered down her spine, washing her in a myriad of emotions as her heart rolled and her pulse quickened. But she didn't turn to face him because she was afraid if she actually glimpsed

James for even a fraction of a second, all of her steely re-solve to work things out with his brother would melt like gelato in the sun. And the leftover hot sticky mess would be difficult to clean up indeed.

"Would you stop me?" she murmured.

"No. I'd hold your hand all the way down, though."

Her eyelids fluttered closed. How had he managed to make that sound so daringly romantic?

The atmosphere shifted as he moved closer. She could feel him behind her, hear the intake of his breath. A sense of anticipation grew in the silence, peppering her skin with goose pimples and awareness.

Before it grew too intense, she blurted out, "I called Will."

James wasn't for her. She needed to keep reminding herself that.

"I gathered that." He sounded amused and reckless si-multaneously. "I plan to personally drive him to the eye doctor tomorrow."

"Oh? Is he having problems with his eyes?"

"Obviously. Only a blind man would let you out of his sight, especially if he knew you planned to be alone on a moonlit terrace. Any plonker could be out here, waiting to ravish you."

She'd been so wrong. Other than a similar accent, James's voice was nothing like Will's. Will had yet to lose the ice while James breathed pure fire when he spoke.

"Good thing his moral, upstanding brother is the only one out here. He wouldn't dare lay a finger on me."

Maybe James needed a reminder that Bella and Will were supposed to get married, too. After all James had been the one to cool things off between the two of them, which had absolutely been the right thing to do.

"Yeah? While Will's having his eyes examined, maybe I'll get my IQ checked, then," James said silkily.

"Feeling a little brainless this evening?"

"I definitely feel like my brain has turned to mush. I think it's that dress. Your bare back framed by that little bit of fabric…it makes me imagine all sorts of things that probably aren't very smart." The frank appreciation in his voice floated through the still night, wrapping around her deliciously. "Let me see the front."

"No." Feeling exposed all at once, she crossed her arms. "I didn't wear this dress for you."

"Shame. I'm the only one here who fully appreciates what's underneath it."

In a flash, her core heated with the memory of being in James's arms on the beach, his hard body flush with hers.

"You shouldn't speak to me like that," she said primly, and nearly gasped as he drew achingly close to her back. She could sense his heat and it called to her.

"Because you don't like it?" he murmured, his mouth not two inches from her ear in a deliberate tease that shot sensation down the back of her throat.

Her breath caught and she gripped the railing lest her weak knees give out. "Because I do."

He laughed and it spiked through her with fingers of warmth.

"That's right," he said smoothly, as if recalling something critically important. "You're weak and liable to give in to temptation. Everything I've always wanted in a woman."

"That's so funny. I'd swear you brushed me off at our last meeting," she couldn't help but reply. It still stung, despite all the reasons why she suspected he'd done so.

"I did," he admitted in an unprecedented moment of honesty. Most men she'd ever met would have tried to pass it off, as if she'd been mistaken. "You know why."

"Because you're not interested."

The colorful curse he muttered made her smile for some reason. "You need *your* IQ checked if you believe that."

"Because my father scared you off?"

"Not even close."

"Because I'm supposed to be with Will," she said definitively and wished it hadn't come out sounding so bitter.

"Yes." James paused as if to let that sink in. "Trust me. It was not easy. But he's my brother."

"So you're okay with it if I marry Will?"

She imagined Christmas. That would be fun, to sit next to her boring husband who was screwing another woman on the side while the man she'd been dreaming about sat across the room. As Mr. Rowling carved the turkey, she could bask in the warm knowledge that she'd furthered a bunch of male ambition with her sacrifice to the royal cause.

"Is that what you want?" he asked quietly, his voice floating out on the still night air.

The question startled her. She had a choice. Of course she did. And now she needed to make it, once and for all.

The night seemed to hold its breath as it waited for her to speak. This was it, the moment of truth. She could end this dangerous attraction to the wrong brother forever by simply saying yes. James would walk away.

Something shifted inside, warring with all the sermons on responsibility and family obligations. And she couldn't stand it any longer.

She didn't want Will.

Whirling, she faced James, greedily drinking him, cataloguing the subtle differences in his features. He and Will weren't identical, not to her. The variances were in the way James looked at her, the way her body reacted. The heat in this man's gaze couldn't be mistaken. He was all James and 100 percent the object of her desire.

She let her gaze travel over his gorgeous body, clad in a tuxedo that fit like an extension of his skin, fluid and beautiful. And she wanted nothing more than to see the secrets it hid so carefully beneath the fabric.

He raked her with a once-over in kind that quickened her

core with delicious tightness. *That* was how a man should look at you in such a dress. As if he'd been presented with every last fantasy in one package.

"The back was good," he rasped, his voice clogged with undisguised desire. "But the front…"

Delighted that she'd complied with Isabella's fortuitous request to wear red, she smiled. "I do like a man at a loss for words."

Moonlight played over his features and glinted off the obscenely expensive watch on his wrist as he swept up her hand and drew her closer. So close, she could almost hear his heart beating.

"Actions speak louder and all that." His arm slid around her waist, pulling her to within a hairsbreadth of his body and she ached for him to close the distance. "Plus, I didn't want to miss your answer."

"Answer to what?"

He lowered his head to murmur in her ear, "What it is that you want."

If she wanted Will, Bella had about two seconds to say so, or James would be presenting the woman in his arms with some hot and heavy temptation. He preferred to get on the same page before that happened because he had a bad feeling *he* might be the weak one on this terrace.

With so much forbidden fruit decked out in a mouthwatering dress that screamed sin and sex, he'd rather not put his ability to resist Bella to the test. But he would resist if she said no, regardless of whether he'd been baiting her in hopes of getting her to break first. Because then he'd be in the clear if she came on to him, right?

The sharp intake of her breath and a sensuous lift of her lips gave him all the nonverbal communication he needed. Then she put the icing on it with a succinct, "Will who?"

The gap between their bodies slowly vanished until their torsos brushed, but he couldn't have said if he closed it or she did. This was not what he'd planned when Bella had inadvertently joined him on the terrace, but it was certainly what he'd fantasized might happen if she'd given him the slightest encouragement.

With her lithe little body teasing his, her curves scarcely contained by that outrageous dress, he could hardly get his mind in gear long enough to form complete sentences. "You could have just said that from the outset."

"You could have said *call me instead of Will* on the boardwalk."

Not if he'd hoped to sleep at night he couldn't have. Of course, he'd done little of that anyway, tossing and turning as he imagined this gorgeous, vibrant woman with his brother.

He nodded in concession, hardly breathing for fear of alerting her to how very turned on he was. "It was my one noble gesture for the decade. Don't expect another one."

She laughed and he felt it vibrate against his rock-hard lower half, which did not improve matters down below. Dangerous and forbidden did it for him in the worst way and when both came in a package like Bella, he might as well surrender to the moment right now. They were both aware of where this was headed, weren't they?

"You know, you spend a lot of time blabbing about how wicked you are, but I've yet to see evidence of it." Her brow arched saucily, turning silvery in the moonlight. "What happened to my man of action?"

"You wanna play?" he growled and slid his hand to the small of her back, pushing her deep into the crevices of his body. "Here's round one of How Bad Can James Be?"

Tipping up her head, he captured her smart mouth with his lips, molding them shut while tasting her simultaneously. What started as a shut-up kiss instantly transformed, becoming slow and sensuous and exploratory as he delved into her sweetness. She met him stroke for stroke, angle for angle, silently begging him to take her deeper.

He *finally* had Bella in his arms. Exactly as he'd ached to have her since releasing her from their first embrace.

Still in the throes of an amazing kiss he never wanted to end, he pinned her against the stone railing, wedging their bodies tight and leaving his hands free to roam where they pleased.

And that creamy expanse of flesh from neck to waist had been calling his name for an eternity. Almost groaning with the pleasure of her mouth under his, he slid a palm north to let his fingertips familiarize themselves with her bare back. Heated, smooth flesh greeted his touch. Greedily, he caressed it all and she moaned throatily, flattening her back against his palm, pleading for more.

He gave it to her.

Nearly mindless with the scent of Bella filling his head, he held her closer in his arms, sliding a knee between her legs to rub at her sweet spot. Heavenly. He wanted to touch every part of her, to taste what he'd touched. To take them both to nirvana again and again as the blistering, forbidden attraction between them was allowed free reign once and for all.

Suddenly, she tore her mouth free and moved out of reach, breathing heavily. "That was...um—"

"Yeah." Earthshaking. Unprecedented. Hotter than Brazil in the summer. "Come back so I can do it again."

He reached for her and for a second, he thought she was going to do it. Her body swayed toward him and his mouth tingled in anticipation of locking on to those lips of hers again.

But then she shook her head, backing up another step. "I can't be with you like this. It's not fair to Will. We have to straighten everything out first."

Bloody hell. Will hadn't crossed his mind once while James kissed his brother's date. Any of dear Father's business cronies could have come upon them on the terrace and there were few people in Alma who confused the twins.

Everyone knew James had inherited Grandfather Rowling's priceless antique watch—much to Patrick's chagrin. It was the first thing people looked for when in need of a handy way to identify the brothers.

"Yes, of course you're right." Though his body ached to yank her back into his arms, he gave her a pained smile instead. "This isn't over."

"Oh, no." She shot him an indecipherable look. "Not by half. The next time you and I are together, I will be naked and screaming your name."

His eyelids flew shut and he groaned. "Why can't that happen tonight?"

"Because as far as the rest of the world is concerned, Will is the Rowling I'm supposed to be with. I've had too many scandals mess up my life to knowingly create a preventable one. That's why it must be perfectly clear to everyone that Will and I are not getting married before you and I get naked."

Grimly, he nodded, the photo of the two of them on the front page fresh in his mind. They should probably address that, too, at some point, but he'd topped out on issues he could reasonably deal with.

"You should go. And go fast before I change my mind." Or lose it. "I'm fresh out of nobility *and* the capacity to resist you."

She whirled and fled. He watched her beautiful back as she disappeared inside the house, and then went in search of a bottle of Jameson to get him through what promised to be a long night indeed.

Five

James cornered Will in his Rowling Energy office at 9:05 a.m. This was the earliest James could recall being awake, dressed and out of the house in quite some time. But this cat-and-mouse game had grown tiresome, and the man who shared his last name, his blood and once upon a time, had even shared a womb, had the power to end it.

"Will."

James didn't cross the threshold out of respect for the fact that he was on his brother's turf. Instead, he waited for him to glance up from his report. Will's expression remained composed, though James caught a flash of surprise in the depths of his gaze, which the Master of Calm quickly banked.

"Yes?"

And now they'd officially exchanged two words this week. Actually, James couldn't remember the last time they *had* talked. They'd never been close. Hell, they were rarely on the same continent, but that wasn't really the reason. The divide had started the night their mum died and grown exponentially over the years.

"We have to talk. Can I come in?"

"Since you're here already, I suppose." Will's long-suffering sigh said he deserved a medal for seeing James on such short notice.

James bit back the sarcasm strictly because he was the one with the mission, though his brother's condescension pricked at his temper. The brothers would never see eye to eye, though why James cared was beyond him.

They'd taken different paths in dealing with the single most defining year of their lives, Will choosing to compensate for the loss of everything familiar by becoming whatever their father said, as long as the remaining parent paid attention to him.

James compensated for his mother's death by lashing out at his father, refusing to forgive the ultimate crime—though James could never run far enough or get into enough trouble to drown out the sound of his own conscience. While he'd never forgive his father for driving his mum out into the rainy night, back in the deepest reaches of his soul, he blamed himself more.

Because he'd heard them arguing and hadn't done anything. What if he'd run out of his hiding place to grab on to his mum and beg her not to leave? She wouldn't have. He knew she wouldn't have. But she'd probably assumed both her boys were asleep. One of them had been.

James took a deep, not at all calming breath as he settled into one of the wingback chairs flanking Will's desk. "It's about Bella."

"Ms. Montoro? What about her?"

James rolled his eyes. "Well, I was going to ask how serious you are about her, but that pretty much told me."

"How serious I…" Will's gaze narrowed. "You've got the hots for her."

That didn't begin to describe what had happened on the terrace last night. Or every moment since the princess had blinked up at him with those big eyes after upending his world. "If you're determined to see this arranged marriage through, I won't stand in your way."

Steepling his hands, Will sat back in his chair, contemplating James carefully. "Really? That's a first."

"What's that supposed to mean?"

"When was the last time you considered anyone above yourself? Especially when a woman is involved."

James was halfway out of his seat before he checked himself. Fisting his hand in his lap as he sat back down, he forced a smile. "I won't apologize for looking out for myself. No one else does. But I will concede the point. This woman is different."

He nearly choked on the words he hadn't consciously planned to say. But it was true. Bella wasn't like anyone else he'd ever met.

Smirking, Will nodded once. "Because she's earmarked for me."

Is that what he thought this was about? That James had come to Will in a fit of jealousy?

"Earmarked? Is that how you talk about her? Bella's a person, not a pile of money."

The nerve. Will had spent too much time in budget meetings if he equated a flesh-and-blood woman with reserve funds.

"Yes. But surely you realize we're talking about an arranged marriage. It's a form of currency, dating back to the dawn of time. No one is under a different impression."

James had a sick sort of realization that what Will described was probably quite right. Two fathers had struck a deal, bargaining away their children's future with no thought to what could or should go into a marriage decision. Namely, the desires of the bride and groom in question.

If he didn't miss his guess, Will accepted that. Embraced it. Thought it was a brilliant idea.

If James had known this was the case, he'd have taken

Bella straight to his room last night and skipped the formality of giving his brother a heads-up that things had changed. "Bella has a different impression. She's not interested in being bought *or* sold."

Will eyed him thoughtfully. "Why hasn't she come to me herself?"

"Because this is between you and me, brother. She didn't want to get into the middle of it." Which he fully appreciated, whether Will did or not. James had to look at himself in the mirror for the rest of his life and he'd prefer not to see his own guilty conscience staring back at him. "And she won't. Neither will I allow her to. If you say you're planning to pursue this ridiculous idea of aligning Rowling Energy to the Montoros through marriage, so be it. Just be sure you treat her like a princess."

Maybe James wasn't done being noble after all. He'd fully expected to walk in here and demand that Will release Bella from their fathers' agreement. But somehow he'd wound up caring more about Bella and how she was being marginalized than whether he'd cleared the way to sleep with her.

"I see." Comprehension dawned in Will's gaze. "You're the reason she left the party so quickly last night. Last I knew, she'd gone out on the terrace for some air, and the next, she'd begged off with a headache."

"I'm sorry," James said earnestly. "I didn't plan for any of this to happen. But Bella deserves better than to be thought of as currency. She's funny and incredible and—"

He broke off before he said something he couldn't take back, like *she's the hottest kisser I've ever met.* Somehow, he didn't think that would go over well.

"You've got it bad." Will didn't bother to hide his smirk. "Never would have thought I'd see the day. She's really got you wrapped, doesn't she?"

As if Bella called the shots or something? James tried to do the right thing one time and all he got was grief.

"She's important," James growled. "That's all."

Will grinned mischievously, looking more like Mum than he usually did. "Ha. I wouldn't be surprised if you proposed to her before her brother's coronation."

"Propose? You mean ask her to marry me?" Ice slid down James's spine and he threw up a hand to stave off the rest of Will's outpouring of madness. "That's not what's going on here. We're just... I'm not... It's that I didn't want to poach on your territory. It's not sporting."

"Gabriella. Paulinha. Abril." Ticking them off on his fingers, Will cocked his head. "I think there was another one, but her name escapes me."

Revisionist history of the worst kind. "If I recall, Abril went home with you. Despite the fact that I saw her first."

"But that's my point. We've competed over women in the past. But you have never come to me first." Will's phone rang, but he ignored the shrill buzz. "We've always subscribed to the may-the-best-man-win philosophy. So obviously Bella is the one."

Yeah, the one James wanted in his bed. That was it. Once they burned off the blinding attraction, they'd part amicably. "No way. You're reading into this."

An even worse thought occurred to him then. Did *Bella* think there was more going on here? Like maybe James wanted to take Will's place in the diabolical bridal bargain their fathers had struck? Surely not. There'd been plenty of flirting, and lots of use of the word *naked*. But no one had said anything about being serious.

Will shook his head, a smile still tugging at his lips. "I don't think so. Put your money where your mouth is."

"A bet? Seriously?" All the long hours in the service of Patrick Rowling's ego had obviously pickled his brother's brain.

"As a heart attack." Nodding at James's wrist, he pursed his lips for a beat. "Grandfather's watch. That's how bad I think you've got it. If you propose to Bella before Gabriel Montoro takes the throne, you give it to me, free and clear."

James laughed. "You are so on."

What a stupid thing to ask for. Will knew how much James loved his grandfather's watch. It was one of the few mementos from England that James had left, and Grandfather had given it to him on his eighteenth birthday. Losing it was not happening. Proposing to Bella was not happening, before the coronation or after.

Sucker's bet. James rubbed his hands together gleefully. "If I don't propose, then what? Make this worth my while."

"I'll come up with something."

James and Will shook on it.

"So this means the arranged marriage is totally off, right?" No point in going through all of this just to find out Will was toying with him.

"Totally off."

A glint in his brother's eye caught his crossways. "You were never interested in her."

"Never," Will confirmed solemnly. "Bella's got all the right parts and everything, and she would have opened up some interesting possibilities for Rowling. But she's not my type. I'm fine with cancelling the whole agreement."

Not his type. That was insane. How could Bella not be every red-blooded man's type? "You'll talk to Father?"

"Sure. It's better coming from me anyway. Now get out so I can run this company."

James got out. He had a naked princess in his future after all.

Bella's eyes started to ache after thirty minutes of trying to read the tiny map print.

"I give up," she muttered and switched off the lamp adorning her bedside table.

All of the words were in Spanish anyway. How was she

supposed to use this map Alex Ramon's assistant had given her to find the farmhouse Tía Isabella had mentioned?

When Bella had asked Rafael about it, he sent her to speak with Alex Ramon, Alma's deputy prime minister of commerce. His assistant helped her scour the royal archives until they found one solitary mention of the abandoned farmhouse in a long list of Montoro holdings. But there was little to go on location-wise other than *Aldeia Dormer*, the name of a tiny village.

At least Mr. Ramon's assistant had managed to find the key to the property tucked away in a filing cabinet, a real plus. Assuming the key still worked, that was.

Now she just had to find the farmhouse. Tía Isabella's urgency had taken root, not to mention a healthy dose of curiosity about how an old farmhouse counted as part of a legacy. There was no way Bella would actually give up.

Plus, finding the farmhouse was a project, her gift to Isabella. Bella needed a local with plenty of time on his hands and access to a vehicle to help her scour the countryside for this farmhouse. And who didn't mind ditching her babysitters-slash-security guys.

Her phone rang. She glanced at it and frowned at the unfamiliar number. That was the second time today and the first caller had been Will. Dare she hope this might be the brother she'd rather talk to? "Hello?"

"You haven't been to the beach all day." James's smooth voice slid through her like silk.

"Was I supposed to be at the beach?" With a wide grin, she flipped over on her back to stare at the ceiling above her bed, completely uninterested in cryptic maps now that she had a much better distraction.

"How else am I supposed to run into you?" he pointed out. "You never gave me your phone number."

Because he'd never asked. "Yet it appears I'm speaking to you on the phone at this very minute."

"A bloke has to be resourceful around this island if he wants to ask a princess out on a date. Apparently."

A little thrill burst through her midsection. After walking away from James at the party, she'd mentally prepared for any eventuality. A woman didn't get between brothers, and James, for all his squawking about being a bad boy, wouldn't have pursued her if Will had called dibs.

And then there was always the possibility James would grow weary of all the obstacles between them. She didn't have any guarantees she'd even hear from him again.

"This is your idea of resourceful? What did you do, hit up Will for my phone number?"

James cleared his throat. "I talked to him. About us."

That was pretty much an admission of how he'd gotten her number. "Yeah. He told me."

"Well, half my battle is won. My day will be complete if you would kindly get your gorgeous rear down to the beach."

Scrambling from the bed, Bella tore off her shorts as she dashed for the dresser and wedged the phone under her chin to pull out a bikini. "What if I'm busy?"

"Cancel. In fact, cancel everything for the rest of the day."

The rest of the day with James? She was so on board with that plan, she could hardly keep the giddiness in check. But she couldn't let *him* know how much she was into him. That was rule number one.

"You'll have to give me more than that in order for me to clear my schedule." She whipped her shirt off one-handed, knocking the phone to the floor. She cursed and dove for it. "I'm American. We invented high-maintenance dating. Make it worth my while."

Head tight to her shoulder so the phone didn't try another escape attempt, she wiggled out of her underwear.

"Trust me, sweetheart," he said with a chuckle. "I've been all over the world. I'm more than capable of handling one tiny American. If you want to find out how worth it I am, walk out the door."

"I'm not dressed," she informed him saucily. Even someone as fashion savvy as Bella couldn't tie a bikini with one hand. And for some reason, now that he knew she was naked, it was an oddly effective turn-on.

"Perfect," he purred. "I like a woman who can read my mind. What am I thinking right now?"

If it was anything close to what she was thinking, a public beach was not the best place for them to be together. "You're thinking that you'd better hang up so I can, you know, leave the house."

His laugh rolled through her and then cut off abruptly as the call ended. She hummed as she threw on her bikini and covered it with a short dress made of fishnet weave.

She hit the foyer in under three minutes and almost escaped without her security detail noticing her stealthy exit, when she heard the voice of doom call out behind her.

"Isabella."

Groaning, she turned to face her father since the cover up was just as see-through from the front as the back. The faster she withdrew from his clutches, the better. "Yeah, Dad."

"I understand you told Will Rowling you weren't interested in him. I'm very disappointed."

Of course he was. He'd have to smooth things over with Patrick Rowling and figure out another way to make everyone miserable.

"That's me. The disappointing daughter," she admitted lightly, hoping if she kept her cool, the extraction might go faster. She had a man waiting patiently for her on the beach.

"You cannot continue behaving this way. Marriage to Rowling will settle you and nothing else seems to work to that end. You must repair your relationship with him."

His hand flew up to staunch the protest she'd been about to voice.

"No, Isabella. This is a serious matter, among other serious matters I must discuss with you. However, I'm expected to accompany Gabriel to a royal function. Be here when I get back," her father commanded.

"Sure, Dad." She fled before he could tell her when he'd be back because then she could claim ignorance when she wasn't here.

Her stomach tightened as she walked down the narrow cliffside stairs to the beach. Why couldn't she have timed that better? The encounter put a damper on the joy she'd had since the moment she'd heard James's voice.

When her toes sank into the sand, she scoured the sun-worshippers for a glimpse of the whipcord physique she couldn't erase from her mind. James was easy to spot in a turquoise shirt that shielded his British complexion from the rays. Sunglasses covered his beautiful eyes and as always, he wore the expensive watch he never seemed to leave home without. He lay stretched out on a towel off to the side of the crowd, lounging in his own little cleared area.

"Thought you'd never get here," he commented when she flopped down next to him. He paused and whipped off his glasses to focus on her intently. "What's wrong?"

How bad was it that he made her so mushy just by noticing that she was a little upset? "Nothing. My father."

"Say no more." James shook his head and sat up to clasp her hand in his, squeezing it once. "I've been avoiding mine since the pictures hit."

"What pictures?"

"You don't know?" When she shook her head, he rubbed his face with his free hand. "Someone snapped us with me on top of you when you tripped over my chair the other day. We were on the front page of the Playa Del Sol newspaper. And probably all the other ones, too. I'm sorry, I figured you'd seen them. Or had a confrontation with your father about them."

Oh, that explained a lot, especially Rafael's use of his boardroom voice. "I learned the hard way to never search my name on the internet, so no, I haven't seen the pictures. And I think I just narrowly missed that confrontation. The one I had was bad enough, but fortunately, he was too busy to give me a proper talking to. I'm supposed to be home when he gets back so I can obediently listen to his lecture. Oops."

James flashed a quick grin. "You're my kind of woman."

"We seem to have a flagrant disregard for authority in common, don't we?"

"When it makes sense," James corrected. "You're not sixteen. You're a grown woman who can make her own choices. If you want to be with me, you should get that opportunity, authority figures aside."

As much as she liked his point, she was still a member of the royal family and the idea of smarmy pictures floating around upset her, especially when the actual event had been so innocuous.

"So we're both rebels, but only when presented with pigheaded fathers?"

"Exactly." His thumb smoothed over hers and he had yet to return his sunglasses to their perch over his eyes. The way he was looking at her, as if he understood her so perfectly, they didn't even need words—it took a massive amount of willpower to not throw herself into his arms.

Why were they outside in plain sight again? Her babysitters could lumber down the stairs from the house at any moment, squelching what promised to be an adventurous day.

"This wasn't exactly what I had in mind for our first date," she remarked with an exaggerated glance around. "Too many people and I'm pretty sure I remember something about getting naked. I readily admit to bucking authority when called for, but I am not a fan of sand in certain places. What shall we do about that?"

James's blue eyes went sultry and he gripped her hand tighter. "A little bird told me you were high maintenance, so I was going to take you to dinner later at Casa Branca in Del Sol. But I see the huge gaping flaw in that plan since you would indeed have to be dressed for that."

"It's also pretty public. I'd love to escape prying eyes, security details and cameras for at least one night." She frowned. Was nowhere sacred enough to spend time with a man she was just getting to know without fear of creating a whole brand-new scandal? "Can we go back to your place?"

They certainly couldn't go to hers, not with the royal lecture pending.

"Ha." James rolled his eyes, turning them a myriad of blues in the sunlight. "I can only imagine dear old Dad's aneurism when I walk through the front door with you."

No, neither of them were sixteen but it felt that way when they couldn't even find a place to be alone without overbearing parents around. So it was time for an adult solution.

"New plan," Bella chirped. "I've heard a rumor of an abandoned farmhouse that's part of our family's royal property. But I don't know where it is. I need someone with a car and a good knowledge of the roads in Alma to help me find it. Know anyone like that who's also free to drive around with me?"

"James's Abandoned Farmhouse Locators, at your service." He bowed over her hand with mock ceremony. "Let's plan on making a night of it. We'll get some takeout. Do you want to run back upstairs to grab a few things?"

"Give me five minutes." She mentally packed an overnight bag. Had she brought that smoking hot lingerie set she hadn't worn yet?

"Four." He raised her hand to his lips and kissed it. "That bikini is killing me. I want to untie it with my teeth and take a good hard look at what's underneath. Then my mouth will be busy getting acquainted with every inch of your naked body."

She shuddered as his words lanced through her core with a long tug. "I'll be back in three."

Six

The small cockpit of James's car filled with the scent of Bella instantly. It was exotic, erotic and engaging, flipping switches in his body he'd have sworn were already wide open from the visual of Bella at the beach in that little bikini.

How was it possible to be even more turned on when you were already blind from lack of release?

She'd changed into a little white sundress that hugged her curves. The tiny straps begged for a man's hands to slip them off her shoulders, kiss the smooth flesh and then keep going into the deep V of her cleavage.

It was going to be a long, long drive through the interior of Alma as they looked for an abandoned farmhouse Bella insisted they could find. Problem was, he wanted her now, not in two hours after they crisscrossed the island in his green Lamborghini, which was hardly invisible.

As they clicked their seatbelts, his phone buzzed and he glanced at it out of habit, already planning to ignore whatever it was. Nothing could be more important than Bella.

Except it was a text message from Will. Who never texted him. Frowning, James tapped the screen of his phone and read the message.

I had nothing to do with this, but thought you should know.

Nothing good was going to come of clicking the link Will had sent, but forewarned was forearmed, so James did it anyway.

Montoro Princess to Wed the Heir to Rowling Energy.

The headline was enough. He didn't need to read the rest.

With a curse, he tilted his phone toward Bella. "Now taking bets on which of our fathers is behind this."

She glanced at it and repeated his curse, but substituted the vilest word with a more ladylike version, which put a smile on his face despite the ill-timed, fabricated announcement.

"Mine," she announced with a snort. "Control and dictate is exactly his style."

"Sure you're not describing my father?" James returned. "Because that's his MO all day long."

"No, it's my father. Definitely. But it doesn't matter." She grabbed his phone, switched it off and stuffed it in the bag at her feet. "You can't have that back. No more scandals, interfering fathers and marriage alliances. Just drive." She glanced over her shoulder. "And now. Before my babysitters figure out I'm not in the house."

Since that sounded fine to him, he backed out of his beachside parking place and floored the gas pedal, heading west out of Playa Del Onda.

"This is a gorgeous car," she commented with apparent appreciation as she caressed the dashboard lovingly in a way that immediately made him want her hand in his lap instead of on his car. "I dated a guy in Miami with an

Aventador, but it's so flashy without any real substance. The Gallardo is more refined and I love the color."

God, she *was* going to kill him before the day was over. "You know cars? I can't begin to tell you how hot that is."

She shrugged with a musical laugh, knocking one of the straps of her dress askew and drawing his attention away from the road. Dangerously.

"It's hard to live in a place like Miami without gaining at least some passing knowledge. I'll let you in on a secret, though. We girls always judge a man by his car. Mercedes-Benz? Too serious. Porsche? Works too hard. Corvette? Too worried about his hair."

James laughed in spite of the discomfort going on down below that likely wouldn't ease for an eternity. "So my Lamborghini is the only reason you wanted to go out with me?"

"The car test only works if you haven't met the guy yet. We're strictly talking about taking someone's measure in the parking lot."

He shifted to take a hairpin curve as they wound away from the beach into the more sparsely populated inland roads of Alma. Since he had no idea what they were looking for, he'd drive and let her do the surveying.

"Then I'll go with my second guess. You wanted to go out with me because I'm a witty conversationalist." He waggled his brows and shot her a sly smile. "Or door number three—I know a trick or two between the sheets."

He'd meant to be flirtatious, but now that it was out there, he realized the conversation with Will still bothered him a bit. Bella had said on numerous occasions that marriage wasn't her thing. Regardless, establishing the ground rules of what they were doing here couldn't hurt.

"Both." Blond hair swinging, she leaned on the emergency brake between them, so close he imagined he could hear her heart beating. "We have all night long and I do love a good conversation, especially in the dark. But if you forced me to choose, I'd go with door number three."

Brilliant. So they were both on the same page. They were hot for each other and wanted to burn it off with a wild night together. "Just so you know, with me, sheets are optional."

Awareness tightened the atmosphere as she let her gaze travel down his chest and rest on the bulge in his pants. He could hardly keep his attention on the road. Who wanted to watch the scraggly countryside of Alma when a goddess sat in the adjacent seat?

"By the way," she said. "I think we just passed the road we were supposed to take."

With a groan, he did a quick U-turn and drove down the street barely noticeable in the overgrowth of trees and groundcover. "I didn't know we had directions. Maybe you could speak up earlier next time?"

"Sorry, I'm a little distracted. Maybe you could stop being so sexy for a couple of minutes." Fanning herself as if he'd heated her up, she trailed a finger down his bicep muscle and toyed with the crook of his elbow.

"Me?" he growled. "You're the one in that knockout dress. All I can hear in my head is your voice on repeat, when you said the next time we were together, you'd be naked."

"Oh, did I forget to tell you?" She kissed the tip of her finger and pressed it to his lips, but she pulled away too quickly for him to suck the finger into his mouth the way he wanted to. "I'm naked under this dress. Wanna pull over?"

He nearly whimpered. "I cannot possibly explain how much I would like to do exactly that. But we are not getting it on in the car like a couple of horny teenagers. You deserve to be treated right and that includes a bed and me taking my time enjoying you."

Besides, they might be headed into the heart of rural Alma, but the roads were not deserted. They passed cars constantly. People knew who drove the only green Lamborghini on the island and all it would take was one idiot with a camera phone for another risqué picture of James and Bella together to land in the public eye. It was a dirty shame he hadn't tinted the windows on his car.

Until they straightened out the marriage announcement, it would create so much less of a jumble if they kept a low profile.

"Then drive faster," Bella suggested, and her hand wandered over to rest on his inner thigh, where she casually stroked him. Innocently, as if she touched him all the time, except she hadn't touched him like *that* before and his vision started to blur with unrequited lust.

He stepped on the gas. Hard.

"Where are we going?" Driving around until they stumbled over a farmhouse that may or may not exist had started to sound like the worst idea he'd ever agreed to.

"This is the main road to Aldeia Dormer, right?" When he nodded, she pointed at the horizon. "The assistant I talked to thought she remembered that the farmhouse was on the outskirts, before you hit the village. If you keep going, we'll find out."

"What if I just take you to a hotel and we check in under an assumed name?"

He had plenty of practice with parking in an obscure place and passing out discrete tips to the staff so he and his lady friend could duck through the kitchen entrance. Why hadn't he insisted on that in the first place? The text from Will had muddled him up, obviously. There was a former castillo-turned-four-star-bed-and-breakfast on the south side of Playa Del Onda that he wouldn't mind trying.

She shook her head with a sad smile and it was so much the opposite of her normal sunny demeanor, he immediately wanted to say something to lighten the mood. But what had caused such an instant mood shift?

"My aunt asked me to find the farmhouse. It's important to her and maybe to Gabriel. She said it was part of the Montoro legacy. We're already so close. I promise, if we don't find it soon, I'll reconsider the hotel."

Her earnestness dug under his skin and there was no way he could refuse. "Sure. We'll keep going."

Okay, maybe she was a little different from other women he'd dated. He certainly couldn't recall catering to one so readily before, but that was probably due to the degree of difficulty he'd experienced in getting this one undressed and under him.

They drove for a couple of miles, wrapped in tension. Just when James started to curse his flamboyant taste in cars, they crested a hill, and she gasped as a white farmhouse came into view.

Wonders of wonders. "Is that it?"

"I'm not sure." Bella pursed her lips as he drove off the main road onto the winding path to the farmhouse and parked under a dangerously dilapidated carport.

Would serve him right if this ill-conceived jaunt through Alma resulted in a hundred grand worth of bodywork repairs when the carport collapsed on the Lamborghini. "I thought you said it was off this road."

"Well, it's supposed to be. But I've never been here before," she pointed out. "Maybe there are a hundred white farmhouses between here and Aldeia Dormer."

"Only one way to find out." He helped her from the car and held her hand as they picked through the overgrown property. "Don't step in the tall weed patches. There might be something living in them you'd rather not tangle with."

She squeezed his hand. "I'm glad you're here, then. I'll let you deal with the creepy crawly stuff."

"I'll be your hero any day."

Her grateful smile made his chest tight with a foreign weight because he felt like a fraud all at once. The only heroic thing he'd ever done in his life was give Bella an opportunity to be with Will if she chose. When had he last expended any appreciable effort looking out for someone else's welfare?

He could start right now, if he wanted to. No reason he couldn't keep an eye out for opportunities to throw himself in front of a bullet—figuratively speaking—for an amazing woman like Bella. If she'd smile at him like that again, the payoff wasn't too shabby.

The farmhouse's original grandeur still shone through despite the years of neglect. Once, the two-story clapboard house had likely been the home of a large family, where they gathered around an old wooden table at supper to laugh and tell stories as dogs ran underfoot.

As if he knew anything about what a family did at supper. Especially a family whose members liked each other and spent time together on purpose. Did that kind of lovely fairy tale even exist outside of movies? He swallowed the stupid lump in his throat. Who cared? He had no roots and liked it that way.

The property spread beyond the house into a small valley. Chickens had probably clucked in the wide backyard, scolding fat pigs or horses that lived in the wooden pens just barely visible from the front of the house. The fences had long fallen to the weed-choked ground, succumbing to weathering and decay.

James nearly tripped over an equally weathered rectangular wooden board hidden by the grass and weeds. He kicked at it, but it was solid enough not to move much despite the force of his well-toned football muscles. Metal loops across the top caught his attention and he leaned down to ease the board up on its side.

"It's a sign," Bella whispered as her gaze lit on the opposite side.

James spun around to view the front. In bold, blocky letters, the sign read *Escondite Real.* "In more ways than one."

Unless he missed his guess, this was indeed the property of royalty. Or someone's idea of a joke.

"No one told me to brush up on my Spanish before I came here. What does it say?" Bella asked with a mock pout.

"Royal Hideaway. Is this where your ancestors came to indulge in illicit affairs?"

Mischievously, she winked at James. "If not, it's where the current generation will."

"Illicit affairs are my favorite." Taking her hand again, he guided her toward the house.

"Look. It's beautiful."

Bella pointed at a butterfly the size of his palm. It alighted on a purple bougainvillea that had thrived despite the lack of human attention, the butterfly's wings touching and separating slowly. But the sight couldn't keep his attention, not when Bella's face had taken on a glow in the late afternoon sunlight as she smiled at the butterfly.

God, she was the most exquisite woman he'd ever seen. And that was saying something when he'd been hit on by women renowned the world over for their beauty.

"Let's check out the inside." He cleared the catch from his throat, mystified by where it had come from. Women were a dime a dozen. Why didn't Bella seem like one of the legion he could have in his bed tomorrow?

It didn't matter. Will hadn't seen what he thought he'd seen when James cleared the air with him. The watch on his wrist wasn't going anywhere anytime soon.

Bella fished a set of keys from her bag. The second one turned the tumblers in the padlock on the splintered front door. It opened easily but the interior was dark and musty. Of course. There wouldn't be any electricity at an abandoned farmhouse. Or a cleaning crew.

"I guess we should have thought this through a little better," James said. "At least we know we're in the right place since the key worked."

Any hope of stripping Bella out of that little dress and spending the night in a haze of sensual pleasure vanished as something that sounded as if it had more feet than a football team scrabbled across the room.

"Yeah. It's a little more rustic than I was anticipating." She scowled at the gloom. "I'm not well versed in the art of abandoned farmhouses. Now what?"

Bella bit her lip to staunch the flow of frustrated tears. Which didn't exactly work.

This was all her fault. She'd envisioned a romantic rendezvous with a sexy, exciting man—one she'd looked forward to getting to know *very* well—and never once had it crossed her mind that "abandoned" didn't mean that someone had picked up and left a fully functioning house, ready and waiting for her and James to borrow for a night or two. The most strenuous thing she'd expected to do before letting James seduce her was kill a spider in the shower.

Graying sheets covered in cobwebs and dust obscured what she assumed must be furnishings underneath. The farmhouse hadn't been lived in for a long time. Decades maybe. The property may not even have running water. She shuddered. What had Isabella sent her into?

One tear shook loose and slid down her face.

Without speaking, James took her hand and drew her into his embrace, which immediately calmed her. How had he known that was what she needed? She slid her arms around his waist and laid her head on his strong chest.

Goodness. His athlete's physique did it for her in so many ways. He was shockingly solid and muscular for someone so lean and her own body woke up in a hurry. Sensation flooded her and she ached for him to kiss her again, as he'd done on the terrace—hot, commanding and so very sexy.

But then he drew back and tipped her chin up, his gaze serious and a bit endearing. "Here's what we're going to do. I'll drive into the village and pick up a few things. I hate to leave you here, but we can't be photographed

together. While I'm gone, see if you can find a way to clean
up at least one room."

His smile warmed her and she returned it, encouraged
by his optimism. "You do have a gift for uncomplicating
things. I'm a little jealous," she teased.

"It'll be smashing. I promise."

He left and she turned her attention to the great room of
the farmhouse. Once she pulled the drapes aside, sunlight
shafted into the room through the wide windows, catching on the dusty chandelier. So the house was wired for
electricity. That was a plus. Maybe she could figure out
how to get it activated—for next time, obviously, because
there was a distinct possibility she and James might make
long-term use out of this hideaway. Being a princess had
to be worth something, didn't it?

Holding her breath, she pulled the sheets from the furnishings, raising a tornado of dust that made her sneeze.
Once all the sheets were in a pile in the corner, she dashed
from the room to give all the flurries a chance to settle.
Using her phone as a flashlight, she found a broom in one
of the closets of the old-fashioned kitchen.

"Cinderella, at your service," she muttered and carried
the broom like a sword in front of her in case she ran into
something crawly since her knight had left.

By the time he returned, the sun had started to set.
She'd swept the majority of the dust from the room and
whacked the cobwebs from the corners and chandelier.
The throaty growl of the Lamborghini echoed through the
great room as James came up the drive and parked. The
car door slammed and James appeared in the open doorway, his arms weighted down with bags.

"Wow." He whistled. "This place was something back
in the day, huh?"

She glanced around at the rich furnishings, which were
clearly high-end, even for antiques, and still quite func-
tional if you didn't mind the grime. "It's a property owned

by royalty. I guess they didn't spare much expense, regardless of the location. I wonder why no one has been here for so long?"

And why all these lovely antiques were still here, like ghosts frozen in time until someone broke the spell.

"Tantaberra liked Del Sol." James set his bags down carefully on the coffee table and began pulling out his bounty. "My guess is this was too far out of the limelight and too pedestrian for his taste."

A variety of candles appeared from the depths of the first bag. James scouted around until he found an empty three-pronged candelabra, screwed tapers into it and then flicked a lighter with his other hand. He shut the front door, plunging the room into full darkness. The soft glow of the candles bathed his face in mellow light and she forgot all about the mystery of this farmhouse as he set the candelabra on the mantel behind the brocade couch.

"Nice. What else did you bring me?" Bella asked, intrigued at the sheer number of bags James had returned with. She'd expected dinner and that was about it.

"The most important thing." He yanked a plaid blanket from the second bag and spread it out on the floor. "Can't have you dining on these rough plank floors, now can we?"

She shook her head with a smile and knelt down on the soft blanket to watch him continue unpacking. It seemed as if he'd thought of everything, down to such necessary but unique details as a blanket and candles. It was a quality she would never have thought to admire or even notice. And in James, it was potently attractive.

"Second most important—wine." He plunked the bottle next to her and pulled out two plastic cups. "Not the finest stemware. Sorry. It was the best I could do."

His chagrin was heartbreakingly honest. Did he think she'd turn up her nose at his offering? Well, some women probably would, but not Bella.

"It's perfect," she said sincerely. "If you'll give me the

corkscrew, I'll pour while you show me what else you found in town."

He handed her a small black-cased device of some sort. It looked like a pocketknife and she eyed it curiously until he flicked out the corkscrew with a half laugh. "Never seen one of these before?"

"My wine is typically poured for me," she informed him pertly with a mock haughty sneer, lady-of-the-manor style. "Cut me some slack."

Instead of grinning back, he dropped to the blanket and took her hand. "This is a crappy first date. I wish I could have taken you to dinner in Del Sol, like I'd planned. You deserve to be waited on hand and foot and for me to make love to you on silk sheets. I'm sorry that things are so out of control for us right now. I'll make it up to you, I swear."

"Oh, James." Stricken, she stared into his gorgeous aqua eyes flickering in the candlelight. "This is exactly what I've been envisioning since I got in the car back at the beach. I don't need a three-hundred-euro dinner. I just want to be with you."

"You're a princess," he insisted fiercely. "I want to treat you like the royalty you are."

Good grief. Was all this because of the stupid joke she'd made about being high maintenance? Obviously he'd taken her at her word. Backpedaling time.

"You do that every time we're together. Encouraging me to make my own choices about who I date. Bringing me to the farmhouse simply because I asked, without telling me it was crazy. Holding me when I cry. Being my hero by making this night romantic with ingenuity and flair, despite the less than stellar accommodations. How could I possibly find fault in any of that?"

A little overcome, she stared at him, hoping to impart her sincerity by osmosis. Because he was amazing and somehow verbalizing it made it more real. Who else in her life had ever done such wonderful things for her? No one. Tender, fledgling feelings for James welled up and nearly splashed over.

He scowled. "I did those things because you needed me to. Not because you're a princess."

Silly man. He didn't get what she was saying at all. "But don't you see? I need someone to treat me like *me*. Because you *see* me and aren't wrapped up in all the royal trappings, which are essentially meaningless at the end of the day."

That was the mistake her father had made, trying to pawn her off on Will. And Will was nearly as bad. Everyone was far more impressed with her royal pedigree than she ever was. Everyone except James. And now he was being all weird about it.

Just as fiercely, she gripped his hand. "I wasn't a princess last year and if you'd met me then, wouldn't you have tried to give me what I needed instead of trying to cater to some idea you have about how a girl with royal blood should expect you to act?"

"Yeah." He blew out a breath. "I would. I just didn't want this to be so disappointing for you. Not our first time together."

Seriously? After the way he'd kissed her on the terrace? There was no freaking way he'd disappoint her, whether it was their first time or hundredth time. The location hardly mattered. She wanted the man, not some luxury vacation. If he thought dollar signs turned her on, she'd done something wrong.

"Our first time together cannot be disappointing, because you're half the equation," she chided gently. "I expect fireworks simply because you're the one setting them off. Okay?"

He searched her expression, brows drawn together. "If you're sure."

She caressed his arm soothingly, hoping to loosen him up a little. The romantic candlelit atmosphere was going to waste and that was a shame. "Yeah. Now show me what else is in your magic bag."

With a grin, he grabbed the last bag. He fished out a roll of salami, which he set by the wine, then lined up a wedge of cheese, boxed crackers and a string of grapes. "Dinner. I wish it—"

"Stop. It's food and I'm hungry. Sit down and let's eat it while you tell me stories about growing up in Alma." Patting the blanket, she concentrated on opening the wine, her one self-appointed task in the evening's preparations. It was tougher to pierce the cork than she'd anticipated.

Instead of complying with her suggestion, he took the bottle from her hands and expertly popped the cork in under fifteen seconds.

"You've done that before," she accused with a laugh as he poured two very full glasses of the chilled white wine. It was pretty good for a no-name label and she swallowed a healthy bit.

"Yep. I'm a master of all things decadent." He arched a brow and plucked a grape from the bunch to run it across her lips with slow sensuality that fanned heat across her skin instantly. "Hurry up and eat so I can show you."

Watching him with unabashed invitation, she let him ease the grape between her lips and accepted it with a swirl of her tongue across the tips of his fingers. His eyelids lowered, fluttering slightly, and he deliberately set his glass of wine on the coffee table, as if to silently announce he planned to use both hands in very short order.

She shuddered as all the newly-awakened feelings for this man twined with the already-powerful attraction. She wanted to explore his depths and let the amazing things happening between them explode. Simple desire she understood and appreciated, but this went beyond anything simple, beyond anything she'd experienced before.

"Or we can do both at the same time," she suggested,

her voice dropping huskily as he trailed his wet fingertip down her chin and throat to trace the line of her cleavage.

"There you go again reading my mind," he murmured and captured another grape without looking away, his gaze hot and full of promise. "Let's see if you can guess what I'm thinking now."

Seven

James outlined Bella's full lips with the grape and then ran it down her throat, resting it in the hollow of her collarbone. Slowly, he leaned over and drew the fruit into his mouth, sucking at her fragrant skin as he crushed the grape in his teeth simultaneously.

The combination of Bella and sweet juice sang across his taste buds. She was exquisitely, perfectly made and he wanted her with an unparalleled passion that wiped his mind of everything else.

Flinging her head back to give him better access, she gulped in a breath and exhaled on a low moan that tightened his whole body.

"Instead of reading your mind," she said, her low voice burrowing into his abdomen, spreading heat haphazardly, "why don't you surprise me with a few more strategically placed grapes?"

"You like that?"

Grapes as a seduction method—that was a first. And now he was wishing he'd bought a bushel. Gripping another one, he traced it between her breasts and circled one of her nipples. It peaked beautifully under the filmy sundress.

How had he gotten so supremely lucky as to have such a beautiful, exciting woman within arm's reach? One who didn't require him to rain expensive gifts down on her, but seemed perfectly content with simple trappings and a man paying attention to her.

All the talk of heroics made his skin crawl. She was sorely mistaken if she thought of him as a hero, but the look in her eyes—well, that made him feel ten feet tall, as if he could do anything as long as she believed in him.

The power of it emboldened him.

Urgently, he lunged for her, catching her up in his arms as he laid her back on the blanket. Her lips crashed against his in a hot, wet kiss that went on and on as their tongues explored and dipped and mated. Her body twined with his and finally, she was underneath him, his thigh flush against her core. Her hands went on a mission to discover every part of his back and he reveled in the feminine touch he'd been craving for so long.

Hooking the neckline of her dress, he dragged it from her breast. As her flesh was revealed, he followed the trail with his mouth, nibbling and kissing until his lips closed over her nipple.

She arched against his mouth, pushing herself deeper inside as he reached for a handful of grapes. With little regard for decorum, he lifted his head and crushed the fruit savagely, letting the juice drip onto her peaked nipple. The liquid wetted the tip as she watched with dark eyes; her glistening breast was so erotic, he groaned even as he leaned forward to catch an errant drop on his tongue.

Licking upward until he hit her nipple again, he sucked all the juice off to the sound of her very vocal sighs of pleasure. That nearly undid him.

"I want to see all of you," he murmured and his need was so great, he didn't even wait for her reply. Peeling off that little dress counted as one of the greatest pleasures of his life as inch by inch, he uncovered her incredible skin.

"You're so beautiful," he told her with a catch in his throat.

Something unnamable had overcome him. Something dramatic and huge. But he liked it and before whatever it was fled, he pulled a string of condoms from his pocket and rolled to the side to shed his own clothes so he could feel every gorgeous bit of her against him.

When he was naked, he rolled back, intending to gather up that bundle of heaven back into his arms, but she stopped him with a palm to his chest. "Not yet. I want to see you, too."

Her gaze roved over his body and lingered in unexpected places. His thighs. His pectorals. Her palm spread and flattened over his nipple, as if she wanted to grab hold.

When she couldn't, she purred. "Hard as stone. I like that."

"I like you touching me."

"Allow me to continue." Wicked smile spreading across her face, she ran both hands down the planes of his chest and onto his thighs, right past the area he'd hoped she was headed for. Which of course made him anticipate the return journey.

Her fingernails scraped his leg muscles lightly, and she trailed one hand over his hip to explore his butt, which tightened automatically under the onslaught. *Everything* tightened with unanswered release, including the parts he'd have sworn were already stretched to the point of bursting.

He groaned as heat exploded under her hands. His hips strained toward her, muscles begging to be set free from the iron hold he had on them. "Are you trying to make me barmy?"

"Nope. Just looking for the best places for when it's my turn with the grapes."

"Oh, it's totally your turn," he countered. "This is your dinner, too, and you must be hungry."

"At last." She knelt, grabbed a grape and eyed his splayed body. "Hmm. Where to start? I know."

She stuck the grape in her mouth and rolled it around with her tongue, her hot gaze on his erection. Somehow that was more arousing than if she'd actually tongued *him*. She caught the small globe in her front teeth and bent to run it over his torso, dipping into the valleys and peaks, her hair spreading out like a feathery torture device across his sensitive skin. When she accidentally—or maybe on purpose—dragged her hair over his erection, the light touch lit him up. Fire radiated from the juncture of his thighs outward and just as he was about to cup her head to guide her toward the prize, she leaned up on her haunches.

Plucking the grape from between her lips, she grazed his length with the wet grape, nearly causing him to spill everything in one pulse.

"Enough of that," he growled, manacling her wrist to draw it away from the line of fire. "You've obviously underestimated my appetite. Time for the main course."

She grinned. "I thought you'd never say that."

Fumbling with a condom, he somehow managed to get it secured and then rolled her underneath him. He'd been fantasizing about taking her exactly this way for an eternity. Soft and luscious, she slid right into the curves of his body as she had that day in the sand, except this time, nothing separated their skin and it was every bit as glorious as he'd imagined.

"You—" He nearly swallowed his tongue as she shifted, rolling her hips against his. The tips of her breasts ground into his torso, and it all felt so amazing, he couldn't speak.

And then he didn't have to speak as he gazed down into her blue eyes. Candlelight danced in their depths and he caught a hint of something else that hit him in the gut. As if she'd seen pieces of him that he'd never realized were there and she liked what she'd found. As if she truly saw him as a hero. Maybe she was the only one who could relate. They were both rebels—to the rest of the world—but his pain and difficulties behind the rebellion made total sense to her.

"Bella," he murmured and that was the extent of what he could push through his tight throat.

"Right here." Her low, husky voice became his favorite part of her as it hummed through him. "I was really afraid this would never happen. Make it worth the wait."

It was already so worth it. Worth the lectures from his father, worth the uncomfortable nobleness he'd somehow adopted when around her. Worth sending her away from him on the terrace when all he'd wanted to do was pull that outrageous red dress up to her waist and make her his under the moonlight.

This way was better. Much better. No fear of being caught. No loaded landmines surrounding them, no paparazzi lying in wait to cause a scandal just because they wanted to be together.

He laid his lips on hers and fell into a long sigh of a kiss that grew urgent as she opened her mouth and dove in with her tongue, heightening the pleasure.

And then with a small shift, they joined. Easily, beautifully, as if she'd been specially crafted for James Rowling. It was almost spiritual and he'd never felt such a weight to being with a woman.

He froze for a moment, just letting her essence bleed through him, and then, determined to get her to the same place of mystical pleasure, he focused on her cries, her shifts, her rhythms. He became an instant student of Bella's pleasure until he could anticipate exactly what she wanted him to do next to drive her to release.

And then she stiffened as a volatile climax engulfed her that he felt all the way to his soles. He let go and followed her into oblivion, holding her tight because he couldn't stand to lose contact with her.

As he regained cognizance, he realized she was trying to get closer, too. He settled Bella comfortably in his arms and lay with her to watch the candle flames flicker, throwing shadows of the heavy furniture on the walls of the farmhouse they'd turned into the safest of havens.

This time with Bella…it was the most romantic experience he'd ever had, which sat strangely. For a guy who loved sex and abhorred roots, romance was difficult to come by. Not only had he never had it, he'd never sought it.

Why did something as normal as sex feel so abnormally and hugely different with this woman? He couldn't make sense of it and it bothered him. As the unsettled feeling grew, he kissed Bella's forehead and separated from her.

Bustling around to gather up their abandoned wine glasses and remnants of their dinner, he threw a forced smile over his shoulder. "Ready to finish eating?"

She returned the smile, not seeming to realize that he was trying to mask his sudden confusion. "Depends. Is that code for round two? Because the answer is yes, if so."

Round two. He chugged some wine to give himself a second. Normally, he went for round two like a sailor on shore leave, but the thick, romantic atmosphere and the crushing sensation in his chest when he looked at Bella made him question everything.

What was going on here? This was supposed to be nothing but an opportunity to have fun with Bella, no expectations, no proposals before her brother took the throne.

"No code. Let's eat."

What was his *problem*? A beautiful woman who rocked his world wanted him to make love to her again. Maybe he should just do that, and everything would make sense once they were back to just two people having smashing sex. Will's bet had hashed everything.

"For now," he amended. "Got to keep up our strength."

She grinned and shoved some crackers in her mouth. "All done," she mumbled around the crackers.

Groaning around a laugh, he sat close to her on the blanket and shook off his strange mood. After all, she was Alma's only princess. What role did a disgraced football player have in the middle of all that? Especially when he didn't plan to be living in Alma permanently. In fact, a new contract would get him out from under all of this confusion quite well. He could enjoy a fling with Bella and jet off to another continent. Like always.

Obviously, there was no reason to give any more credence to the heavy weight in his chest.

There was a huge crick in Bella's neck, but she actually welcomed the pain. Because she'd gotten it sleeping in James's arms on a blanket spread over a hardwood floor.

That had been delicious. And wonderful. And a host of other things she could barely articulate. So she didn't, opting to see what the morning brought in this unconventional affair they'd begun.

Once they were dressed and had the curtains thrown open to let sunlight into the musty great room, she turned to James. "I don't know about you, but I'm heavily in favor of finding a café that'll give you a mountain of scrambled eggs, bacon and biscuits in a takeout box. I'm starving."

He flashed a quick grin. "Careful. That kind of comment now has all sorts of meaning attached. You better clarify whether you want me to feed you or strip you."

Laughing, she socked him on the arm. "You're the one who started that with the grapes. And the answer to that is both. Always."

He caught her hand and held it in his. "I'm only teasing. I'll go get breakfast. I wish you could come with me. Is it too much to ask that we go on a real date where I sit with you at an actual table?"

"We'll get there." She kissed him soundly and shoved

him toward the door. "Once I have food in me, we can strategize about the rest of our lives."

Item number one on the agenda: get this farmhouse in livable shape.

The strange look he shot her put a hitch in her stride and she realized immediately how he must have taken her comment. Okay, she hadn't meant it like that, as if she was assuming they'd become a dyed-in-the-wool couple and he needed to get down on one knee.

But what was so bad about making plans beyond breakfast? She'd had some great lovers in the past, but what she'd experienced with James went far beyond the category of casual. Hadn't he felt all the wonderful things she'd felt last night?

She rolled her eyes to make it harder for him to detect the swirl of emotion going on underneath the surface. "You can stop with the deer-in-the-headlights, hon. I just narrowly escaped one marriage. I'm not at all interested in jumping right into another one, no matter how good the prospective groom is at *feeding* me."

Which was absolutely, completely true. Saying it aloud solidified it for them both.

With a wicked smile, he yanked on her hand, pulling her into his embrace. His weird expression melted away as he nuzzled her neck.

Foot-in-mouth averted. Except now she was wondering exactly what his intentions toward her were. A few nights together and then ta-ta?

And when did she get to the point where that wasn't necessarily what *she* wanted? She didn't do all that commitment-and-feelings rigmarole. She liked to have fun and secretly felt sorry for women on husband-hunting missions. Her mother had gotten trapped in that cycle and lived a miserable existence for years and years as a result. *No, thank you.*

Nothing had changed just because of a few emotions

she had no idea what to do with. Her affair with James had begun so unconventionally and under extreme circumstances. If they'd been able to go out on a real date from the beginning, they'd probably have already moved on by now.

Good thing she'd made it clear marriage wasn't on her mind so there was no confusion, though a few other things could be better spelled out.

James sucked on her tender flesh, clearly about to move south, and she wiggled away before her body leaped on the train without her permission.

"That wasn't supposed to be a code word." She giggled at his crestfallen expression but sobered to hold his gaze. "Listen, before you go get breakfast, let's lay this out. Last night was amazing but I'm not done. Are you? Because if this thing between us was one night only, I'll be sad, but I'm a big girl. Tell me."

He was already shaking his head before she'd finished speaking. "No way. I'm nowhere near done."

Her pulse settled. *Good answer.* "So, if you want a repeat of the grapes-on-the-floor routine, I'm all for it. But I'd prefer a real bed from now on. My plan is to put some elbow grease into this place, preferably someone else's, and create a lover's retreat where we can escape whenever we feel like it."

"Are you expecting us to have to hide out that long?" Wary surprise crept into his tone, setting her teeth on edge.

"I don't know. Maybe." What, was it too much trouble to drive out here just to have a few stolen hours together? "Is what I'm suggesting so horrible?"

"No. Not at all. My hesitation was completely on the issue of hiding out. I want to be seen with you in public. I'm not ashamed of our relationship and I don't want you to think I am."

Her heart squished as she absorbed his righteous indignation and sincerity. He wanted their relationship to be aboveboard, just as he'd wanted to clear things with Will before proceeding. And that meant a lot to her. He kept trying to make her think he didn't have a noble bone in his body when everything he did hinged on his own personal sense of honor.

"I didn't think that, but way to score major points." She batted her eyelashes at him saucily. "But that aside, I don't even know if I'm staying in Alma permanently or I'd get my own place. I suspect you're in the same boat."

He'd told her he hoped to get another contract with a professional soccer—sorry, *football*—team, and that the team could be in Barcelona or the UK or Brazil or, or, or... He might end up anywhere in the world. And probably would.

"Yeah. I haven't made a secret out of the fact that I don't plan to stick around," he agreed cautiously.

"I know. So do you really think there's a scenario where either of us would be willing to parade the other across the thresholds of our fathers' houses even if we do clear up the engagement announcement?"

He sighed. "Yeah, you're right. Let's rewind this whole conversation. Smashing idea, Bella. I'd love to help you get this place into shape so I can take an actual shower in the morning."

That was the James she knew and loved. Or rather, the James she...didn't know very well, but liked a whole lot. With a sigh, she let him kiss her again and shoved him out the door for real this time because her stomach was growling and her heart was doing some funny things that she didn't especially like.

Space would be good right now.

The sound of the Lamborghini's engine faded away as she went about taking inventory on the lower floor. Apparently most, if not all, of the original furnishings remained, as evidenced by their arrangement. Bella had been in enough wealthy households to recognize when a place had been artfully decorated and this one definitely had.

The pieces had been placed just so by a feminine hand, or at least she imagined it that way. That's when it hit her that this farmhouse had probably once belonged to an ancestor of hers. Someone of her blood.

A long gone Montoro, forgotten for ages once the coup deposed the royal family. She'd never felt very connected to the monarchy, not even at the palace in Del Sol where some of the original riches of the royal estate were housed. But the quieter treasures of the farmhouse struck her differently.

She picked up a filthy urn resting on a side table. White, or at least it was under the grime. She rubbed at it ineffectually with her palm and managed to get a small bit of the white showing. The eggshell-like surface was pretty.

Maybe it wasn't priceless like the Qing Dynasty porcelain vase sitting in an art niche at the Coral Gables house. But worth something. Maybe it was actually worth more than the million-dollar piece of pottery back in Miami because it had been used by someone.

She'd never thought about worth being tied to something's usefulness. But she liked the idea of having a purpose. She'd had one in Miami—wildlife conservation. What had happened to that passion? It was as if she'd come to Alma and forgotten how great it made her feel to do something worthwhile.

With renewed fervor, she dove into cleaning what she could with the meager supplies at hand, and revised her earlier thoughts. It would be fun to put some elbow grease of her own into this house. Whom else could she trust with her family's property?

When the purr of James's car finally reverberated through the open door, she glanced at her dirty arms and her lip curled. Some princess she looked like. A Cinderella in reverse—she'd gone from the royal palace to being a slave to the dust. A shower sounded like heaven about now.

The look in James's eye when he walked in holding a

bag stenciled with the logo of the only chain restaurant in Alma had her laughing. "There is no way you're thinking what I think you're thinking. I'm filthy."

"Yes, way." He hummed in approval. "I've never seen a sexier woman than you, Bella Montoro. Layer of dirt or not."

There he went again making her insides all melty and that much more raw. She always got the distinct feeling he saw the real her, past all the outside stuff and into her core. The outside, inconsequential stuff was invisible to him. Coupled with the hard twist of pure lust she got pretty much any time she laid eyes on him, she could hardly think around it.

She shook it off. This fierce attraction was nothing more than the product of their secret love affair. Anticipation of the moment they'd finally connect, laced with a hint of the forbidden. It had colored everything and she refused to fall prey to manufactured expectations about what was happening between them.

Get a grip. "Smells like ham and biscuits," she said brightly.

He handed her the bag. "I hope you like them. I had to drive two towns over to find them."

The first bite of biscuit hit her tongue and she moaned. "I would have paid three hundred euros for this."

He laughed. "On the house. You can pay next time."

"Oh?" She arched a brow, relieved they'd settled back into the teasing, fun vibe she'd liked about them from the beginning. "Are you under some mistaken impression that I'm a liberated woman who insists on opening her own doors and paying her own way? 'Cause that is so not happening."

"My mistake," he allowed smoothly with a nod and munched on his own biscuit. "You want a manly bloke to treat you like a delicate hothouse flower. I get it. I'd be chuffed to climb all the ladders around here and wield the power tools in order to create a luxury hideaway, as ordered. You know what that means I get at the end of the day in return, right?"

"A full body massage," she guessed, already planning exactly how such a reward might play out. "And then some inventive foreplay afterward."

That was even more fun to imagine than the massage part of the evening's agenda.

"Oh, no, sweetheart." He leaned in and tipped her chin up to capture her gaze, and the wicked intent written all over his face made her shiver. "It means I get the loo first."

Eight

The farmhouse's great room looked brand-new and James couldn't take all of the credit. It was because the house had good bones and old-world charm—qualities he'd never appreciated in anything before.

Hell, maybe he'd never even *noticed* them before.

Bella finished polishing the last silver candlestick and stuck it back on the mantel of the humongous fireplace, humming a nameless tune that he'd grown a bit fond of over the past day as they'd worked side by side to get their lover's retreat set to rights.

"Did you hear that?" she asked with a cocked head.

"Uh, no." He'd been too busy soaking in the sight of a beautiful woman against the backdrop of the deep maroon walls and dark furniture. "What was it?"

"The sound of success."

She smiled and that heavy feeling in his chest expanded a tad more, which had been happening with alarming frequency all day. Unfortunately, the coping mechanism he'd used last night—grabbing Bella and sinking into her as fast as possible so his mind went blessedly blank—wasn't available to him at this moment because a workman from the municipality was on his way to restore the water connection.

It was a minor miracle the workman had come out on short notice, given the typical local bureaucracy, but once James had mentioned that he was a representative for the Montoros, everything had fallen into place.

He'd have to make himself—and his distinctive green car—scarce. Just as he'd done this morning when the bloke from the electric company had come. But it was fine. The time away had given him an opportunity to talk through strategy with his sports agent, who mentioned a possible opportunity with Liverpool. No guarantees, but some shifting had occurred in the roster and the club needed a strong foot. Brilliant news at an even better time—the sooner James could escape Alma, the better.

"Yep," he said and cleared a catch from his throat. "Only twenty-seven rooms to go."

They'd started on the downstairs, focusing on the kitchen and great room, plus the servant's quarters past the kitchen, where they intended to sleep tonight if the bed they'd ordered arrived on time, as promised. A lot had been accomplished in one day but not nearly enough.

Once they got the master bedroom upstairs cleaned up, James planned a whole silk-sheets-and-rose-petals-type seduction scene. He owed it to Bella since she'd been such a good sport about sleeping in the room designated for the help.

One thing he immensely appreciated about Bella: she joked around a lot about being high maintenance but she was the furthest thing from it. And he knew a difficult, demanding woman when he saw one, like his last semi-permanent girlfriend, Chelsea. She'd cured him of ever wanting to be around a female for more than a one-night stand, a rule which he'd stuck to for nearly two years.

Until Bella.

Since he couldn't lose his mind in her fragrant skin for…
he glanced at his watch and groaned…hours, he settled for
a way-too-short kiss.

She wiggled away and stuck her tongue out at him. "Yes,
we have a lot of work left. But not as much as we would
have if you hadn't made all those calls. You're the main
reason we've gotten this far."

The hero-worship in her gaze still made him uncomfortable, so he shrugged and polished an already-sparkling
crystal bowl with the hem of his shirt so he had an excuse
not to look directly at her. "Yeah, that was a brilliant contribution. Hitting some numbers on my phone."

"Stop being such a goof." Hands on her hips, she stepped
into his space, refusing to let his attention linger elsewhere.
"You're a great person. I'm allowed to think so and don't
you dare tell me I can't."

That pulled a smile from him. "Yes, Your Highness."

"Anyway," she drawled with an exaggerated American
accent, which only widened his smile, as she'd probably
intended. "When I was cleaning the fireplace, I realized I
really need to call my father. We can't ignore the press release about my engagement to Will much longer."

Though she kept up her light tone, he could tell some
stress had worked its way into her body. Her shoulders
were stiff and a shadow clouded her normally clear eyes.

"Maybe we can wait," he suggested, and laced his fingers with hers to rub her knuckles. "Tomorrow's soon
enough."

"I kind of want to get it over with." She bit her lip,
clearly torn. "But I also really like the idea of procrasti-
nating."

"Why?" he asked, surprising himself. He'd meant to
say they should wait. Why do today what you can put off
until tomorrow?

He, of all people, understood avoiding conflict, especially when it involved an overbearing father. But the distress evident in the foreign lines around her eyes had to go and he would do whatever it took to solve the problem.

Maybe it wasn't a good thing for him to encourage her to wait. Maybe she needed to get the confrontation over with. But how would he know if he didn't ask?

"My father really wants me to fall in line, like Gabriel did. When Rafe abdicated, it was kind of a big deal." She sighed. "I get that. I really don't want to cause problems because of my own selfishness."

"But you're not," he countered. "How is it a problem that you want to choose the bloke you marry?"

"Because my father says it is." Her mouth flattened into a grim line. "That's why I want to put off dealing with all of this. I'm just not ready for all of the expectations that go along with restoring the monarchy. I mean, I always knew our family had come from a royal line, but that was so long ago. Why is it so important to my father all of a sudden?"

She seemed a little fragile in that moment so he pulled her into his arms, shushing her protests over the state of her cleanliness.

"I wish I could tell you why things are important to fathers," he murmured. "Mine has yet to explain why it's so horrifying to him that I don't want a job at Rowling Energy. Becoming a world-class football player might make some dads proud."

"Not yours?" she whispered, her head deep in his shoulder.

Her arms tightened around him, which was oddly comforting. What had started as an embrace he'd thought she needed swiftly became more precious to him than oxygen.

"Nah. Will's his golden boy."

"Why don't you want to work at Rowling?"

It was the first time anyone had ever asked him that.

Most people assumed he wanted to play football and there was little room for another career at his dad's company. But even now, when he had few choices in continuing his sports career, he'd never consider Rowling an alternative.

His father wasn't the listening type; he just bulldozed through their conversations with the mindset that James would continue to defy him and never bothered to wonder why James showed no interest in the family business.

"It's because he built that company on my mother's grave," he said fiercely. "If she hadn't died, he wouldn't have moved to Alma and tapped in to the offshore drilling that was just starting up. I can't ever forget that."

"Is someone asking you to forget?" she probed quietly. "Maybe there's room to take a longer view of this. If your father hadn't moved to Alma, you wouldn't have discovered that you loved football, right?"

"That doesn't make it okay." The admission reverberated in the still house and she lifted her head to look at him, eyebrows raised in question. "I love football but only because it saved me. It got me out of Alma at an early age and gave me the opportunity to be oceans away. I can't be on the same small island as my father. Not for long."

When had this turned into confession time? He'd never said that out loud before. Bella had somehow pulled it out of him.

"I'm sorry," she said quietly and snuggled back into his arms, exactly where he wanted her.

"I'm sorry you've got the same issues with your father. But there's always gossip in a small town. We're going to be dealing with a scandal over the press release once someone catches on to us shacking up in this love nest. But I support whatever decision you make as far as the timing," he told her sincerely, though he'd be heavily in favor of waiting.

He wasn't royalty though. She had a slew of obligations he knew nothing about; he could hardly envision a worse life than one where you had to think about duty to crown and country.

"I think that's the most romantic thing you've ever said to me." Her voice cracked on the last word.

Puzzled, he tipped her chin up, and a tear tracked down her cheek. "Which part? When I called this jumble of a house a love nest or described our relationship as shacking up?"

She laughed through another couple of tears, thoroughly confounding him. Just when he thought he finally got her, she did something he couldn't fathom.

"Neither. The part where you said you support me, no matter what. It makes me warm, right here." She patted her stomach.

He almost rolled his eyes. That was laying it on a bit thick, wasn't it? "I do support you, but that's what peop—lovers…people in a rela—" God, he couldn't even get his tongue to find the right word to explain the status of what they were doing here.

Maybe because he didn't *know* what they were doing here.

"Yeah," she said happily, though what she was agreeing to, he had no idea. "That's what you do. I get that. You've always done exactly the right thing, from the very beginning."

He scowled. "I don't do that."

He didn't. He was the guy who buckled when it mattered most. The guy whose team had been counting on him and he'd let them down. The guy who ran from conflict instead of dealing with it. Hadn't she been listening to anything he'd said about why he played football?

His character had been tarnished further with the hooker incident. James Rowling was the last person anyone should count on. Especially when it came to support. Or "being there" for someone emotionally.

"You do." Her clear blue eyes locked with his and she wouldn't let him look away. "You look in the mirror and see the mistakes your father has insisted you've made. I look at you and see an amazing man. You did hard physical labor all day in a house that means nothing to you. Because I asked you to. You're here. That means a lot to me. I need a rock in my life."

She had him all twisted up in her head as the hero of this story. She couldn't be more wrong—he was a rock, all right. A rolling stone headed for the horizon.

It suddenly sounded lonely and unappetizing. "I can't be anyone's rock. I don't know how."

That had come out wrong. He intended to be firm and resolute, but instead sounded far too harsh.

"Oh, sweetie. There's no instruction manual. You're already doing it." She shook her head and feathered a thumb over his jaw in a caress that felt more intimate than the sex they'd had last night. "You're letting someone else cloud your view of yourself. Don't let your father define who you are."

He started to protest and then her words really sank in. Had he subconsciously been doing that—letting his father have that much power over him?

Maybe he'd never realized it because he'd refused to admit the rift between him and his father might be partially his own fault. James had always been too busy running to pay attention. Even now, his thoughts were on Liverpool and the potential opportunity to play in the top league. But more importantly, Liverpool wasn't in Alma—where the woman who had him so wrongly cast in her head as the hero lived. He was thinking about leaving. Maybe he was already halfway out the door.

Which then begged the question—what if he buckled under pressure because he always took off when the going got tough?

The new bed was supremely superior to the floor. Bella and James christened it that night and slept entwined until morning. It was the best night of sleep she'd ever had in her life.

But dawn brought a dose of reality. She hadn't been back to the Playa del Onda house in almost forty-eight hours. The quick text message to Gabriel to explain her absence as a "getaway with a friend" hadn't stopped her father from calling four times and leaving four terse voice mail messages. She hadn't answered. On purpose.

With the addition of running water and electricity, the farmhouse took on a warmth she enjoyed. In fact, she'd rather stay here forever than go back to the beach house. But she had to deal with her father eventually. If this matter of the engagement announcement was simply a test of her father's resolve versus her own, she wouldn't care very much about the scandal of being with James.

But it wasn't just about two Montoros squaring off against each other. It was a matter of national alliances and a fledgling monarchy. She didn't have any intention of marrying Will, but until the Montoros issued a public retraction of the engagement story, the possibility of another scandal was very real. This one might be far worse for Gabriel on the heels of the one Rafe had caused. And hiding away with James hadn't changed that. She had to take care of it. Soon.

"Good morning," James murmured and reached out to stroke hair from her face as he lay facing her on the adjacent pillow. "This is my favorite look on you."

"Bedhead?" She smiled despite the somberness of her thoughts.

"Well loved." He grinned back. "I liked it yesterday morning, too."

Speaking of which… "How long do you think we can reasonably hole up here without someone snapping a picture of us together?"

He shrugged one shoulder. "Forever." When she arched a brow, he grinned. "I can fantasize about that, can't I?

As long as I keep jetting off when people show up, what's the hurry?"

Her conscience pricked at her. James was leaving the timing of forcing the issue to her, but a scandal could be damaging to him as well. It was selfish enough to refuse to marry Will, but she wasn't really hurting him as long as they were up front about it. A scandal that broke before the retraction could very well hurt James and she couldn't stand that.

"I think I need to talk to my father today," she said firmly. "Or tomorrow at the very latest."

James deserved what he'd asked for—the right to take her out in public, to declare to the world that they'd started seeing each other. To take her to a hotel, or dinner or wherever he liked. It wasn't fair to force him to help her clean up this old farmhouse just so she could avoid a confrontation.

Except she wasn't only avoiding the confrontation. She was avoiding admitting to herself that her own desires had trumped her responsibilities. Hurricane Bella had followed her across the Atlantic after all.

"I'll drive you back to Playa Del Onda," he said immediately. "Whenever you're ready."

A different fear gripped her then. What if they got everything straightened out and she and James could be together with no fear of scandal—only for her to discover things between them were so amazing because of the extreme circumstances? The white-hot attraction between them might fizzle if their secret affair wasn't so secret any longer.

That was enough to change her mind.

"I'll probably never be ready. Let's shoot for tomorrow." That was too soon. The thought of losing her allure with James made her want to weep. "Let's get some more work on the house done today. It'll give me time to gear up. Is that okay? Do you have something else you need to be doing?"

"Nothing I would rather be doing, that's for sure. I'm completely open."

"Me, too."

And for some reason, that didn't sit well, as if she was some kind of Eurotrash princess who had nothing better to do than lie around all day getting it on with a hot athlete. That was like a tabloid story in and of itself.

The urn from the great room popped into her head. Usefulness created worth and she wanted to feel that her life had worth.

"You know what I'd like to do?" she said impulsively. "Find out if there's a wildlife conservation organization in Alma."

James, to his credit, didn't register a lick of surprise. "I'll help you find one."

Of course he'd say that, without questioning why. His unwavering support was fast becoming a lifeline. "I was involved in one back in Miami. I like taking care of poor, defenseless creatures. Especially birds. We had wild macaws on the grounds at our house and I always felt like they were there as a sign. I miss them. I miss feeling like I'm doing something to give back, you know?"

"It's a good cause," he agreed. "There are some estuaries on the east side of the main island. Lots of migratory birds and fish live there. Surely there are some organizations devoted to their preservation. If not, you're in the perfect position to start one."

Her breath caught. At last, a use for the title of princess. If her brother was running the show, he could give her backing in parliament to get some state money set aside. Fund-raisers galore could come out of that. "Thanks. I love that idea."

"If we're going to Playa Del Onda tomorrow, you want to swing by the Playa branch of the Ministry of Agriculture and Environment and see if they have any information on wildlife conservation?"

"Definitely. And then I'd like to come back and put together a serious renovation plan for the house. But I'm not suggesting you have to help," she amended in a rush.

Good grief. Everything that came out of her mouth sounded as if she was ordering him around, expecting him to play chauffer and be a general Alma guide. He might have his own life to live. Or he might realize the thrill had worn off.

"I want to help," he insisted. "My assumption is that we're still planning to lie low, even after you clear things up with your father. So that means we need a place to go. I like it here."

She let out the breath caught in her lungs. She shouldn't read into his response. But for some reason, it made her feel a little better that he wasn't already planning to ditch their relationship once it wasn't secret any longer. "I do, too."

She'd started thinking she might like to live in the farmhouse permanently. It wasn't too far from Del Sol, so she could visit Tía Isabella occasionally. If she planned to stay in Alma, she had to live *somewhere*. Why not here? No one else cared about it.

As she lay in the bed James had ordered and smiled at him in the early morning light, it occurred to her that *he* was the only reason she'd even thought about a permanent place to live. As if James and forever were intertwined.

That was enough to propel her from the bed with a quickly tossed-off excuse about taking a shower now that she could.

As the water heated up, she berated herself for dreaming about life beyond the next few days. It was one thing to question whether James would lose interest once they could go public with their affair, but it was another entirely to assign him a permanent place in her life without even consulting him.

What would his place be? Boyfriend? Official lover? She'd be living in the public eye far more in Alma than in

Miami. What if James didn't want that kind of scrutiny? She wouldn't blame him, especially given the past scandals that dogged his steps.

Of course, she didn't know his thoughts one way or another. Maybe he'd be done with their affair in a few days, regardless of the status of their relationship. Maybe the whole concept of being her long-term lover had little appeal.

What was she *thinking*?

What had happened to the girl who used to flit from one guy to the next with ease? Or for that matter, the girl who flitted from party to party? Living out here in the country would make it really difficult to stay in the scene. No jetting off to Monte Carlo or Barcelona for some fun on the Mediterranean when Alma grew too dull. But when she exited the bathroom and saw the beautiful, surprisingly romantic man still in the bed they'd shared last night, sprawled out under the covers like a wicked fantasy, all of that drained from her mind. What party—what other man, for that matter—could compare to *that*?

"Give me a few minutes and we'll get started," he promised. "Let's check out the upstairs today."

God, she was in a lot of trouble. *She* should be the one thinking about cooling things off, not worrying about whether James planned to.

But the thought of ending things with James made her nauseous.

What was she going to do?

Nine

The upstairs master suite had the most amazing four-poster bed Bella had ever seen. When she drew off the drop cloths covering it, she almost gasped at the intricate carvings in the wood. Delicate flowers in full bloom twined up the posts and exploded into bunches at the top corners.

Once she polished the wood to gleaming and whacked the dust from the counterpane and pillows, the bed took on an almost magical quality, as if it had been a gift from the fairy realm to this one.

The rest of the room was a wreck. Mice had gotten into the cushions of the chairs by the huge bay window and Bella could tell by the discoloration of the walls that some type of artwork had originally hung there, but had disappeared at some point over the years.

The floor groaned behind her and she turned to see James bouncing lightly on a spot near the bed. The planks bowed under his weight and then with a *snap*, one cracked in two. Both pieces fell into the newly created hole. It was a testament to James's superior balance and athletic reflexes that the broken plank hadn't thrown him to the floor.

"Oops," he said sheepishly as he leaped clear. "I was not expecting that to happen. Sorry."

She waved it off. "If that's the worst damage we do today, I'll consider that a plus. Why, exactly, were you jumping up and down on it in the first place?"

"When I walked over it, this section felt different, like it wasn't solid underneath. It turns out it wasn't."

Grinning at his perplexed expression, she joined him to peer into the hole. It was a shallow compartment, deliberately built into the floor. "Looks like you found the royal hiding place. Oooh, maybe there are still some priceless jewels in there."

Eagerly, she knelt and pulled the broken board from the hole. "Hand me your phone."

James placed it in her outstretched hand and when she aimed it into the gap, the lighted screen revealed a small box. Leaning forward slightly on her knees, she stuck her hand down into the space and only as her fingers closed over the box did she think about the possibility of spiders. Ick. Since it was too late, she yanked the box out and set it on the floor next to James.

"Anything else?" he asked, his body hot against her back as he peered over her shoulder, lips grazing her ear.

It shouldn't have been such a turn-on, but then, there was nothing about James that *didn't* turn her on. Warmth bloomed in her midsection and as she arched her back to increase the contact with his torso, the feel of him hummed through her.

"Maybe," she murmured. "Why don't you reach around here and see for yourself."

He must have picked up on her meaning. His arms embraced her from behind, drawing her backward into his body, and his fingers fumbled around the edge of the hole without delving more than half an inch into it.

"Nope. Nothing in there." His lips nuzzled her neck as he spoke and she could tell his attention was firmly on her. The hard length grinding into her rear said he'd lost interest in whatever else might be in the decades-old hiding place as well. "But what have we here?"

"I think you better investigate," she said, and guided his hands under her shirt, gasping as his questing fingertips ran over her sensitive breasts.

"You're not fully dressed," he accused her with a naughty laugh. "Ms. Montoro, I am shocked at your lack of undergarments. It's almost as if you expected a bloke's hands to be under your shirt."

"You say that like it's a bad thing." Her core heated as he caressed her, nudging her rear with his hard erection. "And as you're the only man around, you're welcome."

His laugh vibrated along her spine, warming her further. She loved it when he laughed, loved being the reason he was amused. Loved it when he touched her as if he'd discovered something rare and precious and he planned to become intimately familiar with every nook and cranny.

Then he got serious, palming her aching nipples, massaging and working her flesh until she could hardly breathe from wanting him. Would she *ever* get tired of that, of the gasping need and clawing desire? She hoped not.

She whipped off her shirt and tossed it on the bed, granting him full access. Arching against him, she pushed her breasts into his hands and flung her head back against his shoulder. As if reading her mind, he fastened his lips to her earlobe, sucking on it gently as one hand wandered south in a lazy pattern, pouring more fire on top of the flames he'd already ignited as her flesh heated under his fingertips.

Finally, his fingers slid into her shorts and toyed for an eternity with her panties, stroking her through the fabric, teasing her as he kissed her throat. So hot and ready, she could hardly stand waiting until he'd had his fill of exploring.

When she moaned in protest at the delay, he eased her back against his thighs and slipped off the rest of her clothing. Without a word, he picked her up and spun her around, placing her gently on the bed, his dark gaze worshipping her body.

Even that heaped more coals on the fire and she shuddered.

Through hazy vision, she watched as he knelt between her thighs and kissed each one. His tongue traced a straight line across her flesh and then he glanced up at her under his lashes as he licked her core. His tongue was hard and blistering hot and wet.

The flare of white-hot pleasure made her cry out. He dove in, tasting her in a sensuous perusal that drained her mind. *Yes*, she screamed. Or maybe that had only been in her head. Her body thrashed involuntarily as he pleasured her with his mouth, slight five o'clock shadow abrading her thighs as he moved.

Higher and higher she spun, hips bucking closer to the source of this amazing pleasure with each thrust of his tongue. The light scape of his teeth against her sensitive bud set off a rolling, thick orgasm that blasted her apart faster and harder than anything she'd ever felt before.

"Now," she murmured huskily and lay back on the counterpane in invitation. "I want your very fine body on mine."

He complied, clothes hitting the floor in a moment. He stretched out over her, his lean torso brushing her breasts deliciously. She wiggled until they were aligned the way she wanted, reveling in the dark sensation of this man covering her.

Savoring the anticipation, she touched him, letting her hands roam where they pleased. Fingertips gliding over his muscled back—gorgeously bunching as he held himself erect so he wouldn't crush her—she hummed her appreciation and nipped at his lips until he took her mouth in a scorching kiss reminiscent of the one he'd given her at her core, tongue deep inside her.

Wordlessly, she urged him on by rolling her hips, silently begging him to complete her as only he could. A brief pause as he got the condom on and then he slid into her, filling her body as gloriously as he filled her soul.

She gasped and clung with all her muscles.

James.

Absolutely the best thing that had ever happened to her. The sexiest man she'd ever been with, for sure, but also the only one who *saw* her. No pretense. No games. She couldn't tear her gaze from his face and something shifted inside, opening the floodgates of a huge and wonderful and irrevocable surge of emotion.

She let herself feel, let everything flow as he loved her. She couldn't even find the capacity to be shocked. It was dangerous—she knew that—but couldn't help it. Murmuring encouragement, his name, who knew what else, she rode out another climax made all the more intense by the tenderness blooming in her heart for the man who'd changed everything. But the wonderful moment soured as soon as her breathing slowed and the hazy glow wore off. She couldn't tell him she'd discovered all these things inside that had his name written all over them. Could she?

No. Fear over his reaction gripped her and in the end, she kept her big mouth shut. After their affair became public, maybe she could admit he'd done something irrevocable to her. But now, reeling it all back, she lay in his arms, letting him hold her tight as if he never meant to let go.

Later, when they'd finally gained the strength to dress, she noticed the box still on the floor near the broken boards. "We should open that."

She pushed at it with her bare foot and it tumbled over, lid flying open and spilling its contents all over the hardwood planks. Letters. Ten or twenty of them, old and fragile, with spidery pale blue handwriting looping across the yellowed pages.

Picking one up, she squinted at it but in the low light of the still musty bedroom, it was too hard to read. She flipped it over to see more of the same faded writing.

"What are they?" James peered over her shoulder, breath warm and inviting across her neck. "Front *and* back. Looks like someone had a lot to say."

"Oh, no." She shook her head and moved out of his reach with a laugh that came out a lot less amused than she'd intended. "You are banned from coming up behind me from now on."

She was far too raw inside to let him open her up again. Not so soon.

"What?" His wicked grin belied the innocent spread of his hands. "I was curious. I can't help it if breathing the same air as me gets you all hot and bothered."

It was a perfectly legitimate thing to say. They flirted and teased each other all the time. *All* the time, and she normally loved it.

He was just so beautiful standing there against the backdrop of the bed where he'd made her feel amazing and whole, made her feel as if she could do anything as long as he was by her side, holding her hand.

Suddenly, her throat closed and she barely caught a sob that welled up from nowhere. This was supposed to be a fun-filled, magnificently hot getaway from the world. When had everything gotten so complicated?

"I, um… Tía Isabella will want these." Bella held up the letters in one hand with false cheer. "I'm just going to go put them in my bag so I don't forget them."

She turned away from James and left the room as quickly as she could without alerting him to her distress. Apparently she'd succeeded.

And now she was completely messed up because she'd hoped he would follow her and demand to know why she was crying.

They slept in the servant's quarters again because they hadn't gotten nearly enough accomplished upstairs due to the detour Bella had sprung on James.

Not that he minded. She could detour like that all day long.

When he awoke, he missed Bella's warmth instantly. She wasn't in the bed. Sitting up, he sought a glimpse of her through the open bathroom door, but nada.

Shame. He liked waking up with her hair across his chest and her legs tangled with his. Surprisingly. This was officially the longest stretch he'd spent with a woman in… ages. Not since Chelsea. And even then, he hadn't been happy in their relationship, not for a long time. When she'd broken up with him because she'd met someone else, he'd been relieved.

Wondering where Bella had taken off to, James vaulted from the bed and dressed, whistling aimlessly as he stuck his shirt over his head. He felt a twinge in his back at the site of an old football injury. Probably because he'd spent the past few days using a different muscle group than the ones he normally engaged while strength training and keeping his footwork honed. Cleaning decades of grime from a place was hard work. But he liked the result— both in the appearance of the house and the gratitude Bella expressed.

Strolling out into the newly-scrubbed kitchen, he reached for the teapot he'd purchased, along with a slew of other absolute necessities, and saw Bella in his peripheral vision sitting outside on the back stoop. She was staring off into the distance as if something was troubling her.

He had a suspicion he knew what it was. Today they were supposed to drive into Playa Del Onda. Should he pretend he'd forgotten and not bring it up so they didn't have to go? He hated that she'd worked the whole confrontation over the engagement announcement up in her mind into something unpleasant. It really shouldn't be so complicated.

Demand a retraction. Done. Of course, getting her father to agree wouldn't necessarily be easy, but it certainly wouldn't be complicated.

In the end, he opted to join her on the stoop without comment, drawing her into his arms to watch the sun burst from behind the clouds to light up the back acreage. She snuggled into his torso and they sat companionably, soaking up the natural beauty of the wild overgrowth.

A horn blasted from the front of the house, startling them both. "Expecting someone?" he asked and she shook her head. "Stay here. I'll see what it is."

"You can't." Her mouth turned down. "I have to be the one. It's Montoro property."

Enough of this hiding and watching their step and having to do things separately so no one could take a picture of them together. They were catering to the whims of their fathers, whether she realized it or not.

"We'll go together." He rose and held out his hand.

She hesitated for so long, an uneasy prickle skittered across the back of his neck. It was way past time to dispense with all this secrecy nonsense. He wanted to do what he pleased and go wherever he wished without fear of someone creating a scandal. Today was a perfect day to stop the madness, since they already planned to confront her father.

Firmly, he took her hand and pulled her to her feet. "Yes. Together. If someone takes a picture, so be it. We're talking to your father today, so there's no reason to keep up this game of hide and seek. Not any longer."

Heaving a huge breath, she nodded. "Okay."

Together, they walked to the front, where a delivery driver stood on the front drive, waving.

"Tengo un paquete," he said, and touched his cap.

Smashing. One-day delivery, as advertised. James had been worried the gift he'd ordered for Bella wouldn't arrive in time, but obviously the exorbitant rush charge had been worth it.

"Gracias," James responded immediately. *"¿Dónde firmo?"*

Bella's eyebrows quirked. "When did you learn Spanish?"

"In like grade four," he retorted with a laugh. "I grew up in a Spanish-speaking country, remember?"

The driver held out his clipboard and once James signed, the deliveryman went to the back of the truck and pulled free a large parcel. Handing it over, the driver nodded once and climbed back into his truck, starting it up with a roar.

The package squawked over the engine sound.

"What in the world is in there?" Bella asked, clearly intrigued as James carried the box into the house through the front door, careful not to cover the air holes with his arms.

"It's a gift. For you." James pulled the tab to open the top of the box, as the Spanish instructions indicated. The box side fell open to reveal the large metal birdcage holding two green macaws. They squawked in tandem.

Bella gasped, "James! What is this?"

"Well, I must have gotten the wrong birds if it's not abundantly clear," he said wryly. "You said you missed your macaws so I brought some to you. Are they okay?"

He'd paid an additional flat fee to guarantee the birds would arrive alive. They looked pretty chipper for having been shipped from the mainland overnight.

With a loud sniff and a strange, strangled mumble, Bella whirled and fled the room, leaving James with two loud birds and a host of confusing, unanswered questions.

"I guess I muddled things up," he told the birds.

He put the cage on the coffee table and gave them some water as he'd been instructed when he ordered the birds, but his irritation rose as he poured. More water ended up on the floor than in the container.

If he could just punch something, his mood would even out. Probably.

Was he supposed to chase Bella down and apologize for spending money on her? Demand an explanation for why she'd hated the gift so much, a simple thank you was beyond her?

By the time he'd ripped open the package of bird food and poured some in the dish, she hadn't returned and his temper had spiked past the point of reasonableness. So he went in search of her and found her upstairs lying in a tight ball on the bed in the master suite. Sobbing.

Instantly, his ire drained and he crawled into the bed to cuddle her, stroking her hair until she quieted enough to allow his windpipe to unclench. "What's wrong, sweetheart?"

She didn't answer and his gut twisted.

Maybe she'd been looking for the exit and his gift had upset her. Women were funny about expensive presents, thinking a bloke had all kinds of expectations in mind if they accepted the gift.

"There aren't any strings attached to the birds, Bella. If you like them, keep them. If you don't, I'll…" *No returns*, the place had said. "…sort it."

His throat went tight again. If she was done here, the birds were the least of his problems. He wasn't ready to end things, not yet. Eventually, sure. His agent had a phone call scheduled with Liverpool today, but that was only the beginning of a long process that might not net him anything other than dashed hopes.

Had he inadvertently speeded up the timeline of their parting with his gesture?

"I like them," she whispered, her mouth buried in the bedspread.

His heart unstuck from his rib cage and began to beat again. "Then talk to me, hon. I'll uncomplicate it, whatever it is."

Without warning, she flipped to face him and the ravaged look on her face sank hooks into his stomach, yanking it toward his knees.

"Not this. You can't uncomplicate it because *you're* the complication, James."

Circles again, and they didn't do circles. Not normally. She shot straight—or at least she had thus far. Had things changed so much so quickly?

"What did I do that's so horrible?" he demanded.

The little noise of disgust she made deep in her throat dredged up some of his earlier temper, but he bit it back to give her the floor.

"You came in here," she raged, "and tore down all my ideas about how this thing between us was going to go. You understand me, pay attention to me. And worse than all of that, you made me fall for you!"

The starkness in her expression sealed his mouth shut once and for all, and he couldn't have spoken for a million euros.

"And I'm scared!" she continued. "I've never been in love. What am I supposed to do? Feel? I'm running blindfolded through the dark."

Too much. Too fast. Too...everything. He blinked rapidly but it didn't do anything to ease the burning in his eyes. He couldn't...she wasn't... *Deep breath. Hold it together.*

She was afraid. Of *him* and what was happening inside her. That was the most important thing to address first. Cautiously, he reached out and took her hand. He was so completely out of his depth, it was a wonder his brain hadn't shut down.

This was a challenge. Maybe the most important one of his life, and after all his claims of being able to uncomplicate anything, now was a good time to start. No buckling under the pressure allowed. Bella needed to feel as if she could trust him and obviously she didn't.

Heart pounding—because honestly, the freaking out wasn't just on her side—he cleared his throat. "Look me in the eye and tell me that again. But without all the extra stuff."

"Which part?" she whispered, searching his gaze, her eyes huge, their expression uneasy.

"The thing about falling for me." Her nails cut into his hand as they both tightened their grip simultaneously. This was a tipping point, and the next few minutes would decide which way it tipped. "I want to hear it straight from your heart."

His lungs seized and he honestly couldn't have said which way he wanted it to tip. What did he hope to accomplish by making this request of her? But he'd spoken the honest truth—regardless of everything, he wanted to hear it again.

"I'm falling for you," she said simply in the husky voice that automatically came out when she was deeply affected.

Something broke open inside him, washing him with warmth, huge and wonderful and irreversible. And suddenly, it wasn't very complicated at all. "Yeah. I've got something along those lines going on over here as well."

That something had been going on for a while. And he was quite disturbed that Will had realized it first. Bella was special and admitting it wasn't the big deal he'd made it out to be. Because the specialness had always been true, from the first moment her body aligned with his on the beach. It was as if he'd been waiting for that moment his whole life and when it happened, his world clicked into place.

"Really?" Hope sprang into her eyes, deepening the blue. "Like a little bit or a whole lot?"

"With no basis for comparison, I'd say it's something like being flung off a cliff and finding out exactly what maximum velocity is," he said wryly. "And it's about as scary as cliff diving with no parachute, since we're on the subject."

The smile blooming on her face reminded him of the sunrise they'd just watched together outside, before the birds had prompted this second round of confessions.

"Isn't it against the guy code to tell a woman she scares

you?" She inched toward him and smoothed a hand over his upper arm, almost as if she was comforting him—which was supposed to be his role in this scenario.

"All of this is against the guy code." He rolled his eyes and she laughed, as he'd intended. The harmonious fullness in his chest that magically appeared at the sound was an unexpected bonus. "Can you at least fill me in on why I had to pry all of this out of you with a crowbar?"

She scrubbed at her face, peering at him through her fingers. "This is not how it was supposed to go. We were going to have a couple of hot dates and maybe I would end up going back to Miami. Maybe you'd jet off to another country like you always do. No one said anything about losing my heart along the way."

A little awed at the thought of Bella's heart belonging to him, he reached out and flattened his palm against her chest, reveling in the feel of it beating against his hand. "I'll take good care of it."

He realized instantly that it was the wrong thing to say.

"For how long?" She sat up and his hand fell away. He missed the warmth immediately. "Until you get a new football contract and take off? You don't do relationships. *I* don't do relationships. Are you prepared to figure out why the hard way—with each other?"

"Yes," he said instantly. "Stop making this so difficult. *If* I get a contract, you come with me. Simple."

The alternative was unthinkable. Actually, he'd never thought about these kinds of things. Never had a reason to. Women came, women left. But this one—he had an opportunity here to grab on to her tight with both hands and no matter how much it scared him, he wasn't letting go.

Catching her lip between her teeth, she worried it almost raw. "What if we get my father to retract the engagement announcement and everything is wonderful. We can date in the open. And then we find out the only thing we had going for us was the secrecy?"

"What, you're afraid I won't be keen on all of this if we don't have to sneak around?" A laugh slipped from his mouth before he fully registered the serious set of her jaw. It finally dawned on him. "That's what you're afraid of."

She shifted uncomfortably. "It's a real possibility."

"It's a real possibility that you'll figure out the same thing," he shot back and the wracked expression on her face floored him. "You already thought of that."

Ice formed instantly in his stomach. It had never occurred to him while they were confessing unexpected feelings that he hadn't actually removed the complications. The *real* complications might only be beginning. Falling for each other didn't magically make either of them relationship material and the potential to hurt each other was that much greater as a result.

Sometimes, no matter how much you practiced, you still missed the goal. And neither of them actually had much practice. What were the odds of success?

"Why do you think I got so upset?" she countered. "You're giving me everything I've ever wanted, and then you give me things I had no idea I wanted, and my heart does all this crazy stuff when you look at me, and when you kiss me it's like my life finally makes sense, and what if I'm the one who's building up this relationship into something mythical because I really like my men with a side of forbidden?"

"Okay, breathe."

He half laughed and ran a hand through his hair. This rated as the most honest conversation he'd ever had with a woman. And that made it all the more fascinating that he was still here, determined not to buckle. Bella was worth it.

She breathed. And then dropped the second bomb. "What if I want to get married someday? Is that potentially in the cards?"

He let the idea rattle around inside for a long moment,

but it didn't completely unnerve him to consider it. He wasn't saying yes, but wasn't saying no.

"What if it is?" He captured her gaze and held it, refusing to let her look away, where she might miss the sincerity of what he was telling her. "Will that scare you as well?"

His brother had predicted that, too. Silently, he cursed himself and then his omniscient twin. Well, he hadn't proposed yet and no one was saying he would. Grandfather's watch still belonged to James. For now.

"More than I could possibly tell you," she admitted.

But she didn't have to tell him because he had a pretty good idea that the adrenaline racing around in his body closely matched what was going on with her.

"And," she continued swiftly, "I'm not saying that I will want to get married. To you or anyone. But what if I do?"

"You know what?" He tipped her chin up. "I think it's a safe bet that we have more going on here than a forbidden love angle. And I also think that no matter what, we can be honest with each other about what's going on, whether it's marriage or something else. I might be wrong, but I'm willing to take that risk. Are you?"

"Will you hold my hand?" she asked in a small voice. "When you're holding my hand, I feel like the world is a different place, like nothing bad could ever happen."

Yeah, he got that. If they could do this together, it might actually work.

Tenderly, he laced his fingers with hers and held on. "I'll never let go, not even when we hit the water. Jump with me, Bella."

Her smile pierced his heart and he started to believe they might figure this out after all. There were a lot of unknowns, sure, and they still had to sort their families—which wouldn't be as easy as he might be pretending. But it felt as if they were at the beginning of something wonderful.

It wasn't until they'd climbed into the Lamborghini

an hour later that he glanced at his phone and noted two missed calls, followed by a text message...and had the strangest sense of foreboding, as if he'd vastly underestimated the level and complexity of the complications to come.

Ten

James was quiet during the drive back to Playa Del Onda and Bella left him alone with his thoughts.

After all, she'd been the one to change the game, and while he'd admitted his feelings had grown stronger than he'd expected as well, he hadn't argued when the subject of *what ifs* came up. It was a lot to take in. A lot to reconcile.

She still didn't know how she felt about all of this either. She certainly hadn't intended to blurt out something so difficult to take back as "I'm falling for you," but he'd been so sweet, first with the birds and then the way he handled her half-coherent stream of babbling about her fears. If any man was a keeper, it was James Rowling.

So the question was, how hard was it going to be to keep him? Her father was going to freak and there was no getting around the fact that James was still the wrong brother.

No matter. She wasn't ready to let James go, not yet. Whatever happened between her and James, they had a right to pursue it. And she wasn't leaving here without her father's promise to stop interfering.

When they walked into the house—together—Gabriel and her father were waiting for her in the foyer, thanks to a text message she'd sent on the way imploring her brother to play diplomat if the situation called for it.

Judging by the frown on Rafael's face, she'd made a good call.

"What is *he* doing here?" her father demanded, making it perfectly clear that he knew Bella hadn't brought home the correct Rowling despite their similar appearances— and that Rafael's feelings on the matter hadn't changed.

Bella halted but didn't drop James's hand. He squeezed hers tight in a show of solidarity but remained silent, earning a huge number of points. "James is here because I invited him. You've caused us both problems by announcing my engagement to Will Rowling and therefore, we both have a vested interest in resolving the situation."

"The problems caused by the engagement announcement are one hundred percent at your feet, Isabella." Her father crossed his arms over his expensive suit, presumably to ensure he appeared intimidating, but he'd lost any edge he might have had by using that tone of voice with her—and the man she was pretty sure she was in love with.

"Let's not sling accusations," Gabriel interjected and she smiled at him gratefully. "Listen to Bella, Dad. She's a grown woman and this is a friendly conversation between adults."

Rafael deflated. A bit.

Gabriel's "king" lessons had paid off, in Bella's humble opinion. He'd grown a lot in the past few weeks and no one was confused about Serafia's role in that. Her future sister-in-law—also the future queen—was an inspiration and Bella was happy to call Serafia family.

"You have the floor, Isabella." Her father glowered at James but didn't speak to him again, which was fine by her. For now.

"I don't want to marry Will. I told you this already.

Why in the world would you go ahead and issue a press release saying we were engaged? Do you hate the idea of my happiness so much?" Her voice broke against her will.

Why did she still care so much that her father didn't seem to see her as anything other than a bargaining chip?

James stepped forward and addressed Rafael directly. "Sir, you don't know me and I realize I'm not your first choice for your daughter, but please understand that she makes me happy. I want nothing more than to do the same for her. I hope you can respect that."

Well, if there was any question about whether she was in love with him, that speech pretty much shot all doubt to hell. There might even be swooning in her future. She grinned at him, not even caring that she probably looked like a besotted fool.

Her father sighed and rubbed his head but before he could speak, Gabriel held out his hand to James, shaking it vigorously.

"I can respect that." Her brother nodded once at James. "I didn't get a chance to mention it when we first met, but I occasionally watched you play for Real Madrid. Bum deal that they released you. Big mistake on their part, in my opinion."

"Thanks." James smiled and bowed slightly to Gabriel, despite being told the prince didn't like formality. "And good luck to you. Alma is in brilliant hands with you at the helm."

Now that all the small talk was out of the way... "Dad, James and I are going to be a couple. You have to retract the engagement story or we're going to have a scandal on our hands. I don't want that for Gabriel or the Montoro family as a whole."

"All of which would have been avoided if you'd simply gotten with the program," Rafael insisted. "We're all making sacrifices for Gabriel—"

"Hold on a minute." The future king threw up his hands

with a frown. "Don't drag me into this. I never asked Bella to marry Will Rowling and frankly, an arranged marriage is ridiculous in this day and age. I've never understood the reasoning."

"You need the alignment with Rowling Energy," her father sputtered and might have gone on if Gabriel hadn't interrupted again.

"Yes. I do. But Bella is asking us to find another way. What kind of king would I be if I didn't at least try to take her wishes into account?" Gabriel asked rhetorically, his regal voice echoing with sincerity in the grand foyer. "Dad, I think you should consider the retraction, especially if Bella and James's relationship is what they say it is."

Gabriel shot Bella a look that said he'd taken one look at her dopey face and made all kinds of assumptions about the nature of her relationship with James. But then, bringing James with her to the showdown had probably tipped her brother off to that the moment they'd crossed the threshold. "I don't kiss and tell, so you can forget any juicy details, if that's what you're after."

Gabriel mimed putting his fingers in his ears and shook his head with a shudder.

Clearing his throat in his no-nonsense way, Rafael put on his best disappointed-father face. "It's not just the alignment with Rowling Energy that's at stake here, Isabella. You have a tendency to be flighty. Irresponsible. Marriage will be good for you, if you choose someone who settles you. Will is as steady as they come."

The unvoiced and pointed barb directed at James was: *and the man you waltzed in here with is the opposite of steady*. The sting of hearing her father's unvarnished opinion of *her* was totally eclipsed by the negativity directed toward James, who was nothing like what her father assumed.

"That's where you're wrong, Dad. Will might be good at holding a company together, but James is good at holding *me* together. He settles me in a way I've never felt before. I'd rather spend an evening with him washing windows than at a party."

The words were out of her mouth before she consciously planned to say them, but once they took root in her heart, she recognized the truth. She didn't have any desire to be the party girl she'd been in Miami. Her boredom at Will Rowling's party hadn't had anything to do with the difference in party styles across the ocean, but in the subtle changes already happening inside *her*.

"By the way," she threw in. "You haven't asked, but in case you're wondering, your irresponsible daughter has spent the past few days restoring the old farmhouse near Aldeia Dormer that's part of the Montoro holdings. It looks really amazing so far and I couldn't have done it without James's help. I've also spent almost one hundred percent of that time with him, yet I dare you to find one illicit photograph of the two of us."

"What's this about a farmhouse?" Gabriel's eyebrows drew together as he homed in on her.

"I'll fill you in later," she promised. "Can you try to be happy for me, Dad? If you can't do that, I'll settle for that retraction. I do have a strong sense of my royal obligations. I'd just like you to respect the fact that I feel differently about what they are than you do."

"I'll issue the retraction but only to avoid the potential scandal. I cannot condone this relationship. I would prefer that you do not continue seeing him." Her father's sidelong glance at James spoke volumes. There was no doubt he still considered the wrong Rowling a terrible influence.

"I can't do that, Dad. And I'm disappointed that you still can't see the value James brings to my life." Her voice cracked and she cursed herself once again for caring. Regardless, she was getting the retraction she asked for, and she'd take it.

"You're right, I can't. I fully expect that once the thrill

wears off, you'll be back to your former ways, Isabella."
With that vote of no confidence ringing in her ears, her
father motioned to James. "And if you're not, *he* will be.
This is a disaster in the making. Will it do any good for
me to warn you to keep your brother's reign at the fore-
front of your thoughts?"

"I always keep Gabriel in mind," she countered.

"Good, then the three of you can deal with Patrick Rowling." Her father wheeled on Gabriel with a scowl. "Since
you're taking Bella's side in this, I'll let you handle the
delicate matter of ensuring the alliance I painstakingly
put into place won't suffer."

Her father stalked off to go terrorize the staff or something.

"Sorry," Bella said to her brother with a scowl. "I didn't
mean for you to get in the middle of this. At least not that
way. Are you okay with talking to Mr. Rowling?"

Unfortunately, thanks to the hours upon hours of conversation with James at the farmhouse, Bella knew exactly
why Patrick wasn't going to be pleased with the develop-
ments.

"I'll talk to him," James volunteered, and Bella shot
him a small smile.

"That's a good idea." Gabriel's expression reflected the
gravity of the situation. "I'll speak with him as well. But
it's sticky. We have business agreements in place that could
be in jeopardy. You should lie low for a while longer until
matters are a bit more settled."

Great, more hiding. Why was it such a problem that two
people wanted to spend time together? But the mention of
things like business agreements clued her in that there was
more at stake than she might have supposed.

At least her father hadn't forbidden her to see James.
He just said he didn't want her to and made his disappointment in her clear. Fortunately, she had a lot of practice at
living with her father's disappointment. If Gabriel worked

things out with Mr. Rowling, maybe her father would come around. It could happen.

Gabriel and James talked a bit more about the logistics of their impending conversations with Patrick Rowling until James's cell phone rang.

He glanced at it and excused himself to take the call. Based on his expression, it must be shocking news indeed. Gabriel went off to do king stuff as James ended the call.

"What is it?" she whispered, almost afraid to ask. They'd barely confessed their fledgling feelings to each other, their fathers were still potential stumbling blocks in their relationship and she didn't know how many more hits they should be expected to take.

"Liverpool." His tone couldn't have been more stunned. "Management wants to meet with me. Tomorrow."

"Liverpool? Isn't that a city in England?" Then it dawned on her that he meant the football team. "They want to talk to you about a contract? That's great!"

"I have to fly to London." His enthusiasm shone from his face. Then he grew serious. "I don't know what they're going to say. But if it's an offer, it would be hard for me to turn down."

"Why would you turn it down? You can't."

"I would have to live in England for most of the year." His gorgeous eyes sought and held hers as the implications weighed down her shoulders.

This was serious, life-altering stuff, the kind of thing couples with a future considered. While she thought that was where they were headed—thought that was where she *wanted* them to go—it was another matter entirely to have Big Decisions dropped in your lap before you were ready. It was far scarier than accidentally revealing your feelings.

"We'll figure it out," she murmured, as though she knew what she was talking about. "We're jumping together. Just don't let go of my hand, remember?"

Instead of agreeing, or grabbing her hand and shooting

her a tender smile, he scrubbed at his eyes with stiff fingers. "Everything is moving too fast."

Her heart froze.

Everything? As in their relationship, too? He'd volunteered to come with her, to talk to his father and work out the issues between the Montoro family and Rowling Energy—was he having second thoughts now? "One step at a time, James. Go to England and see what they say. Then we can talk."

He nodded and swept her up in a fierce hug. She inhaled his familiar scent, soaked in his essence. That at least felt somewhat normal and it calmed her a bit.

"I'll call you the moment I know something. Guess I'll be gone a couple of days."

Watching him drive away wrenched something loose inside her and the place ached where it used to be attached. She rubbed at her chest and perversely wondered if it would get better or worse if he called with the news that Liverpool wanted to sign him. Because that's when she'd find out once and for all whether removing the temptation of the forbidden caused him to completely lose interest.

James resisted pulling at his starched collar. Barely. If he'd had more notice that Liverpool wanted a meeting, he might have scared up a more comfortable suit. Contract negotiations rarely included the player and the fact that Liverpool specifically asked for James to attend meant... what? He didn't know and it was weighing on him.

The small room got smaller the longer Liverpool's management murmured behind their cupped hands. James could tell from their less-than-impressed faces that his agent's opening pitch hadn't won anyone over.

So maybe the comfort of the suit didn't matter when your entire future was on the line.

Liverpool had expressed definite interest in picking up

James if the price was right, according to his agent, but they wanted to move fast on making a decision.

James was not leaving here without that contract. It wasn't about the money. It was about putting his mistakes behind him and gaining the opportunity to prove his loyalty to a club. He had to. To show Bella he was really the hero material she saw him as. To prove that he was worth all the trouble they'd gone through to be together.

James cleared his throat. "It's obvious you have reservations about me. What are your concerns?"

The three suits on the other side of the table all stared at him with varying degrees of surprise. Why, because he didn't subscribe to the British philosophy of keeping a stiff upper lip?

His sports agent, Spencer Stewart, shot him an annoyed glance and waved off James. "No one has reservations. We're all professionals here. So, give us your best offer and we'll consider it."

"Yes, we're all professionals," James agreed. "But these gentlemen have every right to question my capacity to act professionally. Let's call a spade a spade. I made mistakes. But I'm ready to be serious about my career and I want to play my heart out for a team willing to give me that chance."

All at once, it occurred to him that Alma's reserve team had already offered him that chance. And he'd turned his nose up at it. As if he was too good for what he considered the small time.

That didn't sit well. No club *owed* him a spot on the roster.

Liverpool's manager nodded slowly. "That's fair. As is our original salary offer. The cap is a concern, after all."

James kept his face straight, wishing he could argue. The cap was only a concern for a risky acquisition. They'd gladly pay the fines for going over the cap to gain a player with a less scandalous past. He'd have to take a pay cut if he wanted to play for Liverpool—and work twice as hard to earn it. Simple as that.

And he'd have to move to England.

A few days ago, he would have already been packed in anticipation of relocating as fast as possible. He could avoid his father for good. That conversation with dear old Dad about the agreements between Rowling Energy and the Montoros—the one he'd promised Gabriel he'd have—never had to happen.

Liverpool was the perfect solution to his relationship with Bella—if they had to lie low, what better place to do it than England?

But he couldn't get enthusiastic about it all at once. Bella deserved better than to be required to hide their relationship because of his past. She shouldn't have to move to England if she wanted to be with him, just because he couldn't get another contract.

How had things grown so complicated so fast? The king of uncomplicating things was falling down on the job.

"I need some time to weigh my options," James announced suddenly. Because he'd just realized he not only had options, he also had other people to consider outside of himself. "I appreciate the offer, and it's generous under the circumstances. Mr. Stewart will update you soon on my decision."

Liverpool wasn't the right club for him. Not yet, maybe not ever. Not until he'd proven to everyone—Bella, his father, hell, even himself—that he could stop running away from conflict and deal with the consequences of his actions. He needed to be in Alma to do that. Permanently.

Actually, this wasn't very complicated at all.

James loved football. He'd thought for so long that a professional league contract was his goal, only to find the game had completely changed on him. Bella had changed it. He wanted to be a better man for her. She was the best reason of all to find out whether he could finally stand up under extreme pressure and come out a winner.

James hurried to Heathrow, eager to get back home and tell Bella that her belief in him wasn't misplaced. That he could be the hero she saw him as. He wanted to commit to her, to have a future with her.

As he settled back in his seat and switched off his cell phone in accordance with the flight attendant's instructions, he glanced at his watch. And cursed as he realized what was happening—it looked as if Will was going to be the lucky recipient of Grandfather's watch after all.

When James got off the plane in Del Sol, he powered up his cell phone intending to call Bella immediately. *Surprise. I'm home early.*

But the first text message that popped up was from Will.

Chelsea is here. You better come talk to her. She's camped out in the lobby disrupting business.

What the hell? He swore, dove into his Lamborghini and then drove to Rowling Energy at double the speed limit. The harrowing hairpin turns should have put a smile on his face the way they normally did, but Will's text message had effectively killed any cheer he might have taken from the thrill.

If only he'd called Chelsea back yesterday, when he'd seen the missed calls on his phone, the ensuing fiasco could have been avoided. But Bella had been nervous about confronting her father and he really didn't want to talk to Chelsea in the first place. So he'd ignored her. What could they possibly have to say to each other?

Apparently that had irritated his ex-girlfriend enough for her to go to Rowling Energy and bother his brother. James had dated her for…what, four months? Not long enough for her to remember that James hated Rowling

Energy so much that he rarely set foot in the place. It had taken something as important to him as Bella to get him through the door last week.

His phone beeped. Will had texted him again. Hope you're almost here. Your ex is a piece of work.

Still fuming, James screeched into a parking spot and stomped into the elevator. Why in the hell had she taken it upon herself to disrupt an entire company in order to speak to an ex-lover she'd had no contact with for almost two years? When a bloke didn't ring you back, it meant he wasn't into you.

But when he arrived in the reception area, some of the pieces fell into place. Chelsea, looking less glamorous and far more worn than he recalled, sat on the leather couch bouncing a baby.

A baby.

Obviously she'd been busy since they'd broken up and was clearly hard up for money. What, did she think James was going to fund her for old times' sake? How dare she bring a kid in here as a sympathy ploy? His ire increased exponentially. She *was* a piece of work.

"Chelsea." She glanced up. "Can we take this outside please?"

She nodded, hoisted the baby to her hip and followed him out of the building to a shaded courtyard around the side of the building where employees sometimes ate lunch. It was thankfully deserted.

"You have a lot of nerve barging into my father's company to extort money from me," he said by way of greeting to the woman he'd had only marginal affection for once upon a time.

"That's not why I'm here and besides, you didn't call me back," she reminded him as she settled onto a bench with the baby. "How else was I supposed to find you?"

He bit back a curse. "You're barking up the wrong tree if you think I'm going to give you a dime out of the goodness of my heart because some plonker knocked you up and you're short on cash."

That would explain why she had a bargain basement fashion statement going on. When they'd dated, she spent thousands on clothes and jewelry, usually with his credit card.

"Not someone." Chelsea peered up at him, totally cool. In her element because she'd gotten his attention after all. "You. This is your daughter."

His vision blacked out for a moment as all the blood rushed from his head.

I have a baby daughter. None of those words belonged in the same sentence. Blindly, James felt for the bench so he could sink onto it before the cramp in his stomach knocked him to the grass.

"What are you talking about?" he demanded hoarsely over the street sounds floating through the privacy bushes. "I haven't even seen you in almost two years. That's a baby and they only take nine months to make."

Chelsea smirked and flipped her lanky brown hair behind her back. "She's almost a year old, Daddy. Do the math."

Daddy. His brain couldn't—*could not*—keep up, especially when she insisted on throwing inflammatory monikers onto the woodpile. And now she wanted him to do subtraction on top of it all?

"Why...wha— How...?" Deep breath. His tongue couldn't seem to formulate the right questions. "Paternity test? I want one."

Okay, now he was on top of this situation. Get to the bottom of this pack of lies and toss her out on her no-longer-attractive rear end.

She rolled her eyes. "Fine. I'll arrange one as soon as possible. But there's really no question."

The little girl picked that moment to turn her head, peering directly at James for the first time.

Aqua eyes the exact color of his beamed at him through fringed lashes. Not only the exact color of his, but both Will and their late mother shared the rare shade.

His world tilted and slid quickly off the rails. The paternity test would be superfluous, obviously.

He couldn't tear his gaze away from the baby. His baby. It was real. This was his child, and until five minutes ago he'd had no idea she existed. He'd missed his daughter's birth, along with a ton of other milestones, which he mourned all at once. Chelsea could never rectify that crime.

"Why now, Chelsea? You should have bloody well shown up long before today with this news."

"I thought she was Hugh's." Chelsea shrugged nonchalantly as if they were discussing a pair of pants she'd found in her closet after they'd broken up. "He's the guy I left you for. I must have miscalculated my conception date, but I didn't realize it until recently when her eyes changed color. And I knew I couldn't keep this from you."

There was so much wrong with all of that, he hardly knew where to start. "What happened when her eyes changed color, Chelsea? Did you see dollar signs that Hugh couldn't match?"

"No." She frowned, pulling her full lips into a pout. "I thought it was right that you know about Maisey."

Maisey. His daughter's name was Maisey. And he'd had no say in it. Not that it was a horrible name, but if Chelsea had told him when she got pregnant, he might have been able to participate in the selection process. He'd have liked to name his daughter after his mum. Yet another thing this woman had stolen from him.

"If you thought about me at all, I'm sure it had more to do with things like child support."

He had to get over it and figure this out. Chelsea was his daughter's mother. Period. Like it or not, they were going to have some type of relationship for the next eighteen years, at least. Maybe longer.

Before she could deny her selfishness again, he eyed her. "What did Hugh think about your little error in calculation? Bet he wasn't so thrilled."

Chelsea looked away quickly but not before he saw the flash of guilt in her expression.

"He left you," James concluded grimly. "And you're skint."

She sighed. "Hugh refused to keep taking care of a kid that wasn't his and he might have been slightly ticked to find out that I fudged the details a little about the last time you and I slept together. So yeah, I'm low on money."

God, did the string of dumb decisions this woman had made ever end? This was his daughter's life Chelsea was playing around with, but she seemed to be treating it all like a big game.

The baby made a noise that sounded like a cross between a sob and a sigh and she captivated his attention instantly.

"What was that? Is she okay?" he whispered.

"She's a baby," Chelsea snapped impatiently. "That's what they do. Make noise. And cry. And poop."

This conversation had passed surreal ten minutes ago.

"What do you want from me?" he demanded.

Well, hell. It hardly mattered what she wanted. If this little breathing bundle of hair and pink outfit was his daughter, there was a lot more to consider than what the woman who'd given birth to her hoped to achieve. He had rights. He had options. And he would exercise both.

"I want you to be her father," Chelsea said simply.

"Done. We need to discuss child support and custody arrangements."

Reality blasted him like a freight train whistle. What was his life going to look like from now on? Did he need to reconsider Liverpool so he could be close to Chelsea in England? How would Bella feel about spending weekends with his infant daughter from now on?

He scrubbed at his face. *Bella*. God, this was going to be exactly what her father had predicted—a disaster. She deserved so much more than to be saddled with a boyfriend who had a kid. And what kind of new problems might this cause for her? An illegitimate child surely wasn't going to make her father suddenly approve of James.

"Nothing to discuss." Chelsea shook her head. "I don't want either one. I want you to take her. Forever. I'm signing over all my rights to you."

"You...what?"

Arms crossed mutinously like the immature woman she was, Chelsea scowled. "I'm done being a mum. I hate it. This is your fault, so you take her."

She said it as if they were discussing a stray dog. And she was making his choice easy. He didn't want such a selfish mum raising his daughter anyway. Sickened that he could have ever been intimate with this woman, he nodded grimly. "Seems like the best idea all the way around, then."

Single dad. The voice in his head wouldn't stop screaming that phrase, over and over, and the place in his heart that belonged to Bella ached at this new reality. Just as he'd accepted that he not only *could* do a long-term, roots-into-the-ground relationship, he wanted to. But not like this, with such a huge complication as a surprise baby.

The timing was horrific. Because he'd just realized why this was so difficult, why he couldn't take the Liverpool contract. Why he was so worried about dropping this news on Bella—he was in love with her.

Eleven

By evening, James hadn't called.

Bella tried not to think about it. He was busy with Liverpool. She got that. The one time she'd tried to call him, it went straight to voice mail. Maybe his cell phone had died and he'd forgotten his charger.

If not that, there was a simple explanation for his silence and when he got her message, he'd call. No one would willingly face down her father without having some skin in the game. James had said he'd call and he would. He cared about her. She knew he did.

After a long night of tossing and turning, she had to find something to do to keep busy and the farmhouse still needed work. It kept her mind off the disloyal thoughts that had crept in overnight—that the distance between here and England had given James some perspective and his feelings had cooled after all. Just as she'd feared.

Or he'd decided a princess with a scandal-averse family was too much work for a guy who liked to play the field.

Discovering a bird's nest in the tree close to the back

steps finally pulled her attention from her morose thoughts. She missed her own birds— she'd moved the macaws James had given her to the Playa Del Onda house since she hadn't planned to continue traveling back and forth. These baby birds filled the silence with high-pitched cheeps and she smiled as she watched them from an upstairs window.

It was a much-needed sign. Regardless of what happened with James and the news regarding his contract with Liverpool, she should go forward with conservation work. Birds would always need her and she liked having a purpose.

When she returned to Playa Del Onda, a maid met her in the foyer and announced Bella had a visitor in the salon. *James.* Her heart did a twisty dance move in her chest. Of course she'd blown his silence out of proportion and they'd laugh over her silliness. Maybe he'd come straight from the airport and somehow she'd missed his call. As she dashed into the salon, she palmed her phone, already checking for the errant message.

It wasn't James, though, and the man standing by the window almost rendered her speechless. But she found her manners somehow.

"Mr. Rowling," Bella greeted James's father cautiously. "How nice to see you."

They'd met formally once before and she'd greeted him at Will's party, but this was the first time they'd spoken without others in attendance. Did James know he was here? Had he already talked to his father? If Gabriel had spoken to Mr. Rowling, he would have mentioned it to her. She was flying completely blind and nothing good could possibly come of this surprise meeting.

James's father didn't offer his hand but instead bowed as if they'd stumbled into a formal setting without her realizing it. "Princess Isabella. Thank you for seeing me on short notice."

"Of course." Mindful of her father's warning to watch

her step when dealing with matters important to the crown, she inclined her head graciously. "What can I do for you?"

"May we take a seat?" Mr. Rowling indicated the over-stuffed and incredibly uncomfortable couch.

Sure, why not add more formality on top of the already overbearing deference of the elder Rowling? She perched on the cushion and waited for Patrick Rowling to get to the point.

He cleared his throat. "I realize that you and Will have agreed to part ways and that you are seeing my other son. You've made a terrible mistake and I'm here to ensure you understand the full extent of it."

Geez, first her father and now Patrick Rowling? It was as if everyone thought she could be talked out of her feelings if they just tried hard enough. "Will would be a bigger mistake. We aren't interested in each other."

Mr. Rowling held up a conciliatory hand. "I'm not here to talk about Will. Granted, there is sound sense in a match between you and my son, but even I understand that the heart isn't always sensible."

Confused and suspicious, she eyed James's father. "Then why are you here?"

That had come out a little more bluntly than intended, but he didn't seem bothered by her lack of decorum.

Clearing his throat, he leaned forward as if about to impart a secret. "The mistake you're making, the one I'm here to help you avoid, is putting your faith in James. He is not a good choice for any woman, least of all you."

Her temper boiled over but she schooled her features and bit back the nasty phrase she'd been about to say. This man didn't know her and he had a lot of nerve assuming he had insight into what kind of man would be good for her.

But the worse crime was that he didn't know his own son either. That, she could correct.

"James is an amazing man. I'm shocked his own father doesn't recognize that, but since it's clear you don't, despite ample opportunity to come to know your son, I'll tell you. He has a good heart, a generous nature and most of all, he cares about me."

Her voice rang with sincerity. Because she believed what she was saying. He'd call soon and they'd talk about the future. Everything was going to work out.

Mr. Rowling frowned. "I do so hate to disagree. But my son is a notorious womanizer with little regard for anyone's feelings other than his own. Surely you're aware of his indiscretions." He swept her with a pitying once-over. "God help you if you're not."

Foreboding slid down her spine and raised the hair on the back of her neck.

"You mean the photographs in the tabloids?" She crossed her arms, wondering if it would actually protect her against this man's venom. "I'm aware of them."

James had been very upfront about his brush with scandal. Whatever his father thought he was going to accomplish by bringing up the pictures wasn't going to work.

"Oh, no, Princess Isabella." He shook his head with a *tsk*. "I'm talking about James's illegitimate daughter."

Bella's skin iced over. "His…what?" she whispered.

Mr. Rowling watched her closely through narrowed eyes, and she suspected he'd finally come to the meat of the reason he'd casually dropped by.

"James has an infant daughter he fathered with his last girlfriend. Shall I assume from your reaction that he hasn't mentioned any of this to you?"

"No," she admitted quietly as her pulse skipped a whole lot of beats. "I wasn't aware."

And of course there was a reason James hadn't told her. There had to be. Her mind scrambled to come up with one. But without James here to explain, she was only left with huge question marks and no answers.

In all that time at the farmhouse together, he'd never once thought to mention a baby he'd fathered with the girlfriend he'd stopped seeing nearly two years ago? Had she completely misread what he'd confessed to her about his feelings? None of this made any sense. Why would he talk about the implications of moving to England but not tell her he had a daughter?

It was a lie. Mr. Rowling was trying to cause problems. That was the only explanation.

Mr. Rowling eyed her and she didn't miss the crafty glint in his gaze. Neither of his sons took after this schemer in any way and it was a testament to James that he'd ended up with such an upstanding character.

"It's true," he said, somehow correctly interpreting the set of her jaw. "James will confirm it and then you might ask why he's kept it from you. It's a consideration for a woman when choosing whom she has a relationship with, don't you think?"

Yes, a huge consideration. That's what he'd meant by James not being a good choice for her. Because he wasn't trustworthy.

She shook her head against the rebellious thoughts. This was a campaign to poison her against James, plain and simple, but why, she couldn't fathom. "He has his reasons for not telling me. Whatever they are, I can forgive him."

Because that's what people in a relationship did. Not that she had any practice—she'd never had one, never dreamed she'd have one that tested her in quite this way. But James was worth figuring it out.

"You realize, of course, that his daughter is illegitimate." Mr. Rowling countered smoothly. "You're still in line for the throne should something happen to Gabriel. Alma doesn't cater to that sort of impropriety in its monarchy, and citizens have no patience for royal scandals. Frankly, neither do I."

It was a veiled threat, one she understood all too well after the discussion with Gabriel and her father about business between the crown and Rowling Energy. And blast it, he wasn't overstating the point about her position or potential to be queen one day. A princess couldn't drag an illegitimate child through the world's headlines.

Her head started to pound as her father's warning played over and over on an endless loop in her mind. Gabriel wouldn't be on her side with this one, not after what happened with Rafe and Emily and their unexpected pregnancy. Not after she'd already forced her brother to renegotiate agreements with Rowling, which would be very difficult to wade through indeed if Mr. Rowling's threat was to be believed.

If she continued to be with James, the entire future of Gabriel's reign—and indeed perhaps her own—might be in jeopardy.

"Let me ask you another question, Princess Isabella."

The way he said that made her spine crawl but she didn't correct him. Only her friends called her Bella and this man was not in that group. A shame since she'd hoped he would become her father-in-law someday. That dream had rapidly evaporated under his onslaught.

She nodded, too miserable to figure out how to make her voice work.

"What if she's not the only illegitimate child out there?"

God, he was right. The reality of it unleashed a wave of nausea through her stomach. James had made no secret of his playboy past. Since she'd never sat around in virginal white gowns either, it hadn't troubled her. Until now.

She very much feared she might throw up.

"If you weren't aware of the baby, you also probably aren't aware that her mother is here in Playa Del Onda visiting James." Mr. Rowling leaned forward, apparently oblivious to the hot poker he'd just shoved through Bella's chest. "I know you'd like to think that you're special. James has a particular talent with women. But the fact of the matter is that he still has very deep feelings for the mother of his child. Their relationship is far from over."

"That's not true," Bella gasped out. It couldn't be. She wasn't that naïve. "Anyway, James is in England."

The pitying look Mr. Rowling gave her nearly stopped her heart. "He's been back in Alma since yesterday."

"I trust James implicitly," she shot back and cursed the wobble in her voice. She did. But he'd come home from England and *hadn't called* and his silence was deafening. "Why are you telling me all of this?"

Mr. Rowling pursed his lips. "I'm simply making sure you are aware of what you are getting yourself into by refusing to see the truth about James. I have your best interests at heart."

She doubted that very much. But it didn't negate the accusations he'd brought against James. Her throat burned as she dragged breath into her lungs.

No. This was propaganda, plain and simple. She shook her head again as if she could make it all go away with the denial. "I need to talk to James."

"Of course," he agreed far too quickly. "I've said my piece. But before I go, please note that Will is still open to honoring the original marriage agreement."

With that parting comment, Mr. Rowling followed the butler out of the salon, leaving Bella hollowed out. She crawled onto her bed to lie in a tight ball, but nothing could ease the sick waves still sloshing through her abdomen.

Lies. All of it was lies. James could—and would—straighten all of this out and then they'd deal with the issue of his illegitimate child. Somehow.

Except he still didn't answer her call. Twice.

This silence…it was killing her. If he was done with her, she deserved to hear it from him, face-to-face. Not from his father.

She had to know, once and for all. If he wouldn't answer the phone, she'd go to his house.

The Montoro town car had long been on the list of instantly admitted vehicles at the Rowling Mansion gates, so the driver didn't have to announce Bella's presence. As Mr.

Rowling had said, James's green Lamborghini sat parked in the circular drive of the Rowling mansion.

Bella climbed out of the car, her gaze fastened to the Lamborghini, her heart sinking like a stone. James was home. And hadn't called. Nor would he answer his phone. The truth of Mr. Rowling's revelations burned at the back of her eyes but she refused to let the tears fall.

James would explain.

A woman's laugh floated to her on the breeze and Bella automatically turned toward the gazebo down the slope from the main drive. It was partially obscured by foliage but James was easy to make out. Even if she couldn't plainly see the watch on James's arm, Will didn't live here, and neither would he be at his father's house in the middle of the work day when he had a company to run.

The dark haired woman sitting in the gazebo with James faced away from Bella, but she'd bet every last euro in the royal treasury it was his former girlfriend. It didn't mean anything. They were probably talking about the daughter they shared. Patrick Rowling wasn't going to ruin her relationship with James.

Bella had come for answers and now she'd get them.

Feeling like a voyeur but unable to stop herself, she moved closer to catch what they were saying but the murmurs were inaudible. And then James threaded his fingers through the woman's hair and pulled her into a scorching kiss.

And it was a *kiss*, nothing friendly about it.

The back of Bella's neck heated as she watched the man she loved kiss another woman.

James was kissing another woman.

Brazenly. Passionately. Openly. As if he didn't care one bit whether anyone saw him.

His watch glinted in the late afternoon sun as he pulled the dark-haired woman closer, and the flash blinded Bella. Or maybe her vision had blurred because of the tears.

How long had she been playing the fool in this scenario—and was she truly the last to find out? Was everyone giggling behind their hands at her naïvety? Mr. Rowling had certainly known. This was going on in his house and as many times as she'd accused him of not knowing his son… *she* was the one who didn't know James.

It all swirled through her chest, crushing down with so much weight she thought her heart would cease to beat under the pressure.

Whirling, she fled back to the car, only holding back the flood of anguish long enough to tell the driver to take her home.

But when she finally barricaded herself in her room, it didn't feel like home at all. The only place she'd ever experienced the good, honest emotions of what a home should feel like was at the farmhouse. But it had all been a complete lie.

Still blinded by tears, she packed as much as she could into the bag she'd lived out of during those brief, precious days with James as they cleaned up the Montoro legacy. Alma could make do without her because she couldn't stay here.

Everything is moving too fast, he'd said. He'd meant *she* was, with her expectations and ill-timed confessions. The whole time, he'd had a woman and a baby on the side. Or was *Bella* the side dish in this scenario?

Horrified that she'd almost single-handedly brought down the monarchy with her own gullibility, she flung clothes into bags faster. New York. She'd go to New York where there were no bad memories. Her friends in Miami would only grill her about James because she'd stupidly kept them up to the minute as things unfolded with her new romance.

And her brother Rafe would see through her instantly. She couldn't stand to be around people who knew her well.

Within an hour, she'd convinced Gabriel to concoct

some story explaining her absence and numbly settled into the car as it drove her to the private airstrip where the Montoro jet waited to take her to New York. It was the perfect place to forget her troubles among the casual acquaintances she planned to look up when she got there.

The shorter her time in Alma grew, the more hollowed out she felt.

When her phone beeped, she nearly hurled it out the window. *James*. Finally, he'd remembered that she existed. She didn't care what he had to say, couldn't even bear to see his name on the screen. But a perverse need to cut her losses, once and for all, had her opening up the text so she could respond with something scathing and final.

I'm home. Came by, but Gabriel said you left. When will you be back? We need to talk.

She just bet he'd come by—to tell her he was in love with his daughter's mother. Or worse, to lie to her some more.

Bella didn't think twice before typing in her reply.

Not coming back. Have a nice life with your family.

Now she could shake Alma's dust off her feet and start over somewhere James and his new family weren't. New York was perfect, a nonstop party, and she intended to live it up. After all, she'd narrowly escaped making a huge mistake and now she had no responsibilities to anyone other than herself. Exactly the way she liked it.

But Bella cried every minute of the flight over the Atlantic. Apparently, she'd lost the ability to lie to herself about losing the man she loved.

Twelve

The Manhattan skyline glowed brightly, cheering Bella slightly. Of course, since leaving Alma, the definition of cheer had become: *doesn't make me dissolve into a puddle of tears.*

She stared out over the city that never slept, wishing there was one person out there she could connect with, who understood her and saw past the surface. None of her friends had so much as realized anything was wrong. They'd been partying continuously since this time last night. It was a wonder they hadn't dropped from exhaustion yet.

"Hey, Bella!" someone called from behind her in the crowded penthouse. "Come try these Jell-O shots. They're fab."

Bella sighed and ignored whomever it was because the last thing she needed was alcohol. It just made her even more weepy. Besides, they'd go back to their inane conversations about clothes and shoes whether she joined them or not, as they'd been doing for hours. That was the problem with hooking up with casual acquaintances—they didn't have anything in common.

But neither did she want to call her friends in Miami. The problem was that she didn't really fit in with the wealthy, spoiled crowd she used to run around with in Miami either. Maybe she hadn't for a long time and that was why she'd felt so much like a hurricane back home— she'd never had enough of a reason to slow down and stop spinning.

In Alma, she'd found a reason. Or at least she'd thought she had. But apparently her judgment was suspect.

The party grew unbearably louder as someone turned up the extensive surround sound system that had come with the condo when Rafael had purchased it from a music executive. A Kanye West song beat through the speakers and Bella's friends danced in an alcohol-induced frenzy. All she wanted to do was lie on the wooden floor of a farmhouse eating grapes with a British football player who'd likely already forgotten she existed.

Barricading herself in her room—after kicking out an amorous couple who had no sense of boundaries—she flopped onto the bed and pulled the bag she'd carried from the farmhouse into her arms to hold it tight.

The bag was a poor substitute for the man it reminded her of. But it was all she had. When would she stop missing him so much? When would her heart catch a clue that James had not one, but two females in his life who interested him a whole lot more than Bella?

Something crumpled inside the bag. Puzzled, she glanced inside, sure she'd emptied the bag some time ago.

The letters.

She'd totally forgotten about finding the cache of old, handwritten letters under the floorboards of the farmhouse. She'd meant to give them to Tía Isabella and with everything that had happened…well, it was too late now. Maybe she could mail them to her aunt.

When she pulled the letters from the bag, the memories of what had happened right after she'd found the letters flooded her and she almost couldn't keep her grip on the string-bound lot of paper.

James holding her, loving her, filling her to the brim. They'd made love on that gorgeous bed with the carved flowers not moments after discovering the hiding place under the boards.

She couldn't stand it and tossed the letters onto the bedside table, drawing her knees up to her chest, rocking in a tight ball as if that alone would ward off the crushing sense of loss.

The letters teetered and fell to the ground, splitting the ancient knotted string holding them together. Papers fluttered in a semicircle. She groaned and crawled to the floor to pick them up.

Indiscretion. Illegitimate. Love.

The words flashed across her vision as she gathered the pages. She held one of the letters up to read it from the beginning, instantly intrigued to learn more about a story that apparently closely mirrored her own, if those were the major themes.

She read and read, and flipped the letter over to read the back. Then, with dawning horror and apprehension, she read the rest. *No!* It couldn't be. She must have misread.

With shaking fingers, she fumbled for her phone and speed-dialed Gabriel before checking the time. Well, it didn't matter if it was the middle of the night in Alma. Gabriel needed to make sense of this.

"What?" he growled and she heard Serafia murmur in the background. "This better be good."

"Rafael Montoro II wasn't the child of the king," she blurted out. "Grandfather. Our father's father. He wasn't the king's son. The letters. The queen's lover died in the war. And this means he was illegitimate. They were in love, but—"

"Bella. Stop. Breathe. What are you talking about? What letters?" Gabriel asked calmly.

Yes. Breathing sounded like a good plan. Maybe none of this would pan out as a problem. Maybe she'd read too much into the letters. Maybe they were fake and could be fully debunked. She gulped sweet oxygen into her lungs but her brain was still on Perma-Spin.

"I found some old letters. At the farmhouse. They say that our grandfather, Rafael the Second, wasn't really the king's son by blood. Wait." She pulled her phone from her ear, took snapshots of the most incriminating letter and sent the pictures to Gabriel. "Okay, read the letter and tell me I misunderstood. But I couldn't have. It says they kept the queen's affair a secret because the war had just started and the country was in turmoil."

Gabriel went quiet as he waited for the message to come through and then she heard him talking to Serafia as he switched over to speakerphone to examine the photo.

"These letters are worth authenticating," he concluded. "I'm not sure what it means but if this is true, we'll have to sort out the succession. I might not be the next in line."

"Why do you sound so thrilled?" Bella asked suspiciously. That was not the reaction she'd been expecting. "This is kind of a big deal."

"Because now there's a possibility that after the wedding, I might be able to focus on getting my wife pregnant instead of worrying about how to hold my head so the crown doesn't fall off."

Serafia laughed and she and Gabriel apparently forgot about Bella because their conversation was clearly not meant for outsiders.

"Hey, you guys, what do we do now?" she called loudly before things progressed much further. Geez, didn't they ever give the lovey-dovey stuff a rest? "We need to know if this is for real, preferably before the coronation. But who would be the legitimate heir if it's not you?"

God, what a mess. Thankfully, she wasn't in Alma, potentially about to be swept into a much larger scandal than any she'd ever created on her own.

"Juan Carlos," Serafia confirmed. "Of course. If Rafael's line is not legitimate, the throne would fall to his sister, Isabella. I don't think she'd hesitate to pass it to her grandson. It's perfect, don't you think? Juan Carlos has long been one of the biggest advocates of the restoration of the monarchy. He'll be a great king."

Gabriel muttered his agreement. "Bella, send me the letters overnight, but make copies of everything before you do. Can you send them tonight?"

"Sure." It wasn't as if she had anything else to do.

And that was how an Alman princess with a broken heart ended up at an all-night Kinkos on Fifth Avenue, while her so-called friends drank her vodka and ruined her furniture.

When she got home, she kicked them all out so she could be alone with her misery.

JFK Airport had it in for James. This was the ninth time he'd flown into the airport and the ninth time his luggage had been lost.

"You know what, forget it," he told the clerk he'd been working with for the past hour to locate his bags. "I'll call customer service later."

After two delays at Heathrow, all James wanted to do was crawl into a hole and sleep, but he'd spent close to thirty-six hours already trying to get to Bella. He wasn't flaking out now.

The car service ride to the address Gabriel had given him took another forty-five minutes and he almost got out and walked to Bella's building four times. He worried his lip with his teeth until he reached the building and then had to deal with the doorman, who of course wasn't expecting anyone named James Rowling.

"Please," he begged the doorman. "Buzz Ms. Montoro and tell her I'm here."

It was a desperate gamble, and she might very well say, *James who?* But he had to see her so he could fix things. He might be too late. His father might have ruined everything, but he had to take this shot to prove to Bella that she could trust him. That he'd absolutely planned to tell her about Maisey but everything had happened too fast.

"No need. Here I am."

Bella's voice washed over him and he spun around instantly. And there she was, wearing one of those little dresses that killed him every time, and he wanted to rush to her to sweep her up in his arms.

But he didn't. Because he didn't understand why she'd left Alma without at least letting him explain what was happening with Maisey or why his life had spiraled out of control so quickly that he'd managed to lose her or why just looking at her made everything seem better without her saying a word.

"Hi," he said, and then his throat closed.

He'd practiced what he'd say for a day and a half, only to buckle when it mattered most. Figured.

"Hi," she repeated, and glanced at the doorman, who was watching them avidly. "Thanks, Carl. It's okay."

She motioned James over to the side of the lobby, presumably so she could talk to him with a measure of privacy. "What are you doing here?"

"I wanted to talk to you." *Obviously.*

Off kilter, he ran a hand over his rumpled hair. Now that he was here, flying to New York without even calling first seemed like a stupid plan.

But when his father had smugly told him that he'd taken the liberty of informing Bella about Maisey, James had kind of lost it. And he'd never really regained his senses, especially not after his father made it clear that Bella wasn't interested in a bloke with an illegitimate child. As though it was all sorted and James should just bow out.

That wasn't happening. Because if Bella was indeed no longer interested in him because of Maisey, he wanted to hear it from Bella.

"So talk." She crossed her arms and he got another clue that things between them had progressed so far past the point of reasonable, there might be no saving their relationship. He was on such unfamiliar, unsteady ground, it might as well be quicksand.

The damage was far more widespread than he'd hoped. "Why did you leave before I could explain about Maisey?"

"Maisey? Is that your girlfriend's name?" Her eyes widened and she huffed out a little noise of disgust. "Surely you didn't expect me to sit around and wait for you to give me the boot."

"Maisey is my daughter," he countered quietly. "Chelsea is her mother. I'm sorry I didn't get a chance to tell you about this myself. I'm very unhappy with my father for interfering."

"Well, that couldn't have happened if you'd just told me from the beginning." He could tell by her narrowed gaze that she'd already tried and convicted him. "Why couldn't you be honest with me?"

"I was going to tell you. But you left first." With no clue as to where she was going. Was that her way of saying a lover with a kid was *no bueno*? Sweat dripped between his shoulder blades as he scrambled for the right thing to say. "Why didn't you wait for me to call like we discussed?"

"Wait for you to—are you mad at *me*? You're the one who should be on your knees begging my forgiveness. And you know what else? I don't have to explain myself to you!"

She stormed to the elevator and he followed her, only just squeezing through the doors before they closed.

Obviously *that* hadn't been the right thing to say. And she was far more furious than he'd have ever dreamed.

Yeah, he'd messed up by giving his father an opportunity to get between them, but hadn't he just flown thousands of miles to fix it? Shouldn't he at least get two minutes to make his case?

Or was it too late and was he just wasting his time?

"Actually," he countered as anxiety seized his lungs. "An explanation would be smashing. Because I don't understand why you don't want to hear what I have to say. I thought we were a couple who dealt with things together."

And now he was shouting back at her. Good thing the elevator was empty.

He'd thought they were headed for something permanent. He had little experience with that sort of thing, but he didn't think jetting off to another continent without so much as a conversation about the potential complexities was how you did it.

He'd *wanted* to talk to her about Maisey. To share his fears and ask her opinion. To feel less alone with this huge life-altering role change that had been dropped on him. Even the simple logistics of flying to New York hadn't been so simple, not the way it used to be. It had required him to sweet-talk Catalina, one of the Rowling maids, into babysitting Maisey—totally not her job, but Cat was the only person James trusted implicitly since they'd grown up together. As soon as he got back, finding a nanny for his daughter was priority number one.

She wheeled on him, staring down her nose at him, which was an impressive feat since he was a head taller. "A couple? Really? Do you tell Chelsea the same thing? I saw you two together. You must have had a good laugh at my expense."

"You saw me and *Chelsea* together? When?"

"The day I left Alma. Don't shake your head at me. I *saw* you. You were very cozy in that gazebo."

Gazebo? He'd never set foot in any gazebo.

"That would be a little difficult when Chelsea and I

were in my lawyer's office signing paperwork to give me sole custody of Maisey." They'd obtained the results of the fastest paternity test available and then James had spent a good deal more cash greasing the works so he could be rid of Chelsea as soon as possible. "And then she immediately left to go back to England."

He'd been relieved to have it done. The meeting with his lawyers had taken far longer than he'd expected but he had to deal with that for his daughter's sake before he could untangle himself to go talk to Bella. Unfortunately, those few hours had given his father the perfect window of opportunity to drive a wedge between James and Bella.

"She...what?" For the first time since he'd entered the elevator, Bella's furious expression wavered.

"Yeah. I came to tell you everything but you'd apparently just left. Gabriel gave me some lame explanation, so I texted you, remember?"

The elevator dinged and the doors opened but Bella didn't move, her expression shell-shocked. Gently, he guided her out of the elevator and she led him to the door of one of the apartments down the hall.

Once they were alone in the condo, James raised his brows in silent question.

"I remember your text message. Clearly," Bella allowed. "If Chelsea left, who were you kissing in the gazebo?"

"Kissing? You thought I was kissing someone?" His temper rose again. "Thanks for the lack of trust, Bella. That's why you took off? Because you thought I was two-timing you?"

Suddenly furious he'd spent almost two days in pursuit of a woman who thought so little of him, he clasped his aching head and tried to calm down.

"What was I supposed to think, James?" she whispered and even in his fit of temper he heard the hurt and pain behind it. "Your father told me you still had feelings for Chelsea. I thought he was lying, so I went to the Rowling mansion to talk to you. Only to see you kissing a dark-haired woman. I wouldn't have believed it except for your watch."

She glanced at his bare arm and her face froze as he held it up. "You mean the watch I gave to Will?"

"Oh, my God."

In a flash, she fell to the ground in a heap and he dashed to her, hauling her into his arms before he thought better of it.

"Are you okay?" he asked as he helped her stand, his heart hammering. "Did you faint?"

"No. My knees just gave out." She peered up, her gaze swimming with tears as she clutched his shoulders, not quite in his embrace but not quite distancing herself either. "It was Will. The whole time."

He nodded grimly. Such was the reality of having a brother who looked like you. People often mistook them for each other, but not with such devastating consequences. "Welcome to the world of twins."

Now he understood her animosity. No wonder he'd felt as if he was on the wrong side of a raging bull. His father's interference had caused even more damage than James had known.

And who the hell had *Will* been kissing in the gazebo?

"Why didn't you tell me you gave him your watch? You always wore it. I know how much it means to you and I just…well, I never would have thought you'd…" Her eyes shut for a beat. "I know, I left before you could tell me. I'm sorry. I shouldn't have jumped to conclusions."

"Yeah, on that note. Why did you?"

His temper hadn't fully fled but it had been so long since he'd been this close to her, he couldn't quite make himself let her go. So he sated himself on the scent of her and let that soothe his riled nerves.

"You said everything was moving too fast," she reminded him. "It's not that I didn't trust you. You've always been honest with me, but… Chelsea's your child's mother. You didn't call and your father said you were home from England. Your car was in the drive and he dropped the news about a baby and tells me you have feelings for your old girlfriend. Maybe you thought it was the right thing to try again with her."

That was so far off the mark…and yet he could see the logic from her perspective. It was maddening, impossible, ridiculous. "Not for me. I love *you*."

"You do?" The awe in her face nearly undid him. Until she whacked his shoulder with her fist. "Then why didn't you call me when you got back from England?"

"Blimey, Bella. I'd just had the news about the baby dropped on me, too."

She recoiled. "Wait. You mean you *just* found out you had a daughter?" Her eyelids flew shut for a moment. "I thought…"

"What, you mean you thought I knew from the very beginning?" He swore. Everything made so much more sense. Scowling, he guided her to the couch. "We need to get better at communication, obviously. Then my father wouldn't have been able to cause all of these problems."

She nodded, chagrin running rampant across her expression. "I'm sorry. I told you I wasn't any good at relationships."

"We're supposed to be figuring it out together. Remember?" Without taking his gaze from hers, he held out his hand. "I promised not to let go. I plan to stick to that."

She clasped his hand solemnly, no hesitation. "Are you really in love with me?"

"Completely." Tenderly, he smoothed a stray hair from her cheek. "I'm sorry, too, sweetheart. I was trying to get everything settled in my barmy life before I settled things with you. I jumbled it all up."

This was entirely his fault. If he'd told her every minute what she meant to him, she might have very well marched up to Will and demanded to know what he was doing. And realized it wasn't James. None of this would have happened.

He'd been missing this goal since day one, yet kept kicking the ball exactly the same way. No wonder she'd assumed he didn't want her anymore.

"So are things settled?" She searched his gaze and a line appeared between her eyes. "What did you mean about Chelsea signing over custody? What happened?"

And then reality—his new reality—crashed over him. They'd only dealt with the past. The future was still a big, scary unknown.

James shook his head. "She dumped the diaper bag in my lap and told me she was too young to be tied down with a baby she hadn't asked for. Being a mum is apparently too hard and it's interfering with her parties."

"Oh, James." Her quiet gasp of sympathy tugged at something in his chest.

"I'm quite gobsmacked." This was the conversation he'd intended to have when he went to her house in Playa Del Onda. Only to find that she'd taken off for New York. "I have a daughter I never knew existed and now she's mine. I'm a single father."

And he'd have to relinquish his title as the king of uncomplicating things. There was no way to spin the situation differently. No matter how much he loved Bella, she had to decide if he was worth all the extra stuff that came along with the deal.

Now the question was...would she?

James was a single father.

When she'd seen James across the lobby, she'd assumed he'd come to grovel and planned to send him packing. But then the extent of his father's lies and manipulation had come out, changing everything. The instant James had held up his bare wrist, she'd known. He wasn't the man his father made him out to be. The explanation she'd sought, the forgiveness she knew she could offer—it had all been right there, if only she'd stayed in Alma.

Part of the fault in all of this lay with her. She shouldn't have been so quick to judge, so quick to believe the worst in him. So quick to whirl off and leave broken pieces of her relationship with James in her wake.

And still James had said he loved her. Those sweet words…she'd wanted to fall into his arms and say them back a hundred times. If only it were that simple.

But it wasn't.

"That's…a lot to take in," Bella allowed with a small smile. Her mind reeled in a hundred directions and none of them created the type of cohesion she sought. "How old is she?"

"Around ten months. I wish I knew what that meant in terms of development. When will she start walking, for example? It's something I *should* know, as a father. But I don't." He shut his eyes for a beat. "I'm learning as I go."

Her heart dipped. This must be so hard. How did you learn to be a father with no warning? James would have to get there fast and probably felt ill-equipped and completely unready. "You'll be a great father."

He'd stepped up. Just as she would have expected. James always did the right thing.

"I'd like you to meet her. If you want to."

"I do," she said eagerly and then the full reality of what was happening hit her.

Dear God, was *she* ready to be the mate of a single father? She barely felt like an adult herself half the time. When she'd confronted her father to demand her right to see James, she'd taken huge steps to become the settled, responsible person she wanted to be.

But she wouldn't exactly call herself mother material, not yet. Maybe in the future she could be, after she'd spent time alone with James and they'd both figured out how to be in a relationship. But they didn't have the luxury of that time. She couldn't decide in a few months that it was too much responsibility and whirl away, leaving a broken family in her wake. Like her own mother had.

She loved James. After everything, that was still true.

But was love enough when their relationship had so many complications, so many things going against it? Adding a child into the mix—an illegitimate one at that, which would reflect poorly on the royal family—only made it worse.

And in the spirit of figuring it out together, they had to talk about it.

"Your daughter is a…" She'd almost said a *problem*. "A blessing. But I'm a princess in a country very unforgiving of indiscretions. I'm still in line for the throne. You realize there's a potential for our relationship to…go over very badly, right?"

The tabloids would have a field day, eviscerating the royal family in the press. She was supposed to be forging alliances and solidifying the new monarchy in the country of her heritage. Not constantly dodging scandals.

"Yeah." He sighed as she gripped his hand tighter. "I know. We don't make any sense together and you should toss me to the curb this minute. I'm a lot of trouble."

Her heart fluttered in panic at the thought. But that's what they were talking about. Either they'd make a go of it or they'd part ways.

"Seems like you warned me how much trouble you were once upon a time."

Continually. He'd told her he was bad news from the start. She hadn't believed him then and she still didn't. James Rowling had character that couldn't be faked. His father couldn't see it, but Bella did. He was every inch her hero and the rest of the world would see that, too. She'd *help* them see it. And that decided it.

She smiled as she cupped James's face. The face of her

future. "Turns out I like my man with a side of trouble. We have a lot of obstacles to leap. We always have. But I think you're worth it, James Rowling. Jump with me."

"Are you sure?" he asked cautiously even as he pressed his jaw more firmly into her hand. "You don't worry about losing out on your fun lifestyle and how Maisey will tie you down?"

Once, that might have been her sole consideration. No longer.

"The party scene is empty and unfulfilling." As she said the words, they felt right. She'd been growing up all along, becoming a woman she could be proud of, one ready for new challenges. "Maybe someone who hadn't had a chance to sow her wild oats might feel differently. But I don't regret moving on to a new phase of life. Just don't let go of my hand, okay?"

"Never." He grinned back. "You're right, by the way. My grandfather's watch is very special to me. Will bet me that I would ask you to marry me before Gabriel's coronation and the watch was the prize. I fought like hell to keep it, but in the end, it was only fair to hand it over."

"But you haven't asked me to marry you." Because she'd run off and almost ruined everything.

"No, I haven't. Allow me to rectify that." He dropped to one knee and captured her hand. "Isabella Montoro, I love you. I don't deserve a minute of your time, let alone forever, but I'm so lost without you. I have sole custody of my daughter and it's selfish to ask you to be an instant mother. Despite all of that, I'm asking you to marry me anyway. Let me treat you like a princess the rest of your life."

Just when she'd thought he couldn't possibly get any more romantic, he said something like that. How could she say no? "Before I decide, I have a very important question to ask."

"Anything," he said solemnly.

"Do I have to move to England?"

His laugh warmed her. "No. I turned down Liverpool. My heart is in Alma. With you."

"Oh." And then her ability to speak completely fled as she internalized what she'd almost missed out on—an amazing man who'd quietly been making her his top priority all along. "Then yes," she whispered. "The answer is always yes."

He yanked on her hand, spilling her into his lap, and kissed her breathless, over and over until she finally pushed on his chest.

"I love you, too," she proclaimed. "Even though you made a stupid bet with your brother that lost you a watch and almost lost you a fiancée. What if I'd said no? Would you still ha—?"

He kissed her. It was a very effective way to end an argument and she hoped he planned to use it a whole lot in the future.

Epilogue

Bella still loved Miami. Thanks to the double Montoro wedding that had concluded a mere hour ago, she'd gotten an opportunity to come back, see her friends and spend some alone time with James. Which was much needed now that they were settling into life with a baby.

James's arm slipped around her waist as he handed her a glass of champagne. Still a little misty from the ceremony where her brothers had married their brides, she smiled at the man she loved.

Bella sighed a little over the romantic kiss her brother Rafe shared with his new wife, Emily, as they stole a few moments together in a secluded corner. Of course, they probably didn't intend for anyone to see them, but Bella had been keeping her eye on her new sister-in-law. She'd been a little unsteady due to her pregnancy.

Serafia Montoro, Bella's other new sister-in-law, toasted Gabriel and laughed at something her new husband said. They were going to be just as happy together as Rafe and Emily, no question.

The reception was in full swing. Five hundred of the world's most influential people packed the party. The governor of Florida chatted with Bella's father, Rafael III, near the bar and many other of Montoro Enterprises' key partners were in attendance.

"You ready to do this with me soon?" James murmured in her ear.

She shivered, as she always did when he touched her. Looked at her. Breathed in her general direction. Oh, she had it bad and it was delicious.

But who could blame her when she'd fallen in love with the only man in the world who got her? The only man who settled the hurricane in her heart. She'd returned to Alma to meet his daughter, who was the most precious thing in the world. And she looked just like her father, which was a plus in Bella's book. She'd instantly bonded with the little sweetheart.

Then James had helped Bella launch a fledgling organization dubbed the Alma Wildlife Conservation Society. A graphic with twin macaws served as the logo and no one had to know she'd secretly named them Will and James.

It was a healthy reminder that things weren't always what they seemed. As long as she always communicated with James, no one could tear them apart. It was their personal relationship credo and they practiced it often.

Bella smiled at James. "I'm afraid I'm out of siblings so our wedding ceremony will have to star only us. And Maisey."

James cocked his head. "You'd want her to participate? Babies and weddings don't necessarily mix."

"Of course," Bella insisted fiercely. "She's my daughter, too."

Maisey had surprised everyone by uttering her first word last week—*bird*. Her proud father couldn't stop smiling and Bella had decided then and there to have another baby as soon as possible. *After* she and James got married.

The Montoros didn't need any new scandals.

Not long after she'd returned to Alma, Gabriel had appointed a royal committee to authenticate the letters Bella had found at the farmhouse. After careful and thorough examination and corroborating evidence culled from the official archives, the letters proved valid.

The late Rafael Montoro II wasn't the legitimate royal heir, which meant no one in his line was either. His grandson, Gabriel, and granddaughter, Bella, weren't eligible for the throne. The legitimate line for the throne shifted to Isabella Salazar nee Montoro, Rafael's sister, who was unfortunately too ill to take on her new role. Therefore, her grandson, Juan Carlos II, long the only Montoro with the right heart to lead his country, became the sole legitimate heir.

Despite Bella's willingness to brave the tabloids with James, to weather the storm over the unfortunate circumstances of his daughter's birth, in the end, no one paid much attention to Bella and James as the world's focus shifted to Juan Carlos.

Bella wasn't the only Montoro to express relief. Gabriel looked forward to spending time with his new wife instead of balancing his personal life with his public reign. Their cousin would take the throne of Alma, leaving the three Montoro siblings to their happily-ever-afters.

* * * * *

CLAIMING HIS REPLACEMENT QUEEN

AMANDA CINELLI

For Emily

CHAPTER ONE

'I'D RATHER DIE than be your wife a moment longer.'

Khal opened his eyes, clean cool air filling his lungs with painful force. His surroundings were a jolt to his system, the sleek interior of the royal jet's main cabin so far apart from the angry red sands and fathomless black water of his dream. It had just been a dream. He sat back, looking up at the ceiling as his heartbeat found its rhythm once more.

His subconscious had long ago stopped tormenting him with every detail of his last conversation with his wife before her death. Or so he had believed.

He unbuckled his seat belt and stood, stretching out the painful tightness in his shoulders. He could have chosen to sleep in any one of the three luxurious bedrooms on board, but sleep had not come easily of late. The dreams were back with a vengeance. The same dreams that had plagued him for an entire year after his wife's death. Stress seemed to be a trigger and the past few weeks had most certainly not been a relaxing time.

He pressed a button on the panel by his side and, as if by magic, two flight attendants emerged from the end of the cabin. A tray bearing hot towels and fresh ice water was placed on the nearest table without a word.

His chair was returned to the upright position and a pot of hot coffee set down within reach.

'That will be all, thank you,' he said, his voice unintentionally gravelly from sleep. He glanced up just in time to see one of the women visibly flinch as he waved one hand in dismissal. He fought the urge to roll his eyes with irritation. Without another word, they hurried back behind the curtain and he was alone once more. Just as he preferred it.

Most of his staff knew him well enough to disregard the rumours that had spread upon his wife's untimely passing. Disgusting, slanderous rumours that he had worked hard to dispel even while in the first days of his grief. But still, whispers spread and somehow the idea that he was a man to be feared had stuck.

People believed him to be a villain and it suited him to keep it that way. He was not forced to make idle conversation, to pretend to care. He did not throw social functions nor did he attend a great many.

Or at least he hadn't until recently.

Khal opened his laptop and scanned an assortment of international news articles that his press team had collated from the past week. *The Most Romantic Royal Love Story of the Decade*, one headline proclaimed. It was any news reporter's dream, Princess Olivia of the tiny European kingdom of Monteverre turning her back on her lofty title to marry a man her family deemed unsuitable. One picture showed Khal's close friend Roman Lazarov as he walked hand in hand with the beautiful redhead. What a cruel twist of fate it was that the woman he had finally chosen as his second wife, the answer to all his economic woes, would be snatched up at the last moment. And by his best friend, no less.

Remarrying had never been in his plans for his reign as Sheikh. He had been a young man on his first wedding day, filled with naïve hope for the future. That version of himself was long gone. He had no desire to find a woman to mend his broken heart, or any of the other schemes he had heard whispered by his mother and sister when they thought he could not hear. Thanks to his sister, he had two strong nephews that would carry on the Al Rhas bloodline and therefore he'd believed he had absolutely no need for a wife.

But he could no longer deny that the rumours surrounding his wife's demise were affecting Zayyar's international image. His country had been peaceful for over two decades, his father and grandfather before him credited with having brought their small Middle Eastern kingdom back from the brink of complete ruin. Khal had no wish for fame or a place in the history books, but he refused to be remembered as the Sheikh who had ruined all of their hard work.

Known for his careful planning, he had spent months drawing up an arrangement with Monteverre, one of the oldest and most financially troubled kingdoms in Europe. It was a deal that would solve all his problems in one fell swoop. He would provide the Monteverrian economy with a very healthy injection of capital and in return he would gain a loyal alliance in the form of the perfect bride with the perfect amount of political influence and public appeal.

By now the whole world knew that the Princess had given up her formal title to be with her scandalous Russian lover. There was no mention of a failed engagement to the Sheikh of Zayyar in any newspaper, nor would there ever be, thanks to his team. His name rarely graced any of the world media sources, nor did paparazzi images. He paid handsomely for his privacy. And a good thing too, considering he was about to arrive unannounced into a foreign country to retrieve his replacement bride.

He knew nothing of the youngest Sandoval Princess, only that she had been studying abroad in England for many years and had agreed to his offer of a royal marriage of convenience with very little hesitation. She had even agreed to sign a formal engagement contract without first meeting in person. He should feel relieved that his plans had not been completely derailed, and yet something seemed off.

He had amended the terms of the agreement from its original form, limiting the deal to five years of marriage in name only, followed by an easy divorce settlement. With such a solid link to European royalty provided by his bride, five years would be more than enough time for him to repair the bridges that had been burned by his reputation. Divorce was a common occurrence across the globe; Zayyar was no different. Still, he knew he would not truly rest until he had spoken to his fiancée in person.

He spent the remainder of the flight in quiet contemplation, barely noticing that they had landed until his pilot announced the incredibly low temperature in the city of London. It was the middle of May and yet he felt the need to pull up the collar of his impeccably tailored wool coat as he made the short trip from jet to limousine, grateful that he had chosen to change into Western-style clothing mid-flight. His usual flowing white robes were perfect for the desert heat, but not designed for the chilly, wet weather so common in this part of the world.

His Chief of Security sat waiting in the car, his expression stressed—Sayyid never looked stressed. Immediately Khal's instincts stood to attention.

'There has been a small problem,' Sayyid said solemnly.

Khal kept his features expressionless as his trusted servant outlined the events of the past twenty-four hours' surveillance operation. Finally, he closed his eyes, fighting the urge not to slam his fist into the door panel. 'You believe she is a flight risk?'

'She shows all of the signs of it, Sire.' After a prolonged silence, Sayyid cleared his throat quietly. 'If you give me the order, I will have the Princess collected immediately and delivered to the jet.'

'Your men are currently in pursuit?' Khal spoke with quiet control, hardly believing history was repeating itself so blatantly.

'She is safely surrounded and unaware of their presence.'

Khal nodded, running a hand across the light stubble on his jaw. He had already taken King Fabian's word once and been burned, but this time it was different. He had sent his personal secretary to London with official documents and ensured that Her Highness signed them herself in person. He had done everything within his power to ensure her complete consent before entering into a legally binding engagement to protect his investment. If she walked away from their engagement now, the repercussions for her kingdom were grave.

Surely she realised that?

But of course he had to be prepared for the fact that

maybe she did not care. Nonetheless, at this moment in time she was his fiancée. And in Zayyar that was as good as already being his wife. He had a duty to ensure her safety. Princess Cressida might be having second thoughts about their marriage, but he'd be damned if he would send anyone in to talk her round this time, other than himself.

'I'll handle this myself.' He spoke with a calm he did not feel. 'Take me to her.'

The exclusive club was a secret to most Londoners, hidden away behind the rather nondescript black door of a Georgian townhouse in Mayfair. The chilly breeze brushed across her skin as Cressida Sandoval stepped out onto the pavement and looked up at the building's dimly lit facade. The urge to abandon her plans and retreat to the warm interior of the limousine was strong. Frank, her loyal chauffeur of five years, was not happy with her insistence that he remain behind and he'd made his disapproval known by slamming the door audibly behind her.

'Your Highness, are you sure you don't want me to escort you inside?' He spoke quietly, worrying his black tie with one hand.

Cressida stiffened at the honorific. The title that set her so far apart from every other twenty-four-year-old woman seeking a night of freedom. She inhaled softly, reminding herself that her freedom relied entirely on the driver's discretion. 'I have never asked for a favour before now.'

He shook his head, leaning back against the car bonnet. 'Five years of driving you from home to Oxford,

Oxford to home, like blimmin' clockwork. Last night on the job and you've decided to give me heart failure.'

'Two hours alone, Frank. That's all I want.' She understood his worry; his job would be on the line if anything happened to her on his watch. If she'd had any street sense she would probably have taken a cab, but princesses did not take cabs, nor did they sneak out unaccompanied to secret clubs in the dead of night. She'd had to dodge her two bodyguards and beg Frank, just to get him to agree to drive her and wait outside. Once the time was up, she would return to reality. Or at least the suffocating reality of what her life had recently become.

Her father's voice rang in her ears.

'Politically advantageous...royal duty...for the good of the kingdom.'

Tomorrow she would become Princess Cressida Sandoval once more, returning to her kingdom after five years of self-imposed exile. Her father, the King of Monteverre, had barely listened to her weak argument about the European languages doctorate she had signed up for or the assistant teaching position she had been offered. 'Princesses do not *teach*, Cressida,' he had boomed in his usual way. 'I'm sure the Sheikh will have plenty of dusty old books for you to bury your nose in, or whatever it is that you've been wasting your time with for the past five years.'

The Sheikh. Her future husband.

She should not feel so nervous about something that was essentially just a business arrangement. Five years of service, her father had said. How utterly romantic. Not that romance had ever played a part in her life so far, but still... She had been comfortable here in London, away from the watching eyes of the public. Was she truly ready to become a queen?

A fresh wave of anxiety fuelled her with adrenaline as she met the eyes of the burly man guarding the door to the club. She quietly spoke the code word she had overheard three nights before from one of her bodyguards. The door was opened without comment, revealing plush red carpeted stairs with sleek chrome handrails descending downwards. She paused for a moment, fear of the unknown snaking around her chest and pulling tight. The low hum of music and conversation drifted upwards like a siren's song.

This was her last night in London, she reminded herself as she took the first step downwards. She owed it to herself to experience at least a taste of the freedom she had stupidly taken for granted before her face graced the front of every newspaper on the globe.

She had felt the walls closing in on her as she'd signed her name on each document that had been presented to her, precious control slipping through her fingers. Perhaps that was why she was acting on impulse for the first time in her life. She was overcome with the need to go somewhere new and be someone anonymous for just a few short hours before doing The Right Thing.

Because, when it came to royal duty, she always did what was asked of her. Whether she liked it or not.

She had felt on edge from the moment she'd ended that fateful phone call with her father. Knowing that she would do as he asked, even if it was not what she wanted. He knew it too. He knew that she always felt the pressure to measure up to her older sisters. It was so much more than simple sibling rivalry. He had always made it clear that she was his least favourite, the daughter he simply tolerated. Her thoughts turned dark, thinking of that fateful day when, as a twelve-year-old, she had finally found out why...

Pausing at the end of the stairway, Cressida took in the image of a sultry blonde in red and took a deep breath as she realised it was her own reflection. Her dark blonde locks fell in soft waves around her face, free from their usual tight ponytail. Her plain black glasses had been replaced by contact lenses. Her jeans and sneakers gone, in favour of a stylish red dress and heels slightly too high for comfort. She had devoted more time and research to tonight's outfit than she'd given to her most recent thesis. She was good at research. It was the practical application that made her insides shake. But suddenly, standing looking at this strange, almost pretty version of herself, the bands around her chest loosened a little and she felt a hint of that freedom she so craved.

The club was deceptively spacious inside, much larger than it seemed from the narrow building facade. The décor was a modern monochrome with a hint of old world glamour in the large sparkling chandeliers that hung from the ceiling at various points. A small stage with a live jazz band dominated one corner of the large space while a double-sided bar with floor-to-ceiling mirrors glittered in the middle. It was like walking into an old black-and-white movie.

Cressida walked towards the bar as confidently as she could muster, ignoring the painful beat of her heart high up in her throat.

The music was fast paced but sensual, accentuated by a husky-toned singer in a scandalously short dress and elbow-length gloves. As she slid onto a bar stool she spied a line of strategically roped-off areas towards the back, some filled with very beautiful but rather bored-looking people. The nameless secret basement club was known for its A-list clientele and its air of anonymity, according to the conversation she had overheard between her two bodyguards. No paparazzi allowed.

Even though it was a weeknight, the club was filled with people dancing and moving to the music as the lighting curved around them. As she looked on, a famous blonde singer stood up on a table and began to pour a bottle of expensive-looking champagne over the people around her. The group of men and women began dancing and gyrating under the spray, laughing and singing along to the music.

She found herself smiling in wonder at the sight of such ridiculous behaviour. If she were to truly enjoy her freedom, she would just stand and join in with the dancing and no one would look twice at her... The thought came and passed as she took a seat at the end of the long bar, comfortably on the outskirts of the action.

Soon she would probably need to ask for permission before doing something so daring as dancing in public; she felt her mouth curve downwards.

She could refuse the match, of course. This was not some medieval drama where she would be bound and dragged down the aisle, whether she agreed to the union or not. She adored the simple life she had begun to carve out for herself here in London but of course she knew it was not allowed for a member of royalty to take a paid job. She was not meant for such blissful normality as being a teaching assistant, much as she had been delighted to be offered the position. She had a duty to serve the people of Monteverre.

She ordered a white wine, not feeling confident enough to order anything else. She occasionally drank a glass with dinner, but never more. Alcohol dulled her senses in a way that simply did not appeal to her orderly nature. She sipped slowly, feeling slightly at sea amidst the raucous dancing and groupings of people. Mingling had never been a forte of hers. The word itself made her feel twitchy. She remembered herself as a young girl, wishing she was more confident, more natural at being a princess. She had always felt so different to her older sisters, the stereotypical mousy wallflower to their flame-haired beauty. And then one day everything had changed and she had simply stopped trying. She had found comfort in blending into the background where it was safer, where no one looked too closely at her...

You came here to feel free and here you are, hiding in the corner feeling sorry for yourself. She bit her lip hard, swirling the golden liquid in her glass and watching the light play on the surface. She became suddenly aware of a shadow in the reflection of the glass and the delicious scent of a warm, distinctly male cologne.

She looked up.

Goodness...

Tall, dark and handsome simply did not describe the man standing a mere foot away from her. This man was broad, exotic and breathtaking. She swallowed hard as dark, hooded eyes met hers. He didn't make a move to speak and after a long moment her awkward nature interfered, her voice trembling slightly as she asked, 'Can I help you?'

His expression changed fleetingly to one of mild surprise, making her wonder if he had mistaken her for someone else. His gaze moved down to take in her long legs crossed on the high barstool before returning to her face. She half hoped he had made a mistake, then perhaps he would leave and she might be able to breathe normally again.

'Are you expecting someone?' He gestured to the empty barstool beside her. His voice was a deep accented rumble.

'No. I'm here alone,' she said quickly, then worried if that made her seem a little bit needy. 'I mean, the seat is yours. If you want it, that is. It's…not mine, either way.' She felt her cheeks heat. She was a babbling idiot.

A tension-filled silence followed and the stranger's eyes narrowed slightly as though he were waiting for her to say something more. A strange bewildered expression crossed his face as he moved to sit back onto a barstool, leaving the seat between them empty.

Cressida frowned, one hand idly tracing the edge of her glass as she shot a sidelong glance towards the mysterious hunk. Nipping at her bottom lip with her teeth, she took a slow sip of her wine to cool her suddenly dry throat. He was handsome, there was no denying it, with warm mahogany-toned skin and jet black stubble shadowing his jawline.

The shadow that began on his jawline continued down a strong throat to disappear into the open collar of a perfect white shirt. A white shirt that covered the broadest shoulders she had ever seen…

She moved her gaze back up to find a pair of dark eyes watching her. Startled, she inhaled sharply and promptly breathed in a mouthful of wine. Her throat convulsed in a series of loud embarrassing coughs and she was vaguely aware of a napkin appearing in her peripheral vision. She prayed her eye make-up hadn't run and silently willed the dark stranger to disappear so that she didn't have to continue her embarrassment any longer.

She froze as he placed a glass of water into her hands, the heat of his fingers scorching her skin for a few short seconds. The cold water calmed both her raw throat and her overheated brain.

Cressida looked up to find he had moved to the seat directly beside her. This close, she could see tiny flecks of gold in his deep brown irises. The way he was looking at her so intently made her feel as though she had walked under a spotlight. She was too warm, too exposed.

'Thank you,' she blurted, forcing herself to meet his eyes. 'For the water.'

'It's my pleasure.' His eyes did not leave hers. 'However, I believe it is now irresponsible of me to leave you unsupervised while you finish your drink.'

'I must seem quite ridiculous, really.' Cressida half laughed, feeling rather blinded under the intense spotlight of his attention.

'That's the last word I would use,' he said silkily, tilting his head to one side.

She managed a slight smile, wondering again why he had chosen to sit with her. Men like him did not show interest in women like her; it was hard not to be suspicious. Not that she was here seeking male attention; far from it. Tonight was simply about freedom, she reminded herself with a firm shrug of her shoulders.

'I find myself wondering…' his dark voice rumbled somewhere close to her ear '…what might have brought you here tonight to this particular club?'

Cressida felt the vibration of his deep voice travel

down to her toes. She shifted in her seat. 'The same reason as everyone else, I assume. It's an escape.'

'You are looking to escape something?'

'If I say the outside world, is that rather a cliché?' She grimaced with a half laugh, feeling herself relax slightly. 'I must go back eventually, of course.'

He seemed thoughtful for a moment. 'While you are here, what do you plan to do?'

'I hadn't really thought that far ahead.' She laughed, shocked at how feminine she sounded. 'I'm trying to be spontaneous for once. Perhaps I might dance?'

'Alone?'

'If no one asked me, I suppose I would have to dance alone.' It was hardly a suggestive statement, but still she felt herself blush a little, knowing she suddenly wanted him to ask her to dance. What on earth had come over her?

She had never flirted with a man before—she wasn't even sure if this qualified as flirting—but it definitely felt different to any previous conversations with a member of the opposite sex. What was she even doing? She was promised to another man, both morally and legally. She might not have met her fiancé yet, but she still knew where the boundaries stood. But a simple dance…that was hardly improper. Maybe it was the wine, though she knew herself that two sips could hardly provide enough stimulant. It was becoming intoxicating, feeling so free. That was the only explanation. It was making her feel different, bolder.

'By all means, then. You should dance,' he said.

'Yes, I would love to.' She smiled, feeling the sense of bravado heighten further. She slid off the barstool, biting her lower lip as he made no move to stand.

You should dance, he had said, not *we*. Silly girl.

She smiled a little too widely before turning to take a few steps towards the crowded dance floor. Throwing a final look over her shoulder as she walked away, she found herself momentarily pinned by a dark gaze. Heat sizzled through the air, seeming to settle somewhere in the region of her solar plexus.

Her painfully shy nature and workaholic tendencies had stopped her from ever having a dating life. So much so that the opposite sex might well have become a foreign species altogether, apart from her interactions with her bodyguards and driver. She could read and write fluently in eight languages and yet she could not formulate a simple sentence in English to ask a man if he wanted to dance with her. It was so utterly ridiculous that she laughed. Her laughter caught the attention of a blond-haired man nearby and he moved to dance beside her.

She smiled back briefly and continued dancing, distracted by wondering if *he* was still sitting at the bar, watching her. It was a ridiculous thought, that a complete stranger might feel the same hum of attraction after a moment of idle conversation. It was not as though she planned to do anything about it, but she had to admit it felt nice being noticed.

In the background, she registered the beat shifting seamlessly into a soft, seductive ballad. She let her gaze drift around the dance floor just as a handful of couples moved close and began moulding their bodies together sensually. She looked away for a moment then looked back, transfixed by the sight of a couple melting together in a haze of locked lips and intertwined limbs, all the while maintaining a perfect rhythm.

Without warning, the blond man moved close. A chunky arm snaked around her waist and she froze. She took a step away, trying to think of a kind way to decline the dance without hurting his feelings, but he moved with her, not forcefully but still determined to get close. Needing to be free of the situation, she placed her hand calmly against the man's chest, shaking her head to show that she was leaving. Worried he wasn't going to take the hint, she turned fully and took a few steps away from the dance floor, only to be blocked by a wall of warm, hard muscle.

'Waiting for me?' The stranger's deep voice was like a balm to her nerves as he extended a hand towards her. To her surprise, she instantly placed her hand in his, allowing herself to be drawn into the delicious warm scent of his cologne until their bodies were mere inches apart. She was vaguely aware of the other man disappearing into the crowd, but it was becoming increasingly harder to form a coherent thought as a strong male arm moved slowly around her waist.

The smooth, steady rhythm of the music seemed to pound through the wall of her chest before joining her own erratic heartbeat. He pulled her close. So close that the smooth dark skin of his open collar was directly in her eye line, mere inches away. The tips of her breasts pressed momentarily against a wall of warm hard muscle before he moved back slightly. Her free hand hovered uncertainly for a moment before she bravely moved it upwards to link around his neck, her fingers resting between warm skin and the thick dark hair of his nape as he led her into an easy rhythm.

She had been given the finest dancing lessons as a young teenager to prepare her for the many occasions that a princess was required to perform a simple waltz or foxtrot. Nine times out of ten she tripped over her own feet, of course, but she knew the basics. But none of that could have prepared her for this moment. They seemed to dance for hours, moving in perfect unison. He was an excellent lead, confident and strong. He held her in such a way that she almost felt graceful for the first time in her life. His hands did not wander from their place on her waist; he didn't even try to pull her too close against him. She felt safe, she realised. What a strange thing to feel in the arms of a man she barely knew.

Her dark stranger bent his head and for a moment she wondered if he planned to kiss her. She held her breath, relaxing when instead his mouth stopped somewhere just above her earlobe.

'In my country, dancing like this is considered a very intimate act.' His voice was a soft rumble that sent an earthquake of shivers down her spine.

'Is that so?' Cressida breathed, hardly believing that such a husky murmur had just escaped her own suddenly dry throat. 'I can't imagine why.'

A mischievous smile played on his lips. 'You can't?'

'People dance all of the time. It's hardly dangerous.'

'I'm not so sure,' he murmured. 'Swaying like this... pressed so close... I can see how it would be seen as temptation.'

'Temptation for what...?' Her feverish brain wondered momentarily at his choice of words before realisation dawned with all the grace of a sledgehammer. She clumsily missed a step but her dancing partner barely reacted, correcting her misstep with graceful ease and continuing as though nothing had occurred.

'It is usually only married couples who might dance like this,' he continued, oblivious to her embarrassment. 'Or perhaps those who are engaged to be married.'

She barely registered his words as her mind focused on the heat of his hand as it began to move higher on her waist, resting ever so slightly on the bared skin of her lower back. It was as though the movement of his hand shifted some kind of invisible barrier between them. She looked up, meeting the visible heat in his eyes for a long silent moment. The air seemed to pulse with heat along with the slow seductive crooning of the jazz in the background.

Suddenly it felt as though every inch of her front was glued to a wall of warm hard muscle. Her body felt heated and loose in his arms, her mind telling her to move closer. A tiny fragment of her logical brain warned her to walk away. She ignored it.

'I doubt anyone else in here considers slow dancing to be such an important act.' She kept her tone even, trying to maintain some level of worldly composure in the face of her body's ridiculous reaction.

'I had quite forgotten that there was anyone else here at all,' he said softly.

Cressida looked up to meet his eyes; they were dark and earnest, no trace of humour or sarcasm. She felt her cheeks heat, her eyes lowering to rest comfortably on his chin. This was it, she told herself sternly—this was the moment where she should thank him for a lovely dance and make a calm and graceful exit.

The dance had been perfect, she told herself sternly—exactly what she had needed. She had sought a little excitement on her night of freedom and now she would leave London tomorrow and go happily to her duty. She could forget about this night, forget about this handsome stranger and easily go on for ever without wondering...

Suddenly she became aware that they had stopped dancing. The music had got faster and the other couples moved around the spot where they stood, entirely still in their embrace. She looked up. He was still watching her with that impenetrable gaze in a moment that seemed to stretch on as though separate from time entirely. His fingers flexed slightly at her waist, sending tingles up her spine.

What would it be like to feel his mouth on hers and his hands roaming over her body? The thought caught her by surprise, her cheeks heating as she ran the tip of her tongue along her suddenly dry lips. Her sister had described a kind of madness that had taken over when she'd met the man who was now her fiancé, an attraction that had overcome logic and reason. She doubted she could ever harbour such a passion. All of a sudden she despised the calm, rational Cressida who lived in fear of straying too far from her comfort zone. What would it feel like to simply have a thought pop into one's mind and act on it? To be a different version of herself, even for just a moment?

He cleared his throat and she felt the moment slipping away; the small window of time she had been granted seemed to be disappearing, leaving nothing but the promise of tomorrow. Of the life being forced upon her. The choices she would no longer be free to make. *But not yet...*a small voice inside whispered.

She looked up into the deep brown of his gaze, catching her breath at the blatant heat she saw there. Madness indeed, she thought as her breath stopped completely, realising what she was about to do. Letting impulse take the lead, she flexed her body upwards and pressed her lips to his.

Soft, firm lips remained still under the clumsy touch of her inexperienced kiss. The hands on her waist applied pressure, holding her where she stood as his lips began to move against hers, hard and fast. Suddenly the kiss was demanding and filled with a hunger that took her breath away. It was intoxicating and overwhelming and…utterly perfect.

Was this what everyone felt when they kissed a man for the first time? Was this what she had been missing out on all these years? It felt as though she was waking up from a deep sleep and feeling her body come to life for the first time.

When he pulled his mouth from hers all too soon, she felt the loss keenly, as though going from the warmth of a fire to the bitter cold.

He uttered something harsh and guttural in a foreign language before she felt herself being unceremoniously hauled away from the dance floor towards the private area at the back of the club. Still dazed by the earth-shattering kiss, she didn't think to protest, allowing herself to be steered into a semi-private booth shielded partially from view by a thick red velvet curtain.

'I didn't mean for that to happen.' He spoke harshly, his breathing slightly laboured. 'I didn't intend to—'

'Please, don't apologise,' she blurted, not wanting his regretful words to taint what had been such a wonderful moment for her. One half of her prayed silently that he would leave, while the other half wanted nothing more than for him to take her in his arms again. 'I kissed you, after all.' She forced a smile. 'And I'm glad that I did.'

'You might not feel that way if you knew who I was.' He spoke evenly, but his expression held a trace of darkness that had not been there before.

'Maybe it adds to the sense of mystery.' She attempted a smile.

'Is this what you were seeking tonight, coming here?' His voice was a low rumble as he took a step closer. 'Kissing strangers on a darkened dance floor?'

Something in his eyes brought gooseflesh to her exposed skin. She couldn't put her finger on it but the atmosphere no longer felt warm and anonymous; she felt suddenly exposed and thoroughly out of her depth. The realisation of what she had just done came crashing upon her like a cold shower and she took a few slow backwards steps.

'Thank you for the dance,' she murmured, avoiding his eyes. 'It was…wonderful.'

He raised one brow, leaning against the side panel on the wall. 'Time to return to reality already?'

Cressida nodded once, feeling a strange pull between needing to get away and desperately wanting to stay. She wondered what his name was, where he came from. So many questions would be left unanswered once she left.

And still she walked away.

She left the club and its swaying music behind as she emerged into the night, the sharp wind making her wish she had brought a jacket. As she looked around to find where her chauffeur had got to, a trio of men in dark suits seemed to appear from nowhere.

'Your Highness,' the tallest one said in accented English, 'do not be frightened. We are ordered here to assure your safety.'

'My safety?' she breathed, looking around the street wildly. 'Where is my driver? How do you know who I am? Ordered by whom?'

'Ordered by me,' a familiarly accented voice rang out in the silent night from the nightclub doorway.

Cressida whirled, inhaling hard as she was met by the sight of the dark stranger from the dance floor walking towards her. Wordlessly, he draped a heavy woollen coat across her shoulders, guiding her a few steps away from the small army of what she presumed to be bodyguards.

His accented voice rang in her ears, intensifying the sensation of unease along her spine that warned her she had made a grave mistake tonight. She had overlooked something important. Her heart beat frantically in her chest as she met his dark gaze. 'Who *are* you?'

'I am Sheikh Khalil Al Rhas, ruler of Zayyar.' He held her pinned with his dark gaze. 'And you, Princess, are in a world of trouble.'

CHAPTER TWO

CRESSIDA FELT THE weight of his words settle somewhere in her chest. His accent, the way he had looked at her when they'd first spoken—it all fell horribly into place. 'You can't be him,' she breathed.

'And yet I am,' he said smoothly.

Disbelief held her body frozen for what felt like an eternity. Gone was the warmth from his eyes, replaced by a hardness that sent prickles along her skin.

She had sourced a few photographs online of the notoriously private Sheikh Khalil but the images she had seen had shown pictures of a man who seemed older, dressed in traditional white robes, his features obscured by a headdress and sunglasses. Not smooth shaven in a sleek open-collared suit, practically vibrating the air around him with a dark virility that made her knees weak.

This was her *fiancé*? The man her father had described as old-world and ruthless? She thought of all the anxiety that had plagued her, worrying what to say when they first met or how she should behave...

'Was this a game to you?' Her voice was suddenly ice-cold. 'Was it some kind of test to see how I might... perform?'

'No,' he said simply, a strange look crossing his features. 'This was most definitely not a part of my plan for our first meeting.'

Cressida swallowed hard. 'Did you know who I was from the start?'

His jaw seemed to tighten before he answered. 'Yes.'

'Well, then, I fail to see how you weren't toying with me.' She shook her head, unable to stand still a moment longer. She had taken no more than two steps towards the street and he was by her side. A muscular hand encircled her wrist, stopping her progress.

'Let me go,' she gritted, snatching her hand from him with force.

'You will not walk away from me, Princess,' he said softly. 'We have not yet finished our conversation.'

'I most certainly am finished. I never want to see you again.'

His mouth hardened into a thin line. 'You can come with me calmly so that we can resolve this privately, or you can make things needlessly difficult.'

As she watched, his eyes drifted to the handful of men surrounding them. She felt the distinct sensation of being caged in and it was not pleasant. 'Where is Frank?' she asked quietly, suddenly worried for her loyal chauffeur.

He raised one dark brow. 'Your driver has been relieved of his duties, along with your incompetent bodyguards.'

'You can't do that,' she breathed, aghast. 'They are not at fault for my actions.'

His head cocked to one side. 'It's a little late for remorse now, don't you think? If a driver can be persuaded to overlook protocol by a pair of fluttering lashes, then he has no business being entrusted with the responsibility.'

'You can't do this.'

'Oh, I most certainly can,' he purred, encircling her wrist with his strong hand.

'For tonight, at least, your safety is my responsibility.'

She did not know why, shock perhaps, but she put up virtually no fight as he guided her into the limousine that lay in wait by the roadside. The team of guards retreated into their own imposing vehicles to the front and behind. Even when it became clear that they were driving in completely the opposite direction to her apartment, she could not speak. She felt cold, the skin on her arms prickling with gooseflesh.

If her driver and guards had truly been dismissed, then that meant they would have already alerted King Fabian. Her father had already made it clear that he was depending on her to ensure this union went ahead at any cost. Guilt gnawed at her stomach as she closed her eyes, focusing on the gentle sway of the car to distract herself from the many reasons why, once again, she was an utter disappointment to her parents. This was the first and only thing the King had ever asked of her directly, the first time he had spoken to her since...well, since he had decided she was no longer worth speaking to. She had finally been given an opportunity to prove herself, to save her kingdom. And, as per usual, she had failed spectacularly.

'Are we to travel in silence?' The Sheikh was facing her, one long leg propped over the other, making him seem larger and more imposing in the small space.

'I fail to see how making idle chit-chat with you

will make this situation any easier.' She purposefully directed her gaze out at the passing blur of streetlamps and shadows.

'You seem quite indignant for someone who chose to run away from her guards for a wild night out.' His voice held only the smallest hint of impatience.

'I am not the one who did anything wrong here.'

'Aren't you?' He met her gaze evenly.

Before she could retaliate, the car came to a stop outside one of the most exclusive hotels in London. They were escorted inside by the Sheikh's entourage, who shielded them both from view until they were safely inside a private lift.

The Sheikh's suite spanned the entire top floor of the building, offering a breathtaking view of the London skyline. She was instantly drawn to look out at the majestic sea of lights of the city she had spent virtually no time exploring in the past five years.

She was aware of the bodyguards moving around as they performed a thorough check of the rooms. A handful of other men and women appeared briefly, speaking to the Sheikh in a language she assumed to be Zayyari. Her studies had included most European languages, along with ancient Greek and Latin, but she had no experience of Middle Eastern tongues. The way the syllables cut and rolled off their tongues was fascinating; it was a struggle not to turn and observe the conversations.

After a while she became aware of the lack of noise in the open-plan living space. She turned just as he reached her side.

Sheikh Khalil cleared his throat gently. 'Have you

spent all of this time appreciating the view or plotting on ways to escape, I wonder.'

She turned to face him fully. 'At what point did I become your prisoner?'

'Despite how others may portray me, I am not a tyrant. I assured your family that I would escort you to Monteverre personally and I will not go back on my word, even if you choose to end our arrangement.'

His gaze travelled briefly to her mouth before returning upwards. Did she imagine the slight dart of his tongue to moisten his lips before he spoke again?

He took another step so that he was by her side, one hand braced on the glass. 'I came to London to meet my future Queen on neutral ground. To ensure that we might begin our union on equal footing and avoid history repeating itself. It seems I'm destined to fail on that point.'

Cressida lowered her gaze, knowing he was referring to his failed engagement with her older sister, Olivia. The fact that she was a replacement bride should offend her, but she couldn't blame him for wanting Olivia as his first choice. Her sister was graceful and beautiful with a flawless talent for public speaking. Who wouldn't want her as their Queen? The arrangement between Monteverre and Zayyar had been in negotiations for months until her sister had chosen to walk away before accepting the proposal.

'You are our last chance, Cressida. Make me proud.'

'Tell me why you didn't reveal yourself straight away,' she said, ignoring the echo of her father's voice in her mind and firmly throwing down the gauntlet between them. She simply could not go ahead with the deal if tonight had been some kind of practical joke.

She had *some* pride. But could she truly return to Monteverre a failure?

'It was interesting to find myself meeting you without the complication of my own identity in the way,' he said simply.

'You see yourself as a complication?' she asked quietly, mulling over his words.

'When seeing a person as they truly are, yes.'

She raised her brows at his honesty. She knew all too well how the world changed once people knew you had a title in front of your name. Sometimes for the better, sometimes for the worse.

'I am not in the habit of using women as toys to amuse myself—was that what you accused me of?' He raised one brow in challenge. 'However, I will admit when I am wrong. I should have immediately announced my identity once I realised you had no idea who I was.'

'Yes. You should have.' She bit her bottom lip, trying not to look at him directly lest she be overtaken by another flashback to what it had felt like to be in his arms.

'But perhaps none of that matters, as you have said you are finished with all of this and never wish to see me again.' There was no playfulness in his words as he moved across the room to take a seat in the living area. 'Truthfully, this entire deal has been a fiasco from the start, with your father's lies and manipulations. It's clear to me now that you can't have been entering into this marriage willingly if this is how you choose to spend your free time.'

Cressida felt a prickle of irritation rise within her at his easy reclined posture and flippant judgement. There was no way she was going to beg this arrogant man to honour their agreement. And yet she was not

quite ready to return to Monteverre if that meant her
father lost the deal that would salvage their kingdom's
failing economy.

She settled for a nonchalant shrug of her shoulders.
'This is an unusual situation for me, Your Highness,
not that it's any of your business.'

'Perhaps both of us acted on impulse, Princess. But
still, now I've met you I can't see how you will be happy
away from the freedom and thrills of this kind of life.
I have a duty to my people to give them a Queen who
will be fulfilled by her role.'

'Why not just leave me here, then?'

'I am taking you back to your kingdom, just as I
promised I would.' He watched her, his expression entirely unreadable. 'Your father made it very clear that
your time in London had come to an end. But, considering recent events, I also made sure to consult my own
sources. They told me that you are no longer enrolled
with the university and the lease on your apartment has
been cancelled.'

Her father had been quite busy this past week. He
had not been happy when she'd told him of her wish
to accept the teaching position, even before Olivia had
walked away from the deal with the Sheikh. Cressida
swallowed hard, moving to take a seat directly across
from him in the luxurious living area. She had been
fully prepared to return to her home country right up
until approximately two hours ago. Why all of a sudden
did it seem more favourable to walk through hot coals
than to set one foot on Monteverrian soil?

She straightened her shoulders, making direct eye
contact with the man across from her for the first time
since they had entered his suite. 'I know that you have

spent months on these negotiations. My father told me that you had already begun to invest millions, according to the deal, before my sister walked away from the arrangement.'

His eyes narrowed slightly, the rest of his expression utterly still. Clearly he'd had practice in holding his reactions in check.

Cressida crossed one leg idly over the other. 'It's clear to me that both our kingdoms stand to lose if we walk away.'

He was thoughtful for a long moment. 'There is much at stake. But tonight has made me question some things. I did not expect you to be a saint, Princess. You have clearly lived a life of…freedom…during your time here.' He looked at her pointedly. 'But a man in my position requires one hundred per cent loyalty from the woman by his side. To project an image of stability and unity.'

She chewed on the inside of her lip, fighting the urge to shout that she had never even kissed a man before tonight, but she resisted. 'I would like to propose that tonight should not have any bearing on our arrangement.'

'And yet it does.' He cleared his voice, angling his face away from her. 'There was something between us tonight—an attraction. A political agreement such as this one does not mix well with emotional involvement.'

'You think I am emotionally involved after one kiss?' she asked.

He tensed. 'I mean that sometimes people tend to read more into simple physical chemistry.'

And by *people* he meant *women*, clearly. She fought against the urge to roll her eyes. 'I am not one of those *people*,' she said pointedly. 'I don't particularly do emotional connections. I have always been perfectly happy with my own company.' She didn't tell him that it wasn't really her choice to be so cold, simply a part of her make-up.

The Sheikh stood, pacing to the sideboard at the corner of the room and pouring himself a glass of iced water. 'So if I am willing to go ahead with the arrangement, you wish to uphold your end of the bargain?'

Cressida took a deep breath, mulling over her words carefully before she spoke. 'I think I would be willing, but only once I know that the terms will remain the same. That it will not be a…a true marriage.'

Khal paused at the slight tremor in the young Princess's voice. She sat perfectly poised on the low-slung sofa, long slim legs tucked demurely to one side. One would never guess she had been virtually plastered to his front less than an hour before. He cleared his throat, pushing the images from his mind. 'The legal agreements you have already signed state the general terms of the union. What they do not overtly mention is that absolute fidelity is required, along with every effort to maintain the perfect image. So while we might not be sharing a bed as man and wife, I assure you that I would still expect a true marriage.'

A strange look crossed her features. She took a moment of pensive silence before looking up to meet his gaze head-on. 'Are those rules the same for you?'

Khal let a moment of silence hang in the air. 'In my country, the act of marriage is not one that is entered into lightly, even one of a political nature. So yes, the terms of the union would apply equally to both parties.'

She stood, pacing towards the window and wrapping

her arms around herself before turning back to him. 'Well, then, I suppose I don't have any other questions.'

'You sound very eager to become my Queen, I must say.'

'It has always been part of my duty to my kingdom to marry advantageously, if required.' She shrugged.

'And abandoning your studies? That does not bother you?'

She frowned, looking away for a moment. 'It's almost as though you are trying to talk me out of this.'

'I'm making sure you won't bolt at the last minute,' he said plainly, seeing no need to mince his words considering the turn the night had taken.

Understanding dawned in the depths of her blue eyes. 'You are concerned that I will act as my sister did.'

'I am protecting my own interests, yes.'

She nodded, biting her lower lip. 'I don't think that my sister intended to behave as she did. The Olivia that I know was always true to her word.' She shook her head once, a frown marring her brow. 'I understand that you have a vision for your future wife. That Olivia fitted a certain mould. I must warn you that I have not been a part of public life for many years—'

'My team are aware of this and are prepared to help you in your new role.' He watched as she moved back to sit delicately on the sofa once more. It seemed as if she were unable to be still. 'You seem quite eager to perform your royal duties; it surprises me in someone who has not set foot in their kingdom for such a long time.'

Her shoulders stiffened slightly at his words. 'Of course I have personal reasons for agreeing to this marriage, Your Highness. They are my own, not ones forced upon me or held over me. All I can do is assure you wholeheartedly that I'm here because I choose to be.'

'That's more than enough for me,' he said smoothly as he stood and took the few steps to close the space between them so that he stood over her. She inhaled sharply, freezing as he reached into the pocket of the coat he had draped across her shoulders earlier. He withdrew a small black box and sat on the seat alongside her.

'I understand that this is the tradition in Monteverre?' He opened the ring box, revealing a delicate vintage ruby ring set in the finest gold.

'Oh...' Her eyes widened. 'There is really no need for...'

He took her hand, cutting off whatever she'd been about to say as he slipped the ring onto the correct finger and surveyed his handiwork. 'A perfect fit.'

She cleared her throat, frowning slightly as she blinked down at the sparkling gem nestled against her pale skin. 'Thank you.'

Khal was suddenly very aware of the intimacy of their position. He stood, clasping both hands together. 'We will stop first in Monteverre for a brief press conference, followed by an engagement party. The wedding will take place as quickly as possible, but likely will be in a few months' time to allow for planning and invitations.'

Cressida frowned. 'Oh... I hadn't realised the wedding would be a big event.'

'There is usually some fanfare when a King takes a woman to be his Queen.' Khal fought the urge to laugh.

'I was under the impression from your secretary that we would be married quickly, that's all. That time was important to you.'

'You have an objection to the timing of the marriage?'

'No, not at all. The sooner the better, really.' She shrugged. 'I just thought there would be some kind of spin put on it. A secret elopement or something.'

'You do not want a big public wedding?'

'Well, it's just… No offence, but you are hardly the most public of figures and I clearly have not lived in the spotlight. It might seem odd if we suddenly announce a big wedding. I don't even know who I would invite, other than my family.'

Khal frowned, considering the logic in her words. The plan had originally been formed to account for his first bride—it was true that Princess Olivia was much more of a public figure in the media than her reclusive sister. Once again, it seemed his plans were being thrown to the winds. But perhaps, this time, a change in direction might benefit him and help him to make up for lost time.

Cressida noticed that the Sheikh seemed suddenly distracted as he called for one of his assistants to show her to her room. She barely had a moment to bid him goodnight before she was swept away and shown into a luxurious bedroom. A fresh silky towelling robe and slippers lay draped on the bed and she wasted no time in stripping out of her tight dress and heels before flopping onto the giant bed in the most un-princess-like manner possible.

The events of the night seemed surreal in her exhausted state. Almost as if she was living in some alternate reality of her own life. She raised her hand into the air above her head, staring at the ruby glinting on her finger. He had slid the ring on her finger with such businesslike finality, and yet the touch of his skin on hers had set her pulse racing.

She closed her eyes against the onslaught of memories from the hours before. The feel of his hands on her waist as they'd moved to the music, that first electric touch of his lips against hers. She would never let him know that he had been her first kiss; that would make it matter somehow.

Which it didn't. It had just been a kiss. She closed her eyes, repeating the words silently to herself and letting the tiredness take over.

She was awoken before dawn and told that they would be travelling to the airfield immediately. The sky was still jet-black and the air frosty as she ascended the steps to a luxury jet bearing the Royal insignia of Zayyar. The Sheikh was already on board and conversing with a team of men and women in traditional Zayyari attire. He had changed into white robes and the elaborate headdress she had seen in pictures.

She was thankful that he'd had the foresight to have a small case of her belongings collected and delivered to her room during the night so that she didn't have to wear the red dress again. She had not expected him to think of her comforts. Or, more realistically, it was his assistant who had thought of her. She took a seat near the front of the plane, swiping through the news on her phone as she waited for the meeting to end.

'Cressida,' a familiar deep voice called to her from within the cocoon of staff.

She stood, making her way down the wide aisle to the long conference table in the middle of the aircraft.

The men and women of his staff bowed their heads, moving away and revealing their King, seated at the top of the table surrounded by official documents and paraphernalia.

'I had not realised you planned to fly to Monteverre at first light,' she said breathlessly, fidgeting with the hem of her simple white blouse. She felt ridiculously underdressed in her blue jeans and worn sneakers. Her more expensive royal attire was sadly out of date, considering she had not attended anything as Princess Cressida in years.

'Change of plan.' He looked up for the first time, pausing to sweep his gaze over her briefly. 'We fly directly to Zayyar.'

'You are not taking me home first?'

'I thought it best to take you home after we are married. Which will now be in two days' time.'

CHAPTER THREE

'TWO DAYS? AS IN forty-eight hours from now?'

Khal had kept his tone deliberately neutral, taking in her pleasantly flushed cheeks and tied back hair. She looked younger without all the make-up from the night before, her ash-blonde hair was now swept neatly back from her face in a tight elastic band. The austere style only served to draw more attention to her wide-set blue eyes and porcelain skin. Of course, the red dress of last night had been more expertly cut to show off her curves than the plain blouse and casual jeans she now wore but he could still see the delicate dip and flare of her waist. If he thought hard enough, he could remember how good those curves had felt under his hands only hours before…

Redirecting his wayward thoughts, he cleared his throat and focused on the papers in front of him. 'That is correct,' he said coolly. 'I ran your suggestion past my team last night, after you went to bed, and they took it quite to heart. It seems you may have averted us from a mistaken course of action indeed.'

'My suggestion?' she breathed, her eyes growing wider still.

'The change in PR operation, of course. You alone

spotted the likely backlash in public opinion. You were absolutely right to question it.' He nodded in her direction as though congratulating her on acing a project rather than bumping forward an entire wedding. 'You did say that you would prefer to get married as soon as possible.'

'Yes... I did say that.' She moved to a nearby seat and sat down heavily. She looked ashen all of a sudden, small and fragile in the large leather chair that cocooned her.

'You have an entire bedroom to yourself for the duration of the flight,' he said, motioning to a set of doors at the end of the main cabin. 'You can't have got very much sleep last night.'

She pursed her lips slightly. 'Thank you. I could do with some more rest.'

Khal felt a momentary flash of conscience as she disappeared through the doors but pushed it away. He had done what was necessary in bringing forward the date. He had made the best decision to protect his deal. The sudden sense of urgency he'd felt—to take her far away from the life she had led in London and back to his kingdom—was purely down to expediting matters and avoiding any more risk of her going back on the agreement. The sooner Princess Cressida was his wife, the sooner he could get back to the business of growing his kingdom's influence and doing what he did best.

Khal took the time alone to gather his thoughts, trying to shift the uncomfortable sensation that had settled in his gut. He felt completely unhinged, as though everything he had believed of himself was being challenged. This entire marriage debacle had done nothing but challenge him from the moment his advisors had suggested it as a solution to their problem with European trade.

From the start he had not been able to deny that an alliance with Monteverre made sense. The global perception of his country was vastly outdated, harking back to their war-torn history. Zayyar had enjoyed an age of peace and prosperity for almost a quarter of a century and still they hit wall after wall when it came to foreign politics. Monteverre was one of the oldest nations in the Western world; it had influence and sway and, best of all, it desperately needed help in the form of cash investments, due to years of spending far beyond its means. It was simple mathematics.

What was not quite so simple was the old Zayyari law that demanded a marital alliance between two highborn members of aligning kingdoms. His advisors had already been fighting a backlash from the older generation, who disagreed with their country's changing landscape. He needed a bride if he wished to avoid public uproar. Thankfully, King Fabian had assured him that arranged marriage for the royal descendants was still a firm practice in his kingdom. Khal was not overly fond of the King, but he had not believed him capable of coercing his own daughter to the point that she would run away to avoid a proposal.

Cressida had assured him that she was not being coerced as her sister had been, yet still he wondered what personal reasons drove her to accept a political arrangement. Clearly she had a strong sense of loyalty to her kingdom and her family. It did not take much imagination to picture her by his side, swathed in silks and jewels, hosting lunches and balls in the Zayyari grand palace for hundreds of guests from all over the globe.

The trouble was, he had imagined a cold marriage. So far, his response to his fiancée had been far from cold. He'd had a true marriage once, built on the foundations of love and companionship. He had no desire to try to recreate that, for many reasons.

But the attraction between them was a complication he had not foreseen. Five minutes with her in his arms and he had practically pulled her to the nearest private area, needing more. She had felt so good in his arms. Too good.

The moment that he had realised she was completely oblivious to his identity he had felt something awaken inside him that he had long buried. Suddenly his quiet political marriage had seemed a lot less straightforward. He had planned to sit and keep watch until she decided to leave of her own accord. Then someone had tried to dance with her and that small primitive part of him he tried his best to suppress had roared to life, moving in to claim what was *his*.

So much for changing his image of ruthless desert King.

He had not expected to be physically interested in the woman he married; it was not necessary to the arrangement, after all. His head was not usually turned by long legs and a short dress. But the moment he'd had her body pressed against his, he had felt his libido emerge from its self-imposed hibernation with a vengeance. He'd been possessed by the mad urge to press his lips to the soft parts of her neck and continue down… It had shocked him, the need.

The wedding would take place in two days. This time he had made sure of it. An iron-clad contract of law bound Princess Cressida to their agreement. If she went back on her promise, his financial investments into Monteverre's failing economy became null and void. Perhaps it was severe, but he couldn't take a chance on her backing out of the marriage just like her sister had. Not when the future of two countries lay in the balance. He was not a patient man, quite the opposite. He liked things to be done precisely when he planned. Soon he could get back to more important matters in his own kingdom.

Cressida tried to stifle a gasp as the helicopter lowered swiftly to the ground, depositing them on a crop of barren flatlands on the very outskirts of the Zayyari desert. Despite her attack of anxiety at the news that she would become Queen so soon, she had surprisingly managed to sleep for almost five hours before waking with a ferocious hunger. The rest of the flight had been spent nibbling on snacks and perusing some of the books she had found on board about her new home, the desert kingdom of Zayyar. It had been a smooth trip from the private airstrip and she had presumed that they would arrive directly at the palace in the centre of Zayyar's capital city of the same name. Her Internet research had provided her with some basic facts of what to expect from her new home, but nothing could have prepared her for the heat. Her blouse already felt damp on her back as Khal helped her out of the SUV and into the direct glare of the burning hot sun.

She had covered her hair with a pale pink scarf before they exited the jet, provided by one of his many assistants. In general, Zayyar was rather cosmopolitan for the Middle East; they did not enforce modesty among the women of its population. But apparently where they were going for their wedding ceremony was a sacred place. It was all very mysterious.

'We continue on horseback from here.' Khal's voice was gruff and sleep-worn as he gestured to where his guards had already begun to mount impressively large dark steeds. 'You will ride with me.'

She gulped, taking in the sheer size of the animal before her. She had never been one for horseback riding as a girl. But, before she could object, strong arms gripped her hips tight and she felt herself being swung up onto the saddle as though she weighed nothing at all. The hard warmth of the Sheikh's chest pressed tight to her back as he settled behind her and she felt her body tense. The effort of keeping her eyes on the horizon was a welcome distraction as they began a swift gallop across the sand. There was no sound around them other than the beating of hooves on the dry desert plain. Gone was the hustle and bustle of city life she had grown used to, the noise she had used to distract her just as much as the books she lived inside. The air she breathed in was warm and fragrant, reaching deep within her and calming her raging heartbeat.

The thought that she had spent the past five years in one city was suddenly ludicrous. There had been a whole world outside her self-imposed cage, waiting to be explored. They crossed the endless expanse of sand for almost an hour; her thighs ached from stopping herself from relaxing back into the warmth of the hard male chest behind her. She still thought of him as the Sheikh, she realised. Surely one should be on first name terms with the man you were about to marry? He shifted his body behind her in the saddle, keeping the horse in pace. She felt gravity press her backwards until every inch of her back was plastered to his hard torso. All at once she felt the heat of him seep into her skin, sending goosebumps down her arms. It took all her strength not to dart away from the sensation, away from the overwhelming urge to sink further into it.

Clearing her throat, she turned her head to dart a quick look up at him. Her throat dried at the vision of his hard jaw in profile as he focused on guiding the powerful stallion up the dunes. Clearly he was not as affected by the ride as she.

All thoughts of him were momentarily curbed as their small party crested the last dune and a vision of beauty spread out in the valley below them. Golden sands gave way to the lush green paradise of a small oasis. Nestled in the middle of trees and ancient stone pillars were colourful Bedouin-style tents and temporary structures.

'Welcome to the sacred ground of Old Zayyar,' the Sheikh announced beside her ear. One strong arm snaked around her waist to hold her in place as they began their descent down the steep rocky hillside. They were greeted by a crowd of men and women in traditional robes and clothing, the men in elaborate headdresses and the women adorned in beautiful paints and jewels.

Men banged drums as the Sheikh dismounted and lifted her down to the ground in one powerful movement. She felt entirely out of place in her T-shirt and jeans combo.

'This is your bridal party,' the Sheikh said softly in her ear over the sound of the music and babbling. 'My young cousins speak a little English. You will be taken care of.'

A young woman stepped forward as if on cue, bowing low. Cressida shook her head and raised her hand, preparing to tell the woman not to make such a fuss.

'You are to be my Queen, Cressida.' He spoke once more. 'Be prepared to be treated as such.'

She nodded, straightening her shoulders as the rest of the women in the crowd bowed low in the same fashion. Her chest tightened with anxiety, feeling so many eyes on her, but she forced herself to take a step forward and then another, following the young woman into a large tent and leaving the rest of the crowd, and the Sheikh, behind.

Evidently it was customary for her to meet and join hands with every single woman in the tribe, each one offering what she hoped were kind words in their native tongue as they inked delicate patterns of henna on her skin. The women seemed warm and welcoming, despite the language barrier between them. She was acutely aware of her own plain Western clothing amongst their colourful draped fabrics. She caught more than one woman staring or whispering behind her hand when they thought she was not looking.

Her self-appointed assistant, Aisha, was a young woman of around twenty who had begun studying English only the year before. In between the courses of their evening meal, Aisha told her how she had sourced books and studied alone for a time before applying for a scholarship to university.

'The Sheikh's first wife was a great patron of female education. I thank her in my prayers each morning and night,' Aisha gushed before biting her lip suddenly. 'Oh, how thoughtless of me to mention such a delicate matter on the eve of your wedding!'

Far from being offended, Cressida's curiosity was piqued. She had already seen from her online research that the Sheikh had been married once before. That his wife had died in a tragic car accident four years previously. He had not mentioned her in any of their conversations so far and she did not see the point in bringing up what was likely to still be a delicate subject. 'I confess that I don't know very much about the late Sheikha. I have read that she was much beloved?'

'Sheikha Priya.' The young girl nodded, a wistful smile crossing her lips. 'She was…truly beautiful. She helped many people…' Tears filled the young woman's eyes and she wiped them away, apologising profusely.

'Please, don't apologise. Her death must have come as quite a shock to everyone.' Cressida felt her chest tighten as she offered a napkin to the young woman.

'It was a terrible time for Zayyar. Her Highness was so young. And of course His Highness was the victim of such scrutiny afterwards…because of the rumours.'

Cressida nodded, not wanting to admit that she had no idea what these rumours entailed. She felt the urge to press further, to find out exactly how many secrets lay buried under the facade of her simple marriage of convenience. She allowed the temptation to pass, exhaling as the conversation flowed amongst the women around her and the meal was served.

After dinner she was inundated with gifts of vibrant fruit baskets, decorated sweet cakes and fragrant teas, flowers and little bottles of oil as traditional music floated on the air. Aisha dutifully explained the symbolism behind each of the gifts, how they strengthened the couple's love for one another or brought fertility to the marriage. Cressida tried her best to ignore her discomfort at the thought of accepting such beautiful gifts, as neither love nor fertility would play a part in her marriage. She wished she could just tell them all not to make such a fuss, that she was not a real bride. That this was not the romantic fairy tale elopement that it seemed. She had always hated being in the spotlight and it seemed impossible to avoid as the women argued over her hairstyle and made final adjustments to her wedding clothes.

As night fell across the encampment, Cressida was finally left alone in her bridal tent. She could feel the strain in her cheeks from the polite smile that she had kept plastered on her face all afternoon. Her reflection in a nearby mirror showed dark shadows under her eyes, making her already pale skin seem even more translucent. She exhaled slowly, removing the pink scarf that covered her hair and combing it out with her fingers while ignoring the rising anxiety within her.

She had not been aware of any scandal in Zayyar's past when she'd committed to the marriage, but it made sense if that was the reason why Sheikh Khalil would go so far for a bride with Western ties. She had known from the bare facts available on the Internet that he was a widower, but, apart from a few vague news articles, that seemed as far as the information went. There was no further mention of the Sheikh's activities in the years since then. But she had noticed the way his staff hurried around him on the plane...as though he was a man to be feared.

So why did she not feel that same fear when she looked at him? She thought of the shivers that had run down her spine as he'd held her close on the horse ride across the desert, mere hours before. She had felt the opposite of fear; she had never been more excited in her life. She closed her eyes, placing one hand on her chest to feel the steady beat of her heart. No, she most definitely was not afraid to marry the Sheikh. She was more afraid of the intense attraction she felt every time he came close. Five years was a long time to spend trying to maintain her distance. He would find it easy, no doubt.

She straightened her shoulders, meeting her own gaze in the mirror once more. This was a job, she reminded herself. This was her duty. She would prove her loyalty to her family once and for all and make up for the mistakes she had made in her youth. Then she would be free to live her own life without guilt. She would be free of constantly feeling like a failure.

She moved to her bed, burying herself under the silk coverlet and closing her eyes tight. He had been her first kiss—it was only natural that she would be slightly affected by that milestone. She was not made of stone, much as she had tried to pretend she was. But she would not fail at this. If a cold, distant marriage of convenience was what the Sheikh of Zayyar wanted, then that was exactly what he would have.

The royal events team had worked quickly under pressure, creating a simple space that mixed elements of Western and Zayyari wedding cultures. Already the PR officials were drafting articles for the handful of magazines and newspapers who would be 'leaked' the news of the secret nuptials. The Princess had been right.

A large wedding would not have had half as much impact as this would.

Their marriage was to be a seamless union of east and west, a romantic desert fairy tale...or something like that. He had stopped listening to the event planner after she had begun talking about using sand as symbolism for their everlasting love. Little did they know how very far from the truth that was.

Khal stood in the heavy stillness of the desert air, watching as the sun began to dip low in the sky as evening fell upon them. The sand burned orange outside the intimate wedding tent and on the light breeze he could smell the fragrant pink flowers that had been arranged in vases and overflowing baskets all around the encampment in celebration. He picked one from a basket, simply to have something to do with his hands while he waited.

Priya had ordered similar flowers for their wedding day, he mused, the thought catching him off guard. He had ordered thousands of the blooms to celebrate their first anniversary. He crushed the delicate blossom in his hand, letting it fall to the ground as though it burned him. Of all the places for this farcical ceremony to take place, of course it would be here—they were in the very spot his parents had married. The sacred heart of his tribe and all the beliefs they held dear. A grand statement to the people of Zayyar, according to the team of advisors who had planned everything.

Priya had wanted a grand event, opting for a lavish three-day celebration in the Grand Palace. He steeled himself, willing his mind to change course. He could not think of his first wife, not when he was set to marry another at any moment.

Once they had arrived in the camp the day before, he had not wasted time in dispatching his fiancée to the women of the tribe, simply to put distance between them after the torture of the journey from the jet. In hindsight, opting to have her soft warm curves cradled between his thighs on horseback for an hour had not been his cleverest idea. He'd spent the afternoon riding across the desert to clear his head, cursing the lack of freezing cold lakes in their vicinity. He was not a teenager. He would not have his position made weak by his physical desire for the woman set to become his wife.

It was his own fault, for not taking a mistress in the years since Priya's death. He had always found an excuse not to move on—there had always been some battle to fight. Whether it was trying to find out the truth behind his wife's death or working against the economic repercussions of the rumours that had plagued him in the aftermath—that he had somehow been responsible for his wife's sudden demise.

He exhaled hard. He was a man. He had needs. And this was clearly the result when one suppressed those needs for too long. His fiancée was the very last person he could afford to desire right now. And the duty their marriage was based on made his situation even more difficult. He had demanded fidelity of her for the duration of their marriage; it was only fair that he offer the same loyalty himself. He would not risk the credibility of their union simply to slake his lust elsewhere.

His jaw felt as if it was made of stone as he heard a hush fall around the small gathering inside the tent. The event planners signalled that the bride was about to arrive. Khal stepped directly underneath two pillars swathed in snow-white gossamer fabric and watched as the small congregation of people appeared over the dunes. The single photographer who had been granted press access to the camp stepped forward, lens primed to catch the story of the year.

Khal kept his breathing steady, determined to play the part of calm groom. The people believed this to be a true marriage, after all. A romantic elopement between their King and his beautiful Western Princess. She was somewhere in the middle of the women, walking the same path that this tribe had walked for centuries. His jaw tightening painfully, he turned away and waited.

She reached his side with a whisper of silk flowing in the breeze, bringing the scent of jasmine and vanilla to his nostrils. Khal looked down and felt his breath catch for a moment. She was beautiful; there was no doubt. Pale porcelain skin offset by a shimmering golden wedding robe and heavy bejewelled veil. Was it a trick of the light or did her blue eyes seem to glow as she met his gaze?

Inhaling past the sudden tightness in his chest, he took his bride by the hand and began repeating his vows, his eyes never leaving hers. Part of the vows included a short sentence in Zayyari; he watched the concentration on her face as she vowed to be his for the remainder of their lives, a strange feeling within his chest as she did not stumble over the thick syllables of his native language. Their eyes met as the celebrant spoke of loyalty and devotion, of sharing a lifetime with one another. He looked in her eyes as the weight of their vows hung heavy in the air. And yet, as she promised to be true, he knew she spoke the truth. A strange feeling of calm came over him as he slid a wedding band onto her slim finger. A sense of complete victory.

Kisses not being customary at Zayyari weddings, they sealed their vows with a symbolic touching of foreheads. All too soon, he left the wedding tent with his new wife by his side to the rapturous applause of the small crowd. He watched as the new Sheikha bowed her head in delicate thanks as men and women complimented her beauty and good fortune in a language she did not understand.

Sayyid appeared by his side, clapping one hand on his back in solidarity. 'You seem happy, my King.'

'Do I?' he murmured, keeping watch as Cressida bent to take the hands of a group of children gathered around her. Security was tight and the people of the camp were peaceful, but still he resisted the urge to drag her away to privacy.

'You have barely taken your eyes away from your new bride. Am I to assume your concern is that she does not run away?' Sayyid smiled good-naturedly.

Khal smiled at the joke, brushing it off. He watched her because she was in a new country, entering a new life. He wanted her to feel at ease. And if he seemed happy it was because everything was going to plan, the lightness in his chest was a result of sealing a deal months in the making and securing the political future of his kingdom. Nothing more. He ignored his Chief of Security's raised eyebrow and returned to his wife's side as they continued to the celebration.

She had been told that celebrations in the camp usually lasted well into the night but not long after they had finished dining Khal leaned into her ear. 'Now it is time for us to make our exit and move to the ceremonial wedding tent.'

Her eyes snapped up to meet his. 'Just the two of us?'

'Don't look so excited, my Queen.' He made a motion with his hands to his guards that they were leaving before extending his hand to her. 'We must at least appear to be newlyweds who cannot wait to tear each other's clothes off.'

Cressida cleared her throat, staring at his outstretched hand and willing herself to stop being such an absolute coward. 'Can the King not make an exception to tradition?'

'Tradition is important to me,' he said simply. 'And it is even more important to the people of this sacred tribe. My family's tribe.'

'Of course.' She nodded, looking around at the small gathering of men and women, seeing how they looked towards their Sheikh's every move. And hers too, she realised with a sudden jolt. She had not thought much of the responsibility that came with her marriage. She was the Queen now, Sheikha of the realm.

Gulping, she stood as gracefully as she could muster. Khal bowed his head to the crowd once and she copied the motion, trying not to jump as the men suddenly shouted their approval in guttural tones. Raucous applause and what she presumed to be words of encouragement followed them across the sand as she followed Khal, flanked by four silent guards. The jewels on her veil tinkled gently as she moved forward, her skirts gathering around her legs with the effort of trying to keep up with the pace of the men and their much longer legs. Thank goodness she had not been forced to wear heels as well as the intricate dress.

From the outside, the tent had seemed just like the one she had stayed in the previous night. But as they stepped through the entryway Cressida went completely still.

If she had ever been the kind of person to hold romantic notions about her wedding night, this would probably be a fairy tale come to life. Swathes of jewel-toned fabrics cascaded from the intricately patterned roof, softly lit by traditional lamps and coloured lanterns. More lanterns provided a glow at strategic points around the space. Warm, luxurious Persian-style rugs carpeted the entire floor and the sensual scent of incense wafted through the air. But what drew her eye most was the enormous canopied bed of luxurious shimmering golden cushions that dominated the room. Filled with satin tasselled throw pillows and covered in bright red rose petals, it was as though it were created simply for the act of deflowering one's new bride. The thought made her gulp audibly.

'Leave us,' Khal commanded after two of his men performed a sweep of the tent's surprisingly large quarters. Once again, she felt slight unease at the level of security that preceded every move they made. She wondered at the reason for it; Zayyar had been at peace for almost a quarter of a century. But, before she could think too much of it, two things suddenly stopped her in her tracks. One, they were completely alone in the most romantic place in the entire world. And two, her new husband had removed his headdress and was shrugging out of his robe with surprising speed.

CHAPTER FOUR

NAKED FROM THE waist up, the man was like one of the statues she would stare at in the palace gardens when she lived in Monteverre. He had the body of a warrior, not a pampered king. He wore his hair long and unruly under the traditional head covering. Cressida whirled to put a few more feet of space between them, pretending to be suddenly interested in the array of fresh drinks and fruit laid out in the small dining area.

When she looked up once more, he had changed into a simple robe and loose drawstring pants, leaving only part of his chest bare. She gulped, looking away from the smooth mahogany skin and wondering when on earth she would regain control of her mind again.

'A robe has been laid out for you as well, and a private area for you to change.' He remained facing away from her, of which she was thankful. She moved quickly behind the screen, immensely grateful that her Zayyari bridal gown was nothing like the Western million-buttons-down-the-back variety. One simple zip ran down the side seam and she was free, stepping out of the pool of fabric and hanging it carefully.

It was a beautiful gown, so simple and elegant that she had almost felt beautiful for the first time in her life.

She had spent a lifetime being the ugly duckling, always comparing herself to her more attractive sisters. Eleanor and Olivia had vibrant red hair like their famous grandmother, the late Queen Miranda, who had once been named the most beautiful woman in the world. Cressida hadn't even inherited her mother's pale blonde locks, instead ending up with an in-between shade of ash-blonde that was entirely forgettable. But the shade of her wedding gown and the sparkling amber jewels that adorned it had made her glow from head to foot.

A standing mirror faced the screen; she angled her body sideways, hardly believing that the woman in the glass was her own reflection. Her lingerie was the same dusky golden shade as her dress but stitched with shimmering embroidery that drew the eye to the illusion of her much fuller breasts. Closing her eyes firmly at the thought, she pulled the buttery soft silk robe over her shoulders, crossing it at the waist and noting that it was significantly shorter than the male version. No drawstring trousers were provided for the bride, it seemed, leaving her legs completely bare from mid-thigh downwards.

Perhaps it was the sensually charged décor of the tent or simply the overwhelming romance of the day in general, but suddenly she felt flushed and hyper-aware of the silk material as it moved against her skin. She felt a strange tightening in her solar plexus at the thought of stepping beyond the screen and revealing her ensemble to the man who was now her husband. She wanted him to see her, she realised with sudden heat in her cheeks.

She wanted him to look at her like he had in London and she wanted to find out just what it felt like to have his hands on her again. But it was unlikely that whatever madness had existed in the dark in London would be present now. He had made it clear that they would not have a true marriage, had he not? With a shake of her head she pulled the robe as tight as it would go, successfully covering most of her cleavage but still leaving much of her legs on show. Opting to leave her hair down, she took a deep breath and stepped back into the open space of the tent, only to find Khal standing opposite her, the ridiculously sensual bed spread out between them like a battlefield.

If only she could have simply turned tail and ducked back behind the screen, just to avoid the treacherous pang of heat that ran down her spine. His eyes raked over her, moving slowly to take in her hair, her breasts, then finally resting upon her bare legs.

Unable to stand still under his scrutiny, Cressida willed herself to move past the bed, turning her back on him on the pretext of pouring herself a glass of water.

'If you plan to continue skittering around me it is going to be a long night.' He sat down and sprawled back on the bed, hands interlocked behind his head as he surveyed her.

She moved forward, stumbling over her words as she nervously twisted the tie of her robe between her fingers. 'I can sleep on the futon if you'd like to take the bed.'

'And have all of the servants know we spent our wedding night apart?' He sat up, both hands braced on his knees. 'We will share a bed for tonight.'

Cressida nodded once. 'Of course. I didn't think…'

'Am I so frightening?' He watched her, waiting.

She placed her glass of water on the table, still twisting one ribbon of her robe around her finger. 'I am not afraid of you. I suppose I'm a little overwhelmed by all of this.'

His brow furrowed. Without warning, he stood and walked to a low table in the middle of the tent where an elaborate tea service had been laid out. He poured the steaming dark liquid into traditional cups and handed her one. 'You seemed to enjoy the festivities this evening. I had worried the Old Zayyari style might be a little far from what you are used to.'

Cressida smiled. 'I adored every moment. I have not travelled much before so this is all so new, but in a good way.' She took a sip of the strong brew, feeling it warm her through. 'I'm impressed at how quickly your team arranged everything.'

'The clandestine photographs will probably be making their way into the wrong hands as we speak,' he mused, one corner of his mouth lifting.

Cressida noticed a tiny dimple appear in his cheek, but it was gone almost before it appeared. He never smiled fully, she realised. It was as though he did not allow himself to. She pushed the thought away, realising that he was still speaking of the ceremony, oblivious to how her thoughts had wandered.

'They simply made some modifications where needed. This tent in particular was redesigned to be larger but the sanctity still lies in the markings on the cloth itself.' He pointed upwards to the domed roof.

She looked up, squinting at a jumble of blurry shapes on the cloth. She could not make out a single thing at a distance without her glasses.

'Looking for these?' He extended the blurry outline of her glasses towards her. She took them quickly as though any prolonged contact might ignite the spark that she was quite happy to ignore.

Cressida adjusted the frames on her nose, craning her neck upwards. Sure enough, the pattern was made up of more than just an arbitrary design. Spread out above them were thousands of intricate symbols and markings painted in burgundy-coloured ink on the raw canvas material. An ancient language. Her mind soared to life, all other thoughts abandoned as she kneeled on the edge of the bed to get a closer look. 'Fascinating...' she breathed. 'What do they all mean, I wonder.'

'I have absolutely no idea,' he said, shrugging. 'The markings are very old; they can be traced back to the first Zayyari tribe that made their settlement in this exact spot. Spending the wedding night here is an ancient custom that goes back to the very dawn of my people.'

'Absolutely fascinating,' she said, mostly to herself.

'Yes, you've said that already.'

She brought her gaze back to him. 'I'm sorry but this kind of stuff is exciting for me. I'm trying my best not to get out my phone to research ancient symbols on the university library database.' She paused, realising with a pang of sadness that she no longer had access to the database as she was no longer a student. Still, she forced a smile. 'Don't worry, I won't.'

'I'm thankful. What would my guards think of me if they walked in here and you were on your phone on our wedding night?'

'Oh, I doubt the signal is strong enough in the middle of the desert, anyway.' She smiled, hardly believing that they were having light conversation after the hyper intensity of the past two days. He still did not smile but his eyes seemed warmer at least, more inviting, like they had at the bar the first time they'd spoken. It seemed like another life, rather than mere days ago.

'I can assure you the signal would be perfect,' he said, offhand. 'Zayyar trades in technology; it is the lifeblood of our economy right now.'

'I read an article that called you an economic genius.'

'The success of this kingdom is a result of the strength and knowledge of the members of government, the money that is put into educating our people and ensuring their quality of life. I believe that when you spend time on nourishing the foundations, growth is inevitable.'

'My father seems to have a very different idea on the measure of economic success,' Cressida said, tracing a circle on the embroidered bedspread. 'When his advisors warned him that economic crisis was forecast, his answer was to buy a new fleet of tanks for the military. A show of wealth, he called it. As though pretending debt was not a problem would simply make it true.'

'There are many leaders who think this way. My great-grandfather was one of them.'

She knew a brief history of the kingdom and the wars that had been waged two generations before. She could see it on his face, the tightness that settled around his eyes at the mention of his ancestor. 'It must be hard, having that history to work against.'

'Not as hard as it must have been for those who lived through it.' He became quiet then, his features turning hard.

'You care a lot about your kingdom,' she said simply.

'The same must be said of you, to have agreed to a marriage in order to save it.'

Cressida shrugged, studying the markings on the ceiling to avoid his knowing gaze. 'There are not many things that third in line to the throne is expected to do, except remain free of scandal and marry according to the King's wishes.'

'And now King Fabian finds himself with only one direct heir...' Khal mused.

Cressida looked up, surprised that she had not thought of that fact. Now that Olivia had given up her place in line to the throne the duty fell entirely upon Eleanor to ensure there was a new generation of Sandovals to carry on the name. And the throne. 'My father is not known for his excellent decision-making skills.'

'Your sister will make an excellent queen,' Khal said earnestly. 'I do not doubt that the future of Monteverre is in competent hands.'

'They just need to survive the remainder of my father's rule.' Cressida smiled ruefully, worrying at her bottom lip. 'But thank you.'

She felt something bloom in her chest at his kind words. She had always looked up to her oldest sister for guidance as a child but she had never envied her position one bit. She had never harboured a desire to become Queen, knowing her strengths lay happily in academic work and keeping a low profile. Just look where that had got her.

'I must point out that you said that it was your duty to remain free of scandal, and yet in London...'

'I was not seeking scandal,' she said, her shoulders straightening. 'I just acted on impulse for the first time in my adult life. It made sense at the time.'

'And now?'

She felt it humming between them again, that sizzle

of awareness that she wished she could ignore. But the events in London had made that entirely impossible. She could not tell herself that the attraction was one-sided any more than she could tell herself that the earth was square. It was simply a fact, heavy in the air between them. Ever present in the tension that seemed to coil tight in her abdomen whenever she was in his presence.

'Now it is irrelevant.' She shrugged. 'I am...your wife.'

Something darkened in his eyes at her words. 'Indeed.'

The large bed suddenly felt too small, her body restless under his heated gaze. She turned her head away, murmuring a hasty goodnight as she tried to relax into the pillows. She was vaguely aware of him moving to extinguish some of the lamps in the tent before returning to the bed but she didn't dare open her eyes. Feigning sleep soon became effortless as the activities of the day caught up with her and sleep claimed her.

It was too hot, Cressida mused, turning over onto her stomach and feeling a sheen of sweat on her skin. The air in her nostrils was white-hot and strangely heavy in her lungs, almost painful. Her eyes snapped open, seeing a strange glow illuminating the room like dancing lights through a fog. Not fog, she corrected herself, smoke.

She felt drunk, consciousness sliding away from her like desert sand through her fingers. Sleep pulled her back, the strange dream melting away.

A man's voice shouted nearby in a language she could not understand, jolting her once more. Then she was being lifted from the bed into strong arms and carried at frantic speed. The strange fog suddenly became recognisable smoke in her lungs, the dancing lights the visible flames of a red-hot fire that was burning up one entire side of the tent. Suddenly the stars were above them and fresh oxygen filled her lungs, making her eyes water. She looked up and found herself eye level with Khal's strong jaw, his powerful body carrying her in a zigzag path through the encampment to where a trio of black dune buggies lay in wait. He deposited her onto the back seat, taking her face in his hands.

'Are you okay?' he breathed, his voice hoarse from smoke and exertion. 'Speak to me.'

'I'm… I'm fine, I think.' She coughed, shivering as realisation of what had just happened began to seep into her consciousness. The look on his face said it all—this was no accident. 'Are we in danger?'

He did not answer her question. 'We will be travelling under darkness but I will protect you. You will not step from my side until we reach the palace, understood?' He turned but did not remove his hand from where it lay on her forearm, waiting for the guards to catch up before he began issuing quiet orders. The men simply nodded, obeying their leader and preparing to depart. Khal slid into the seat beside her, draping one arm over her as they set off, a guard at the wheel. His face was only visible for a few moments before the complete darkness of the desert engulfed them and she couldn't help but grip him tighter. *'I will protect you,'* he had said. And she believed him.

He stayed by her side as they moved from buggy to helicopter, holding the woollen blanket around her the entire time. Preserving her modesty. She tried a few more times to ask what had caused the fire and was met with stony silence from both Khal and his guards. She was not to worry about that, they said. The lack of information only served to heighten her unease. The people of the tribe were peaceful; surely the fire had been accidental? And yet the look she had seen in Khal's eyes as they moved away from the desert was not one of annoyance at someone's foolish mistake. It was a look of absolute rage.

Soon the inky blackness of the desert below gave way to a sea of lights, main roads winding towards a large city. Once they had touched down within the old palace walls she felt Khal visibly relax beside her. Knowing that he had been worried the entire time gave her a sharp pang of anxiety.

An elderly servant appeared and offered, in perfect English, to settle Her Highness in the Sheikha's apartments. The sudden noise that came from Khal's mouth startled her. He gave a few commands in his native tongue and the servant nodded once and disappeared with quiet efficiency.

'Where will I be staying?' Cressida asked, surprised that her voice did not shake after the panic of their ordeal.

'With me. Where you will be safe,' he said simply. His hand was gentle but firm as he gripped her elbow, motioning for her to walk. The first pink fingers of dawn were beginning to snake across the darkness above them. She had barely got a glimpse of the courtyard of her new home before she was being led at speed along winding anonymous stone passageways, deeper into the heart of the palace.

Khal never let go of her arm. She was immediately aware when they entered a more modern wing, more refined and luxurious in its décor. The guards performed a quick sweep of the rooms around them before Khal motioned to dismiss them. He spoke one phrase to his own personal bodyguard; the large man nodded once and closed the door behind him with a soft thud.

'They need to clear the rest of the wing,' he said wearily, running a hand along the stubble on his jaw. 'I would like the doctor to see you before you rest.'

'I'm fine, Khal, honestly.' She shook her head. 'All I need is to sleep.'

'You called me Khal,' he said with surprise.

'I suppose *Your Highness* just seems a little too formal now that we're married. And you did just carry me out of a burning tent.' She felt laughter bubble in her throat, along with the irrational urge to burst into tears at the realisation that this man had probably saved her life tonight.

'You need to be seen by a doctor,' he repeated. 'There was a lot of smoke.'

Cressida nodded, remembering the thickness of the smoke filling her lungs, the burning heat prickling at her skin. Then she remembered how quickly she'd felt safe once she was in his arms, enveloped in his strength. Tears filled her eyes and fell down her cheeks before she even realised what was happening. She turned her face away quickly, not wanting him to see her weakness. But hiding was useless; he was by her side almost before the first tear fell, gathering her in his arms and holding her tight. A few choked sobs escaped her throat; she stifled them with her hand, embarrassed at her complete loss of control. 'I never cry,' she half sobbed, half laughed at herself.

'It's the shock,' he murmured. 'Just breathe.'

She obeyed his command, focusing on the warmth of his arms and the steady beat of his heart somewhere near her ear as she inhaled and exhaled. When she finally felt strong enough to step away, he surprised her by holding her still.

Cressida's stomach flipped at the look in his eyes as strong muscular fingers cupped her jaw. He considered her eyes with such fierce intensity that for one crazy breathless moment she wondered if he might kiss her. No sooner had the thought crossed her mind than his lips were on hers, hot and demanding. His hand fisted in her hair as he angled her to deepen the kiss while the other snaked around her waist to gather her against him.

Perhaps it was the adrenaline still coursing through her veins, or the reminder of her own mortality, but his touch was like kindling to a fire. She wanted to fall into the oblivion of desire and forget all the reasons why it was a bad idea. All she cared about was that there should be less robe between them and more touching. Much more touching. He pressed his thigh between her legs, pinning her to the wall as he kissed her so hard she was light-headed. But no sooner had she begun to sink into him than he was gone. He took two steps away, bracing one hand against the door as he got his breathing under control.

'We have both been through a lot tonight,' he said quietly, not meeting her eyes. 'You should go and get some rest. There are three guest rooms to choose from in my wing; choose whichever you wish.'

Cressida did not trust herself to speak, nodding once as she readjusted the front of her robe to cover herself. Clearly that kiss had just been the result of shock; she knew not to read too much into it. He had been more than clear that they would not behave as man and wife. But it seemed that her body had not received that message. She raised a hand to her face, feeling the blush creep as far as her forehead. The enthusiasm with which she'd kissed him made her blush deepen even further.

Her heart pounded furiously, the remnants of such a sudden flare of passion ebbing slowly away. He, on the other hand, seemed to have regained his composure with complete ease. Anger crept into the corner of her vision. How dare he be so cool and collected while she felt completely turned inside out? It wasn't fair.

A firm knock on the door dissipated what was left of the intimate moment and Cressida spun on her heel to pull her robe tighter around her. She didn't dare to look to see if Khal showed any physical signs of unfulfilled lust, focusing her gaze downwards to take in the patterns on the tiles under her bare feet.

'The adjoining rooms have been cleared.' Sayyid's voice came from behind her, in English for her benefit. 'Come with me, Your Highness.'

Khal made no move to speak or meet her gaze as she passed him; she tried not to feel hurt or rejected at his distance. He probably had many things to attend to other than escorting his new bride to her room. He was King, after all.

Steeling herself, she followed Sayyid to her bedroom and tried to ignore the sense of loneliness that rose in her with each step.

CHAPTER FIVE

'WHAT ON EARTH was His Highness doing sleeping in a tent in the first place? It's utterly ludicrous!' exclaimed the Minister of Defence. 'That encampment was likely filled with thugs and ruffians.'

'It is tradition. Part of the family legacy,' someone at the back of the room added.

Khal made his arrival known by clearing his throat, the sound seeming to cut through the unusual din in his official chambers. The emergency dawn meeting had been assembled by Sayyid, his Chief of Security, who currently looked as though he might like to tear a chunk out of the rather elderly Defence Minister.

'Gentlemen, take your seats,' he commanded, in no mood to deal with the squabbling that ensued with this many egos in one room. He hadn't slept since the encampment; the stench of smoke still clung to his skin, even after showering.

'Your Highness, we are deeply troubled to hear of this unfortunate incident,' the Chief of Police offered respectfully. 'I have assembled a team to investigate the site; they are en route as we speak.'

'Do we really need the police involved?' the minister intervened. 'I mean, we aren't sure of the origin of

the fire. For all we know, it could have been a tribes-
man tripping over a lamp.'

'The King has expressed his wish for a thorough investigation,' Sayyid said loudly.

All eyes moved to him. Khal nodded once to confirm
and watched as the men's attitudes changed instantly to
rapt attention, some even taking notes as Sayyid outlined the security measures taken and the times of guard
check-ins throughout the night.

'Your Highness, are you worried that there is unrest
amongst the old orders?' An elderly man, one of his father's long-time advisors stepped forward. 'You once
expressed the belief that they were behind the death of
the late Sheikha Priya.'

'His Highness made those statements while experi-
encing enormous grief,' another advisor said pointedly.
'The Sheikha's death was deemed accidental.'

Khal felt the casual mention of his wife's death like
a punch to his gut. He stood before he had the sense
to rein in his anger. 'The investigation into my wife's
death is still ongoing,' he hissed.

The elderly man shrank back visibly, realising he
had overstepped the mark.

The Minister for Foreign Affairs spoke softly, ad-
dressing each of the men around the oval table in an effort to calm matters. 'Have a care for the language used
in this chamber, gentlemen. All it takes is one whiff of
scandal to cause an international spectacle.'

Khal turned from the table, unable to stand one more
minute of their so-called politics. 'This meeting is over.
Any questions about the incident will be addressed to
my personal security team.'

He didn't know where he was going, anger powering

him along the ancient passageways until he finally felt the sun on his face. Tension filled his veins, the effort of holding back memories threatening to undo him. He changed direction, moving towards the stables with sudden intent. He demanded his prize stallion to be readied and wasted no time in switching his traditional robes for tight-fitting jodhpurs and well-worn boots. He did not speak to the boy who handed him the reins, impatiently launching himself up into the saddle and taking off in the direction of the sand.

With the wind on his face and the pounding of hooves under him, he finally allowed his spine to relax as he moved with his horse, their bodies in tune as he pushed the great beast to the limit. Takaa was a demon, the fastest horse he had ever owned, and right now he had never been so tempted to test his limits. Knowledge made him slow down as he got close to the boundaries of the old palace lands, veering off down the hill to where an almost dried up ravine formed a small oasis of sorts.

Takaa drank deeply and Khal splashed water onto his sun-warmed face, feeling the midday heat begin to claw at him through his thin shirt. His fists were almost white with the effort of suppressing the rage that had begun to unravel inside him in the chambers. They spoke her name as though it were a trivia, not a bomb that had the ability to tighten his gut with emotion. Grief was an obvious one; he most definitely had allowed grief to sink its mighty claws into him more than once in those first months following Priya's sudden death. She had been his wife for five years, his rock during his father's death and his ascent to becoming the leader he was today.

Everyone had offered him condolences and comfort and in time he had moved past it to the point where he could return to normal life. But the anger was another issue entirely. How did one resolve anger that was soul-deep when the woman who'd caused it was being lamented by their people so much they built shrines to her in the streets? Poetry was written about her beauty, her grace.

He had been left virtually alone with the knowledge of who his wife truly was. How she had betrayed him and everything their marriage stood for. How he had driven her to that betrayal with his own over-controlling measures. How did he resolve the guilt and the regret that ate away at his very soul—that things had not been different?

He growled, throwing the nearest rock at the water so hard that Takaa startled and began to pull back at the reins. He placed his palm flat on the horse's neck, crooning low in his throat until the animal stopped resisting and leaned down to drink once more.

The memory of seeing the smoke last night, of rushing to get Cressida to safety while he was sure his heart would burst through his chest. It had brought him right back to the moment he had been told of the accident. It was as though, for a few moments of madness, both incidents had been one and the same and he was trapped in a nightmare of sorts. And then, when the danger had passed and he was sure she was safe and alive, holding Cressida in his arms while she fell apart had been almost more than he could bear. She was not a woman who lost control of herself easily; that much was painfully evident. And yet she had shown him her weakness. And how had he responded? By ravishing her at the first opportunity, beast that he was.

He had never felt such a challenge to his self-control

than when he was around her. With each encounter, it felt as though he were losing his grip on a cliff face one finger at a time. She was getting under his skin and it simply could not continue. The physical attraction between them was more than inconvenient. It was a risk to the business arrangement of their marriage. They needed to keep their roles clear so that the next five years passed without incident. She would be the perfect Queen as he required her to be and he would break down the various political walls that stood in the way of his development plans with ease. Then, once their time was up, they would part without difficulty or complication.

He mounted Takaa swiftly and kicked off back to the palace, a plan in place. He would resolve this situation just as he did every other area of his life, with careful management and the complete absence of emotion.

While the dramatic details of the reasons behind their late-night arrival were kept carefully under wraps, news of the new Sheikha spread through the palace quickly. Cressida was awoken at dawn by a handful of servants and a young dress maid, who set about draping her in traditional silks and jewels. Zayyari was not one of the languages taught in her university and she found it incredibly frustrating not being able to make out a single word of what the women said as they spoke to one another in low tones, avoiding her gaze. She had the strange feeling of being a new statue on display at a museum.

She made a mental note to begin studying as soon as possible. The thought of having something even remotely connected to her previous academic accomplishments made her feel slightly less at sea in her new life. She had always felt most comfortable when she planned her goals for each term and ticked items off one by one. As she was dressed and styled with hair and make-up, she mentally listed out the materials she would need to get started.

Just as she had begun on the prospect of brand-new stationery, an older woman entered and announced herself in English as her new assistant.

'You are expected to breakfast with the esteemed Sheikha Amala and Princess Nia this morning,' the older woman said, scrolling down the screen of a sleek tablet as she spoke. 'Your new mother and sister-in-law, as they are called in the West.'

'Where will that be?' Cressida asked, trying to conceal the sudden rumble of her stomach along with the fact that she had no knowledge of anyone in her husband's family.

'They live in the palace grounds,' Rana said simply. 'Then this afternoon we will commence your etiquette lessons, followed by cultural and language tuition.'

'Etiquette lessons?' Cressida repeated, her mind stumbling over the sudden weight of having an itinerary handed to her.

'His Highness has arranged for an intensive month of tuition to make you more comfortable in the run-up to your celebration ball.'

She was to be given a ball? As in, an entire event to celebrate her? She fought the urge to flap her arms at the woman currently applying make-up to her eyelids. This was too much to absorb while sitting completely still. Taking one deep breath, followed by another, she waited for the make-up artist to move away for a moment before narrowing her gaze on her new assistant. 'You said the Sheikh has arranged all of this?'

'Along with his team, of course. The priority right now is for you to feel as prepared as possible in your role as Queen.'

Or did the Sheikh himself simply wish for her to be kept as busy and out of sight as possible? Cressida wondered. She didn't know why she felt a sense of rejection that he had not chosen to at least eat breakfast with her in order to inform her of his plans. They had not spoken at all of what the day-to-day workings of their arrangement would be. He was not breaking any promises.

So why did she feel so utterly alone of a sudden?

She simply wished to ask for further news on the fire at the encampment, she told herself. She did not like being left in the dark on the matter. She would seek him out, perhaps. She would ask him for an update and perhaps clarify what was to be expected of her from this point, other than the ridiculous ball and the lessons he and a team of servants and tutors had apparently deemed necessary.

Finally, the make-up artist finished her work and stepped away. Cressida barely even glanced at her own reflection; she needed to stand and move and have a few feet of space to herself for the first time in two hours. The fact that it had taken two hours to get dressed was utterly ridiculous; she had always just put on an outfit, brushed her hair and gone about her day with minimal fuss.

'Is everything okay, Your Highness?'

Cressida looked up from the stifling weight of her thoughts to find all three women looking at her worriedly. She straightened, remembering herself, and plastered on the most serene royal smile she could muster in the face of her inner turmoil. 'I'm fine. Let's get started on the day, shall we?'

* * *

Khal's mother and sister turned out to be surprisingly warm and inviting. Their family apartments were smaller and slightly less formal than the Sheikh's wing. They made their introductions and she was hugged warmly by her new mother-in-law before they sat together to enjoy a warm breakfast of spiced breads, fresh fruit and hot Zayyari tea.

The Sheikha Amala was younger than Cressida had expected, a beautiful woman with perfectly applied make-up and eyes that shimmered with kindness. Princess Nia was only slightly older than Khal, with a family of her own. She spoke fondly of her two young sons, who attended an elite boarding school in Scotland for much of the year but returned to the palace for holidays. Khal's mother did not speak any language other than her own but the Princess conversed easily in both French and English and talked wistfully of her time abroad in Paris when she was younger.

After a time, the Sheikha's mood seemed to change as she began to speak with her daughter as translator, asking for details of the secret wedding ceremony. Cressida described the welcoming environment of the encampment, leaving out the details of the heavy security presence and the fire that brought the night to an abrupt close. No sooner had Cressida begun to describe her fascination with the symbolism on the wedding tent than the older woman stood with a loud sniff and excused herself from the room.

'Did I say something wrong?' Cressida asked the Princess, her worried gaze following her as the door snapped shut, leaving just the two of them.

'My mother is deeply unhappy that Khal did not

allow us to attend the wedding,' Nia said, taking a sip of her tea. 'He explained that it was necessary—it was to be an elopement, and none of the royal family would be present.'

'I am sorry.' Cressida bowed her head. 'It all happened very fast. I'm sure he would have preferred to have you there.'

Nia smiled sadly. 'I think she is upset because she knows that is not the case.' She pursed her lips. 'I have two sons. I know my heart would break to find one of them had shut himself off from me. My brother has been like a stranger to us these past few years. He grieved for a long time. I know it well, such grief. I lost my own husband after only three years of marriage. A loss like that leaves a hole in your soul.' Nia sighed. 'Grief can be so destructive…it takes a part of you with the one you lost.'

The young woman's eyes filled with tears and Cressida felt the urge to reach out and embrace her. Thinking that might be a tad too familiar for a first meeting, she settled for a single solemn pat on her hand. Nia smiled, wiping away the single tear that had escaped her heavily made-up eyes.

'I imagine it is not enjoyable to think of your husband when he was so entwined with another.' She winced. 'I did not think before I spoke.'

'Love is not a fundamental part of this particular marriage,' Cressida said carelessly, regretting the words as soon as they escaped her mouth. 'What I mean is…'

'It has not been disclosed by my brother, but I had a feeling that this had something to do with politics.' The Princess smiled. 'Don't worry; your secret is safe with me.'

'Thank you. And I'm sorry for your loss.'

The older woman shook her head gently. 'I am grateful for my position. I have my brother to watch over my sons as they grow into young men. I have time to spend with my mother, though she can be a little dramatic.' She laughed good-naturedly.

Cressida found herself smiling, a real smile. She liked Khal's sister very much and it was nice to know there was someone here to talk to who was not employed by Khal to watch over her or transform her into the perfect Queen. All too soon, their time was up and Nia rushed off to attend to her mother.

Cressida left the family apartments and trailed behind her assistant for an extensive tour of the palace grounds. The historical Grand Palace compound was almost three hundred years old but showed clear signs of renovation in certain places. Her assistant pointed out the renovations as scars of the wartimes when the palace had been damaged by rebels. Cressida thought of Khal and his determination to have his kingdom accepted by the world despite the violence in Zayyar's past. How many other areas of this beautiful kingdom had been destroyed and rebuilt?

In the cavernous portrait gallery, she was shown depictions of Zayyar's past rulers. Fierce-looking men with long beards and swords sheathed by their sides. As the paintings became more modern, she instantly recognised the face of Khal's mother, by the side of an older man. The old Sheikh had kind eyes, not too different from those of his son. The family resemblance was quite strong.

The next picture portrayed a young Khal alongside a beautiful raven-haired woman. Cressida paused, looking up at the picture of her husband and his original

Queen. She was a stunning beauty, all dark features and effortless grace. He was entitled to still be in love with his dead wife, she reminded herself. Theirs was not a marriage built on the pretence of love or even affection. If anything, it should make things easier knowing that he was emotionally unavailable.

She forced herself to move away from the shadow of the woman who had captured her husband's heart, knowing that such a matter should not concern her. She was an instrument of political influence, not a true wife, and she would be a lot happier if she kept that thought front and foremost in her head.

Learning a new language was her favourite pastime in the whole world, so when she sat down to her first Zayyari lesson with her personal tutor, naturally she expected to feel the same passion and excitement that always came over her with a new academic challenge. But after half an hour she still could not pull her thoughts away from her talk with Nia and the mysterious scandal of the late Sheikha's death. Seeing the picture of Khal with Priya had got under her skin. Why did she feel the urge to compare herself to the dark-eyed beauty? To wonder if Khal compared her too. She had already known that she was second choice to her sister Olivia to be his bride. She had been able to rationalise that as Olivia was older and more famous than she was.

But she could not rationalise how she felt in this moment. A sensation prickled in her chest, peculiarly like jealousy, and she pushed it away, throwing herself into her lessons for the day and determined not to think of the Sheikh at all.

Or his beautiful lost love.

CHAPTER SIX

THE NEXT DAY, once again, the Sheikh was nowhere to be found. Still, he made his presence known by ensuring she had meetings with various advisors whose sole purpose was to groom her to become his perfect Sheikha. She took another more detailed tour of the palace and grounds, accompanied by guards, of course, and tried not to be completely overwhelmed at the prospect of memorising the various winding mile-long corridors.

The royal compound had to be at least twice the size of the palace in Monteverre and it was filled with a history that fascinated her. To her delight, her request for a few books on the history of Zayyar led to her being introduced to an entire wing of the palace filled with the royal collections of art, sculptures and, best of all, books. Thousands and thousands of books.

Still, she spent the afternoon looking over her shoulder, expecting to find him standing in a doorway or walking towards her with that dark unreadable gaze. Not that she was waiting for him, she told herself. Really, she was quite glad to have the time to adjust to her new surroundings without feeling as if he was scrutinising her every move. She dined alone in her suite, a simple meal of traditional slow-cooked meats and fragrant rice. Afterwards she took an idle stroll down the corridor towards the Sheikh's wing, casually slowing as she passed the large gilded double doors.

'His Highness has gone to Valar for meetings,' her bodyguard said quietly.

'Of course.' She nodded, as though she knew exactly where her husband was and what he was doing. 'I thought this was the way to the garden terrace.' When she was kindly redirected to her destination she spent barely a moment looking around the exotic plants before returning to her room, feeling utterly foolish for leaving in the first place.

Valar was the new city on the coast; she had read about it in her studies. It was where her ball was to be held at the beginning of next month. She felt her mild irritation grow into a more solid simmering displeasure at her new husband's disappearing act. Was it so unrealistic to expect a single conversation with one's husband? She set to practising in her mind what she would say when she eventually saw him.

The next day passed in exactly the same fashion; meals were taken alone in her suite, except for a pleasant mid-morning tea with Nia. Aside from that, the only company she had were the various people in the Sheikh's employ, all of whom called her 'Your Highness' and did not make eye contact. Still, she took it in her stride, taking advantage of the pool of knowledge at her fingertips in the library and enjoying the heat of the sun on her face on a leisurely walk in the gardens.

After only two full days at the palace, she found herself longing for the calm of the evening when she could close the door of her private apartment and be completely alone. There were guards outside and a maid came to check in occasionally but, for the most part, she was left to her own devices. So far, that meant immediately changing into her pyjamas and camping out by the open balcony doors to read the books she had found on Zayyar's fascinating history and traditions. Occasionally she would look up and catch sight of the sprawling desert laid out beyond the palace walls, further than the eye could see. It took her breath away every time, the raw beauty of this place and how completely untouched it was. She had not expected to feel so calmed by the desert, or so drawn to it.

Her current reading material consisted mainly of books on the history of Zayyar and its customs but she had also taken time to learn the language of her new home outside the formal tutor-led lessons. She had always enjoyed exploring a new language on her own terms, finding the true rhythm of it by herself. As Sheikha, she would be expected to be knowledgeable and respectful of her nation's traditions but she did not necessarily have to become fluent in their language. She simply could not resist the idea of an entirely new tongue to perfect and actually have the chance to use it on a daily basis. It was something to keep her mind busy, she told herself, as her husband seemed to have zero interest in her company.

Despite her best attempts to fill her time, she felt loneliness begin to set in. She had always been comfortable with her own company, but suddenly being alone with her books didn't feel the same. Perhaps it was the fact that she was in a new country, in a new routine and surrounded by people who barely spoke to her. It was as though she had stepped into a glass cage surrounded by people. She was alone.

Her mobile phone seemed strangely unable to pick up a signal since they had touched down in Zayyar. It felt like a lifetime ago since she had stepped off the jet in the heart of the desert, but in reality it had only been three days. She was by no means a techno junkie but still, it was very isolating not being able to just pick up her phone and send an email or call one of her sisters on the odd occasion. After a few minutes investigating, she discovered it was most likely that the number was no longer in service. Probably, her father had cancelled it, a passive aggressive punishment for disobeying his orders to return to Monteverre for the engagement announcement. She presumed he knew by now that she had eloped with the Sheikh, rather than follow his plan for a grand wedding. That would have been a sight to behold.

It was no big deal; surely she could simply ask Khal's team what the protocol was for obtaining a new phone? A small laugh escaped her throat at the realisation that she was the Queen of an entire kingdom and she couldn't even obtain her own phone without permission. The restlessness that had plagued her all day intensified and she stood, stretching the muscles in her back and looking towards the clock on her bedside table to check the time. It was almost midnight, local time.

She calculated the time zones for a moment. Last she had heard, her sister Olivia was in New York. It was still a semi-reasonable hour there… She hadn't spoken to Olivia at all since recent events had begun to transpire. There simply hadn't been an opportunity. Unable to resist, she took a quick peek into the corridor outside her apartments and bit her lip as she found it deserted. Perhaps the guards switched shifts at midnight. She knew there was a phone in the small office beside the library. She could wait for permission…or she could just go. She was an adult, after all.

Not able to shake the sensation that she was a naughty teenager breaking the rules, she set off quickly for fear she might change her mind. Heart beating fast, she moved soundlessly in her bare feet, so eager she made a few wrong turns and wound up hopelessly lost. She cursed her own sense of direction, wishing she had paid more attention to the corridors in daylight. Still, it was a rather nice change from the monotony of the past few days. She actually felt a little bit free, wandering unchaperoned in the semi-darkness.

By the time she found her way back to the library, she had a little bounce in her step. She had forgotten what it felt like to walk around without guards following her every move like shadows. Even in university, she had been free to move about the campus by herself for most of the time.

Disappointment coursed through her when Olivia's phone number also turned out to be cancelled. Not wanting to waste her time alone, she turned on the computer on the desk. It had always been occupied by a guard on her previous visits to the library. Miraculously, she found the option for guest mode with a decent Internet connection and hurriedly set about signing into her email server. To her surprise, her inbox was flooded with concern from some of the members of her research team at university. With horror, she realised she had never said goodbye before unenrolling from her courses.

She made quick work of finding the number of the head of her research team in London and breathed a sigh of relief when he answered on the first ring. He brushed off her hurried apology at the late hour and seemed genuinely relieved to hear that she was well. He told her of the rest of the team's efforts to get in contact with her; naturally, all of their enquiries to the palace in Monteverre had been met with silence.

After a few minutes she learned that the team was coping quite well in her absence; it seemed she wasn't quite as indispensable as she had believed. She ended the call with a fond farewell, promising to try to arrange a trip to London in the future, although deep down she knew that if she did return it would be so far in the future that they would probably have all moved on further in their careers and forgotten her completely.

She turned to exit the office, stopping with a squeak at a looming figure leaning against the doorway.

'Thought you were all alone?' Khal drawled.

She was just as beautiful in her pyjamas as she had been in her wedding dress. That was Khal's first thought upon finding Cressida sneaking gracefully through the library in semi-darkness. It had been late when he'd returned to the palace so he had opted to wait until morning to alert his new bride to his presence. He had been sitting in a corner alcove, taking in the mountains of books she had been studying, when she'd entered, oblivious to his presence. He'd had every intention of leaving to allow her to complete her phone call in private... Until he'd realised the person she was speaking to in such hushed tones was another man. He had found his fists clenched tight as he'd stalked soundlessly closer to the office doorway.

'You startled me,' she breathed. 'I didn't know you had returned.'

'Do you usually wait until the middle of the night to call your friends?' he asked calmly, ignoring the knot of tension in his abdomen.

Her eyes widened slightly at his tone. 'I never said goodbye to some friends in London. I was just checking in…with my research team.'

'You are the Sheikha of Zayyar.' His voice clipped each word out like a gunshot.

Cressida's eyes widened with surprise. 'I am quite aware of my own title by now, thank you,' she said tightly. 'You sound angry. Why do I feel like I'm being scolded when I have not done anything wrong?'

'Perhaps you mistake anger for simple confusion as to why I just walked in on my wife having a hushed midnight conversation with an unknown man.'

'I will not be told who I can or cannot speak to. Especially when I have been here for days without anyone to speak to at all.'

Khal was silent for a moment, his jaw tight. 'This man. He is a close friend?'

'I've known him a few years through my work at the university,' she said. 'But no. I don't have many friends.'

Silence fell between them and Khal saw a flash of sadness in her eyes before she quickly turned her face from him.

'If that's all you want to ask, I've got an early start in the morning.' She took a couple of steps towards the door.

Khal moved sideways to block her way. 'Being Sheikha is a full-time job, Cressida,' he said, noting the way she tilted her stubborn chin upwards in answer to his tone. 'I need to know that you are prepared for the responsibilities of this life.'

'I've been feeling a little isolated so I made a phone call. I suppose I did miss my old life for a moment.' She half laughed. 'I always felt such happiness in the corner of my small apartment, working at my computer or reading. It keeps my mind working. Makes me feel like I'm achieving something, maybe. But anyway, I needn't have bothered because it seems my departure has not left any lasting impression.'

A faraway look crossed her delicate features, the barest sheen of moisture seeming to brighten her eyes for a split second before she hastily blinked it away. She took a deep breath, pinning him with a brave smile. 'I'm hardly planning to give up and run away after one difficult week.'

He took a step towards her. 'I'm sorry that you felt isolated here. I did not mean to...'

'To leave me completely alone in a new country less than twelve hours after our wedding?' she finished helpfully.

Khal winced, knowing her words were entirely true. He had abandoned her to his staff, believing she would find comfort enough in a busy routine while he dealt with the aftermath of the investigations into the tent fire, among other things. Perhaps there was also a small part of him that wished to put some distance between them after the familiarity of their wedding night. She was his wife. It was only natural he would feel some level of protectiveness towards her. The memory of the kiss they had shared in his suite after the fire had plagued him, sending him to bed each night in a sweat, sleep the furthest thing from his mind.

Almost as though she heard his thoughts, her tongue darted out to moisten her lips, leaving a glistening sheen along the plump pink flesh. He felt his body react instantly, heat rushing downwards. Clenching his fist, he cleared his throat. 'I have not been very attentive so far, it seems.'

'No, you have not,' she agreed, moving past him in the doorway to walk into the library beyond. 'But I understand that you had sudden matters to address that could not be ignored. Have you any update on what caused the fire in the encampment?'

Khal pursed his lips, trying and failing not to notice the gentle sway of her hips in her loose-fitting pyjama bottoms. 'It has been deemed accidental. I was just informed this afternoon, in fact.' He watched as her face visibly relaxed; she had been worried about the fire then. Of course she had.

He wished that the news had given him the same relief. The fact that his security team and the police had no idea who had been behind it and had no leads was frustrating. But he could not think of it now, not when she so clearly needed reassuring.

'You enjoy reading books about Zayyar,' he said, changing the subject, gesturing to where he had found her little nook in the corner.

She smiled, walking over to straighten the small mountain of books with an almost lover-like caress. 'It's a beautiful kingdom.'

'You weren't lying when you said that you consider reading a sport. I'd bet you've made your way through a quarter of my collection already.'

She blushed, turning away as she flicked idly through a volume on Zayyari etiquette and traditions. 'I suppose I just like to feel prepared in a new situation. To arm myself with as much knowledge as possible when I'm feeling out of my depth.'

Of course she was feeling overwhelmed. He had rushed ahead with their wedding without a second thought, put her life at risk in the encampment and then abandoned her at the first opportunity. As far as husbands went, he was already a spectacular failure.

'That is to be expected. Not many people would be quite so composed in the face of such upheaval in their normal routine.' He met her eyes. 'You may brush off my compliment but know that I mean it earnestly. And I would like to make this transition as easy as possible for you as you find your feet here. Starting with your own personal phone line in your suite, perhaps?'

'Thank you. That's very kind.' She smiled. 'My father had my mobile phone account cancelled at some point since we eloped.'

'King Fabian is not known for making direct statements when he is displeased.' Khal spoke thoughtfully. 'I will also have a top-of-the-range device delivered to your suite tomorrow.'

'Really, a simple landline is fine,' she argued.

'You are the Sheikha of Zayyar now, Cressida. If you want something, anything at all, it will be obtained for you. You need only ask.'

For a moment, he thought she might argue. He watched the delicate play of emotions cross her features as she bent to retrieve a book from the pile at their feet. When she stood up straight again, her face was a polite mask of control. Something inside him briefly wondered what lay underneath that mask, what she was truly feeling about her situation, but he brushed away the sentimental thought.

He escorted her back to her suite, making idle conversation about the various parts of the palace she had seen in his absence. As he listened to her genuine appreciation of his ancestral home, he found himself inwardly making plans to show her the hidden gems that few knew about. To play tour guide in his own kingdom and show her the true Zayyar.

He simply wanted her to feel at home here, he told himself, but a strange sensation seemed to envelope him in her presence. The physical attraction was there, of course, but something else had joined it. He wanted her to feel at ease with him, he realised.

After he bade her goodnight at her door and returned to his own adjoining suite, he sat at his desk and idly shuffled through official papers. His mind was not with his work tonight, nor had it been for the entire day. He had been eager to return to the palace almost from the moment he had left it. The chemistry between himself and his new bride was an unwelcome complication and until now he had not known how to manage it, except to keep a distance between them. But perhaps all he needed was a simple redirection. It was not weak or emotional to wish for an accord with the woman who would stand by his side for the next five years. It was practical and far more realistic than his original plan.

Humming to himself, he made a neat, concise list of plans and felt the dark mood that had plagued him begin to lift. Everything was still perfectly in order.

Cressida dreamt of her father, his face contorted with anger as he shouted down at her. She was small in the dream, afraid to speak but feeling his words pierce holes in her delicate skin. She woke with her throat parched dry as though she had been screaming. Dawn had just begun to break over the city; she could see the first flickers of pink light spreading out over the desert in the distance.

She took pleasure in dressing herself without an audience, much to the confusion of her maids, who entered her sitting room to find her fully clothed in one of the loose silk kaftans that had been provided as part of her new wardrobe. The material was a jade-green chiffon with satin lining, decorated with sparkling beads and tiny stones around the collar and cuffs. She had showered and allowed her long ash-blonde hair to dry naturally so it wasn't quite straight but still fell in pleasing waves down her back.

When she entered the dining room of the royal apartment she was surprised to find Khal already seated. He stood while she took her seat at the opposite end of the table, offering a pleasant good morning before returning to his coffee and newspaper. She ate quietly, glancing up every now and then to watch with fascination as he switched between his tablet computer and the broadsheet spread out across the table by his side. Taking notes, by the looks of it, she mused. It should not surprise her that his working day would begin the moment he opened his eyes.

When she had finished eating, he was still absorbed in his reading so she stood up quietly, intending to leave him in peace.

'My apologies for being so distracted; I'm not used to sharing breakfast with anyone.' Khal stood, neatly folding his paper and folding up the cover of his device before tucking it under his arm.

'There's no need for you to change your morning

rituals simply because I am here,' Cressida said earnestly. 'I have a morning packed full of lessons and dress fittings and goodness knows what else. I'm kept quite busy around here.'

'Yes, that's what I wanted to talk to you about. My advisors told me that so far you have been using the main library for all of your studies.'

'The library is wonderful. I'm happy to continue there.'

'I wanted to show you something, before you start your day.' He motioned for her to follow him out of the main door of the apartment, a strange lightness in his usually austere expression. 'It's just something I thought of after our conversation last night.'

Cressida kept her expression neutral as she followed him down the halls of the royal wing of the palace in the direction of the Sheikh's formal offices and library. She had been given a tour of this area of the palace but told that it was for official use only.

'This is my office and official rooms through here,' he said idly, gesturing to a door that led onto a room as big as a basketball court. She had not been permitted inside, but she had been told that many more rooms spread out from there, a library, secretarial offices and such. The Sheikh walked across the large sunny vestibule to a door tucked away at the end of the hallway. He hesitated for a moment before pushing it open and allowing her to enter first.

At first she wasn't quite sure if it was an office or a library. Books lined three of the four walls but there was also a working area on one side with a large cherrywood desk, complete with a computer, phone and pens. A long plush sofa occupied the other side of the room, facing a large arched window that overlooked the gardens beyond.

'I decided you needed a place of your own for your studies,' Khal said matter-of-factly. 'It used to be my office when I was the Crown Prince.'

Cressida walked over to one of the bookcases and ran her fingers along the spines. A place of her own. Her own little sanctuary. She had made one comment to him about missing her tiny study space back in London and he had gone and given her an entire office of her own. She darted a look over her shoulder to see him still standing in the doorway, watching her with hooded brows.

'You can have it redecorated to your own personal taste, of course. I won't be offended if you don't like the décor. And I will arrange to have whichever books you prefer transported here from the main library if the selection here is lacking—'

'It's perfect.' Her voice sounded surprisingly calm, in contrast to the alarming burst of emotion swelling in her chest. 'Thank you.'

He waved off her gratitude good-naturedly before glancing at the watch on his wrist. 'I must start my working day officially, but feel free to stay here and settle in if you wish. If you need anything at all, there is an intercom on the desk and an assistant assigned to you.'

'An assistant?' Cressida gasped.

'The Sheikha always has a personal assistant once royal duties commence,' he replied easily, as though it should have been obvious to her. 'You have three weeks until you officially enter into public life. The calendar of a Sheikha can be quite demanding.'

They were interrupted by two palace officials, seeking the Sheikh's urgent attendance in his office. Cressida motioned for him to go, thanking him once more before he disappeared through the door and closed it behind him with a gentle click.

She wandered over to the desk and sat slowly into the buttery soft leather swivel chair behind it. He had thought of her. He had put thought into her comfort beyond what was necessary. It was a strange feeling, having someone else looking out for her.

Placing both hands on the wood, she glanced down and smiled as she noticed the slim mobile handset that had been placed on top of a sheaf of papers. She lifted it, finding it had already been pre-programmed for her ease of use. She sighed with pleasure, hardly knowing where she would begin with all these wonderful gifts. She wondered if he even considered them gifts.

A wind blew gently through the open window, shuffling some of the papers across the desk. She gathered them back, noticing for the first time that they were stamped with the royal Zayyari crest on top in their signature wine and gold leaf design. But when she noticed the signature underneath, her breath caught completely. A feeling strangely like pride filled her chest as she ran her fingers over the ornate lettering, feeling the weight of the words press much further than just her fingertips.

From the desk of Her Royal Highness,
Sheikha Cressida Al Rhas of Zayyar

CHAPTER SEVEN

KHAL MADE A point of eating with Cressida each morning, inwardly congratulating himself as he noticed her mood lightening with each passing day. He told himself that it was simply in his best interests to ensure that she was comfortable at the palace, but truthfully he looked forward to their morning conversations. Soon, he began to forget to take his usual notes from the political broadsheets, abandoning the task to one of his secretaries in favour of occupying his time hearing about Cressida's progress in her studies. She showed a remarkable aptitude for retaining information, relaying some of her difficulties with the Zayyari language with humour and a total lack of self-consciousness.

On the rare evenings that he did not have meetings or functions to attend, they dined together in the apartment. It was far from an effort to keep his mind focused on the conversations that flowed with surprising ease between them; he enjoyed the new perspective of seeing his beloved kingdom and all of its traditions through her eyes. But still, beneath the iron of his control he fought the urge to let his gaze wander over her tempting curves or to linger when he bid her goodnight at the door to her room.

It seemed that married life made the time pass quickly and he found himself thinking less of his investigations into the fire at the encampment or his suspicions about who might have started it. Exactly two weeks had passed since their wedding when Khal found his good mood completely thrown off course by a single piece of information let slip by one of his secretaries. He called for his Chief of Security immediately, sitting behind his desk with clenched fists as he waited for Sayyid to arrive.

'You wished to see me, Your Highness?' Sayyid entered, a heavy look in his eyes.

'Close the door.' Khal spoke slowly, taking every ounce of his effort to control the temper that threatened to spill over at any moment. He gestured for the other man to take a seat before he stood and paced to the other side of his desk.

'Is there a problem, Sire?'

'One might say that, yes,' Khal gritted. 'If you would describe finding out that there has been yet another incident a *problem*.'

'If you mean the small situation that was contained last week…'

'I will decide what situation is considered small,' Khal growled. 'What makes you believe that your King should not be informed of any kind of threat in his own kingdom? That I should find out a week after the fact that there was an intruder apprehended in the middle of the night, scaling the palace walls?'

'With the utmost respect, Sire, there have been instances of people trying to climb the palace walls in the past. The man did not breach the security fences and did not carry any weaponry; therefore it was classed as a non-dangerous incident.'

'Was he questioned? Did he have ties to any rebellious factions?' Khal felt pressure build in his temples as he noticed Sayyid's mouth tighten.

'We questioned him and ascertained that he was a youth on a foolish dare. Even Lazarov agreed that it was best not to make an incident of something so mundane.'

'Roman was informed of this incident, was he?' Khal fought the annoyance that rose in his chest at the mention of his friend's name. Roman's security firm had trained the entire palace guard; of course they would go to him if there had been an attempted breach. No one dealt with high profile risk assessment and security better than The Lazarus Group. Khal had called upon Roman himself within hours of the fire in the encampment. It had been Roman who had informed him that the private investigation had been classed as one hundred per cent accidental, with no sinister or deliberate intention.

In that same phone call his friend's tone had become concerned as he had reminded Khal of instances in the past where his need for heightened security had been extreme. Of how he needed to trust his team to do their job and stop looking for threats where none existed.

Khal felt anger rise within him once more as he heard that same tone of concern in Sayyid's voice.

'Sire, I can assure you that the Sheikha is safe—'

'I have not mentioned the Sheikha once,' Khal fumed. 'This is about your complete insubordination in not reporting a potentially dangerous matter to your King.'

Sayyid stood suddenly, open defiance on his face.

'There was no danger; that is what I am trying to make you see. What many have tried to make you see.'

Khal turned and took a few steps away, feeling the anger within him reach its peak. Truthfully, perhaps he'd been thinking of Cressida's safety when he'd imagined the unknown intruder scaling the walls in the dead of night. But this was not just about possible danger to his wife. This was about Zayyar.

His father had always made a point of reminding him how quickly rebellion could resurge when one rested in a state of peace. It was his duty to ensure his staff did not take that peace for granted and make mistakes. He inhaled deeply, his jaw pulsing with the effort of keeping his tone measured. Of keeping his control. 'You will take a leave of absence from your duties to account for this error in judgement. One week, effective immediately.'

Sayyid's eyes narrowed. For a moment Khal wondered if the line was about to be crossed. If the other man would openly defy his King's orders.

'As you wish, Your Highness. I'll make the arrangements,' Sayyid finally said. He bowed low before turning and exiting the room without another word.

Khal paced the floor of his study for what felt like hours in the aftermath of the confrontation with his trusted employee, feeling the pressure in his head pulse and thrum with every step. He sat down in a high-backed armchair, resisting the urge to fling the nearby coffee table across the room. He would not allow his staff to decide what he could and would not be told. He had the right to know everything that happened within his own palace. Roman's calm voice popped into his head once more. Was this one of those situations he'd referred to? Was he seeing danger where it did not exist? Should he simply trust his security team to do their job and stop trying to control every single thing in his orbit? He did kick out in frustration then, his foot making hard contact with the heavy marble leg of the coffee table in front of him.

'Having a tantrum?'

A quiet voice shook him from his brooding; he silently hoped it was not Cressida but at the same time knew that it was. She stood a few feet away, wrapped in a pale pink silk robe. He leaned his head back, allowing himself a moment to take her in before he spoke. 'Sheikhs do not have tantrums. We have momentary losses of composure.'

'Ah.' She hovered nervously in the doorway. 'I came back down to get a book and I saw your light still on. Am I interrupting?'

'Come in. Though I might not be the best company.'

He stood up, taking a long languorous stretch and covertly watching as her gaze rose to follow his movements before darting away. Khal felt the beginning of a smile tease his lips. It dawned on him that this was the first time she had set foot inside his office.

Her eyes wandered to his desk, where a handful of professional photographs of their wedding ceremony were scattered. Khal had just received them that morning and hadn't quite decided what to do with them yet. She moved closer, her fingertips trailing over the images delicately.

'I look…completely different,' she said in that same quiet voice. Her brow was furrowed as she picked up a shot of them both with their foreheads touching.

'You don't like them?' he asked, genuinely eager to know the answer.

'They are very well done.' She smiled.

'That is not what I asked.'

'I suppose they're quite convincing. Romantic and dreamy. But when one knows the truth, the illusion is spoiled a little.' She placed the photo back down and arranged the others in a square formation, avoiding his gaze. 'It's a strange feeling, being married but not actually being married, isn't it?'

'We are married,' he said with a hint of irony. 'I have photographic evidence.'

'You know what I mean—we have this arrangement.' Cressida sighed, moving over to inspect the collection of tiny ships in bottles that adorned the shelves of his study. 'I never understood how they got such detailed works inside these things without breaking it,' she said absentmindedly, running a fingertip along the glass that encased a large rare Marlin.

'It's a hobby of mine,' he said idly, wondering why her comment about not actually being married stuck in his mind.

'You made all these?' Her eyes widened as she took in the wall of shelves. 'How on earth do you find the time?'

'It calms my mind.' He shrugged, not quite sure why he'd shared something so personal. A king did not struggle with an overactive mind. A king had complete control over his thoughts at all times.

'It looks incredibly complicated.' She was still peering at various models, genuine appreciation on her features.

'It's simple enough once you approach it from a point

of logic. My father introduced me to it at a young age.' A smile teased the corner of his lips as he remembered some of the tantrums he had thrown when he'd continued to fail at lifting the mast of the tiny ship. His father had always remained seated, never raising a hand or losing his temper. 'Go over your plan and begin again,' he would say calmly. Now, as a grown man, he could see that his father had given him the tools to harness the anger and uncontrolled nature that he had shown even as a young boy. There was no place in Zayyar's future for another king without self-control. For another king ruled by his own selfish desires.

'I was just about to order some tea,' he said brusquely, walking away from her to gather his thoughts for a moment. 'You are welcome to join me.' He kept his tone light, telling himself he was inviting her to stay because he was simply not in the mood to be alone with his own thoughts. She was a good conversationalist. He had no ulterior motives for wanting to be alone with his wife in his study at night…

Clearly, she was having a similar thought process, considering she took a full two minutes to come to a decision before lowering herself into the armchair opposite his own. He had not been lying; he had been about to order tea. It was the only thing that calmed him in a mood such as this one.

His staff were efficient, laying out the perfectly polished pots and utensils between them, hot steam rising from the ornate copper teapot.

To his surprise, Cressida began the service, performing the Zayyari ritual with seemingly effortless movements. It was only because he studied her so closely that he noticed the slight tremble of her fingers, or the way her brow creased momentarily as she focused on her performance. He reached out to accept his cup from her fingers, deliberately brushing his thumb across her skin.

'And you say that you do not feel like you are truly married?' He sat back, savouring the taste of the sweet traditional brew on his tongue. 'This seems like very wifely behaviour to me.'

'Well, you would know more about that than I do.' She focused on stirring her tea, taking a moment to realise what she had said. 'Oh, I'm sorry. I'm so thoughtless...'

'Don't apologise.' Khal shook off the comment, but still he found himself fighting the sudden sharp jab of discomfort with the reference to his first marriage. Perhaps because, since they'd sat down, he had been acutely distracted by the woman who sat across from him. Or maybe it was because his ring now lay upon her finger and so to think of another time seemed inappropriate somehow. Truthfully, he'd thought of his first wife less and less as the years passed. And, even then, only to ponder a new lead in his investigations into her accident. It had been five years, after all. He knew he could not feel the same intense emotions for ever, but still it brought guilt to realise he had truly accepted her death and moved on.

'It seems morbid to ask if you sat like this in the past.' Cressida spoke softly. 'You have never spoken of your first marriage. I'll admit that I am curious.'

'My first marriage was very different for many reasons,' Khal said simply, taking another sip of his tea. 'I was very different.'

'Your sister told me that you grieved for a long time. I got the impression that you were both very much in love.' She met his eyes, a strangely guarded expression on her usually open features.

'We were.' He flexed the tightness from his fingers, laying his palm down flat on the arm of the chair. 'In the beginning, at least.'

'Oh.'

One syllable was all she needed to portray that she understood. She did not push the subject further and for that he was grateful. It was only the beginning of the myriad secrets of his seemingly perfect marriage to Priya. He had never spoken to anyone of the fact that all was not as it seemed. But now he felt strangely lighter having spoken of it, never having considered that there might be weight to carrying secrets.

'My parents' marriage was arranged,' Cressida said after a while. 'My grandmother always said they were lucky to have fallen madly in love as a result.' She pursed her lips, meeting his eyes for a moment before looking away. 'Seeing what falling out of love has done to them, I have always been of the opinion that it was better to have a marriage free of emotions.'

Khal frowned at her admission, picturing King Fabian and his cold, uninterested wife. He had been in their company on a number of occasions, and each time he had become more aware of the deep well of problems in the royal marriage. He was of the opinion that the issues ran far deeper than simply falling out of love, but he kept that thought to himself.

'Is that why you agreed to marry me?' he asked. 'Other than your extreme devotion to your kingdom, of course.'

Cressida seemed to shift in her seat slightly, one hand

adjusting the material of her nightgown. 'I had many reasons for accepting this…arrangement.'

'This is a marriage, *habibti*. Make no mistake.' He did not mean for the hardness to creep into his voice but all of a sudden the idea that she saw their union as some kind of cold business arrangement was not palatable to him, for reasons unknown. After all, political marriages such as theirs were essentially built on business, were they not?

'I'm not saying that we each aren't bound by the same rules as usual marriages,' she said hurriedly. 'I just mean that, behind closed doors, we both know different.'

'Do you feel bound by the rules, Cressida?' he said silkily, feeling a pang of irritation at the feelings her words evoked. The memory of a similar conversation in the past came to the surface, another woman's voice.

'I have never been good at playing by the rules, Khal. I'm sorry.'

'I have no desire to enter into a verbal sparring match at midnight,' Cressida said, standing up and shaking out the fabric of her nightgown. 'You were clearly aggravated by something before I came in here and I think it's best that I say goodnight.'

'Oh, no, you don't.' Khal stood, moving so that he blocked her way. 'You see, I like to finish conversations, not walk away from them if they get a little uncomfortable.'

'I don't feel like this is a conversation any longer. I feel like you are putting words into my mouth.'

She'd mentioned her mouth and, sure enough, that was where his eyes wandered, the perfect pink flesh teasing him. 'Do you feel bound by the rules of this marriage?' he asked again, softer this time. The air between them thrummed with awareness.

'Sometimes.' She half whispered the word, her breath seeming slightly laboured all of a sudden. 'But perhaps not quite in the way that you think.'

'Do you feel unhappy here with me, Cressida?' he asked, feeling the sizzle of something dangerous in the air between them. He wanted to know the answer to his question, the honest answer. To allow him to see beneath the facade she always wore around him.

He wanted something real.

Cressida shook her head once, her eyes meeting his. 'I don't feel unhappy when I'm with you. I feel...frustrated.'

He wasn't sure who leaned in first, but suddenly their mouths were locked and it was like the first drink after weeks in the desert. He feasted on her, taking every ounce of the longing that he could feel in her kiss and giving back in equal measure. He felt the weight of her arms around his neck, her chest pressed tightly against his, and yet it still wasn't enough. He pressed her back against the bookcase, ignoring her sharp intake of breath as he raised her arms above her head and began a slow trail down her neck.

Her groans sent the blood rushing straight to his groin, not that he hadn't already lost control of that particular piece of his anatomy. She moved against him, consciously or unconsciously coming into contact with his arousal and giving a slight gasp. Khal looked down into her widened eyes, tension furling and unfurling in his lower abdomen.

'Tell me to stop,' he commanded. 'Tell me that you don't want this.'

'I can't,' she whispered, lowering her face into the curve of his neck and pressing a hot kiss to his skin. 'I think I have wanted this from the first moment I saw you.'

The kiss undid him completely, along with the words. He waited a moment as she kissed along his clavicle, running her hot tongue along his skin. Unable to cope with the torture of standing still, he ran his hands over her shoulders, gently spreading the delicate vee of her robe wide enough to lower the neck of her nightgown and expose the porcelain skin of one breast. He let his hands explore one hardened peak until she leaned her head back in sensual abandon. Then he leaned down to replace fingers with lips and tongue. He thoroughly pleasured one delicate breast before moving on to afford the same attentions to its twin. Each movement of his tongue brought forth groans of pleasure, which Cressida tried to stifle with her fist. They were in his study, after all.

She moved against him again, more impatiently this time, as though she knew exactly what she wanted. Her pelvis fitted in line with his so perfectly. It would be so easy to just wrap her legs around his waist and slide himself inside her. He would take her rough and hard, sliding in and out of her moist heat until neither of them could remember their own name...

'Don't stop, Khal.' Her hushed plea threatened to undo him. 'Please.'

Spurred on by the raw need in her voice, he continued his explorations, removing her robe and letting his fingers gather her nightgown up until it bunched just under her hips. Pinning the fabric with one hand, he found the lace-covered centre of her and applied a gentle pressure.

* * *

Cressida's attempts to remain quiet were short-lived; soon her loud gasps and stifled moans filled the room. She had never felt such unbearable pleasure as she did with his hands on her, touching her. It was as though he knew exactly how she liked it, exactly how she touched herself in the dark of night when no one was watching. Khal let out a deeply male groan of pleasure as she moved herself against his hand, wanting more than he gave.

He pulled the lace down over her hips, watching her eyes the whole time. Perhaps he was waiting to see if she had finally come to her senses and decided she didn't want this, after all. She did not falter. She had made her decision the moment he stood in front of her, all male sexual energy. Perhaps tomorrow she would remember why this was such a bad idea but in this moment she had never wanted anything more in her life.

She became impatient with his slow movements and kicked the material off the rest of the way, enticing a husky laugh from his throat. She smiled, amazed that this felt so right all of a sudden when moments ago they had been talking about practicality. There was nothing practical about what they were doing right now and they both knew it.

His fingers came into contact with her bare flesh and within seconds she could feel her body begin to pulse and tighten as it began to ascend towards climax. He must have sensed it too because, just as she had almost reached the peak, he stopped.

'What are you—' Her stunned words were stifled by his kiss as he gathered her up into his arms and carried her a few steps across the room to a long sofa. The cushions were soft underneath her but the fabric of her nightgown bunched uncomfortably around her waist.

As though he read her mind, he helped her to be rid of the pesky layers. All of a sudden she was completely naked, spread out before him while he was still completely clothed. He paused for a moment, eyes darkening with pleasure as he drank her in, then he set about removing his own clothing. By the time he was completely naked, Cressida's throat had gone dry. He was... magnificent. There was no other way to describe the hard expanse of copper-toned skin on show. He was well built in a suit but nude, he was powerful. Muscles rippled along a trim abdomen, leading to trim hips and... She gulped, wondering how on earth that was going to fit anywhere belonging to her.

'I have dreamed of doing this,' he murmured, moving over her so that their bodies were entwined. She could feel the heat of him pressing between her thighs, her own excitement slightly embarrassing now that no clothing was between them.

She was nervous but definitely ready. As he poised himself over her, she was struck by the weight of this moment. He moved against her with such slowness, she felt a lump in her throat. She could feel his hard heat as he slid the first inch inside; there was only slight pain as he moved further, stretching her to accommodate him. His eyes widened for a moment as some of her discomfort must have showed on her face. He made to pull away but Cressida gripped his hips with her thighs, holding him tightly against her. Keeping their bodies joined.

He uttered a curse under his breath, his breathing laboured as he gently pressed his forehead against hers, holding his body still with impressive control.

'Don't stop.' Cressida breathed. She arched herself against him and felt the join of their bodies pulse pleasurably. To her relief, he moved once more in response, then twice, placing one hand between them to slide his thumb against that part of her that drove her wild. What little pain there had been soon receded completely and only pleasure remained as her body quickly got the hang of what to do. She felt pleasure like nothing she had ever experienced building deep within her with every thrust. Her body seemed to move against him of its own volition and she noticed Khal hiss between his teeth.

'Oh, yes, *habibti*, just like that,' he practically growled as he spread her legs wider, moving even deeper, increasing his pace.

She felt him begin to lose control, his neck straining as his own climax approached. The sight of this powerful man at her mercy seemed to spur her on, bringing pleasure like she had never experienced crashing down upon her and sending her body into waves of absolute bliss. Cressida felt a moment of confusion as he pulled away from her at the last moment then bit her lower lip as she realised that he had only withdrawn just in time before his own climax hit him.

Khal fell back against the cushions of the sofa, head arched back in the pose of a man completely exhausted and satisfied. His chest rose and fell in a steady rhythm, the barest sheen of sweat glistening on his dark skin. Cressida could not look away, wanting to remember every detail of this perfect moment. She had never imagined that her first time would be quite so intimate and filled with passion.

Not only had she just made love for the first time, she had made love with her husband. The thought brought gooseflesh to her skin and she cursed herself for having such a sentimental reaction.

Truthfully, Cressida had absolutely no idea what one was supposed to say in this situation. Should she make small talk? Should she tell him that she had enjoyed it, they should do it again some time? It was insane, she had stood in front of a crowd and pledged her devotion to this man and he to her. The entire world now believed them to have had a secret love story worthy of movies and magazine spreads. And yet, in this moment, as the silence stretched onwards, she realised that they were just two people who had finally given in to a passion that neither of them quite understood.

Khal felt as though he had just run a marathon, but in the best way possible. He lay back on the sofa, eyes closed, but sleep was the furthest thing from his mind. He was avoiding the woman who lay alongside him, delaying the moment when he would have to confront the reality of what had just transpired between them.

First, he had not used any protection. Second, his wife had clearly been an innocent and he had crudely deflowered her on a sofa.

Suppressing the urge to growl at his own loss of control, he stood up and began to gather up their clothes.

There could not be a child. He could not bear the thought of history repeating itself... He paused for a long moment at his desk, his body seemingly frozen. He felt such an acute loss of control it was as though his thoughts swam away from him every time he tried to grasp them.

'Could you hand me my nightgown?' a quiet voice

came from the sofa. He turned, not knowing how long he had stood immobile and silent while she waited.

Guilt engulfed him as he saw the uncertainty on Cressida's features as she accepted the nightgown and hurriedly shielded her naked body from him.

'You were a virgin,' he said softly, sitting alongside her and turning her cheek so that she met his eyes. 'I would have taken more time, had I known. Made it better for you.'

'We didn't exactly plan for this, either of us.' She spoke with quiet sincerity. 'But it was quite pleasurable...for me, anyway.'

Khal looked down at the bare skin of her thighs, which had been wrapped around his waist mere minutes before. God, but he wanted her all over again. He exhaled a long breath, astounded at the complete deterioration of his adult mind to that of a lust-crazed youth.

Suddenly, Cressida stood up and pulled her arms through her nightgown, shielding her body from view. Khal fought the urge to pull her back down.

'I understand that you might be worried that this... that tonight would complicate matters between us.' She spoke with a strange coldness in her voice.

'Do you believe that it won't?' Khal asked. 'Tonight was irresponsible on my part, in more ways than one.'

She busied herself by pulling her hair back from her face, twisting it around itself in a neat trick that kept it secured atop her head with no clasps or ties. Next, she retrieved her robe, slipping her arms into it quickly.

Khal stood, quite aware that he had not yet bothered to put on his own clothing. He watched as she lowered her gaze for a split second before hurriedly looking away to focus on the wall behind his head as she spoke.

'We were both irresponsible. We are both adults. We got carried away tonight but we can simply agree that this need not happen again.'

'When I say irresponsible, I mean that I didn't use protection, Cressida.' Khal took a step towards her.

'That won't be an issue.' She straightened her shoulders, lifting her hand almost as a barrier between them. 'Presuming that you are…healthy?'

'Of course I am healthy,' he growled.

'Good. Well, I take medication to regulate my cycle,' she said matter-of-factly, tying the sash of her robe with an almost vicious precision. 'So it seems we have nothing else to worry about.'

She made to step away from him. Khal grabbed her by the wrist. 'Just like that? You've forgotten about what just happened in here?'

Her sharp intake of breath was loud in the silence of the night. 'We both agreed that this marriage was to remain free of complications.'

'And you immediately feel confident that you can go back to that plan?'

Cressida frowned. 'Did you not make it clear to me in the beginning that you were not seeking a true wife?'

Khal stepped back as though burned. 'Of course.'

'Then I think it's probably best for us to go back to our rooms…separately. Perhaps take some distance from each other over the next few days.'

'Yes, of course. Retreat and regroup,' Khal murmured, confused at his own irritation at her calm approach. He did not wish to have to dampen down the hopes of an overly sentimental virgin. He should be thanking his lucky stars at his good fortune. She nodded once, bidding him a very civilised goodnight before disappearing through the door of his office with seemingly effortless composure.

Khal waited until her footsteps had disappeared completely before leaving the office himself.

His feet seemed to know where to take him even before his brain registered where he was going. The open courtyards past the eastern wing of the palace led out onto a long tropical garden. Khal followed a marble path inset with aqua-blue stones that sparkled in the light of the full moon. The path sloped downhill to where a small stone fountain took precedence. It had been many years since he had come here. For a long time this had been his preferred place to sit and brood. Perhaps brooding was the wrong word to use—sorrow was the real emotion that one felt at this fountain.

A small marble square adorned the front of the fountain's stone facade. A single aquamarine stone glittered in the centre of the square. Khal placed his hand over the stone, feeling the warmth of it seep through his skin. He had chosen this spot because the sunshine was uninterrupted here during the day. At the time, that had seemed important. There was no name inscribed on the stone, no words to mark the sorrowful reason this fountain stood on this particular spot.

His son had never taken his first breath, and in Zayyari culture that meant that he had not existed. There was no grave. No tomb at which to kneel and pray.

But he had prayed.

He had prayed for the infant son he would never know, and for the wife who had changed for ever. Something had died inside him the day he had been told that Priya had lost their child. He had been on the other side of the world, and protocol had meant he was not able to return for days after. By the time he had finally reached her bedside, the woman looking back at him was not his Priya any longer. Her own death had come less than a year later.

He had not discussed with Cressida the reasons why he had no desire for an heir of his own. For those brief moments, imagining that she might carry his child had made his insides turn to stone. He'd told himself time after time that a leader did not show his fears. This was a half-truth—just because he did not show it, did not mean that he didn't harbour fears that ran deep into his soul.

CHAPTER EIGHT

CRESSIDA GASPED AS the helicopter swooped low to give them a panoramic view of the spectacular coastline of Valar. The city's skyline was impressive, dominated by silver and glass high-rise buildings and ornate hotels. Further down in the distance she could see the swimming pools of the beach-side resorts, tourists no more than tiny black dots on the white sand. They set down on top of a building so high Cressida felt every muscle in her body clench. Reminding herself not to look down, she was jolted when Khal's warmth slid closer to her on the leather seats as he spoke to the pilot, his voice barely audible over the roaring din of the chopper blades slowing to a stop.

She had barely seen him in the week that had passed since the night in his study. He did not eat breakfast with her, nor did he make any impromptu invitations to dine together in the evenings. She had missed the ease of their conversations but told herself it was for the best. He would never want a relationship with her beyond the sexual chemistry between them. A casual sexual relationship was simply not an option for a woman who was already married to the man in question. It would be utter madness to expect things to remain free of emotions, no strings attached.

She was escorted down from the helicopter by two of the security team but it was Khal who took her hand in his and guided her across the blustery rooftop to the lift. Once inside, she released a breath she hadn't realised she'd been holding and heard a rumble of quiet male laughter erupt alongside her.

'Did you fear I would allow you to fall off the rooftop?' he asked, his hand still holding hers captive within his own. He spoke idly, his gaze fixed on the numbers on the display panel as the lift came to a stop and the doors slid open to reveal a square windowless hallway.

'I'm glad you find my fear of heights entertaining,' she quipped, a reluctant smile crossing her own lips as she looked up into a pair of dark brown eyes filled with mirth.

As usual, part of the security detail had already performed a sweep in preparation for their arrival. They were escorted into a spacious foyer and promptly left alone.

All thoughts momentarily left her brain as she was greeted with the most spectacular view she had ever seen. The large open-plan space was sumptuously decorated in bright modern monochrome and sky-blue, but the main attraction was the double height wall of curved plate glass that offered an unobstructed view of the entire city skyline, beautifully framed by a glimpse of the Arabian Sea on one side. The window was so wide and so clear, it was as though the marble tiles simply ended on a precipice, leaving the viewer at the risk of toppling over the edge. It made her stomach tighten, but still she could appreciate the view.

'This city is…breathtaking…' Cressida murmured, still making sure that she remained firmly in the centre of the room.

'This city will soon be the future of Zayyar, thanks to you,' he said, warmth in his eyes. 'News of our marriage has already opened doors that once were firmly closed. Tonight's celebration will solidify many new connections for us.'

Cressida had already been told by her advisors of the progress that had been made since their marriage had become public knowledge. Tonight's formal celebration would bring politicians and foreign dignitaries from across the world here to show their support. However, there would not be a single member of her own family at the event. A fact that did not surprise her in the slightest. Her older sister, Eleanor, was on a charity mission in North Africa but had promised to come and visit soon, while her middle sister, Olivia, was busily setting up the headquarters of her literacy foundation in New York.

Her parents had openly refused the invitation, stating a scheduling conflict. They had half-heartedly organised an event to be held in Monteverre over the coming week and invited her and Khal for an official visit. A pathetic attempt at a show of power by her father, but still Cressida knew that his alliance was vital to Khal so she would dutifully attend.

She was to be on show to the world tonight for the first time as Sheikha. The thought terrified her almost as much as being up at this height did.

'Come and see the view. The window is bulletproof, shockproof—very safe, I assure you.' Khal moved to knock one hand against the glass pane.

Cressida raised one hand instinctively. 'There is *really* no need to demonstrate!'

A dimple appeared in the corner of his mouth again, that mischievous half smile that made her stomach flip. He braced one hand on the glass wall, shifting so that his weight leaned against it as he looked out into the distance. 'You get a much better view of the coastline over here than from all the way across the room. Just a suggestion.'

He was utterly mad; that was the only explanation for it. Who on earth could manage to look so serene and relaxed while seeming to hover on the edge of falling to their death?

'Is this your way of proving what a fearless leader you are? It's really not necessary.'

'I am simply trying to show you that you will not fall.' He spoke with surprising softness as he turned to face her. 'The danger exists only in your mind.'

In a few long strides he was beside her, taking her gently by the wrist. Her breath caught painfully in her throat at the heat of his skin on her own. She did not resist as he gently pulled her, step by torturous step, across the marble-tiled floor until she stood in the exact same spot as he had. He took her hand and placed her trembling palm against the cold glass. Cressida felt her insides tremble as she tried not to look down, focusing on the sensation of his hand still pinning her own in place.

'Open your eyes.' The command was gentle, but a command nonetheless. She gingerly fluttered one eyelid open, feeling as though her heart was about to beat straight out of her chest. He had not been lying when he said the view was better over here. On one side she could see the entire coastline stretching out into the distance, the sun sparkling on the water like a thousand diamonds. They were otherwise surrounded by a sea of sleek modern buildings and hotels, with the barest glimpse of unspoiled desert peeking out in the distance.

'Just don't look down.' Khal's voice came from somewhere near her ear as he removed his hand from hers and stood alongside her.

'You just reminded me that there is a down to look at.' She exhaled a little harder but resisted the urge to step back.

'Your composure is effortlessly regal, Your Highness.' She could hear the smirk in his voice as he placed one hand on the glass and faced away from her.

She couldn't help but let the corner of her own mouth turn up. 'I think all these brave masculine displays of royal window-leaning have reassured me.'

He turned to face her, a strange expression on his face. 'Now, you see, describing it as brave and masculine strokes my ego. Why lessen the effect by making it a royal activity?'

'I doubt most people would think that being royal lessens anything at all.'

'Ah, but we know better, don't we?' he said softly, his gaze travelling down her body for a split second. He swallowed, a frown creasing his brow.

The way he used the word 'we' so easily, she could almost imagine for a moment that they were a normal couple sharing a quiet moment of intimacy. She looked away, feeling the acute sting of awareness that she was looking for something that would never exist. Strange that, no matter what situation she was in, this feeling was always familiar, like an itchy blanket. The feeling of wanting more from someone but knowing she would never have it. Feeling as if she should be grateful for whatever small sliver of attention she had been given. The old pain threatened to overwhelm her until a silky voice invaded her reverie.

'Your mind has wandered away.'

Pulling herself back to the moment, she nodded, avoiding his gaze. 'I must be tired,' she offered, knowing she was lying but just wanting to retreat to her own space and analyse whatever she was feeling.

'You should rest, then. We leave for the ball at eight.'

Cressida nodded, making a mumbled show of thanks as he escorted her to her bedroom door before practically darting from his side. With the door firmly closed between them, she leaned back against the solid wood and waited for her heartbeat to return to normal.

Suddenly she longed for the solitude of the palace and the comfort of not being in such close proximity to the man who set her heartbeat racing and her stress levels rising. It was just simple chemical awareness, she told herself. He was the only man she had ever been close to, the only man who had ever kissed her or touched her. She had been married for less than a month. There was still another four years and eleven months to survive.

Unsurprisingly, she spent the following few hours in a less than restful state. As the sun began to dip in the evening sky, Cressida forced a smile as she took in her reflection in the floor-length mirror of her dressing room. The dress her team had chosen for the ball was a deliberately Western-styled design of midnight-blue lace, elegant and figure-hugging. If she could have chosen a gown to wear upon her first formal occasion as Queen, she could not have chosen one more perfect than this.

The silhouette made her appear more womanly, without making her feel self-conscious. The delicate capped sleeves were adorned with tiny seed pearls and the tiniest glints of sapphire. The same gems adorned her ears and her wrist, designed in Monteverre she was told, which was a nice touch. East meets West, she thought wryly as she gave a little turn in the mirror. She looked up, noticing that the door had opened, and was met with the dauntingly attractive sight of her husband in his formal robes. The King, she corrected herself sternly. The more she thought of him as her husband, the harder it was to forget what she wanted to forget. Taking a couple of breaths before she turned, she steeled herself for the onslaught of simply being in his presence. They were not alone in the room by any means, surrounded by the remnants of her wardrobe team, her assistant and members of her security detail. And yet she felt overheated and on edge.

'You look…beautiful,' he said, sincerity in the deep baritone of his voice.

'Thank you.' Cressida bowed her head slightly, clasping her hands in front of her. 'I thought we were meant to meet in the foyer?'

'I thought it best that I escort you down myself.' He extended his hand. 'That is, if that is all right with you?'

Cressida fought the urge to roll her eyes at the strained formality of it all. Instead, she straightened her spine and placed her hand in his.

Apart from a near miss when her heel got caught in the train of her dress coming down the stairs, their entrance to the ball was utterly flawless, as planned.

Cressida bowed and curtsied to various foreign dignitaries as needed, projecting what she hoped was an air of calm regal elegance when internally she felt far from it. Khal remained by her side as they were met with a queue of guests waiting for introductions to the new Queen of Zayyar.

As she'd expected, most of the guests commented on her appearance while choosing to compliment her husband on his most recent accomplishments. With her, they gushed over her designer jewellery and fawned over how utterly flawless her skin was. As though she had any control over the fact that her skin was pale and clear.

After a time, the smile she had pasted on her face began to hurt her cheeks so she simply stopped smiling. Apart from noticing Khal staring at her on a number of occasions, no one else seemed to notice. She was grateful when they sat down finally, having not eaten since breakfast in preparation for the event. Apparently it was customary to starve oneself before wearing a designer gown in order to achieve maximum leanness and avoid bloating. She had developed a new appreciation for what her sisters must have gone through in the past while she had avoided occasions such as this.

The menu was a mixture of traditional Zayyari meats and spices arranged in various European-style dishes. It was an ingenious incorporation of textures and flavours on the part of the Michelin star chefs who had been employed for the occasion. But, honestly, she could have been eating plain porridge and it would have tasted like sweet ambrosia.

'I see you have found your appetite.'

Cressida looked up, trying in vain to hide the gigantic mouthful of chicken she had just placed in her mouth. It was entirely impossible to appear ladylike or delicate when one's mouth was full of food. Khal smiled, stifling laughter with his hand as he leaned close.

'You will start a rumour that the King of Zayyar routinely starves his new bride.'

'I forgot to eat,' she said quickly, grabbing a napkin to dab the corners of her mouth. The man had barely spoken two words to her since escorting her into the banquet; of course he would choose now to begin a conversation. 'I had hoped nobody was looking.'

'I sincerely doubt that is the case. The entire gathering is captivated by you,' he said in a low voice, leaning in so that it seemed perhaps that they were having an intimate moment. 'You look...exceptionally regal this evening.'

Cressida felt a shiver run down her spine, having him so close, having his delicious scent invading her senses. The way he was looking at her, the depths of his dark eyes seeming to bore deep into her soul, she could not decide if he was continuing the show for the benefit of their guests or if perhaps he was feeling the same pull that she did, considering what had transpired between them a week ago. Or perhaps her hormones were simply not getting the message yet, she thought wryly.

Before he had a chance to dazzle her with any more of his flowery compliments, they were discreetly interrupted by one of Khal's assistants. A quick conversation passed in hushed tones before Khal turned back to her, a crease furrowing his brow.

'We are needed for a moment outside—nothing to worry about, just formalities.' He extended his hand to her, making quiet apologies to the handful of guests at their table before escorting her out through a set of double doors and into a sitting room of sorts.

There were a handful more assistants waiting for them, each of whom began talking in Zayyari so quickly that Cressida found it difficult to even catch a single word she recognised.

'English, please, for the benefit of your Queen,' Khal said briskly.

Cressida's eyes widened slightly at the tone he used. She had never heard him sound so impatient.

'There has been a report in the media...' one of the female assistants began, averting her eyes from Cressida's worried gaze as she spoke.

The chief of the team, a man with greying hair and beady eyes, moved from the side of the room, a large file in his hands. 'Your Highness, I apologise sincerely for disturbing your dinner, but protocol demands that you be alerted immediately to a report of this nature. When it is in the national interest.' He extended the black file to Khal, who took it immediately, opening it and scanning it.

Cressida felt the slight ball of tension in her stomach turn into a full-blown quake as she watched Khal's features turn from mild concern to disbelief before his gaze slowly rose to settle pointedly on her.

'Leave us,' he said quietly, his eyes never leaving her. It was the kind of quiet, firm voice he used when he was barely controlling his temper. The staff around him bowed their heads and left the room immediately, obeying their King's orders.

Cressida fought the urge to turn tail and run. 'What is it?' she asked, hearing the tremor in her voice.

'Why don't you read it for yourself?' He placed the file in her hands and turned his back to her, walking to the window, allowing her a moment.

Cressida scanned the file. It held an article dated that morning from an American publication, outlining very clearly a witness account to a royal scandal in the mysterious European kingdom of Monteverre. The royal scandal that had shaped her entire life.

Cressida felt a lump form in her throat as she took in the salacious headline in bold black ink.

Newly Crowned Queen of Zayyar's Illegitimate Past: the secret behind the scandalous Sandoval family revealed.

The tremor in her stomach turned to full-blown nausea as she felt her breath leave her lungs. Well, here it was, the moment she had prayed would never come to pass. Perhaps it was simply a gossip article; perhaps it was one of those rare cases where the media actually got quite close to the truth by accident but didn't actually have the evidence.

But, as she scanned through the rest of the article, she saw the name that haunted her. A name that she had found by chance at twelve years old, unknowingly setting the cogs in motion that would lead to her feeling ostracised and unwanted for evermore. She could still remember the smell of alcohol on her mother's breath the day she had told her that she was the product of an affair. Unwanted. A shameful reminder of her own mistake.

'Is this true?' Khal asked, still facing out of the window.

'Am I the shameful secret of the Sandoval royal family?' she heard her own voice say, as though from far away. 'Yes, unfortunately it's true.'

Khal turned around, reaching up to pinch the bridge of his nose. 'You did not think to disclose this information upon our marriage?'

'This information was never to be disclosed. My father… King Fabian, I mean, he and his team took extreme legal measures to ensure that it would never see the light of day.' She felt cold, her skin prickling, her insides shaking. She couldn't look at him; she couldn't see whatever expression might be in his eyes as he looked at her.

'Legal measures?'

'As far as I understand, a very large amount of money has been paid annually to this man to keep his silence on the matter.'

'Your biological father?'

Cressida nodded, the discomfort on hearing those words far too much for her to keep eye contact at all.

'You read the article?' A strange note had entered his voice. 'The last paragraph in particular?'

Cressida picked the file up from where she'd laid it on the coffee table, scanning down to the end of the article. 'Posthumous request?' she said numbly. 'He's dead?'

'The interview was released by his family, who are in control of his estate since his death, it seems.'

'It says here that he passed away four years ago.' Cressida shook her head. 'Why release this now? If they were able to break his nondisclosure upon his death.'

'Four years ago you were not the Queen of Zayyar,' Khal said with cold derision.

Cressida took a deep breath, feeling it shudder into her lungs. She closed her eyes, trying to calm the panic that was rising swiftly inside her to a raging storm. 'What are you going to do?'

Khal did not answer; instead he walked to the door and instructed his team to re-enter. The men and women filed in one by one, each one avoiding her eyes, but Cressida could feel them watching her. Judging her. All of a sudden the air was stifling in the sitting room.

'I need to go to the restroom for a moment,' she mumbled quietly, Khal barely looking her way as she slipped out of the door into the hallway beyond. Once alone, she lifted her dress up from the floor and moved quickly. She had no idea where she was going; she just had to get far away from the room full of knowing eyes that lay behind her.

CHAPTER NINE

'WHAT IS THE PLAN?' Khal addressed the head of his team. 'We have a room full of foreign dignitaries and politicians. They each have assistants and smartphones and instant updates. It's a fiasco.'

His head of PR spoke first. 'I think you need to speak on the matter as soon as possible, Your Highness. The longer it is left unaddressed, the weaker our position.'

'And what you propose I say, exactly?' Khal half laughed. 'This information comes just as much of a surprise to me as it would to them.'

'Yes, but the world cannot know that. We must act as though the Sheikha's parentage was known to you. That it was a matter of delicacy that you chose not to disclose for your wife's privacy.'

'And what is Monteverre's position on the matter?' Khal asked, feeling his fists clench at the thought of King Fabian and his underhand measures. It was likely the man did not care one ounce that his daughter had been publicly humiliated in the media. She was no longer a Sandoval, after all.

In the short time that he had been acquainted with Cressida's father, the man had shown him nothing but dishonesty and a ruthless greed that turned his stomach. King Fabian was not the kind of leader who put his people first. He was not even the kind of man to put his family first, given recent events.

And yet, when he had been contacted with the news that the youngest Princess was willing to accept the marriage, he had not hesitated to accept. Khal thought of the first night that he had met Cressida, once she had realised who he was, and he remembered her words. 'It has always been part of my duty to my kingdom...'

He had asked her numerous times if she had been forced into accepting this marriage. He had wanted to make sure that she was not entering into their union under duress...

Ignoring the sudden niggling feeling in his stomach, he looked up just as one of the junior assistants entered the room.

'The Sheikha has retired to her suite,' the young woman said.

Khal raised one brow. 'Retired? We are in the middle of a function.'

The young woman winced. 'Her Highness was quite adamant that she would not be returning, Sire. I was simply asked to convey the message.'

'I see.' Khal stood, walking towards the door before he even knew what he had planned to do. 'Keep the guests entertained. It seems I must retrieve my wife.'

Long strides and a rush of adrenaline had him at the door of Cressida's room within minutes. He did not knock, entering and closing the door with a thud behind him. She had been standing at the window but whirled around at his sudden entrance.

'I will not be abandoned in the middle of dinner.' Khal spoke evenly. It was taking all his self-control not to let his voice boom across the room with the force of his irritation. 'I understand that this situation is uncomfortable—'

'I can't go back in there.' Cressida's voice cut across him, loud and clear. 'I cannot sit and eat my dessert, knowing that the entire room is whispering about my secrets.'

The slight tremor in her voice unwound some of his irritation. She was upset; of course she would be. She had not known that her biological father was dead, that much was clear. But, apart from that, he realised that he had absolutely no idea what the rest of the story was. He had been too preoccupied with the scandal, and how to contain it. He had been Khal, Sheikh of Zayyar. While right now his wife had just needed support from her husband.

'The whole world will know within the next twenty-four hours, *habibti*.' He was surprised at the softness in his voice as he spoke. 'It is not going to go away. And it is definitely not going to get any easier just by hiding yourself away in your rooms.'

'I'm not cut out for this; I told you that before you married me. I was not given the same training to live in the limelight that my sisters were.' She inhaled deeply, turning her face away from him to look out at where the sun was setting on the horizon of the desert. 'Nothing about me is the same as my sisters, and now you know why.'

'How long have you known the truth of your parentage?'

'On some level, perhaps I always knew. Physically, I never inherited the famed Sandoval beauty. I always had the feeling that my father looked at me differently.

Almost like he held me in disdain, no matter how I behaved.' She moved towards the window, her long skirt blowing slightly in the breeze that drifted in. 'When I was twelve, I found a box hidden away in the back of my mother's dressing room. It was filled to the brim with letters and some photographs of a man I didn't recognise. My father found me trawling through these love letters and images. Nothing was particularly graphic or inappropriate, of course; my mother is a queen, after all.' A cruel laugh escaped her throat, or perhaps it was a sob.

'What did your father do?' Khal asked.

'Oh, he never punished me, if that's what you're thinking. He's not one for physical punishment or outward displays of aggression.' Her eyes narrowed slightly. 'I wonder if perhaps a good spanking might have left less scars; I don't know. He grabbed the box, he took me by the hand and he brought me to my mother. I remember she was sitting drinking brandy in the salon. She smiled at me after he made her tell me the truth. It was the saddest smile I have ever seen.

'And then I just stood there, twelve years old, and listened to my father spout rage and venom while my mother stared blankly out of the window. At one point he turned to me, photograph in his hand, and he said, "I am not your father. He is." I will never forget that moment as long as I live. His eyes were almost black with rage, spittle flying out of his mouth as he spoke. I remember flinching as he held the photograph inches from my nose, screaming at me to look at it, to look at him. Him being the man my mother had betrayed our family with.'

Khal let the silence fall between them, amazed at the

lack of emotion on her pale features as she recounted such awful memories. For a moment he felt the urge to close the space between them, to reach out and take her in his arms. It was too intimate, too much emotion tangling up the logical side of his brain that he knew was the priority right now. But his wife was hurting, that much was clear. She might not show her pain, but he could see it in the way she held her shoulders pulled straight, in the way she held her chin high but her lip quivered slightly.

Making his decision, he moved to her side and took both of her hands in his own.

'When you said that you were marrying me as part of your duty,' he began, tilting her chin up so that he could see her face, 'did this secret have anything to do with it? Were you blackmailed?' He did not know what he would do if the answer was yes.

She met his eyes for a moment, the sadness he saw there so profound that he felt his breath catch.

'I was not blackmailed, Khal. My father was already planning to cancel my research work and call me back to Monteverre, whether I agreed to this marriage or not. I made the mistake of sending him a letter around the same time that Olivia had run away from your engagement offer. I told him of a job offer I had received at the university. He was furious. I might not be a Sandoval by blood but I still held the name and title. By agreeing to marry you…he said it would make him proud.' Her voice broke on the last word.

Khal felt his chest constrict, his arms surrounding her as she finally melted into him and let the tears fall. Hearing the evidence of yet more emotional manipulation by such a cruel man made the primal beast within him growl even louder. To use his daughter's love against her, to manipulate her… He took a breath, loosening his hold on her and creating enough space between them so that he could look down into her eyes.

'I will make an excuse for you; there is no reason to force you to return to the function in this kind of emotional state.'

'No.' She shook her head, standing up straight and blotting her eyes lightly with the tips of her fingers. 'It was childish of me to run off like that. Tonight is about taking my place as Sheikha. It's better if we maintain a united front, like the team said. I can hold myself together for another hour or two.'

'You are sure?' Khal frowned at the sudden change in her posture, the way she seemed to so easily switch off such deep pain and anguish.

She nodded, all the weakness from a moment before gone. Aside from a slight smudge at the corner of one eye, it would take very close scrutiny to know that she had been crying at all. She was practised in hiding her pain, he knew now. It made something inside him clench to know that she was now hiding it from him too.

The rest of the dinner passed in a blur. Cressida did not know if perhaps the news had not broken as quickly as they expected it to, or perhaps their guests were simply putting on a very convincing front. But it was a relief that no one seemed to be looking at her differently, no hushed conversations seemed to occur in her vicinity. Or perhaps her inner turmoil was such that she simply did not notice or care.

It felt as though all the energy in her body had been depleted, leaving her weak and tired. So, so tired.

The news that her biological father was dead had shocked her, even though she had never met the man. She had only ever seen his picture, and read the beautiful letters sent to her mother. Vincent was his name, a humble chauffeur. How utterly clichéd that her mother would have a sordid affair with her driver. This really was the media's dream scandal. Most likely, there would be books written. Hollywood probably had someone penning a script as they spoke.

She kept her polite smile in place as the guests began to filter out, taking the chance to slip quietly away. She had fulfilled her duty, she had sat and eaten and listened to speeches and applauded at the correct times. Now, she wanted nothing more than to collapse in her bed and bury herself beneath the covers until the rest of the world was no longer talking about her.

Khal had not spoken to her since they'd returned to the banquet; clearly he was far too preoccupied in ensuring that they retained the power in this awful situation she had created. Poor him, having shackled himself to such an unworthy bride. Heaven only knew what the Zayyari public would make of this scandal. Perhaps there would be call for an annulment of the marriage, now that it was public knowledge that her parentage was illegitimate. She was polluting the royal image of the kingdom with her scandal and secrecy.

Once in her room, she went about the ritual of allowing her maid to assist her with the more difficult garments, then dismissed the young woman for the night so that she could take her time getting ready for bed. She removed the pearl earrings from her ears, placing them delicately into the small box on her dressing table. Next, she removed the heavy necklace from her neck, taking a final moment to admire the glitter of the sapphires in the lamplight.

Standing up from her table, she took a moment to take in the designer lingerie that had been paired with her evening gown. Apparently a dress like hers required a specific cut of bra and underwear to achieve maximum effect. She had just been grateful that she wasn't forced to wear some sort of medieval corset.

The bra was definitely designed well, she smiled to herself. A movement in the mirror caught her eye, and she looked up to see Khal standing in the doorway. They both stood frozen for a moment, Cressida with one hand awkwardly cupping the lace of her bra.

'I came to talk.' He averted his eyes, seeming suddenly transfixed upon a spot on the floor. 'I'll wait in the living room.' With that, he turned around and closed the door behind him.

Cressida exhaled slowly, dropping her hand from her breast to rest at her side. A bubble of nervous laughter rose in her chest. If he didn't already think she was odd, after walking in to find her examining her own bra...

Not wanting to keep him waiting, she threw on her dressing gown, making sure it was closed tight at the front, and tied a double knot at her waist. Slipping on her silk slippers, she contemplated tying her hair into a loose bun but decided against it, considering that it had been pinned up already all evening. Most likely Khal simply wanted to give her an update on the media situation and he would be gone, leaving her free to fall into bed alone as usual.

He sat in an easy repose on her small settee, long legs casually crossed one over the other as he flipped through the fashion magazine that had been left on her coffee table.

'I just want to clarify that I don't usually stand and examine myself in the mirror like that, in case you think me awfully vain.' She kept her tone light in an effort to appear easy and unaffected by the fact that he had just witnessed her half naked. Not that that exactly mattered, considering that he had already seen her fully naked once before, but she wouldn't dwell too much on that thought if she planned to get through this conversation.

'And here I was thinking I had stumbled upon another little secret of yours.' He attempted a smile.

Cressida appreciated his attempt at humour, considering he was not usually one for jokes. She took a seat on the other side of the settee, carefully keeping the folds of her dressing gown together. For a moment she thought she saw his eyes scanning her body slowly, then he blinked and looked away.

'You disappeared tonight before I had the chance to talk further,' he said. 'I wanted to express my admiration for you this evening. Returning to that dinner could not have been easy.'

'It's easier than sitting alone with my thoughts at the moment.' Cressida shrugged.

'Why do you do that?' he asked quietly. 'I offer you a compliment and you shrug it off as though it makes you uncomfortable.'

Cressida fought the urge to squirm in her seat, feeling as though he was doing that thing where he saw right through her. He had always seen her, the real her, so much more than anyone else had. 'Okay, how about I go back in time thirty seconds and I simply say thank you?'

One corner of his mouth raised slightly, his gaze never leaving hers. 'What else would you do if you could go back in time, I wonder?'

'According to my lessons in royal interview tactics, that is the kind of question the Sheikha must never answer.'

'Never has a question been deflected with more skill.' Khal half laughed, giving her mock applause. It was strange, laughing with him after the strain of the past few hours, but at the same time it was just really nice too.

'Why did you come here?' Cressida asked. 'I mean, of course you are welcome to come here whenever you like. I just meant tonight in particular. You must have something specific you wanted to talk about.'

'I did come here to talk further about the plan for the next few days, the strategy to contain the story in the media…' He met her eyes, uncrossing his legs and sitting forward with his hands on his knees. 'My team want us to lie low for a couple of days while they assess the situation and make plans with the relevant team in Monteverre. Then we will travel over for our official visit and address the matter.'

Back to Monteverre. To confront the truth. Cressida felt anxiety rise swiftly within her but she pushed it back down.

'Are you okay? Honestly?' His eyes held hers as he reached between them to grasp her hands. 'It is all right to show me your weakness, Cressida. I won't judge you.'

Cressida felt her heart pump in her chest, hearing the gentle tone of his voice. 'I'm sorry I didn't tell you. I understand if you see me differently now. If you regret our marriage.'

His grip on her hands tightened. 'Is that what you think?'

'You seemed angry all evening. Agitated. It's an entirely valid way to feel, finding out that your wife is even less perfect than she already was.'

'I do not expect you to be perfect, Cressida. This news has come as a shock but, more than anything, I am angry for you, not towards you,' he said passionately. 'And as for regretting our marriage...' He shook his head.

She inhaled deeply, hardly believing, as a rueful smile crossed his lips.

'Some of my agitation likely stems from how utterly beautiful you look tonight and how frustrated I am at not being able to touch you. I haven't been able to take my eyes off you all evening,' he said evenly, his gaze locked on hers. 'It has been a week since I had you in my arms and I still remember every single moment with painful clarity.'

Cressida took a deep breath, the intensity of his gaze on hers making her heart skitter uncomfortably in her chest. She felt restless and yet glued to the spot all at once.

'We said that we would stick with the original plan. But I think that my plan changed the moment I danced with you in the club in London.' His voice seemed lower all of a sudden...huskier. 'I held on to my plan because that's simply what I do. I keep things under control. But it seems that my control does not exist when it comes to you, Cressida.'

'What are you saying?' she asked nervously, not exactly sure what she wanted to hear. She wanted him to want her, but not just as a sexual distraction until they wore each other out or got sick of each other.

'I'm saying that the tidy little red line that I drew around both of our separate circles has been blurred and broken to a point where they seem to be melding into one, whether we will them to or not. So now it seems we face a choice. We can choose to completely separate our lives in such a way that we are very rarely in each other's presence at all. Or we can ignore the red lines completely and see what happens.'

'A world without red lines…' Cressida said slowly, seeing the tension in his body as he awaited her response. 'It seems very uncertain for a man who loves certainty.'

'The only thing that I'm certain about at the moment is that if I don't have you in my arms in the next five seconds I may very well burst out of my skin or erupt into flames where I sit.'

Cressida smiled, a shiver of anticipation running down her spine. 'Oh, don't do that. I've grown quite attached to this sofa,' she said, her voice taking on a sultry tone that shocked her.

A slow smile spread across Khal's lips, 'Well, it seems your choice has been made.' He closed the distance between them in record time, his body covering hers at the same moment his lips moulded against her own.

CHAPTER TEN

THE KISS WAS filled with every ounce of tension and frustration that she had felt herself. She had dreamt of his kisses, had tried her hardest to remember what it felt like to have his lips on hers in case she never felt it again. And yet now that his lips were on hers once more she wondered how she had ever forgotten the feeling. It was so familiar now, like coming home. Dangerously comfortable and yet feverishly exciting all at once.

Cressida felt as though her heart might beat completely out of her chest. What was it about kissing this man that sent every single hormonal impulse in her body into chaos? And not only that, she wanted to say things to him. Do things that made her shocked. She reached out to run her fingers down the bared skin of his chest, spreading his shirt collar wide so that she could touch him just as he had touched her.

Khal's hands encircled her wrists, moving her backwards until she lay back on the sofa, her nightgown spread wide to expose her partially clothed body. He pressed his mouth to the skin above her navel, moving inch by tantalising inch lower, all the while maintaining eye contact. The heat between her legs heightened to a blazing fire and she could not help but reach her fingers towards him, not sure if she wanted to stop him or tell him to move faster to his destination.

'What do you want me to do, Cressida...?' He spoke each syllable with a caress of his lips against her sensitive skin, his large muscular hands gripping her hips.

She breathed hard, hardly able to control the small movements her pelvis made as his lips reached the edge of her lace underwear. 'I want your mouth to touch me... there.' No longer able to be embarrassed by her own words, she moaned as he drew his fingers up along the thin material.

'Right here?' he asked, repeating the movement and groaning as she arched herself against his touch. He stopped speaking then, pulling her underwear down over her hips and throwing them over his shoulder.

The first touch of his tongue along her bared flesh was like nothing she could have ever expected. It was as though her entire body lit up from the inside, warmth spinning upwards along her nerve endings like fireworks. The second touch was even more intense as he drew his tongue slowly along the very centre of her, knowing exactly where would give her the most pleasure. She arched her hips, needing to move against him rather than lying flat and limp. She could not have stayed still if she'd tried, especially once he moved into a smooth rhythm. She had thought the first part was amazing, but it seemed he had more tricks up his sleeve. After a moment, he shifted, looking up at her while he slid his index finger down and slowly into her tight heat. Cressida tilted her head back as he resumed his tongue mastery now with the addition of moving his finger against a spot inside her that she had not known existed. When he added a second finger she thought she might combust on the spot, the feeling of fullness was so intense. Her heart began to pound and she was sure the tension could build no further, the slow tremendous build up like nothing she had ever felt before.

When she finally shattered, she thought she gripped his hair so tightly she was sure it must have been painful. But she was much too busy being overcome by wave after wave of devastating pleasure to care too much. Eyes closed, she was vaguely aware of Khal moving up over her, his mouth laying kisses along her neck.

'You are even more beautiful when you climax.'

She smiled, unable to feel embarrassed after the earth-shattering bliss of what she had just experienced. She felt beautiful when he looked at her this way, as though he could devour her in a single bite.

She reached to his waistband and unzipped the front of his trousers quickly before she lost her nerve. She wanted all of him. It seemed unfair that she was completely nude while he was still dressed. As though reading her thoughts, Khal pulled his shirt over his head and helped her by pulling the trousers off the rest of the way.

She began her exploration on his bare chest, feeling the strength of his pectorals under her fingertips and moving lower to where his abdomen dipped in at the hips. It was the body of a leader, a warrior. Her protector, she thought with a quiet ferocity. She wanted to show him the same care and pleasure that he had shown her, but fear of her own lack of practice made her settle for encircling his length with her hand instead. He thrust forward into her palm, a low hiss escaping his teeth as he exhaled hard. She stroked him, slowly at first then increasing her pace.

'I need to be inside you,' he growled low in his

throat, pulling her hands above her head and moving over her to crush her mouth against his.

She luxuriated in the feeling of all that powerful bare muscle pressed flush against every inch of her. She could feel the heavy heat of his arousal pressing against the top of her thigh and she rocked against him, showing him with her body that she had never wanted anything more in her life.

Khal willed himself to take it slow when all he wanted to do was plunge hard and fast into the delicious heat he knew awaited him. She moved against him again, sliding her slippery heat against him. She was trying to kill him.

He placed one hand on her hip, stilling her as he entered. Her body grasped him so tightly he seriously doubted his ability to last longer than ten seconds.

He wondered if anything on earth was as perfect as the sheer pleasure of being buried fully inside her molten heat. Her body gripped him like a vice, such an absolutely perfect fit it took every ounce of the patience and skill he had to hold himself still and allow her a moment to adjust. The torment of waiting heightened every nerve ending in his body, so much so that he could feel his climax building almost immediately. He leaned down, taking one hard nipple in his mouth and grazing his teeth along the pink flesh. She gasped, her muscles relaxing and tensing as she took him deeper, squeezing him tight.

'You drive me to madness, *habibti*,' he gritted, burying his face in the hollow of her neck as he moved slowly against her. Taking his time to let her catch up, urging her body upwards to join him. He felt her pulse quicken under his lips, her skin salty with the barest sheen of sweat. She was lost to it just as he was, the storm of sensation dancing and growing in the delicious friction of their bodies.

He groaned as his climax approached, moving harder against her and reaching down to caress the sensitive spot he knew would tip her over the edge. He knew the very moment she began to fall, her eyes meeting his for a split second with nothing but raw, primal need in their depths. That was all it took—one look and he could hold out no longer.

Mine, the demon inside him growled. With a hoarse cry he gave in to the pleasure and fully lost himself in Cressida's heat.

There was a man in her bed. Cressida smiled to herself, taking in Khal's glorious muscular form spread out alongside her. Her body felt stiff in places she hadn't known she could strain but nothing could ruin this for her. They had made love once more last night after Khal had carried her to the bathroom and showed her the hidden pleasures that could be found in the shower.

Sex was so much more than she had ever imagined it to be. It had felt like a meeting of their bodies, like two parts joining together in a mutual dance. And what a dance it was with Khal...

She remembered his words the first time he had taken her into his arms on that nightclub dancefloor, about dance being a temptation. The thought made her smile quietly to herself.

He stirred alongside her and she closed her eyes, not quite brave enough to admit she had been awake and ogling him while he slept. A hand splayed across her stomach, sliding across her skin for a moment before she felt his lips touch the delicate skin of her breast.

'Keep your eyes closed,' he murmured. 'We can pretend that you are still asleep and haven't ruined my very specific plans to wake you.'

Cressida shivered, opening her eyes just as he moved over her, kissing a path down the valley of her breasts and over her stomach. His lips were like hot silk moving over her skin, familiar and tantalising. He paid special attention to each hip before deftly bypassing the place she ached for him most in favour of laying a trail of kisses down the insides of each thigh.

'That's not fair.' She tried to laugh but the sound came out a breathy moan. She hadn't even known she was capable of making such feminine sounds until Khal.

'Never let it be said that the great Sheikh is not a fair man,' he teased, moving down to settle between her thighs with dark promise. She did not tense at all as one finger slowly entered her, closely followed by a second. She gasped, feeling him hit just the right spot and begin to work it in a perfect rhythm. Her hips bucked upwards, the pleasure so acute it was almost painful. Spreading her wide, his tongue darted over her sex once, twice...three times, but not quite allowing her to move towards climax.

Cressida sighed, looking up at him just as he moved over her. She pressed her hands on his chest, rising up from the bed so that they both kneeled facing each other. She looked down at his impressive length, running one fingertip along the silky-smooth skin before encircling him with her hand and meeting his eyes purposefully.

'I want to return the favour,' she said boldly.

Khal raised one brow, lying back on the bed in silent invitation. He was not submissive in bed. He was controlled and knew exactly what to do to drive them both over the edge. She wanted the chance to learn how to drive him crazy, just like he did to her. She leaned over him, taking him into her mouth with one smooth movement. He tasted like sex, the action so utterly erotic she felt herself grind her hips a little. One strong hand moved to slide up the outside of her thigh, dropping a light smack on the curve of her behind. He repeated the action and she bit her lip, amazed that she enjoyed it.

'That's it. Just like that.' He exhaled hard.

Typical Khal, she thought, still trying to maintain control. Not this time. She took him deeper into her mouth, feeling his taut stomach muscles shudder beneath her hands.

'I could have you do this all day,' he growled, letting his hand coil into the length of her hair, stopping her movement but still not withdrawing entirely. 'But I cannot wait another moment before I can be inside you again.'

She sat back, running her fingers down his powerful thighs and trying to take a mental photograph of this moment. She did not know how long this mindless passion between them would last. But right now it felt as though they were the only two people in the world and she wanted to savour every moment. His hand encircled her wrist, gently tugging her so that she lay draped over him. She kissed him, softly at first before letting her arousal take over and taking the kiss deeper. Her mind no longer intruded, her body recognising his and knowing just what lay in store.

Strong hands gripped her hips. He thrust upwards, and both of them filled the room with the kind of throaty moan that only came with that very first joining. He thrust deep, filling her to the hilt, and withdrew halfway before he let his hands drift to his sides and went still.

'Show me how you like it,' he said, lying back to watch her with a look of deep male appreciation.

She bit her lip, feeling momentarily vulnerable with his eyes devouring her, but the delicious slide of him inside her was enough to move her thoughts elsewhere quickly enough. She moved over him slowly, finding her rhythm and gasping at the sensation of being filled so very deeply.

She trusted him completely, she realised, suddenly unable to look at him as the force of her emotions began to build, along with her climax. He moved, sitting up so that their chests were only inches apart; his hands on her hips kept her rhythm in check as he thrust in time with her. After the mind-exploding pleasure of their orgasms had passed there was only silence, and then the sound of their laboured breathing. Khal moved away first, darting a quick glance in her direction before lying flat on his back.

Something in his eyes told her that he felt it too, this painful closeness. She inhaled, feeling a lingering tightness in her chest from the force of keeping her emotions in check. She stood from the bed, moving to the bathroom on shaky legs and closing the door gently behind her.

This was so much more than feeling overwhelmed by sex, she thought, biting her lip at her own naiveté. She had known she was in danger from the moment he had looked into her eyes in that wedding tent. He had started out as the man she had been forced to choose and somehow wound up being her perfect fit. Her lover. The word seemed to caress something deep inside her, a tiny speck of romanticism that she would never have dreamed existed within her cynical heart. But there it was, clear as day. And, just as that speck began to glow and blossom, realisation dawned that she had done what she had vowed not to do.

She had let her emotions get involved. She had fallen in love with her husband.

Khal woke with a start, a light sheen of sweat on his chest as he sat up in the unfamiliar bedroom. It took a moment to realise where he was. He stood up, walking to the long terrace doors and opening them a few inches to take in a breath of fresh air. The city of Valar spread out before him in a glittering blanket of lights. The dream had been much the same as it always was. Priya's voice haunting him, reminding him of his unworthiness, only tonight she had not been alone. Beside her, Cressida had appeared, tears falling from her eyes.

He contemplated slipping out to his own room, but immediately disregarded the idea as cowardly. He was not some kind of lothario who slipped in and out of bedrooms in the darkness. He splashed some cold water on his face and went back into the bedroom. The light beside the bed was on and to his dismay he found Cressida was sitting up, waiting for him.

'I had not meant to wake you.' Khal lay heavily back down onto the bed, turning on his side to take in the beautiful sight that greeted him. Cressida lay back against the pillows, ash-blonde hair spilling around her bare shoulders and the satin sheets tucked demurely under her arms to cover her chest. The innocent display of modesty was a delicious distraction from his troubled thoughts; he could think of no better way to redirect his mind than by peeling away those sheets, inch by glorious inch...

'You were talking in your sleep...' Cressida disturbed his train of thought, a nervous tone to her quiet voice '... I was debating whether or not to wake you but then I heard you get up... I wasn't sure if perhaps you were sleepwalking.'

'I hope I at least said something entertaining,' he joked easily, but still he wondered how much she might have gleaned from his night-time ramblings.

Cressida did not smile. 'I believe that you...you were dreaming of your wife.'

He could hear the sadness in her voice, the uncertainty. 'You are my wife. Let us not get mixed up on that fact, *habibti*.'

'You were saying her name.' She took her lip between her teeth, worrying it slightly, weighing up her words before she spoke. 'Priya. Do you dream of her often?'

Khal exhaled, deeply uncomfortable with the turn this conversation had taken. He had never spoken to a soul about the dreams that'd plagued him since Priya's death. How their final conversation seemed to haunt him so heavily. And even now, four years later, the dreams would come back every now and then. It tended to happen at very inopportune times, like when he slept in a jet surrounded by staff or the first night that he slept beside his new wife after making love... He silently cursed himself.

'I'm not exactly sure what triggers the dream, maybe

stress or lack of sleep. It just kind of happens every once in a while.' He curled one arm behind his head and studied the ceiling for a moment, knowing the conversation had only begun, judging by the curious look on Cressida's face.

'No one ever seems to talk of how she died,' Cressida said slowly. 'It's as though it's some great big secret. Ironic, coming from me, I know.'

Khal attempted a smile but found the muscles in his face seemed suddenly tight. He did not speak of Priya's death to anyone. He never had. Other than to aid in the investigations into her accident, no one addressed the subject and he certainly did not bring it into conversation. It felt as though every comfortable boundary in his life had begun to slowly erode from the moment he had met Cressida.

'You don't have to speak about it,' she said quickly, feigning a sudden interest in the pattern on the sheets that covered her abdomen. 'It's probably quite presumptuous of me to even ask. I'm sorry.'

Khal felt like an utter ass, seeing the look on her face. Of course she had the right to ask; they were married and he had just been speaking another woman's name in their bed. The rules surrounding their marriage were still blurred at present, neither of them knowing exactly what was okay or not. The initial agreement for a marriage in name only had most definitely been broken, but it left them in a kind of limbo. They were not man and wife in the truest sense, but neither were they the kind of formal arrangement he had originally envisioned. He knew that right now was most definitely one of those moments where he needed to do the difficult thing.

'It's not something I'm usually comfortable talking

about,' he said slowly, watching as her eyes raised up to meet his. He reached out and laid his hand over hers on the sheets. 'But you spoke through your own discomfort; therefore perhaps it is only fair that I do the same.'

'You don't have to…' Cressida began quickly.

'I want to,' he said, surprised to realise that he was speaking the truth. 'I told you once before that my marriage was not all that it seemed. To the public we were untouchable. I was the picture-perfect husband and she the perfect wife.' He shook his head, a cruel laugh escaping from his lips. 'Not a single soul knows the last words she ever spoke to me… The words that haunt my dreams at night. She told me that she would rather die than be my wife a moment longer.' Khal turned his head, expecting to see disgust in Cressida's eyes. But what he saw there instead was more uncomfortable. Pity. Oh, how he had despised that look of pity on people's faces in the months following his wife's death.

'Couples have arguments all of the time,' Cressida began.

'It was not the first time that she had spoken in that way.' Khal shook his head. 'I was not the best husband, by any standard.' She didn't understand; she didn't realise that when Priya had said those words she had truly meant them.

'How awful, to have that memory in your mind,' Cressida said softly, covering his hand with hers.

Khal inhaled deeply, wanting to recoil from the pity he could hear in her voice. 'You wanted to know how she died. I'll tell you, but you must forgive me if I still hold some anger.' He had unconsciously begun to tap his foot at some point, a nervous gesture that he constantly tried to overcome since teenage years. Kings did not fidget, he remembered his father telling him. Control—it was always about showing control.

'There has never been a definitive answer on how she came to be on the road that she was, at the time that she was. One point of view is that she was on her way to meet her lover. I was aware that she had been unfaithful to me on a number of occasions in the later years of our marriage.' Khal saw a look of shock cross Cressida's features, followed by a brief hint of anger. 'Another view is that she purposely drove her car over the side of the ravine at a high speed in order to end her own life.'

Cressida winced, her grip tightening on his hand.

'In Zayyari culture, both of those possibilities spell out shame. I was not prepared to have her name sullied, so the nature of her death was never disclosed. The perceived secrecy led to speculation and rumours. Most of which involved various theories of how I was a ruthless barbarian who had arranged his wife's murder. Or worse, that I had killed her myself and had the truth covered up.

'I was assured that her death was instantaneous. For that I was grateful.' He closed his eyes for a moment, trying to ignore the onslaught of memories. The smell of burning rubber in the air as he had moved down the side of the sandbank, his guards shouting at him to stop. He remembered watching as one of his sports cars was hoisted from the shallow water. Priya's lifeless body had already been transported to the morgue where he had identified her, but for some reason Khal had needed to see the car. He had needed to see the place where it had happened, to make sense of it all.

'Nothing about it made sense; that was the worst part

to accept. The investigators told me that there was no way to prove if the car had been tampered with, considering it had to be destroyed upon transportation to be impounded.' He shook his head, sitting up straight. 'The idea that her anger at me led to her driving dangerously never sat well with me. I have spent years trying to find evidence that someone deliberately caused the accident other than Priya herself. It's only now...saying it out loud... that I realise maybe that's just my way of coping with my own guilt and sense of powerlessness.'

Cressida leaned forward, pressing her cheek against his bare back and sliding her arm around his abdomen. The gesture was so intimate and so comforting that for a moment he felt himself tightening, the urge to pull away strong. But then the warmth of her skin seeped into his own and he found himself accepting her comfort, grateful for the fact that for once he was not alone in his recollection of these painful memories.

They sat in silence for a while, Cressida listening to the beat of his heart thumping in rhythm with her own. 'I find it hard to believe that you were ever a bad husband.'

To her surprise she felt him tense beneath her skin, pulling away from her slightly. She sat back, wondering if perhaps she had touched a nerve even after all he had just disclosed.

'We had a son,' Khal said, a strange emptiness to his voice as he spoke. 'He never lived, stillborn in the eighth month of pregnancy. But we had a son.'

Cressida felt something inside her break as the words hit her with full force. She had no idea what it was like to bear that kind of tragedy and pain in one's life. The very idea of Khal going through such a loss was unbearable.

'When I say that I was a bad husband, I don't mean that I was a bit selfish or that I forgot to put the toilet seat down. I was a bad husband because my wife's needs were never taken into consideration. All that mattered was ensuring that my need for tight security and safety was prioritised. I overreacted to everything. She got swarmed in the markets once, early on in her pregnancy, and I decided that I needed to keep her under tighter security, even if it meant keeping her confined to the palace. Priya told me on numerous occasions that she was unhappy but the final straw was when she was rushed to hospital, pregnant and terrified. I was halfway across the world being the grand Sheikh of Zayyar. And when I was finally given the news a day later, there was absolutely nothing I could do. We had only been married a year at that point.'

'You blame yourself for so much…' Cressida began, not quite knowing what to say in the face of such an admission.

'I'm sorry. I said that I don't like to share and yet here I am, unable to stop.' He turned, taking her hands in his and looking deep into her eyes.

'There is no need to explain yourself to me,' Cressida said firmly. 'I am simply grateful that you trusted me enough to share what you have.'

He nodded once, taking her in his arms. The embrace began innocently enough, but then the sheet slipped down between them and suddenly she was being swept away on another wave of passion. Their lovemaking this time was slower, a tentative sliver of intimacy seeming to show in the way he held her face in his hands as he kissed her and looked deep into her eyes. Afterwards, he fell into a deep sleep with impressive speed, leaving Cressida staring up at the ceiling, physically satisfied but emotionally distracted.

She found herself absolutely livid that he had been subjected to such harsh scrutiny in his time of grief.

The world lauded her own father, a man who had held his wife and daughters to emotional ransom their whole lives, and yet Khal was shunned, based on rumours and gossip. She felt something within her changing, a strange protectiveness of this new life she had entered into. It scared her, to think that she felt such loyalty to a man she had only known a matter of weeks now. But she did trust him with all of her heart. It was keeping that heart protected when it was becoming more and more in danger of being broken...that was the real problem.

CHAPTER ELEVEN

AFTER THREE FULL days of an impromptu honeymoon spent mostly in bed, Cressida mourned the arrival of their departure for the official visit to Monteverre. They spent a large portion of the flight hidden away in the master bedroom. While Khal might have introduced her to the pleasures of the mile-high club, she had the pleasure of giving him a tour of her home town through her own eyes once they touched down.

Her decision to leave Monteverre at the age of nineteen to study abroad had held no bearing on her love for her kingdom. She had simply needed freedom from the oppressive disdain of her parents and the effort of hiding her secret from her siblings.

Even as their limousine moved slowly around the main square and she pointed out her favourite ice cream shop and the library where she had spent many an afternoon hiding away, she felt anxiety rising steadily within her. The thought of speaking to her sisters now that they had been made aware of the great family secret was daunting. At least, with her parents, she knew what to expect. She didn't know if Olivia and Eleanor would be upset, hurt or even angry at her for keeping such a secret.

Truthfully, she did not know if Olivia would show up at all. Last she had heard, she and her fiancé Roman were sailing around the Caribbean after becoming formally engaged shortly before Cressida had moved to Zayyar.

'You are very quiet, *habibti*,' Khal said as they shared a speciality Monteverrian vanilla ice cream on a narrow side street. 'Don't think I haven't noticed that you are delaying our arrival at the palace.'

Cressida bit her lower lip, hating that he seen through her so easily but also enjoying the fact just a little. 'I'm delaying the unknown. My sisters were always kept in the dark when it came to the secret of my parentage. As far as they knew, there was nothing different about me other than the obvious facts that I have poor fashion sense and a strange attachment to books.'

'I disagree, your fashion sense is no longer poor since you met me.' He jabbed, smiling as she reached out to smudge ice cream on his nose in retaliation. 'Your sisters may be a bit hurt at being kept in the dark, but they will not love you any less.'

'I hope you are right.' Cressida sighed.

They finished their ice creams and finally there was nothing else to do but make their grand arrival at the palace. Usually a high-profile guest was welcomed in grand style, with all the staff lined up at the foot of the wide concrete steps while the Royal family stood waiting at the top. Today, the steps were empty save for a single butler, who stood at the end. Cressida recognised him as Hansel, the second most senior member of the royal house staff. A harsh laugh escaped her throat at the thought that her father had not even deemed her arrival home after almost five years away to be worthy of the head butler.

'Your Highnesses, allow me to be the first to congratulate you on your recent nuptials and to formally welcome you back to Monteverre.' The older man bowed, escorting them inside and down the long familiar corridors to the grand salon.

Inside, the Sandoval family waited, her mother and sister sitting down while her father stood poised at the mantelpiece, just as she'd expected. It was his usual show of force, he was a tall man and he liked to stand in the position of power in a room when welcoming guests.

She had almost forgotten that Khal was by her side until her father stepped forward, greeting him before he greeted his own daughter.

'Welcome back to my humble kingdom, Sheikh Khalil,' King Fabian said loudly. 'I believe you have already been introduced to my eldest daughter, Crown Princess Eleanor.'

Khal glanced uncomfortably from Cressida to her father, before stepping forward and making his introduction to her older sister.

Eleanor was thinner than she remembered; that was the first thought Cressida had before her sister stepped forward suddenly and embraced her.

'Cress, it has been far too long.' Eleanor did not gush; there was nothing false about the way she held the embrace for a long moment before pulling away. For a moment it almost felt as though they were children again, before anything had ever changed.

The moment did not last long, however, her father booming across the little interlude in his usual fashion.

'And here she is, the woman of the hour,' he pronounced
with mock pride.

Cressida felt Khal stiffen beside her, his hand tightening on hers.

'Father, I hope you are well.' She opted for the polite
approach, ignoring the urge to simply speak her mind
and address the very large elephant present in the room.

'I'm quite well, considering the stress that I and the
royal team have been under for the past three days.' His
lips tightened in what she supposed was an attempt at
a smile. 'I doubt you've been put under much pressure,
hiding out there in the desert.'

He looked to Khal in a very male attempt at cama-
raderie, clearly expecting her husband to share in his
joke. Khal did not.

'Perhaps we should take things to a more business
setting. Leave the women to catch up. It has been such
a long time since Cressida has seen her family.'

Cressida tried not to react to the way the King referred to her mother and sister as her family, not his. He
had no need to hide his true feelings now, she supposed.
She had never been a Sandoval by birth but now she was
no longer even a Sandoval by name. He could pretend
that she had never existed and never feel the difference.

'This matter concerns your daughter just as much
as it concerns our kingdoms—' Khal began, his shoulders straightening.

'No, you should go. You are much better at all of
this.' Cressida squeezed her husband's hand lightly. 'I
trust you to speak on my behalf.'

'You are sure?' He dipped his head, speaking quietly near her ear.

Cressida nodded, smiling as he placed a delicate kiss

on her palm and left the room with a few long powerful strides, her father at his heels.

'So you found love, after all.' Her mother's voice drifted across the room.

Cressida had almost forgotten that her mother was there at all, considering she had not stood once since she had entered the room. 'We have a comfortable arrangement. It's more than I could have hoped for, considering the circumstances.' Cressida spoke evenly.

'What your father and I had… Sorry, King Fabian and I…' Her mother cleared her throat suddenly, the first sign of emotion crossing heavily lined features. 'Our arranged marriage was comfortable at best. Dangerously passionate at worst.' She took a long sip of her brandy, rising to her feet and swaying slightly. 'What you want is something in the middle, something warm that will last, not burn itself out before you've even had a chance.'

Eleanor cleared her throat, ever the peacemaker of the family. 'He seems quite fond of you,' she offered kindly. 'I'm happy for you, little sister.'

'I was nervous about coming here today, considering what has been said.' She met her older sister's eyes, feeling her voice quivering slightly. 'You must know that I would have told you, had I been allowed to.'

'Yes, yes.' Queen Aurelia sighed heavily, making her way slowly across the room towards the sideboard and the brandy decanter that stood upon it. 'We would all have done a great many things, had we been allowed to.'

Something within Cressida seemed to stretch thin and snap apart. Years of hurt and emotional pain rose to the surface, her temper rising with it.

'Your attitude is appalling, Mother.' Eleanor spoke

first, surprising Cressida with the backbone in her voice. Her elder sister had always been the strong, silent one. Never sharing the details of her own seemingly perfect marriage. Always simply moving forward with her duty and not getting involved in any of the family politics that might have arisen.

'My attitude?' Queen Aurelia laughed, filling up her glass almost to the top with amber liquid, not seeming to care that it was barely midday. 'At least I did not run away the first chance I got. At least I put my family first.'

'Is that how you justify your actions to yourself?' Cressida asked quietly. 'I have often wondered if you were entirely oblivious or if you simply never cared about your children or the consequences that your selfishness had on them.'

'Selfishness?' Her mother's eyes widened, her hand abandoning the brandy glass entirely as she swung around to face her two daughters across the grand salon. 'I gave up everything for my children. Don't you dare speak of things when you have no idea of the truth.'

'What have you ever given up?' Cressida shook her head, amazed at the vitriol and the energy in her mother's voice all of a sudden. The woman had been a living ghost for as long as she could remember, now all of a sudden she seemed full of life as she defended her own poor choices.

Queen Aurelia shook her head, emotion seeming to overtake her momentarily as she turned her back to them and walked towards the window. Her pale blonde hair caught the rays of sunlight as she stood silently for a moment and looked out at the sea in the distance.

'Did you know that he had died?' Queen Aurelia

finally asked, turning slightly to meet Cressida's eyes for the first time.

Cressida did not need to ask who she was speaking of; the emotion in her mother's eyes spoke clearly enough. By her side she could see Eleanor begin twisting her hands together, a rare show of discomfort from the Crown Princess.

'I think perhaps I will go and sit in on the meeting,' Eleanor said quickly. 'Perhaps you would both like a moment alone.'

Before Cressida had a moment to respond, Eleanor swept from the room. Her mother turned fully to look at her, still waiting for her answer.

'No, I did not know. The newspaper article was the first I had heard of it.'

Silence fell once again in the room, the only sound a gentle sniff as her mother took out a handkerchief and gently dabbed her eyes. 'I did not have lovers, despite whatever poison Fabian may have put in your mind. I had one true love and I never had the chance to say goodbye to him.'

Tears streamed down her mother's face in earnest now, though she tried to turn away.

Cressida took a handkerchief from her purse, walking to her mother's side and offering it.

'You hated me for it. I saw it on your face the day that he dragged you into my room with my letters in his hand.' Pain was evident in her mother's tight features as she reached out to take Cressida's hand in her own. 'I have never been good at communicating with my children. I have never been good at communicating at all. I have wasted so much time.'

Cressida could hardly believe what she was hearing.

This was all she had ever wanted as a child . For her mother to sit her down and explain it to her. To show her that she wasn't the awful mistake that her father saw her as. Even if one of her parents truly loved and accepted her, it would have been enough. It would have made her feel less alone. But seeing her mother now, so broken and lonely, she did not say any of that. Instead she simply embraced her and held her while racking sobs filled the air around them.

'I loved Vincent with all of my heart, you see. He was the only one who listened to me, who made me feel protected. I never told him that he was going to become a father. I think, had he known, he never would have allowed me to stay here. I thought that I was doing what was best for you and your sisters… I thought that I could fix things with Fabian. But he never forgave me, despite me knowing that he'd been taking mistresses for years. He had left me feeling unwanted and abandoned in our marriage long before I strayed. But my mistake carried a lasting consequence, one that he could use against me and hold me to ransom with, and so I drank to avoid the misery. I slowly retreated from my life.

'When you found out the truth, I tried to contact Vincent, fearing what your father might do. I found out that he had married. He was happy, so I stayed away. I dreamed of him coming back for me, fool in love that I was. But I had broken his heart when I refused to go with him before, and so he took the money your father offered and we never heard from him again.'

Cressida fought the lump of emotion in her chest at the pain that spilled from her mother after decades of withheld emotion.

'You could have talked to me,' she said quietly. 'If

anyone in this family would understand feeling alone and unwanted it is me.'

'Cressida… I stayed in Monteverre to give you a better life and it seems as though I achieved the exact opposite. I was selfish. I let my own pain distract me from being there as a mother. You look so much like your father… Every time I looked at you for the first few years I cried. The weight of it was too much for me so I ran from it. I was a coward. I still am, really.'

'You don't have to be,' Cressida said simply. 'Your children are adults now.'

Queen Aurelia shook her head slowly. 'I have nowhere else to be. Not any longer.' She stared out of the window for a moment before turning back. 'I just needed you to understand… I could never regret the choice that resulted in the happiest time in my life, despite the fact that I knew it was wrong in so many ways. That love resulted in you, Cressida.'

They were interrupted by staff coming to ask the Queen for instructions for that evening's dinner. Cressida took the opportunity to slip away under the guise of retrieving her older sister so that she might have a moment to breathe and gather her own thoughts in the aftermath of such a tumultuous conversation.

As she wandered through the halls of her childhood home in search of Eleanor, she found her mind lingering on the first words her mother had spoken to her. *'So you found love after all,'* she had said. Knowing now what her mother had been through in her own pursuit of love, the statement stuck in her mind. She desperately wanted to go back and ask what she had meant. Had she seen something in Khal's face? A gesture perhaps, or the way his eyes lingered on her? Did she know how to tell if a man was falling in love, even if he had sworn against it?

There really was no point in pretending any longer that she was any different to her mother when it came to seeking acceptance and love. And it seemed she had just the same knack for getting herself into trouble.

She had fallen madly, deeply, irrevocably in love with a man who would never feel the same.

'I see no further point in avoiding the reason why we are here. You invited us here to discuss strategy, did you not?' Khal spoke coolly from where he sat in King Fabian's large study. The man had been blathering on in detail about the extremely positive financial reports that had just been published in the Monteverrian parliament. Khal did not have time to soothe the King's fragile ego at present and found his patience had worn utterly thin since entering into his presence.

'We are still awaiting members of your team, I believe,' one of King Fabian's chief aides said in his monotone voice.

'My team will jump in when they arrive.' Khal opened the large black file that his personal secretary handed him. 'I will begin with a report on what Zayyar has done since we received first notification of this breach. Since this story broke my team and I have received minor retractions from three of the major global news sources. We have released intimate photographs of our wedding in order to redirect media attention and we have also initiated investigations into the nature of Queen Cressida's rights with regard to the legal agreements that were signed twelve years ago.'

'Have you indeed?' King Fabian's eyes narrowed.

'I'm glad that you are assuming responsibility for your *Queen*. I had half expected you to try to shirk off the duty to me.'

Khal flattened his palms on the table, inhaling deeply against his sudden urge to resort to physical violence. 'As this matter preceded our union, Cressida was insistent that your government have their say in the PR, considering that it is the Sandoval name being dragged through the mud. Believe me, had the decision been solely mine, I would not have been so merciful.'

'Merciful?' King Fabian's eyes bulged. 'You seem to have developed quite a *tendre* for your convenient bride, considering she was a poor replacement for the one you truly wanted. How is Roman Lazarov these days?'

Khal smiled at the obvious barb. 'If this is how you conduct political meetings, I can see how you brought your kingdom to such a spectacular ruin in such a short time.'

Both men stood up from the table just as the door burst open and the remainder of Khal's team entered.

'Apologies for the delay, Your Highness,' said the chief of his foreign affairs team, out of breath. 'There has been an urgent development from Zayyar.'

'Well, spit it out. We've been waiting long enough,' King Fabian said impatiently.

Khal nodded once to the man. 'If it is urgent and it involves Monteverre, go ahead.'

The man looked momentarily unsure of himself, adjusting his collar as though it was too tight around his neck. 'It seems…that the marriage agreement between Monteverre and Zayyar has been called into question,' he said slowly, drawing a sheaf of documents from his briefcase.

'That agreement has been signed and done with,' Fabian exclaimed, the rims of his eyes turning an angry red. 'Whatever underhand treachery this is, I won't tolerate it for one moment. Not one!'

'Called into question, how, exactly?' Khal ignored the other man's outburst, feeling a strange floating sensation in his solar plexus.

'Well, Your Highness, Zayyari law demands clear and truthful reporting of parentage. Both biological and legal. Parliament has proposed to nullify the marriage on the grounds that your bride forged her documentation.'

CHAPTER TWELVE

'NULLIFY,' KHAL REPEATED, the word tasting sour on his tongue. 'Even if the marriage has been consummated?'

'If you rule in its favour, yes. You hold the deciding vote, Sire.'

'I called this meeting in order to reach an agreement to manage a scandal, not create an entirely new one,' King Fabian's voice growled from the other side of the table.

'Do you deny that you deliberately withheld vital information in order to expedite my marriage to your daughter?' Khal met the King's eyes.

'I am her father by law,' Fabian said rather weakly.

'Funny how you find that so easy to say now that you see your upward financial swing could be at risk.'

'Are you going to do as they say, then?'

Khal could see the barest hint of fear in the slight widening of the other man's eyes. He momentarily contemplated launching into a list of reasons why he would not be discussing his plans with the man who had emotionally blackmailed his own daughter into marrying a stranger, but he found he had suddenly lost all desire to waste his energy a moment longer. He instructed his team to close the meeting on his behalf and quickly excused himself from the room. He knew he should go to Cressida immediately and tell her everything that had been said. But what exactly would he say?

His thoughts took him out into the grounds of the palace, memory directing him to where he knew a small collection of stallions were kept in a paddock. He had spent some time in Monteverre while negotiating the beginning of the marriage deal that would change his life so completely. He chose a large Arabian named Bruno and borrowed a pair of boots from the grooms-man. The paddock was not as long as his desert out-lands in Zayyar but it served its purpose, giving both him and the horse just enough space in which to race out their excess energy and quiet their minds.

He thought of Cressida's face when she'd spoken of her work, of the life she'd lived in London before he'd come crashing into it. She had told him she felt truly happy in that old life. Would she ever truly feel at peace as Sheikha of Zayyar? She had said time and time again that she was not suited to a public role. That she missed the solitude of her library and the simplicity of a pri-vate existence.

Could he really deny her the chance to turn back the hands of time and make a choice based solely on what she wanted to do? These thoughts haunted him even after the sun began to dip low in the sky. Realising he had spent longer than intended out of the palace, he released the stallion to the groomsman and made his way back inside.

They had been assigned a guest suite in the opposite wing to the family; he took the steps up two at a time, eager to get the conversation over with. When he en-tered the bedroom, however, he found Cressida asleep on the bed. He stood in the doorway for a long while, not wanting to wake her. There was a tightness in his chest that he couldn't understand.

He had no way to be sure what she would decide once he told her of the option to annul their short marriage. He could simply make a phone call and have parliament vote against the whole thing, bury the entire idea as though it had never existed. She would never even know it had been spoken of...

But that would be selfish and he had gained enough self-awareness to know that he could not make this kind of choice for her. Lying to her or withholding information was not protecting her, it was something the old Khal would have done from a place of fear. Regressing was not something that he could justify. She had not been shown much kindness in her life, despite her royal upbringing. She had been used as a pawn in battles between her parents and palmed off as a political sacrifice to a man who was far too broken to ever give her the kind of life she deserved. She deserved to live the life she chose, even if that life did not include him.

Cressida stirred in the bed, a smile brightening her entire face at the same moment that she opened her eyes and saw him. 'What time is it?' she murmured huskily, stretching her arms.

'Almost six,' Khal said, forcing himself to remain still when all he wanted to do was close the distance between them and draw her into his embrace.

'Did the meeting go well? Have you come to an agreement for the press strategy?' she asked, standing up to reveal she wore only one of his T-shirts. She smirked as his gaze darkened. 'Sorry, I couldn't bear the thought of digging through half of the gowns in my case to find my own T-shirt so I stole one of yours.'

This image might very well be imprinted on his brain for ever, he thought with a cruel twist of his lips. She had never looked more tempting than at this moment, wearing one of his white T-shirts. The garment went to her mid-thigh, showcasing her long slim legs. But he was not a barbarian, even though the world claimed he was. Putting his libido firmly in check, he took a few steps away, just as they were interrupted by her assistants arriving to begin preparing her for the evening.

Cressida looked at him uncertainly. 'Is everything all right?' she asked with a frown. 'I can have them come back if you need to talk?'

Khal paused, realising that he had just been about to launch into a very heavy conversation less than an hour before they were due to be seen in public. Cursing his own stupidity, he hastily assured her that everything was okay and excused himself to allow her team to go about their preparations. There was plenty of time to talk tomorrow, he told himself. One more night would not change matters. He went about readying himself, ignoring the niggling feeling that he was simply delaying the inevitable.

Cressida moved to the edge of the party; the air had become uncomfortably warm as more and more guests arrived. She had been told there would be a small gathering of Monteverrian dignitaries and wealthy society favourites in order to show that the royal family stood strong against the scandal. But it seemed half of the kingdom had arrived to get a glimpse of the Sheikh of Zayyar and his scandalous wife.

But as she breathed in the night air, looking at the beautiful ornate fountain and surrounding shrubbery, all lit up in pink and orange lights, she wondered if a husband who was simply understanding would ever be enough. Her mother had said that she and her father had experienced a burning passion in the beginning, then that passion had burnt out, leaving nothing but discontent and resentment in its wake. Without a true emotional connection, would she ever feel secure in her marriage?

'It seems desert life suits you,' a familiar voice came from behind her. Cressida turned to find her middle sister, Olivia, standing in the doorway, her silver gown sparkling like an angel. She couldn't help it; she burst into tears just as Olivia's arms surrounded her in an embrace.

'What are you doing here?' she half choked between sobs.

Olivia wiped one of the tears from her cheek, her classically beautiful features filled with concern. 'We saw the news and we came straight here. Did you know about...the affair?'

Cressida filled her sister in on the entire story, beginning with her mother's version of the affair, leading into her own discovery and Fabian's subsequent emotional blackmail. Once she had finished, they sat in silence for a moment, Olivia shaking her head slightly.

'This family is utterly insane,' Olivia said simply. 'I have never been more grateful for my new distance.'

Cressida smiled, leaning her head against her sister's arm for a moment. Olivia had been the only person she had ever felt a true connection with in her family. Eleanor had always been too busy to entertain her, being the oldest and set to become Queen of Monteverre one day. But Olivia had taught her how to braid her hair and told her the latest gossip from school. She had always envied her sister for her natural beauty and easy elegance. She was talented too, having recently taken the reins of their grandmother's literacy foundation after relinquishing her royal status.

'You seem happy,' Cressida said. 'I'm glad.'

'Roman is wonderful,' Olivia said, a dreamy look crossing her features. 'But I'm also feeling fulfilment from working for the first time in my life.' She smiled widely. 'But I'm sure you know all about that, having had years of freedom in London.'

Cressida thought of that time in her life; it seemed so long ago. 'I do miss it,' she said truthfully. 'I envy you.'

'You could always join forces with me; goodness knows I could use someone with your kind of language skills, Cress.' Olivia's eyes lit up for a moment before she frowned. 'But, of course, you have your own set of responsibilities now. I doubt the Sheikha of a country has time to go travelling around the world teaching children to read?'

The sudden mixture of longing and disappointment that filled her chest took her by surprise. The idea of travelling, seeing the world while at the same time using her knowledge and expertise to teach... She sighed wistfully. But, of course, she had her life in Zayyar and her duties as Sheikha. That should be enough for her. She loved Khal and a small part of her hoped that in time he could come to love her too. But the thought of teaching...

Olivia cleared her throat beside her. 'We could join

forces to do a one off event with the foundation, maybe. It would be great to reconnect and spend time together.'

Cressida opened her mouth to speak, but at the same moment Khal decided to make his appearance on the terrace, followed closely by Roman Lazarov. Olivia's Russian fiancé had once been Khal's Chief of Security and best friend. It wasn't exactly clear how he had come to be engaged to her sister, but it was obvious that it had made things strained between the two men. Khal looked from Cressida to her sister, an unreadable expression crossing his features.

'Olivia was just telling me about her work with the literacy foundation,' Cressida said brightly, covertly trying to swipe away the remnants of her crying episode from her cheeks.

'It's nice to see you again, Sheikh Khalil.' Olivia smiled, nodding politely. 'I was just trying to persuade my sister to put her amazing language skills to good use with the literacy foundation.'

A strange expression crossed Khal's dark features as he looked from Olivia to her. 'Cressida is very talented. She would make an excellent teacher.'

Cressida blushed. She had expected to feel some jealousy with Olivia, considering that her sister had been Khal's original intended bride. But for some reason she did not. Maybe it was the way that Roman and her sister looked at each other, so full of love and happiness. Or maybe it was the fact that she still held out hope that Khal might come to look at her in that same way.

A commotion inside the doorway took their attention and Khal moved aside just in time for the terrace doors to swing open and Queen Aurelia to burst through them.

'I'm done! I want divorce papers drawn up immediately in the morning,' the older woman proclaimed, followed closely by Eleanor and King Fabian. A trio of guards closed the terrace doors, blocking out the scene from the rest of the party.

'Mother, please. At least wait until tomorrow,' Eleanor chided in her best peacekeeping voice as she took her mother by the hand.

'I've waited decades!' Aurelia exclaimed.

Cressida was shocked to realise that her mother was sober; she could tell by the lucidity in her eyes and the hint of colour in her cheeks. She could not remember the last time she had seen her mother look so awake and present.

'Another grand debacle for the entire society to talk about,' King Fabian said, bored. 'I suppose it has been a few months since the last embarrassment.' He looked pointedly towards Roman and Olivia.

Khal moved to Cressida's side, taking her by the hand. 'I think it's best if we go back inside,' he said quietly.

'And leave them like this?'

'They are adults, *habibti*. There is nothing we can do to change whatever is about to transpire. You will only put yourself in the firing line by being present.'

Cressida nodded at his sense, feeling a glow of warmth in the way he stood as her protector. She made to move with him towards the doors, whispering a quiet goodbye to her sisters as her mother continued to berate her father loudly in the background.

'Hold on just a moment,' King Fabian cut across his wife's emotional tirade, his eyes black slits as he took a step towards Cressida. 'As I'm apparently about to suffer an embarrassing and probably expensive divorce, can I at least take it that you two lovebirds have decided to remain married after all?'

Cressida frowned at her father's question—what did he mean, *remain married*? She looked up at Khal, seeing that same stressed expression that he had been wearing all evening.

'This is not the time or the place, Fabian,' Khal gritted.

'I want it in writing that you will not nullify the marriage or the financial transactions that came with it, do you hear me? I want it iron-clad or I will make sure that your kingdom suffers every political roadblock possible.'

'What is he talking about?' Cressida turned to her husband.

'We will speak in private,' Khal gritted, his attention still focused on her father. There was a dangerous glint in his eyes, an awful ruthlessness that she had never witnessed before. It made her recoil slightly, taking a step back from him.

'Cressida,' he said sternly, 'I will not discuss this here.' He reached for her but was blocked by her two sisters, who moved in to stand at her sides.

'What is he talking about…a nullification?' Cressida asked, feeling her hands begin to tremble.

'Parliament have undertaken a motion to dismiss our marriage contract on the grounds of forgery.' Khal's voice was emotionless as he spoke. 'They are saying that because you deliberately withheld the truth of your parentage that I can choose to nullify the contract.'

Cressida felt the ground sway beneath her. 'I see.'

'I did not wish to discuss this with an audience.' He met her eyes. 'I think this is a matter that we should weigh up alone.'

Weigh up? He was discussing the possibility of ending their marriage as though the list of pros and cons was endless. Cressida thought that if she could actually feel her own heart breaking, the pain would be unbearable. As it was, she simply felt numb. 'I don't think we need to weigh up much. If parliament says that my parentage is unacceptable then you need to do what is right for your kingdom. I won't contest any nullification.'

Cressida moved past her sisters and went through the terrace doors, needing to be alone before she let herself completely fall to pieces. She heard the commotion behind her but refused to look back, asking a guard to escort her to her suite. She heard footsteps thundering up the stairs behind them but ignored them, hoping her guard would do his job. Apparently the Zayyari guards only served one ruler, she thought wryly as Khal came striding in the door, slightly out of breath from his sprint.

Khal was silent for a long moment. 'You won't contest it…or you are relieved that it is a possibility?'

'I think if either of us is relieved, it's you. I am hardly the golden bride with political influence that you hoped for. I am steeped in scandal, for goodness' sake. I can hardly make a speech without stuttering.' She shook her head wildly. 'I'm not my sister, Khal. I have tried to measure up as her replacement but I simply can't. Maybe this is best for both of us, to end this now before we go any deeper.'

'How much deeper can we get?' he said, exasperated. 'I know that this marriage did not start out in the most conventional way. I may have chosen your sister first out of convenience, Cressida, but I did not even know that you existed at that time.'

'So if you knew about me, if you could go back and make the choice again, you'd choose me? The awkward, nerdy, antisocial anti-Princess?' she said in complete disbelief.

'I cannot promise that I would have chosen you, given my decision to enter into a loveless marriage. All I cared about was that my bride met criteria.' He moved closer. 'But I would never change you, now that I know the real you. Now that we have begun to share our lives.'

Cressida felt her breath catch in her throat at his words. Surely he didn't mean that he didn't want the annulment? Suddenly she wasn't quite sure exactly who was arguing for or against their marriage any more.

He ran a hand across his jaw, shaking his head. 'What I am offering you now is a real life time machine. A chance to change your future if you want it. Your sister has already offered you a teaching position. If you tell me that you want our marriage annulled, I will honour your request. My conscience would not allow me to hide this from you, much as I may have wanted to.'

'You considered not telling me?'

'God, yes. Why on earth would I want to give you a failsafe chance to walk away from this marriage? Away from me?'

'I just presumed…your plans to have the perfect Sheikha have all gone up in smoke. I'm a walking scandal. Why on earth would you stay weighed down by the burden of me?'

He paused for a moment, the air between them frozen in time. Her heartbeat seemed uncomfortably loud in the silent room and she wondered if he could hear it.

'Yes, you may be a walking scandal. And your family may be utterly insane, and your personality may be better suited to the position of librarian rather than Sheikha...but I promise you, after we have grown closer these past weeks, that you are the woman I would choose over and over again.'

She forgot to breathe, hardly believing what she had just heard. As she watched, he moved closer, coming down on one knee in front of her.

'Cressida... If you truly want to end this marriage, I promise that I will not force you to stay. I have spent so long trying to control everyone and everything around me. Trying to find some sort of peace within myself.' He took her hand, his eyes never leaving hers. 'But I cannot promise that I won't spend every day finding new ways to beg you to come back to me for the rest of my life.'

'Why would you do that?' she breathed.

'Because, while I may have been too afraid to realise my feelings for you before, I know them now. I will not give up on fighting to win your heart. I was afraid to let you all the way in, for fear I would need you too much. It seems laughable now, really, trying to resist my own destiny.'

'You said you don't believe in fate or soulmates.' She felt her insides shake at the look in his eyes, at the sensation that the ground might fall away from under her at any moment.

'Is it not more than coincidence that in a club full of people, in a city with a population twice the size of my entire kingdom...that you would choose me?'

He took a deep breath. 'I realised something today. From the moment I held you in my arms on that dance floor the first night we met, I felt peace. That was what I was running from. I had been so used to feeling at war within myself that feeling your warmth calming me was terrifying. It was as though you took a grip of the darkness in my soul and forced me out into the light again. If that is not love, I don't know what is.'

'I don't know what to say,' Cressida breathed, feeling her hands tremble as he raised one to his lips.

'Say that you will stay by my side. Not just as my Sheikha and my wife, but as my true partner in life. My love.'

It was the romantic proposal she had never received, she realised. She pressed her lips together to stop them from trembling.

'Nothing would make me happier than to stay by your side.' She lowered herself to her knees in front of him, placing one hand on his cheek. 'But I need to be true to myself as well as to my love for you.'

He frowned but she continued quickly, 'I cannot just be a silent figure in a pretty dress by your side. I want to use my skills to help people, to do good in the world.'

A slow smile lit up the darkness in his eyes. 'I will support you in whatever you wish to do with that wonderful brain of yours. You may count on me to stand silently by your side and look pretty in the process.'

She felt the last shred of resistance melt away as she leaned in and pressed her lips to his. He responded by pulling her deep into the circle of his arms, surrounding her with his strength. She felt it in his kiss, the raw power of his love for her. She had not known that this was the missing piece of her heart until he had come into her life and showed her what it meant to be supported and loved for who she was. That she was enough. For Cressida, there could be no greater gift.

EPILOGUE

Six months later...

THE PARISIAN HOTEL ballroom was full to bursting with members of royalty and celebrities alike. Everyone had joined to celebrate the wedding of the year with the most scandalous royal family of the decade. Cressida watched as her sister walked onto the dance floor, accompanied by her handsome new husband for their first dance. 'Olivia looks so happy,' she murmured.

'Roman was never much of a dancer; it appears he has taken lessons.' Khal laughed.

'I will never understand the relationship you two have.' Cressida raised one brow.

'Nor would I expect you to.' He smiled. 'We are both as complicated as each other, but underneath we will always be friends. Brothers now, I suppose.'

'A strange family set-up, if ever I knew one.' She laughed huskily in her throat, gasping as she felt Khal lean in and lay a kiss on the nape of her neck.

'The party is practically over now; surely we can slip away unnoticed?' he murmured playfully, his teeth nipping the side of her ear.

'I am not going anywhere alone with you, Your Highness, not after how little sleep I got last night with you sharing my bed once more.'

Khal had been away for a week while he launched the grand tourism season in the now thriving city of Valar. She had been forced to return early from a trip to South America with the literacy foundation and remain on bed rest at the palace for reasons that they could not yet disclose to the public.

'I hope I did not truly exhaust you?' Genuine concern filled his features as he turned her to look at him. 'You know the doctor said that you needed to rest as much as possible for a couple of weeks.'

Cressida found herself laying one hand across the gentle swell of her stomach in an unconscious show of maternal protection. 'The intense sickness has seemed to ease now that we have got through the first few months. I heard the first trimester is the most difficult.'

Khal nodded, a tight smile crossing his features. His change of heart regarding a family of their own had come as an enormous surprise to Cressida. She had fully intended to respect Khal's wishes to remain without natural heirs, despite knowing that deep down she longed to become a mother some day. But as he had relaxed into the ease of their relationship, she had noticed he tended to worry less and less about things he could not control.

It was not effortless for him. He was a natural protector, after all. It seemed his urge to protect those he loved also included a wish to have children of his own. She had been only too happy to fulfil her wifely duties in that regard, rejoicing when she had fallen pregnant almost immediately. She had not told either of her sisters yet, especially knowing that Olivia's wedding was so close. She did not want to detract from the day.

But as she watched the newlywed couple slow dance

together, she thought she could see a similar glow in her sister's cheeks as Roman's hand slid covertly to her stomach for the briefest of moments. Her eyes met Olivia's across the crowded ballroom, her sister's answering smile telling her all that she needed to know.

'Are you nervous?' Cressida asked a while later as she lay cradled in her husband's arms in the master bedroom of their hotel suite. 'For the baby, I mean.'

Khal moved his powerful body behind her, holding her tight to his chest as he drew lazy circles on her abdomen with one finger. 'Of course I'm nervous. But I think most people are, even if they have not been through a loss. My biggest concern is fighting the urge to place you on permanent bed rest and lock you away for the next six months.'

'Six months in bed?' Cressida pretended to seriously consider that scenario. 'Would you be there too?'

'These hormones have turned you into a sex-crazed hellion,' he scolded, flipping on top of her. 'We have already made love twice today and you still have energy.'

Cressida felt a moment of complete happiness wash over her, looking up into the eyes of the man who loved her. It was almost overwhelming.

'What is it?' Khal asked, a furrow forming in his brow as Cressida's eyes welled up with unshed tears.

'I just realised… I have spent my whole life wanting more and feeling like I would never deserve it. And now here I am with everything that I will ever want or need right here in this bed. I never have to feel alone again.'

'Never,' Khal murmured against her lips, drawing her into his embrace. 'As long as you want me I am yours.'

* * * * *

LET'S TALK
Romance

For exclusive extracts, competitions
and special offers, find us online:

facebook.com/millsandboon

@MillsandBoon

@MillsandBoonUK

Get in touch on 01413 063232

MILLS & BOON
A ROMANCE FOR EVERY READER

- **FREE** delivery direct to your door

- **EXCLUSIVE** offers every month

- **SAVE** up to 25% on pre-paid subscriptions

SUBSCRIBE AND SAVE

millsandboon.co.uk/Subscribe

JOIN US ON SOCIAL MEDIA!

Stay up to date with our latest releases, author news and gossip, special offers and discounts, and all the behind-the-scenes action from Mills & Boon...

 millsandboon

 millsandboonuk

 millsandboon

t might just be true love...

MILLS & BOON

HISTORICAL

Awaken the romance of the past

Escape with historical heroes from time gone by.
Whether your passion is for wicked
Regency Rakes, muscled Viking warriors or
rugged Highlanders, indulge your fantasies and
awaken the romance of the past.

Five Historical stories published every month, find them all at:

millsandboon.co.uk

MILLS & BOON

MODERN

Power and Passion

Prepare to be swept off your feet by sophisticated, sexy and seductive heroes, in some of the world's most glamourous and romantic locations, where power and passion collide.